B. M. Bower

The Thunder Bird & Skyrider
(Western Adventure Classics)

OK Publishing 2021

B. M. Bower

The Thunder Bird & Skyrider

(Western Adventure Classics)

Adventures of a Wild West Cowboy Who Wanted to be a Pilot

Published by

MUSAICUM

Books

- Advanced Digital Solutions & High-Quality book Formatting -

musaicumbooks@okpublishing.info

2021 OK Publishing

ISBN 978-80-272-7569-4

Contents

Skyrider

Chapter One. A Poet Without Honor

Before I die, I'll ride the sky;

I'll part the clouds like foam.

I'll brand each star with the Rolling R,

And lead the Great Bear home.

I'll circle Mars to beat the cars,

On Venus I will call.

If she greets me fair as I ride the air,

To meet her I will stall.

I'll circle high-as if passing by —

Then volplane, bank, and land.

Then if she'll smile I'll stop awhile,

And kiss her snow-white hand.

To toast her health and wish her wealth

I'll drink the Dipper dry.

Then say, "Hop in, and we'll take a spin,

For I'm a rider of the sky."

Through the clouds we'll float in my airplane boat —

Mary V flipped the rough paper over with so little tenderness that a corner tore in her fingers, but the next page was blank. She made a sound suspiciously like a snort, and threw the tablet down on the littered table of the bunk house. After all, what did she care where they floated-Venus and Johnny Jewel? Riding the sky with Venus when he knew very well that his place was out in the big corral, riding some of those broom-tail bronks that he was being paid a salary —a *good* salary-for breaking! Mary V thought that her father ought to be told about the way Johnny was spending all his time-writing silly poetry about Venus. It was the first she had ever known about his being a poet. Though it was pretty punk, in Mary V's opinion. She was glad and thankful that Johnny had refrained from writing any such doggerel about *her*. That would have been perfectly intolerable. That he should write poetry at all was intolerable. The more she thought of it, the more intolerable it became.

Just for punishment, and as a subtle way of letting him know what she thought of him and his idiotic jingle, she picked up the tablet, found the pencil Johnny had used, and did a little poetizing herself. She could have rhymed it much better, of course, if she had condescended to give any thought whatever to the matter, which she did not. Condescension went far enough when she stooped to reprove the idiot by finishing the verse that he had failed to finish, because he had already overtaxed his poor little brain.

Stooping, then, to reprove, and flout, and ridicule, Mary V finished the verse so that it read thus:

"Through the clouds we'll float in my airplane boat —

For Venus I am truly sorry!

All the stars you sight, you witless wight,

You'll see when you and Venus light!

But then —I'm sure that I should worry!"

Mary V was tempted to write more. She rather fancied that term "witless wight" as applied to Johnny Jewel. It had a classical dignity which atoned for the slang made necessary by her instant need of a rhyme for sorry.

But there was the danger of being caught in the act by some meddlesome fellow who loved to come snooping around where he had no business, so Mary V placed the tablet open on the table just as she had found it, and left the bunk house without deigning to fulfill the errand of mercy that had taken her there. Why should she trouble to sew the lining in a coat sleeve for a fellow who pined for a silly flirtation with Venus? Let Johnny Jewel paw and struggle to get into his coat. Better, let Venus sew that lining for him!

Mary V stopped halfway to the house, and hesitated. It had occurred to her that she might add another perfectly withering verse to that poem. It could start: "While sailing in my airplane boat, I'll ask Venus to mend my coat."

Mary V started back, searing couplets forming with incredible swiftness in her brain. How she would flay Johnny Jewel with the keen blade of her wit! If he thought he was the only person at the Rolling R ranch who could write poetry, it would be a real kindness to show him his mistake.

Just then Bud Norris and Bill Hayden came up from the corrals, heading straight for the bunk house. Mary V walked on, past the bunk house and across the narrow flat opposite the corrals and up on the first bench of the bluff that sheltered the ranch buildings from the worst of the desert winds. She did it very innocently, and as though she had never in her life had any thought of invading the squat, adobe building kept sacred to the leisure hours of the Rolling R boys.

There was a certain ledge where she had played when she was a child, and which she favored nowadays as a place to sit and look down upon the activities in the big corral-whenever activities were taking place therein-an interested spectator who was not suspected of being within hearing. As a matter of fact, Mary V could hear nearly everything that was said in that corral, if the wind was right. She could also see very well indeed, as the boys had learned to their cost when their riding did not come quite up to the mark. She made for that ledge now.

She had no more than settled herself comfortably when Bud and Bill came cackling from the bunk house. A little chill of apprehension went up Mary V's spine and into the roots of her hair. She had not thought of the possibilities of that open tablet falling into other hands than Johnny Jewel's.

"Hyah! You gol-darn witless wight," bawled Bud Norris, and slapped Bill Hayden on the back and roared. "Hee-yah! Skyrider! When yo' all git done kissin' Venus's snow-white hand, come and listen at what's been wrote for yo' all by Mary V! Whoo-*ee*! Where's the Great Bear at that yo' all was goin' to lead home, Skyrider?" Then they laughed like two maniacs. Mary V gritted her teeth at them and wished aloud that she had her shotgun with her.

A youth, whose sagging chaps pulled in his waistline until he looked almost as slim as a girl, ceased dragging at the bridle reins of a balky bronk and glanced across the corral. His three companions were hurrying that way, lured by a paper which Bud was waving high above his head as he straddled the top rail of the fence.

"Johnny's a poet, and we didn't know it!" bawled Bud. "Listen here at what the witless wight's been a-writin'!" Then, seated upon the top rail and with his hat set far back on his head, Bud Norris began to declaim inexorably the first two verses, until the indignant author came over and interfered with voice and a vicious yank at Bud's foot, which brought that young man down forthwith.

"Aw, le' me alone while I read the rest! Honest, it's swell po'try, and I want the boys to hear it. Listen-get out, Johnny! *'I'll circle high as if passing by, then —v-o-l —then vollup, bank, an' land —'* Hold him off'n me, boys! This is rich stuff I'm readin'! Hey, hold your hand over his mouth, why don't yuh, Aleck? Yo' all want to wait till I git to where —"

"I can't," wailed Aleck. "He bit me!"

"Well, take 'im down an' set on him, then. I tell yuh, boys, this is rich —"

"You give that back here, or I'll murder yuh!" a full-throated young voice cried hoarsely.

"Here, quit yore kickin'!" Bill admonished.

"Go on, Bud; the boys have got to hear it-it's *rich*!"

"Yeh-shut up, Johnny! Po'try is wrote to be read-go on, Bud. Start 'er over again. I never got to hear half of it on account of Johnny's cussin'. Go on —I got him chewin' on my hat now. Read 'er from the start-off."

"The best is yet to come," Bill gloated pantingly, while he held the author's legs much as he would hold down a yearling. "All set, Bud-let 'er go!"

Whereupon Bud cleared his throat and began again, rolling the words out sonorously, so that Mary V heard every word distinctly:

> "Before I die, I'll ride the sky;
>
> I'll part the clouds like foam.
>
> I'll brand each star with the Rolling R,
>
> And lead the Great Bear home.'"

"Say, that's *swell*!" a little fellow they called Curley interjected. "By gosh, that's darned good po'try! I never knowed Johnny could —"

He was frowned into silence by the reader, who went on exuberantly, the lines punctuated by profane gurgles from the author.

"Now this here," Bud paused to explain, "was c'lab'rated on by Mary V. The first line was wrote by our 'steemed young friend an' skyrider poet, but the balance is in Mary V's handwritin'. And I claim she's some poet! Quit cussin' and listen, Johnny; yo' all never heard this 'un, and I'll gamble on it:

"*'Through the clouds we'll float in my airplane boat —'* That, there's by Skyrider. And here Mary V finishes it up:

> "For Venus I am truly sorry!
>
> All the stars you sight, you witless wight,
>
> You'll see when you and Venus light!
>
> But then —I'm sure that I should worry!'"

"I don't believe she ever wrote that!" Johnny struggled up to declare passionately. "You give that here, Bud Norris. Worry-sorry-they don't even rhyme!"

"Aw, ferget that stuff! Witless wight's all right, ain't it? I claim Mary V's some poetry writer. Don't you go actin' up jealous. She ain't got the jingle, mebby, but she shore is there with the big idee."

"*Drink the dipper dry*'—that shore does hit me where I live!" cried little Curley. "Did you make it up outa yore own head, Johnny?"

"Naw. I made it up out of a spellin' book!" Johnny, being outnumbered five to one, decided to treat the whole matter with lofty unconcern. "Hand it over, Bud."

Bud did not want to hand it over. He had just discovered that he could sing it, which he proceeded to do to the tune of "Auld Lang Syne" and the full capacity of his lungs. Bill and Aleck surged up to look over his shoulder and join their efforts to his, and the half dozen horses held captive in that corral stampeded to a far corner and huddled there, shrinking at the uproar.

"*And kiss 'er snow-white ha-a-and, and kiss 'er snow-white ha-and,*" howled the quartet inharmoniously, at least two of them off key; for Tex Martin had joined the concert and was performing with a bull bellow that could be heard across a section. Then Bud began suddenly to improvise, and his voice rose valiantly that his words might carry their meaning to the ears of Johnny Jewel, who had stalked back across the corral and was striving now to catch the horse he had let go, while his one champion, little Curley, shooed the animal into a corner for him.

"*It would be grand to kiss her hand, her snow-white hand, if I had the sand!*" Bud chanted vaingloriously. "How's that, Skyrider? Ain't that purty fair po'try?"

"It don't fit into the tune with a cuss," Tex criticized jealously. "Pass over that po'try of Johnny's. Yo' all ain't needin' it-not if you aims to make up yore own words."

"C'm '*ere*! You wall-eyed weiner-wurst!" Johnny harshly addressed the horse he was after. "You've got about as much brains as the rest of this outfit-and that's putting it strong! If I owned you —"

"*I'd cir-cle high 's if pass-in' by, then vol-lup bank an' la-a-and,*" the voice of Tex roared out in a huge wave that drowned all other sounds, the voices of Bill, Aleck, and Bud trailing raucously after.

Johnny, goaded out of his lofty contempt of them, whirled suddenly and picked up a rock. Johnny could pitch a very fair ball for an amateur, and the rock went true without any frills or curving deception. It landed in the middle of Bud Norris's back, and Bud's vocal efforts ended in a howl of pain.

"Serves you right, you devil!" Mary V commented unsympathetically from her perch on the ledge.

Three more rocks ended the concert abruptly and started something else. Curley had laughed hysterically until the four faced belligerently Johnny's bombardment and started for him. "Beat it, Johnny! Beat it!" cried Curley then, and made for the fence.

"I will like hell!" snarled Johnny, and gathered more rocks.

"Oh, Johnny! Sudden's comin'!" wailed Curley from the top rail. "Quit it, Johnny, or you'll git fired!"

"I don't give a damn if I do!" Johnny's full, young voice shouted ragefully. "It'll save me firing myself. Before I'll work with a bunch of yellow-bellied, pin-headed fools —" He threw a clod of dirt that caught Tex on the chin and filled his mouth so that he nearly choked, and a jagged pebble that hit Aleck just over the ear a glancing blow that sent him reeling. The third was aimed at Bill, but Bill ducked in time, and the rock went on over his head and very nearly laid out Mary V's father, he whom the boys called "Sudden" for some inexplicable reason.

Mary V's father dodged successfully the rock, saw a couple of sheets of paper lying on the ground, and methodically picked them up before he advanced to where his men were trying to appear very busy with the horses, or with their ropes, or with anything save what had held their attention just previous to his coming.

All save Johnny, who was too mad to care a rap what old Sudden Selmer thought of him or did to him. He went straight up to the boss.

"I'll thank you for that paper," he said hardily. "It's mine, and the boys have been acting the fool with it."

"Yeh? They have?" Selmer turned from the first page and read the second without any apparent emotion. "You write that?"

Johnny flushed. "Yes, sir, I did. Do you mind letting —"

"That what I heard them yawping here in the corral?" Selmer folded the paper with care, his fingers smoothing out the wrinkles and pausing to observe the place where Mary V had torn off a corner.

"Poets and song birds on the pay roll, eh? Thought I hired you boys to handle horses." Having folded the papers as though they were to be placed in an envelope, Sudden held the verses out to Johnny. "As riders," he observed judicially, "I know just about what you boys are worth to me. As poets and singers, I doubt whether the Rolling R can find use for you. What capacity do I find you in, Curley? Director of the orchestra, or umpire?"

Curley climbed shamefacedly off the fence and picked up his rope. The business of taming bronks was resumed in a dead silence broken only by the trampling of the horses and a muttered oath now and then. A lump over Aleck's ear was swelling so that the hair lifted there, and Bud limped and sent scowling glances at Johnny Jewel. Tex spat dirt off his tongue and scowled while he did it; indeed, no eyes save those of little Curley seemed able to look upon Johnny with a kindly light.

Mary V's father stood dispassionately watching them for five minutes or so before he turned back to the gate. Not once had he smiled or shown any emotion whatever. But he had a new story to tell his friends in the clubs of Tucson, Phoenix, Yuma, Los Angeles. And whenever he told it, Sudden Selmer would repeat what he called *The Skyrider's Dream* from the first verse to Mary V's last-even unto Bud's improvisation. He would paint Johnny's bombardment of the choir practice until his audience could almost hear the thud of the rocks when they landed. He would describe the welt on Aleck's head, the exact shade of purple in Curley's face when his boss called him off the fence. He would not smile at all during the recital, but his audience would shout and splutter and roar, and when he paused as though the story was done, some one would be sure to demand more.

Then a little twitching smile would show at the corner of Sudden's lips, and he would drawl whimsically: "Those boys were so scared they never chirped when the poet actually went sky-riding to an altitude of about ten feet above the saddle horn, and lit on the back of his neck. Johnny's a good rider, too, but he was mad. He was so mad I don't believe he knows yet that he was piled. Afterwards? Oh, well, they came to along about supper time and yawped his poetry all over the place, I heard. But that was after I had left the ranch."

There were a few details which Sudden, being only human, could not possibly give his friends. He could not know that Mary V went back down the hill, sneaked into the bunk house and got Johnny's coat, and sewed the sleeve lining in very neatly, and took the coat back without being seen. Nor did he know that she violently regretted the deed of kindness, when she discovered that Johnny remained perfectly unconscious of the fact that his coat sleeve no longer troubled him.

Chapter Two. One Fight, Two Quarrels, and a Riddle

Rolling R ranch lies down near the border of Mexico-near as distances are counted in Arizona. Possibly a hawk could make it in one flight straight across that jagged, sandy, spiney waste of scenery which the chance traveler visions the moment you mention southern Arizona, but if you wanted to ride to the Border from the Rolling R corrals, you would find the trip a half-day proposition. As to the exact location, never mind about that.

The Selmer Stock Company had other ranches where they raised other animals, but the Rolling R raised horses almost exclusively, the few hundred head of cattle not being counted as a real ranch industry, but rather an incidental by-product. Rolling R Ranch was the place Sudden Selmer called home, although there was a bungalow out in the Wilshire District in Los Angeles about which Sudden would grumble when the tax notice came in his mail. There was a big touring car in the garage on the back of the lot, and there was a colored couple who lived in two rooms of the bungalow for sake of the fire insurance and as a precaution against thieves, and to keep the lawn watered and clipped and the dust off the furniture. They admitted that they had a snap, for they were seldom disturbed in their leisurely caretaking routine save in the winter. Even Mary V always tired of the place after a month or two in it, and would pack her trunk and "hit the trail" for the Rolling R.

Speaking of Mary V, you would know that a girl with modern upbringing lived a good deal at the ranch. You could tell by the low, green bungalow with wide, screened porches and light cream trim, that was almost an exact reproduction of the bungalow in Los Angeles. A man and woman who have lived long together on a ranch like the Rolling R would have gone on living contentedly in the adobe house which was now abandoned to the sole occupancy of the boys. It is the young lady of the family who demands up-to-date housing.

So the bungalow stood there in the glaring sun, surrounded by a scrap of lawn which the Arizona winds whipped and buffeted with sand and wind all summer, and vines which the wind tousled into discouragement. And fifty yards away squatted the old adobe house in the sand, with a tree at each front corner and a narrow porch extending from one to the other.

Beyond the adobe, toward the sheltering bluff, a clutter of low sheds, round-pole corrals, a modern barn of fair size, and beside it a square corral of planks and stout, new posts, continued the tale of how progress was joggling the elbow of picturesqueness. Sudden's father had built the adobe and the oldest sheds and corrals, when he took all the land he could lawfully hold under government claims. Later he had bought more; and Sudden, growing up and falling heir to it all, had added tract after tract by purchase and lease and whatever other devices a good politician may be able to command.

Sudden's father had been a simple man, content to run his ranch along the lines of least resistance, and to take what prosperity came to him in the natural course of events. Sudden had organized a Company, had commercialized his legacy, had "married money," and had made money. Far to the north and to the east and west ran the lines of other great ranches, where sheep were handled in great, blatting bands and yielded a fortune in wool. There were hills where Selmer cattle were wild as deer-cattle that never heard the whistle of a locomotive until they were trailed down to the railroad to market.

These made the money for Selmer and his Company. But it was the Rolling R, where the profits were smaller, that stood closest to Sudden's heart. There was not so much money in horses as there was in sheep; Sudden admitted it readily enough. But he hated sheep; hated the sound of them and the smell of them and the insipid, questioning faces of them. And he loved horses; loved the big-jointed, wabbly legged colts and the round-bodied, anxious mothers; loved the grade geldings and fillies and the registered stock that he kept close to home in fenced pastures; loved the broom-tail bronks that ranged far afield and came in a dust cloud moiling up from their staccato hoof beats, circled by hoarse, shouting riders seen vaguely through the cloud.

There was a thrill in watching a corral full of wild horses milling round and round, dodging the whispering ropes that writhed here and there overhead to settle and draw tight over some unlucky head. There was a thrill in the taming-more thrills than dollars, for until the war overseas brought eager buyers, the net profits of the horse ranch would scarcely have paid for Mary V's clothes and school and what she demurely set down as "recreation."

But Sudden loved it, and Mary V loved it, and Mary V's mother loved whatever they loved. So the Rolling R was home. And that is why the Rolling R boys looked upon Mary V with unglamoured eyes, being thoroughly accustomed to the sight of her and to the sharp tongue of her and to the frequent discomfort of having her about.

They liked her, of course. They would have fought for her if ever the need of fighting came, just as they would have fought for anything else in their outfit. But they took her very calmly and as a matter of course, and were not inclined to that worshipful bearing which romancers would have us accept as the inevitable attitude of cowboys toward the daughter of the rancho.

Wherefore Johnny Jewel was not committing any heinous act of treason when he walked past Mary V with stiffened spine and head averted. Johnny was mad at the whole outfit, and that included Mary V. Indeed, his anger particularly included Mary V. A young man who has finished high school and one year at a university, and who reads technical books rather than fiction and has ambitions for something much higher than his present calling, —oh, very much higher! —would naturally object to being called a witless wight.

Johnny objected. He had cussed Aleck for repeating the epithet in the bunk house, and he had tried to lick Bud Norris, and had failed. He blamed Mary V for his skinned knuckles and the cut on his lip, and for all his other troubles. Johnny did not know about the coat, though he had it on; and if he had known, I doubt whether it would have softened his mood. He was a terribly incensed young man.

Mary V had let her steps lag a little, knowing that Johnny must overtake her presently unless he turned short around and went the other way, which would not be like Johnny. She had meant to say something that would lead the conversation gently toward the verses, and then she meant to say something else about the difficulty of making two lines rhyme, and the necessity of using perfectly idiotic words-such as wight. Mary V was disgusted with the boys for the way they had acted. She meant to tell Johnny that she thought his verses were very clever, and that she, too, was keen for flying. And would he like to borrow a late magazine she had in the house, that had an article about the growth of the "game"? Mary V did not know that she would have sounded rather patronizing. Her girl friends in Los Angeles had filled her head with romantic ideas about cowboys, especially her father's cowboys. They had taken it so for granted that the Rolling R boys must simply worship the ground she walked on, that Mary V had unconsciously come to believe that adoration was her birthright.

And then Johnny stepped out of the trail and passed her as though she had been a cactus or a rock that he must walk around! Mary V went hot all over, with rage before her wits came back. Johnny had not gone ten feet ahead of her when she was humming softly to herself a little, old-fashioned tune. And the tune was "Auld Lang Syne."

Johnny whirled in the trail and faced her, hard-eyed.

"You're trying to play smart Aleck, too, are yuh?" he demanded. "Why don't yuh sing the words that's in your mind? Why don't you *try* to sing your own ideas of poetry? You know as much about writing poetry as I do about tatting! 'Worry'! 'surrey'! Or did you mean that it should be read 'wawry,' 'sorry'?"

A fine way to talk to the Flower of the Rancho! Mary V looked as though she wanted to slap Johnny Jewel's smooth, boyish face.

"Of course, you're qualified to teach me," she retorted. "Such doggerel! You ought to send it to the comic papers. Really, Mr. Jewel, I have read a good deal of amateurish, childish attempts at poetry-in the infant class at school. But never in all my life —"

"Oh, well, if you ever get out of the infant class, Miss Selmer, you may learn a few rudimentary rules of metrical composition. I apologize for criticising your efforts. It is not so bad-for infant class work." He said that, standing there in the very coat which she had mended for him!

Mary V turned white; also she wished that *she* had thought of mentioning the "rudimentary rules of metrical composition" instead of infant classes. She smiled as disagreeably as was possible to such humanly kissable lips as hers.

"No, is it?" she agreed sweetly. "Witless wight was rather good, I thought. Wight fits you so well."

"Oh, that!" Johnny turned defensively to a tolerant condescension. "That wasn't so bad, if it hadn't shown on the face of it that it was just dragged in to make a rhyme. Do you know what wight means, Miss Selmer?"

Mary V was inwardly shaken. She had always believed that wight was a synonym for dunce, but now that he put the question to her in that tone, she was not positive. Her angry eyes faltered a little.

"I see you don't —of course. Used as a noun-you know what a noun is, don't you? It means the name of anything. Wight means a person-any creature. Originally it meant a fairy, a supernatural being. As an adjective it means brave, valiant, strong or powerful. Or, it used to mean clever."

"Oh, *you*! I hate the sight of you, you great bully!" Mary V ducked past him and ran.

"I'll help you look it up in the dictionary if you don't know how," Johnny called after her maliciously, not at all minding the epithet she had hurled at him. He went on more cheerfully, telling himself unchivalrously that he had got Mary V's goat, all right. He began to whistle under his breath, until he discovered that he was whistling "Auld Lang Syne," and was mentally fitting to the tune the words: *"Before I die, I'll ride the sky. I'll part the clouds like foam!"*

He stopped whistling then, but the words went on repeating themselves over and over in his mind. "And by gosh, I will too," he stated defiantly. "I'll show 'em, the darned mutts! They can yawp and chortle and call me Skyrider as if it was a joke. That's as much as they know, the ignorant boobs. Why, they couldn't tell an aileron from an elevator if it was to save their lives! —and still they think I'm crazy and don't know anything. Why, darn 'em, they'll *pay money* some day to see me fly! Boy, I'd like to circle over this ranch at about three or four thousand feet, and then do a loop or two and volplane right down *at* 'em! Gosh, they'd be hunting holes to crawl into before I was through with 'em! I will, too —"

Johnny went off into a pet daydream and was almost happy for a little while. Some day the Rolling R boys would be telling with pride how they used to know Johnny Jewel, the wonderful birdman that had his picture in all the papers and was getting thousands of dollars for exhibition flights. Tex, Aleck, Bud, Bill-Mary V, too, gol darn her! —would go around bragging just because they used to know him! And right then he'd sure play even for some of the insults they were handing him now.

"Mary V Selmer? Let's see-the name sounds familiar, somehow. O-oh! You mean that little red-headed ranch girl from Arizona? Oh-h, yes! Well, give her a free pass-but I mustn't be bothered personally with her. The girl's all right, but no training, no manners. Hick stuff; no class, you understand. But give her a good seat, where she can view the getaway."

Tex, Aleck, Bud, and Bill-little Curley was all right; Curley could have a job as watchman at the hangar. But the rest of the bunch could goggle at him from a distance and be darned to them. Old Sudden too. He'd be kind of nice to old Sudden-nice in an offhand, indifferent kind of way. But Mary V could get down on her *knees*, and he wouldn't be nice to her. He should say not!

So dreamed Johnny Jewel, all the way to the mail box out by the main road, and nearly all the way back again. But then his ears were assailed with lugubrious singing:

"An' dlead the Great Bear ho-o-ome,

An' dlead the Great Bear hoo-me,

I'll brand each star with the Rollin' R,

An-n dlead the Great Bear home!"

That was Bud's contribution.

"Aw, for gosh sake, *shut up!*" yelled Johnny, his temper rising again.

From the bungalow, when he passed it on his way to the bunk house, came the measured thump-thump of a piano playing the same old tune with a stress meant to mock him and madden him.

"Then if she'll smile I'll stop awhile,

And kiss her snow-white hand."

That was Mary V, singing at the top of her voice, and Johnny walked stiff-backed down the path. He wanted to turn and repeat to Mary V what he had shouted to Bud, but he refrained, though not from any chivalry, I am sorry to say. Johnny feared that it would be playing into her hand too much if he took that much notice of her. He wouldn't give her the satisfaction of knowing he heard her.

"It would be grand to kiss 'er hand,

Her-rr snow-white hand if I had the sand,"

Bud finished unctuously, adjusting the tune to fit the words.

Johnny swore, flung open the low door of the bunk house, went in, and slammed it shut after him, and began to pack his personal belongings. Presently Tex came in, warbling like a lovesick crow:

"I'll cir-cle high 's if pass-in' by,

Then vol-lup bank-an' la-a-and —"

"So will this la-and," Johnny said viciously and threw one of his new riding boots straight at the warbler. "For gosh sake, lay off that stuff!"

Tex caught the boot dexterously without interrupting his song, except that he forgot the words and sang ta-da-da-da to the end of the verse.

"Po'try was wrote to be read," he replied sententiously when he had finished. "And tunes was made to be sung. And yo' all oughta be proud to death at the way yo' all made a hit with yore po'try. It beats what Mary V wrote, Skyrider. If yo' all want to know my honest opinion, Mary V's plumb sore because yo' all made up po'try about Venus instid of about her." He sat down on a corner of the littered table and began to roll a cigarette, jerking his head towards the bungalow and lowering one eyelid slowly. "Girls, I'm plumb next to 'em, Skyrider. I growed up with four of 'em. Mary V loves that there Venus stuff, and kissin' her snow-white hand, same as a cat loves snow. Jealous-that's what's bitin' Mary V."

Johnny was sorting letters, mostly circulars and "follow up" letters from various aviation schools. He looked up suspiciously at Tex, but Tex manifested none of the symptoms of sly "kidding." Tex was smoking meditatively and gazing absently at Johnny's suitcase.

"Yo' all ain't quittin'?" Tex roused himself to ask. "Not over a little josh? Say, you're layin' yoreself wide open to more of the same. Yo' all wants to take it the way it's meant, Skyrider. Listen here, boy, if yo' all wants to git away from the ranch right now, why don't yo' all speak for to stay at Sinkhole camp? Yo' all could have mo' time to write po'try an' study up on flyin' machines, down there. And Pete, he's aimin' to quit the first. He don't like it down there."

Johnny dropped the letters back into his suitcase and sat down on the side of his bed to smoke. His was not the nature to hold a grudge, and Tex seemed to be friendly. Still, his youthful dignity had been very much hurt, and by Tex as much as the other boys. He gave him a supercilious glance.

"I don't know where you get the idea that I'm a quitter," he said pettishly. "First I knew that a bunch of rough-necks could kid me out of a job. Go down to Sinkhole yourself, if you're so anxious about that camp. Furthermore," he added stiffly, "it's nobody's business but mine what I write or study, or where I write and study. So don't set there trying to look wise, Tex-telling me what to do and how to do it. You can't put anything over on me; your work is too raw. Al-to-gether too raw!"

He glanced sidewise at a circular letter he had dropped, picked it up and began reading it slowly, one eye squinted against the smoke of his cigarette, his manner that of supreme indifference to Tex and all his kind. Johnny could be very, very indifferent when he chose.

He did not really believe that Tex was trying to put anything over on him; he just said that to show Tex he didn't give a darn one way or the other. But Tex seemed to take it seriously, and glowered at Johnny from under his black eyebrows that had a hawklike arch.

"What yo' all think I'm trying to put over? Hey? What yo' all mean by that statement?"

Johnny looked up, one eye still squinted against the smoke. The other showed surprise back of the indifference. "You there yet?" he wanted to know. "What's the big idea? Gone to roost for the night?"

Tex leaned toward him, waggling one finger at Johnny. The outer end of his eyebrows were twitching—a sign of anger in Tex, as Johnny knew well.

"What yo' all got up yore sleeve-saying my work is raw! What yo' all aimin' at? That's what I'm roostin' here to learn."

Johnny fanned away the smoke and gave a little chuckle meant to exasperate Tex, which it did.

"I guess the roosting's going to be pretty good," he said. "You better send cookee word to bring your meals to yuh, Tex. Because if you roost there till I tell yuh, you'll be roosting a good long while!" He got up and lounged out, his hands in his pockets, his well-shaped head carried at a provocative tilt. He heard Tex swear under his breath and mutter something about making the darned little runt come through yet, whereat Johnny grinned maliciously.

Halfway to the corral, however, Johnny's steps slowed as though he were walking straight up to a wall. The wall was there, but it was mental, and it was his mind that halted before it, astonished.

What had touched Tex off so suddenly when Johnny had flung out that meaningless taunt? Meaningless to Johnny-but how about Tex?

"Gosh! He took it like a guilty conscience," said Johnny. "What the horn-toad has Tex been doin'?"

Chapter Three. Johnny Goes Gaily Enough to Sinkhole

Johnny Jewel, moved by the fluctuating determination of the young, went to bed that night fully resolved that he would not quit a good job just because untoward circumstance compelled him to herd with a bunch of brainless clowns. He, who had a definite aim in life, would not permit that aim to be turned aside because various and sundry roughneck punchers thought it was funny to go around yelping like a band of coyotes. Mary V, too-he did not neglect to include Mary V. Indeed, much of his determination to remain was born of his desire to crush that insolent young woman with polite, pitying toleration.

Even when the boys trooped in and began to compose what they believed to be rhymes, Johnny did not weaken. He turned his face to the wall and ignored them. Poor simps, what more could you expect? They went so far as to attempt some poetizing on the subject of Johnny's downfall in the corral, but no one seemed able to eliminate the word bronk at the end of the first line, *"Johnny tried to ride a bronk."* No one seemed able, either, to find any rhyme but honk. They tried ker-plunk, and although that seemed to answer the purpose fairly well, they were far from satisfied.

So was Johnny, but he would not say a word to save their lives. In spite of himself he heard a howl of glee when some genius among them declaimed loudly: *"Johnny volluped into Job's Coffin, and Venus she most died a-lawfin!"*

Johnny gave a grunt of contempt, and the genius, who happened to be Bud, lifted his head off the pillow and stared at the black shadow where Johnny lay curled up like a cat.

"What's the matter with that, Skyrider? Kain't I make up po'try if I want to?"

"Sure. Help yourself-you poor fish. Vollup! *Hunh!*" The contempt was even more pronounced than before.

"Well? What's the matter with that? You said it yourself. And look out how you go peddlin' names around here. You think nobody knows anything but you! You're the little boy that invented flyin' —got the idea from yore own head, by thunder, when it swelled up like a balloon with self-conceit! That there gas-head of yourn'll take yuh right up amongst the clouds some day, and you won't need no flyin' machine, neither! Skyrider-is —*right!*" Accidentally Johnny had touched Bud's self-esteem in a tender spot. "And that's no kidding, either!" he clinched his meaning. "Punch a hole in yore skelp, and I'll bet that big haid of yourn would wizzle all up like them red balloons they sell at circuses! You —"

"*Hm-m-m!* Just so it ain't all solid bone like yours," Johnny came back at him with youth's full quota of scorn. "Keep away from pool rooms, Bud. Somebody is liable to take your head off and use it for a cue-ball. *Vollup! Hunh!*"

Bud said more; a great deal more. But Johnny flopped over on the other side, buried his head under the blankets, and let them talk. Cue-balls —that was all their heads were good for. So why concern himself over their senseless patter?

It occurred to him, just before he went to sleep, that the unmistakable, southern drawl of Tex was missing from the jumble of voices. Tex, he remembered, had been unusually silent at supper, also, and twice Johnny had caught Tex watching him somberly. But he could think of no possible reason why Tex should want him to go down to Sinkhole Camp, and he could not see how either of them could effect the change even if Johnny had cared to go. Sudden Selmer did not ask his men what was their desire. Sudden gave orders; his men could obey or they could quit. And if Pete left, as Tex had hinted, Sudden would send some one down there, and that would be an end of it. There was just about one chance in six that Johnny Jewel would be the man to go.

Yet it so happened that Johnny did go-though Tex had nothing to do with it, so far as Johnny could see. For all his determination to stay and tolerate his companions, noon found him packed and out by the gate that opened on the stage road, waiting to flag the stage and buy a ride to town. He had accomplished, since breakfast, two fights and another quarrel with Mary V over that infernal jingle he had written. And though Johnny could not see it, Tex had had something to do with them all.

Tex was not one of these diabolically cunning villains. He did not consider himself any kind of a villain. He accepted himself more or less contentedly as a poor, striving young man who wanted to get ahead in the world and was eager to pick up what he called "side money," which might, if he were on to his job, amount to more than his wages. Tex did not consider that he owed the Rolling R anything whatever save a certain number of days' work in each month that he drew a pay check. He sold Sudden his time and his skill in the saddle —a month of it for fifty dollars. But if he could double that fifty without harm to himself, Tex was not going to split any hairs over the method.

Tex was not displaying any great genius when he edged the boys on to tease Johnny beyond the limit of that young man's endurance, or when he tattled to Mary V a slighting remark about her ability as a poet. Tex was merely carrying out an idea which had come to him when he saw Johnny with his hands full of aircraft literature. If it worked, all right. If it didn't work, Johnny would not be on the Rolling R pay roll any longer, but Tex would not have lost anything. It would be convenient to have Johnny down at Sinkhole Camp, shirking his job while he fiddled around with his flying bug. Tex believed he knew how he could keep the bug very active, and Johnny very much engrossed with it-down at Sinkhole Camp. It was simple enough, and worth the slight effort Tex was making.

So there was Johnny Jewel with his saddle and bridle and suitcase and chaps, waiting out by the mail box for the stage. And there came Sudden, driving back from the railroad-Tex knew he was expected back that forenoon-and reaching the gate before the stage had come in sight around the southwest spur of the ridge it could not cross. Sudden liked Johnny-and Tex knew that too. (Tex made it his business to know a good deal which had nothing to do with his legitimate work.) And good riders who did not get drunk every chance that offered were not to be hired every day in the week.

Johnny opened the gate, but Sudden did not drive through. He stopped and eyed the suitcase and the saddle and the chaps, and then he looked at Johnny.

"Too much song-bird stuff?" he asked, which showed how sensitive was the finger Sudden kept on the pulse of his outfit.

"I've got to work for a living, but I don't have to work with that bunch of idiots," Johnny stated with much dignity.

Sudden rubbed a gauntleted hand across the lower part of his face; and that, I think, is why Johnny saw himself taken as seriously as his young egotism demanded.

"Rather be by yourself, would you? Well, throw your baggage in the back of the car. I want you to catch up a couple of horses and go on down to Sinkhole. You won't be annoyed down there with anybody's foolishness but your own, young man. You'll work for your living, all right! Got a gun? A rifle? Well, there's one at the house you can take. There may not be any Rolling R horses going across the line-but it'll be your business to *know* there aren't. If you see a greaser prowling around, put him on the run. They're paying good money for horses in Mexico, remember. You're down there to see they don't get 'em too cheap on this side. Do you get that?"

"Yes, sir-you bet!"

"Oh. You do? Well, get in."

At the corral he turned again to Johnny. "Stop at the house when you're ready. There's a pile of *Modern Mechanics* you may as well take along. You won't have any too much time for reading, though-not if you work the way you rhyme."

"Well, I hope I work better," said Johnny, his spirits risen to where speech bubbled. "I get paid for my work-and I guess I'd starve writing poetry for a living."

"Yes, I guess you would. Good thing you know it." Sudden swung his machine around and drove into the garage, and Johnny, untying his rope from his saddle, went into the corral to catch two fairly gentle horses.

When he was ready he rode over to the bungalow, leading the gentlest horse packed with bedding roll, "war bag," and a few odds and ends that Johnny wanted to take along. Sudden was waiting on the porch with a rifle, cartridge belt and two extra boxes of ammunition, and a sack half full of magazines. He stood with his hands in his pockets while Johnny tied rifle and sack on the saddle.

"Now I want you to understand, Johnny, that you're going down there on special work," he said, coming down the steps and standing close to the horse. "There's a telephone, and that's your protection if anything looks off-color. Keep the stock pushed back pretty well away from the line fences. There's some good feed in those draws over east of Sinkhole creek. Let 'em graze in there-but keep an eye out for rustlers. Get to know the bunches of horses and watch their moves. You'll soon know whether they are being bothered. Pete leaves camp this afternoon. You'll probably meet him.

"And this gun-well, you keep it right with you. I don't want you to go around hunting trouble, but I want you to be ready for it if it comes. A horse looks awfully good to a greaser, remember. But no greaser likes the looks of a white man with a gun. Now let's see how much brains you've got for the job, young man. If you see to it that no Rolling R stuff comes up missing, and do it without any trouble, I'll call that making good."

"All right, I'll try and make good, then." Johnny's shoulders went back. "When a man's got some object in life besides just earning a living, he —"

From within the house full-toned chords were struck from a piano. Johnny scowled, gave his packed horse a yank, and rode off. Couldn't that girl ever let up on a fellow? Playing that darn fool tune over and over! It sure showed how much brains she had in her head! He hoped she'd get enough of it. If he was her mother or her father, he knew what he'd do with her and the whole outfit. He'd stand 'em all up in a row and make 'em sing that fool song till they were hoarse as calves on the fifth day of weaning. There was a time, too, when he had liked that girl. If she had shown any brains or feeling, he could have loved Mary V. Good thing he found out in time.

Johnny looked back from the gate and heaved a great sigh of relief at his narrow escape. Or was it regret? Johnny himself did not know, but he called it relief because that was the most comfortable emotion a young man may take away with him into desert loneliness.

Yes, sir, he was glad of the chance to stay at Sinkhole for awhile. He wouldn't be pestered to death, and he would have plenty of time to study and read. He'd send for that correspondence course on aviation, and he'd get the theory of it all down pat, so that when he had enough money saved up to go into the thing right, all he would need would be the actual practice in the air. He should think he could go to some school and work his way along; get a little practice every day, and do repair work or something the rest of the time for nothing. A dollar a minute for learning was pretty steep, Johnny thought, but after all it was worth it. A dollar a minute-and four hundred minutes in the air for the average course!

Four hundred dollars, and only half that much saved. And then there would be his fare back east, and his board-Johnny wished that he might cut out eating, but he realized how healthy was his appetite. He counted three meals for every day, at an average of fifty cents for each meal. Well, even so, he could "ride the bumpers" to the school; take a side-door pullman; beat his way; hobo it-or whatever the initiated wanted to call it. He could send his suitcase on by express, and just wear old clothes-send his money on, too, for that matter. He could save quite a lot that way. Or maybe he could get Sudden to let him go back with cattle from the Gila River Ranch-only he wouldn't ask any favors from any one by the name of Selmer. No, he'd be darned if he would! He'd just draw his wages, when he had enough saved, and drop out of sight. He wouldn't even tell Curley where he was going. And then, some day —

There came the air castle again, floating alluringly before his eager imagination, like a mirage lake in the desert. Johnny's eyes stared ahead through the shimmering heat waves-stared and saw not the monotonous neutral tints of sand and rock and gray sage and yellow weeds and the rutted, dusty trail that wound away across the desert. But Mary V's face turned expectantly toward him from the crowd as he walked nonchalantly around his big tractor, testing every cable, inspecting the landing gear and the elevators and the-what-ye-may-call-'ems-and then climbing in and trying out his control-and pulling down his goggles and settling his moleskin cap and all-and then nodding imperiously to his helper-not little Curley; he was not big enough to crank his powerful motor-but some big guy that had a reach like —

And then the buzz and the hum, and fellows braced against the wings to hold 'er till he was ready to give the word! And the dust storm he kicked up behind-he hoped Mary V got her eyes full, darn her! —and then, getting the feel of 'er, and giving a nod to the fellows to let go the wings! And then —

Johnny rode along in a trance. He, his conscious inward self, was not riding a sweating bronk along a trail that wound more-or-less southward across the desert. That was his body, chained by grim necessity to work for a wage. He, Johnny Jewel's ego, was soaring up and up and up-up till the eagles themselves gazed enviously after. He was darting in and out among the convolutions of fluffy white clouds; was looping earthward in great, invisible volutes; catching himself on the upward curve and zigzagging away again, swimming ecstatically the high, clean air currents which the poor, crawling, earthbound ones never know.

Johnny jarred back to earth and to the sordid realities of life. He had ridden half way to Sinkhole without knowing it, and now his horse had stopped, facing another horse whose rider was staring curiously at Johnny. This was Pete, on his way in from Sinkhole.

"Say-y! Yuh snake-bit, or what?" Pete asked. "Ridin' glassy-eyed right *at* a feller! If my hawse had been a mite shorter, I expect you'd of rode right on over me and never of saw me. What's bitin' yuh, Johnny?"

"Me? Nothing!" No daydreamer likes being pulled out of his dream by so ugly a reality as Pete, and Johnny was petulant. "Why didn't you get outa the way, then? You saw me coming, didn't you?"

"Me? Sure! I ain't *loco*. I seen yuh five mile back, about. I knowed it was somebody from the ranch. Sudden 'phoned in and said I could drag it. And you can bet yore sweet young life I hailed them words with joy! What yuh done to 'im that he's sendin' yuh off down to Sinkhole? Me, I 'phoned in and much as told 'em he'd have to double my pay if he wanted me to stay down there any longer. That was a coupla days ago. Didn't git no satisfaction atall till to-day. Me, I'd ruther go to jail, twicet over, than stay here a week longer. Ain't saw a soul in two weeks down there. Well, I'll be pushin' along. Adios-and here's hopin' you like it better than what I done."

Johnny told him good-bye and straightway forgot him. Once he had his two horses "lined out" in their shuffling little trail-trot that was their natural gait, he picked up his dream where he had been interrupted. Where his body went mattered little to Johnny Jewel, so long as he was left alone with his thoughts. So presently his eyes were once more staring vacantly at the dim trail, while in spirit he was soaring high and swooping downward with the ease of a desert lark, while thousands thrilled to watch his flight.

What did he care about Sinkhole Camp? Loneliness meant long, uninterrupted hours in which to ride and read and dream of the great things he meant some day to do.

Chapter Four. A Thing That Sets Like a Hawk

Six days are not many when they are lived with companions and the numberless details of one's everyday occupation. They may seem a month if you pass them in jail, or in waiting for some great event, —or at Sinkhole Camp, down near the Border.

Three days of the six Johnny spent in familiarizing himself with the two or three detached horse herds that watered along the meager little stream that sunk finally under a ledge and was seen no more in Arizona. He counted the horses as best he could while they loitered at their watering places, and he noticed where they fed habitually-also that they ranged far and usually came in to water in the late afternoon or closer to dusk, when the yellow-jackets that swarmed along the muddy banks of the stream did not worry them so much, nor the flies that were a torment.

He reported by telephone to his employer, who seemed relieved to know that everything was so quiet and untroubled down at that end of his range. And once, quite inadvertently, he reported to Mary V; or was going to, when he recognized a feminine note in the masculine gruffness that spoke over the wire. And when she found he had discovered her:

"Oh, Johnny! I've thought of another verse!" she began animatedly.

Johnny hung up, and although the telephone rang twice after that he would not answer. It seemed to him that Mary V had very little to do, harping away still at that subject. He had been secretly a bit homesick for the ranch, but now he thanked heaven, emphatically enough to make up for any lack of sincerity, that he was where he was.

He got out his aviation circulars again and went over them one by one, though he could almost repeat them with his eyes' shut. He tried to dream of future greatness, but instead he could only feel depressed and hopeless. It would take a long, long time to save enough money to learn the game. And the earning was dreary work at best. The little adobe cabin became straightway a squalid prison, the monotonous waste around him a void that spread like a great, impassable gulf between himself and the dreams he dreamed. He wished, fervently and profanely, that the greasers would try to steal some horses, so that he could be doing something.

People thought the Border was a tumultuous belt of violence drawn from Coast to Gulf, he meditated morosely. They ought to camp at Sinkhole for awhile. Why, he could ride in an hour or two to Mexico-and see nothing more than he could see from the door of his cabin. He wished he could see something. A fight-anything that had action in it. But the revolution, boiling intermittently over there, did not so much as float a wisp of steam in his direction.

He wished that he had not "hung up" on Mary V before he had told her a few things. He couldn't see why she didn't leave him alone. The Lord knew he was willing to leave *her* alone.

A few days more of that he had before he saw a living soul. Then a Mexican youth came wandering in on a scrawny pony that seemed to have its heart set on drinking the creek dry, before his rider could drink it all. Johnny watched the boy lie down on the flat of his lean stomach with his face to the sluggish stream, and drink as if he, too, were trying to cheat the pony. Together they lifted their heads and looked at Johnny. The Mexican boy smiled, white-toothed, while deep pools of eyes regarded Johnny soberly.

"She's damn hot to-day, señor," he said. "Thank you for the so good water to drink."

"That's all right. Help yourself," Johnny said languidly. "Had your dinner?"

"Not this day. I'm come from Tucker Bly, his rancho. I ride to see if horses feed quiet."

"Well, come in and eat. I cooked some peaches this morning."

The youth went eagerly, his somewhat stilted English easing off into a mixture of good American slang and the Mexican dialect spoken by peons and some a grade higher up the ladder. He was not more than seventeen, and while Johnny recalled his instructions to put any greaser on the run, he took the liberty of interpreting those instructions to please himself. This kid was harmless enough. He talked the range gossip that proved to Johnny's satisfaction that he was what he professed to be —a young rider for Tucker Bly, who owned the "Forty-Seven" brand that ranged just east of the Rolling R. Johnny had never seen this Tomaso-plain Tom, he called him presently-but he knew Tucker Bly; and a few leading questions served to set at rest any incipient suspicions Johnny may have had.

They were doing the same work, he and Tomaso. The only difference was that Johnny camped alone, and Tomaso rode out from the Forty-Seven ranch every day, taking whatever direction Tucker Bly might choose for him. But the freemasonry of the range land held Johnny to the feeling that there was a common bond between them, in spite of Tomaso's swarthy skin. Besides, he was lonely. His tongue loosened while Tomaso ate and praised Johnny's cookery with the innate flattery of his race.

"Wha's that pic'shur? What you call that thing?" Tomaso pointed a slender, brown finger at a circular heading, whereon a pink aeroplane did a "nose dive" toward the date line through voluted blue clouds.

"That? Say! Didn't you ever see a flying machine?" Johnny stared at him pityingly.

Tomaso shook his head vaguely. "Me, I'm never saw one of them things. My brother, he's tell me. He knows the spot where there's one fell down. My brother, he says she's awful bad luck, them thing. This-a one, she's fell 'cross the line. She's set there like a big hawk, my brother says. Nobody wants. She's bad luck."

"Bad luck nothing." Johnny's eyes had widened a bit. "What you mean, one fell across the line? You don't mean-say what 'n thunder *do* yuh mean? Where's there a flying machine setting like a hawk?"

Tomaso waved a brown hand comprehensively from east to west. "Somewhere-me, I dunno. My brother, he's know. He's saw it set there. It's what them soldiers got lost. It's bad luck. Them soldiers most dead when somebody find. They don't know where that thing is no more. They don't want it no more. My brother, she's tol' me them soldiers flew like birds and then they fell down. It's bad luck. My brother took one hammer from that thing, and one pliers. Them hammer, she's take a nail off my brother's thumb. And them pliers, she's lost right away."

Johnny's hand trembled when he tried to shake a little tobacco into a cigarette paper. His lips, too, quivered slightly. But he laughed unbelievingly.

"Your brother was kidding you, Tom. Nobody would go off and leave an airplane setting in the desert. Those soldiers that got lost were away over east of here. Three or four hundred miles. He was kidding you."

"No-o, my brother, she's saw that thing! She's hunt cattle what got across, and she's saw that what them soldiers flew. Me, I *know*." He looked at Johnny appraisingly, hesitated and leaned forward, impelled yet not quite daring to give the proof.

"Well, what do you know?" Johnny returned the look steadfastly.

"You don't tell my brother —I —" He fumbled in his trousers pocket, hesitated a little longer, and grew more trustful. "Them pliers —I'm got."

He laid them on the table, and Johnny let his stool tilt forward abruptly on its four legs. He took up the pliers, examined them with one eye squinted against the smoke of his cigarette, weighed them in his hand, bent to read the trade-mark. Then he looked at Tomaso. Those pliers may or may not have come from the emergency kit of an airplane, but they certainly were not of the kind or quality that ranchmen were in the habit of owning. To Johnny they looked convincing. When he had an airplane of his own, he would find a hundred uses for a pair of pliers exactly like those.

"I thought you said your brother lost 'em," he observed drily.

Tomaso shrugged, flung out his hands, smiled with his lips, and frowned with his eyes. "S'pose he did lost. Somebody could find."

Johnny laughed. "All right; we'll let it ride that way. I ain't going to tell your brother. Want to sell 'em?"

Tomaso took up the pliers, caressed their bright steel with his long fingers, nipped them open and shut.

"What you pay me?" he countered.

"Two bits."

Tomaso turned them over, gazed upon them fondly. He shook his head regretfully. "*No quero*. Them pliers, she's *bueno*," he said. "You could find more things. My brother, she's tell lots of things is where that sets like a hawk. Lots of things. You don't tell my brother?"

"Sure not. I don't want the things anyway. And I don't know your brother."

Tomaso thoughtfully nipped the pliers upon the oilcloth table cover. He looked at the airplane picture, he looked at Johnny. He sighed.

"Me, I'm like see those thing fly like birds. I'm like see that what sets over there. My brother, she's tell me it's so big like here to that water hole. She's tell me some day it maybe flies. I go see it some day."

Johnny laughed. "You'll have some trip if you do. You take it from me, Tom, I don't know your brother, but I know he was kiddin' you. It was away over east of here that those fellows got lost."

After Tomaso had mounted reluctantly and ridden away, however, Johnny discovered himself faced southward, staring off toward Mexico. It was just a yarn, about that airplane over there. Of course there was nothing in it-nothing whatever. He didn't believe for a minute that an airplane was sitting like a hawk on the sands a few miles to the south of him. He didn't believe it-but he pictured to himself just how it would look, and he played a little with the idea. It was something new to think about, and Johnny straightway built himself a dream around it.

Riding the ridges in the lesser heat of the early mornings, his physical eyes looked out over the meager range, spying out the scattered horse herds grazing afar, their backs just showing above the brush. Behind his eyes his mind roved farther, visioning a military plane sitting, inert but with potentialities that sent his mind dizzy, on the hot sand of Mexico-so close that he could almost see the place where it sat.

This was splendid food for Johnny's imagination, for his ambitions even, though it was not particularly good for the Rolling R. He was not bothered much. Evenings, the foreman or Sudden would usually call him up and ask him how things were. Johnny would say that everything was all right, and had the stage driver made a mistake and left any of his mail at the ranch? Because he had been to the mail box on the trail and there was nothing there. The speaker at the ranch would assure him that nothing had been left there for him, and the ceremony would be over.

Johnny was fussy about his mail. He had spent twenty-five dollars for a correspondence course in aviation, and he wanted to begin studying. He did not know how he could learn to fly by mail, but he was a trustful youth in some ways-he left that for the school to solve for him.

Tomaso rode over again in a few days. This time he had a mysterious looking kind of wrench in his pocket, and he showed it to Johnny with a glimmer of triumph.

"Me, I'm saw that thing what flies. Only now it sets. It's got wheels in front-little small wheels. Dos-two. My brother, he's show me. I'm find thees wranch. It's got wings out, so." Tomaso spread his two arms. "Some day, I'm think she's fly. When wind blows."

Johnny felt a little tremor go over him, but he managed to laugh. "All right; you've been looking at the pictures. If you saw it, tell me about it. What makes it go?"

Tomaso shook his head. "She don't go," he said. "She sets."

"All right. She sets, then. What on, —back of the wheels? You said two wheels in front. What holds up the back?"

"One small, little leg like my arm," Tomaso answered unhesitatingly. "Like my arm and my hand-so. Iron."

Johnny's eyes widened a trifle, but he would not yield. "Well, where do men ride on it? On which wing?"

"Men don't," Tomaso contradicted solemnly. "Men sets down like in little, small boat. Me, I'm set there. With wheel for drive like automobile. With engine like automobile. My brother, she's try starting that engine. She's don't go. Got no crank nowhere. She's got no gas. Me, I'm scare my brother starts that engine. I'm jomp down like hell. I'm scare I maybe would fly somewhere and fall down and keel. *No importa*. She's jus' sets."

Johnny turned white around the mouth, but he shook his head. "Pretty good, Tommy. But you better look out. If there's a flying machine over there, it belongs to the government. You better leave it alone. There's other folks know about it, and maybe watching it."

Tomaso shook his head violently. "*Por dios*, my brother she's fin' out about that," he said. "She's don't tell nobody, only me. She's fin' out them *hombres* what ride that theeng, they go *loco* for walking too much in sand and don't get no water. Them *hombres*, they awful sick, they don't know where is that thing what flies. My brother, she's fin' out that thing sets in Mexico, belongs Mexico. Thees countree los'. Jus' like ship what's los' on ocean, my brother she's tell from writing. My brother, she's smart *hombre*. She's keep awful quiet, tell nobody. She's theenk sell that thing for flying."

"Huh!" Johnny grunted. "What you telling me about it for? Your brother'd skin yuh alive if he caught you blabbing it all out to me."

Tomaso looked a little scared and uneasy. He dropped his eyes and began poking a hole in the sand with his toe. Then he looked up very candidly into Johnny's face.

"Me, I'm awful lonesome," he explained. "I'm riding here and I'm see you jus' like friend. You boy like me. You got picshurs them thing what flies. You tell me you don't say nothing for my brother when I'm tell you that things sets over there." He waved a dirty, brown hand to the southward. "Me, I'm *trus'* you. Tha's secret what I'm tell. You don't tell no-*body*. You promise?"

"All right. I promise." Very gravely Johnny made the sign of the cross over his heart.

Tomaso's eyes lightened at that. More gravely than Johnny he crossed himself-forehead, lips, breast. He murmured a solemn oath in Spanish, and afterwards put out his hand to shake, American fashion. All this impressed Johnny more than had the detailed description of the thing which sat.

If he still laughed at the story, his laugh was not particularly convincing. Nor was his jibing tone when he called after Tomaso when that youth was riding away:

"Tell your brother I might buy his flying machine-if he'll sell it cheap!"

Mary V was indefatigably pursuing a new and apparently fascinating avocation, for which her mother expressed little sympathy, no enthusiasm whatever, and a grudgingly given consent. Mary V was making a collection of Desert Glimpses for educational purposes at her boarding school. She had long been urged to do so by her schoolmates and teachers, she told her mother, and now she was going to do it. It should be the very best, most complete collection any one could possibly make within riding distance of the Rolling R. Incidentally she meant to collect jackrabbit ears and rattlesnake rattles, for the purpose of thrilling the girls, but she did not tell her mother that. Neither did she tell her mother just why her quest always lay to the southward when there was plenty of desert to be glimpsed toward the north and to the east and the west. She did not even tell herself why she did that.

So Mary V, knowing well the terrific heat she would have to face in the middle of the day, ordered her horse saddled when the boys saddled their own-which was about sunrise. She did not keep it standing more than half an hour or so before she came out and mounted him. She was well equipped for her enterprise. She carried a camera, three extra rolls of film, a telescoped tripod which she tied under her right stirrup leather, a pair of high-power Busch glasses (to glimpse with, probably), two duck-covered canteens filled and dripping, a generous lunch of sandwiches and cake and sour pickles, a box-magazine .22 rifle, a knife, a tube of cold cream wrapped in a bit of cheesecloth, and a very compact yet very complete vanity case. Jostling the vanity case in her saddle pocket were two boxes of soft-nose, .22-long cartridges for the rifle. Furthermore, for special personal protection she had an extremely businesslike six-shooter which she carried in a shoulder holster under her riding shirt; a concession to her father, who had made her promise never to ride away from the ranch without it.

For apparel Mary V wore a checked riding coat and breeches, together with black puttees. The suit had grown a bit shabby for Los Angeles, and Mary V's mother believed that town cast-offs should be worn out on the ranch. Mary V did not mind. She hated the cumbersome riding skirts of the range girl proper, and much preferred the breeches. When she had put a little distance between herself and the ranch, she usually removed the coat and tied it in a roll behind the cantle. She looked then like a slim boy-or she would have, except for the hat. Mary V cherished her complexion, which Arizona sun and winds would have burned a brick red. In cool weather she wore a Stetson like the boys; but now she favored a great, straw sombrero such as you see section hands wear along the railroad track in Arizona. To keep it on her head in the winds she had resorted to tying a ribbon down over the brim from the front of the crown to the nape of her neck; and tying another ribbon from the back of the crown down under her chin. Thus doubly anchored, and skewered with two hatpins besides, the hat might be counted upon to give Mary V no trouble, but a great deal of protection. Worn with the checked riding breeches and the heavy, black puttees, it was not particularly becoming, but Mary V did not expect to meet many pairs of critical eyes. Rolling R boys were too much like home folks to bother about, having been accustomed to seeing Mary V in strange and various guises since she was a tiny tot.

Southward she rode, and as swiftly as was wise if she valued the well-being of her horse. Movies will have it that nothing short of a gallop is tolerated by riders in the West; whereas Mary V had been taught from her childhood up that she must never "run" her horse unless there was need of it. She therefore contented herself with ambling along the trail at a distance-devouring trail-trot, slowing her horse to a walk on the rising slopes and urging him a little with her spurred heels on the levels. She did not let him lag-she could not, if she covered the distance she had in her mind to cover.

Away over to the south-almost to Sinkhole Camp, in fact-was a ridge that was climbable on horseback. Not every ridge in that country was, and Mary V was not fond of walking in the sand on a hot day. The ridge commanded a far view, and was said to be a metropolis among the snakes that populated the region. Mary V had, very casually, mentioned to the boys that some day she meant to get a good picture of a snake den. She said "the girls" did not believe that snakes went in bunches and writhed amicably together in their dens. She was going to prove it to them.

A perfectly logical quest it was therefore that led her toward that ridge. You could not blame Mary V if the view from the top of it extended to Sinkhole Camp and beyond. She had not made the view, remember, nor had she advised the snakes to choose that ridge for their dens. She was not even perfectly sure that they did choose it. The boys had told her that Black Ridge was "full up" with snake dens, and she meant to see if they told the truth.

Wherefore her horse Tango laboriously carried Mary V up the ridge and kept his ears perked for the warning buzz of rattlers, and his eyes open for a feasible line retreat in case he heard one. Tango knew just as well as Mary V when they were in snake country. He had gone so far as to argue the point of climbing that ridge, but as usual Mary V's argument was stronger than Tango's, and he had yielded with an injured air that was quite lost upon his rider. Mary V was thinking of something else.

They reached the top without having seen a single snake. Tango seemed somewhat surprised at this, but Mary V was not. Mary V thought it was too hot even for rattlesnakes, and as for the dearth of lizards-well she supposed the snakes had eaten them all. She had let Tango stop often to breathe, and whenever he did so she had looked south, scanning as much of the lower level as she could see, which was not the proper way to go about hunting snake dens, I assure you. But at the top she permitted Tango to walk into the shade of a boulder that radiated heat like a stove but was still preferable to the blistering sunlight, and there she left him while she walked a little nearer the edge of the rimrock that topped the ridge on its southern side.

Once more she scanned the sweltering expanse of sagebrush, scant grass, many rock patches and much sand. She saw a rider moving along a shallow watercourse, and immediately she focused her glasses upon him. She gave an ejaculation of surprise when the powerful lenses annihilated nine tenths of the distance between them. One would judge from her manner and her tone that, while she had not been surprised to see a rider, that rider's identity was wholly unexpected.

She watched him until, having reached a certain place where a group of cottonwoods shaded the gully, he stopped and dismounted to fuss with his cinches. Mary V could not be sure whether he was merely killing time, or whether he really needed to tighten the saddle; but when another rider appeared suddenly from the eastward, she did know that the first rider showed no symptoms of surprise.

She did not know the second arrival at the cottonwoods. She could see that he was Mexican, and that was all. The two talked together with much gesturing on the part of the Mexican, and sundry affirmative nods on the part of the first rider. The Mexican frequently waved a hand toward the south-toward Sinkhole Camp, perhaps. They seemed to be in a hurry, Mary V thought. They did not tarry more than five minutes before they parted, the Mexican riding back toward the east, the first rider returning westward. He had come cautiously, at an easy pace. He went back riding at a long lope, as though time was precious to him.

Mary V watched until she saw him emerge out of that hollow and duck into another which led toward the northwest and, if he followed it, would bring him out near the head of Dry Gulch, which was several miles nearer the Rolling R home ranch than was the ridge where she stood. When he had gone, she turned again to see where the Mexican was going. The Mexican, she discovered, was going east as fast as his horse could carry him without dropping dead in that heat; and he, also, was keeping to the hollows.

"Here's a pretty howdy-do!" said Mary V to the palpitating atmosphere. "I'm just going to tell dad about Tex sneaking away down here to meet Mexicans and things on the sly! I never did like that Tex. I don't like his eyes. You can't see into them at all. I'll bet they're framing up something on Johnny Jewel-they were pointing right toward his camp. There's no telling *what* they're up to! I'm going right and tell dad —"

But she couldn't. Mary V knew she couldn't. In the first place, her dad would ask her what she was doing on Black Ridge, which was far beyond her permitted range of activities. Her dad would foolishly maintain that she could glimpse all the desert necessary without going that far from the ranch. In the second place, he would probably tell her that he was paying Tex to ride the range and, if he met a Mexican, it was his business to send that same Mexican back where he came from. In the third place, he would think she was riding over there for a reason which was untrue and very, very unjust. And he wouldn't fire Tex, because Tex was a good "hand" and hands were hard to find. He would simply make her promise to stay at home.

"He'd say it was perfectly all right for Tex-and perfectly all wrong for me. Dad's *tremendously* pin-headed where I am concerned. So I suppose I'll just have to say nothing, and ride all that long way in the hot sun to make sure that horrid Johnny Jewel is not being murdered or something. It doesn't, of course, concern me personally at all-but dad is *so* short-handed this summer. And he actually *threatened* that he couldn't afford me a new car this winter if wages go up or horses go down, or anything happens that doesn't just please him. And I suppose Johnny Jewel has his uses, in the general scheme of dad's business, so even if he is a mean, conceited little shrimp personally, I'll have to go and make sure he isn't killed, because it would be just like dad to call that bad luck, and grouch around and not get me the car."

Mary V had barely reached this goal of personal unconcern for anything but her own private interests, when Tango began to manifest certain violent symptoms of having seen or heard something very disagreeable. Mary V had to take some long, boyish steps in order to snatch his reins before he bolted and left her afoot, which would have been a real calamity. But she caught him, scolded him shrewishly and slapped his cheek until he backed from her wall-eyed, and then she mounted him and went clattering down off the ridge without having seen any snake dens at all. Doubtless the boys had lied to her, as usual.

To Sinkhole Camp was a long way, much longer than it had looked from the top of Black Ridge. Mary V, her face red with heat, hurried on and on, wishing over and over that she had never started at all, but lacking the resolution to turn back. Yet she was considered a very resolute young woman by those who knew her most intimately.

Perversely she blamed Johnny Jewel for putting her to all this trouble and discomfort, and for interrupting her in her work of getting Desert Glimpses. She repeatedly told herself that he would not even have the common human instinct to feel grateful toward her for riding away down there to see if he were murdered.

She was right in that conjecture, at least. When she rode up to the squat adobe cabin, somewhere near noon, she found Johnny Jewel stretched morosely on his back, staring up at the low roof and thinking the gloomiest thoughts which a lonesome young man of twenty-one or two may conjure from a fit of the blues. That he was not murdered or even menaced with any danger seemed to Mary V a personal grievance against herself after that terrifically hot ride.

Johnny turned a gloomy glance upon her when she walked in and sat down limply on the one chair in the cabin; but he did not show any keen pleasure in her presence, nor any gratitude.

"Well! You're still alive, then!" she said rather crossly.

"I guess I am. Why?" Johnny, his meditations disturbed by her coming, rose languidly and sat upon the side of his bunk, slouched forward with his arms resting across his strong young legs and his glance inclined to the floor.

"Oh, nothing." Mary V took off her hat, but she was too fagged to fan herself with it. Her one emotion, at that moment, was an overwhelming regret that she had come. If Johnny Jewel had the nerve to think that she wanted to see *him* —

"You must love the sun," Johnny observed apathetically. "Lizards, even, have got sense enough to stay in the shade such weather as this." He rumpled his hair to let the faint breeze in to his scalp, and looked at her. "You're red as a pickled beet at a picnic," he told her ungraciously.

Mary V pulled together her lagging wits, marshaled her fighting forces, and flaunted a war banner in the shape of a smile that was demure.

"Well, one must expect to make some sacrifices when one is working in a good cause," she replied amiably, and paused.

"Yeh?" Johnny's eyes lost a little of their dullness. It is possible that he recognized that war banner of hers. "One didn't expect to see one down here-on a good cause."

"No? Well, you do see one, nevertheless. One is at work on an exhibit for one's school, you see. Each of us girls was assigned a subject for vacation work. Mine is 'Desert Glimpses' —a collection of pictures, curios and so on, representing points of interest in the desert country. I've a horned toad at home, and a blue-tailed lizard, and some pictures of jack rabbits, with their ears attached to the frame, and quite a few rattlesnake rattles. So to-day," she smiled again at him, "I rode down here to take a picture of you!"

"Thanks," said Johnny, apparently unmoved. "I didn't know I was a point of interest in your eyes; but seeing I am, I'm willing the girls should have a picture of me framed. If you'll go out and sit in the shade of the shack while I shave and doll up a little, you may take a picture. And I'll autograph it for you. Five years from now," he went on complacently, "you're going to brag about having it in your possession. One of those I-knew-him-when kind of brags. And if you'll bring the girls around some time when I'm pulling off an exhibition flight, I'll let 'em shake hands with me."

"Well, of all the conceit!" By that one futile phrase Mary V owned herself defeated in the first charge. "Of all —"

"Conceit? Nothing like that! When you thought it was a good cause to ride all these miles on the hottest day of the year, just to get my picture —" Johnny smirked at her in a perfectly maddening way. He knew it was maddening to Mary V, for he had meant it to be so.

"I did not!" Mary V's face could not be any redder than the heat had made it, but even so one could see the rise in her mental temperature.

"You said you did."

"Well —I merely want your picture to put with my collection of donkeys! You —"

"You said points of interest," Johnny reminded her. He had lost all his moroseness in the interest of the conversation. He had forgotten what a tonic his word-battles with Mary V could furnish. "You better stick to it, because it will sure pan out that way. You'll hate to admit, five years from now, that you once took me for a donkey. Besides, you can't have my ears to pin to the frame; I'll need 'em to listen to all the nice things some *real* girls will be saying to me when I've just made an exhibition flight."

"Exhibition flight-of your imagination!" fleered Mary V, curling her lip at him. "And I won't need your ears to prove you're a donkey, so don't worry about that."

Johnny Jewel stood up, lifted his arms high above his head to stretch his healthy young muscles, pulled his face all askew in a yawn, rumpled his hair again and reached for his papers and tobacco. He knew that Mary V never noticed or cared if a fellow smoked; she was too thoroughly range-bred for that affectation.

"Good golly! Things must sure be dull at the ranch, if you had to ride twenty miles on a day like this to pick a fight with me," he observed, leisurely singling one leaf out of his book of papers. "Left your horse to bake in the sun, too, I suppose, while you practice the art of persiflage on me."

He finished rolling his cigarette, languidly helped himself to a match from a box on the wide window ledge near him, and sauntered to the door-with a slanting, downward glance at Mary V as he passed her. A little smile lurked at the corners of his lips now that his face was not visible to her. Mary V was studying her wrist watch as though it was vital that she knew the time down to the last second. He judged that she had no retort ready for him, so he picked up his hat and went out into the glaring sunlight.

Tango was sweating patiently under the scant shelter of the eaves, switching at flies and trying to doze. Johnny led him down to the creek and gave him about half as much water as he wanted, then took him to the corral and unsaddled him under the brush shed that sheltered his own horse from the worst of the heat. Whatever her mood and whatever her errand, he guessed shrewdly that Mary V would not be anxious to leave for home until the midday fierceness of the heat was past; and even if she were anxious, common sense and some mercy for her horse would restrain her.

Johnny did not confess to himself that he was glad to see Mary V, but it is a fact that his deep gloom had for some reason disappeared, and that he even whistled under his breath while he untied her lunch and camera and took them back with him to the cabin.

Mary V had been calmly inspecting his new Correspondence Course in the Art of Flying, the first lessons of which had arrived at Johnny's mail box a few days before. She seemed much amused, and she registered her amusement in certain marginal notes as she read. At the top of the first lesson she drew a fairly clever cartoon of Johnny in an airplane, ascending to the star Venus. She made it appear that Johnny's hair stood straight on end and his eyes goggled with fear, and she made Venus a long-nosed, skinny, old-maid face with a wide, welcoming simper. Up in a corner she placed the moon, with one eye closed and a twisted grin.

On the blank space at the end of the first lesson she wrote the following-and could scarcely refrain from calling Johnny's attention to it, she was so proud of it:

"Skyrider, Skyrider, where have you been?

I've been to see Venus, which made the moon grin.

Skyrider, Skyrider, what saw you there?

I saw old maid Venus a-dyeing her hair!"

Having through much industry accomplished all this while Johnny was putting up her horse, Mary V slid the revised lesson out of sight under other papers and was almost decently civil to Johnny when he returned. She did not help him with dinner-which was served cold for obvious reasons-but she divided her sandwiches and sour pickles with him in return for a fried rabbit leg and a dish of stewed fruit. In the intervals of their quarreling, which continued intermittently all the while she was there, Mary V quizzed him about his ambition to fly. Did he really intend to learn "the game"? Had he ever been up in a flying machine? It seemed that Johnny had made two ecstatic trips into the air-for a price-at the San Francisco Fair the fall before, and that his imagination had never quite felt solid ground under it since! Where-or how-could he learn?

If she were secretly trying to inveigle Johnny into showing her his new Correspondence Course, so that she might be a gleeful witness when he discovered her additions and revisions, she must have been a greatly disappointed young woman. For Johnny that day demonstrated how well he could keep a secret. He warmed to her apparent interest in his chosen profession, but he did not once hint at the lessons, and kept rigidly to generalities.

Mary V mentally called him sly and deceitful, and started another quarrel over nothing. While this particular battle was raging, there came an interruption which Mary V first considered sinister, then peculiar, and at last, after much cogitation, extremely suspicious and a further evidence of Johnny's slyness.

A Mexican rode up to the doorway, coming from the east. Not Tomaso, who would have convinced even Mary V of his harmlessness, but a broad-shouldered, square-faced man with squinty eyes, a constant smile, and only a slight accent.

Johnny went to the door, plainly hesitating over the common little courtesy of inviting him in. The man dismounted, announced that he was Tomaso's brother, and then caught sight of Mary V inside and staring out at him curiously.

His manner changed a little. Even Mary V could see that. He stopped where he was, squinting into the cabin, smiling still.

"I come to borrow one, two matches, señor, if you have to spare," he said glibly. "Me, I'm riding past this way, and stop for my horse to drink. She's awful hot to-day —yes?"

Johnny gave him the matches, made what replies were needful, and stood in the doorway watching the fellow ride to the creek and afterwards proceed to eliminate himself from the landscape. Mary V leaned sidewise so that she too could watch him from where she sat at the table. She was sure, when she saw him ride off, that he was the same man who had met Tex away back there in the arroyo.

She watched Johnny, wondering if he knew the man, or knew what was his real reason for coming. Whatever his real reason was, he had gone off without stating it, and Mary V believed that he had gone because she was there. She wished she knew why he had come, but she would not ask Johnny. She merely watched him covertly.

Johnny had turned thoughtful. He did not even see that Mary V was watching him, he was so busy wishing that she had not come at all, or that she had gone before this man rode up. Inwardly Johnny was all a-quiver with excitement. He believed that he knew why Tomaso's brother had come.

Chapter Six. Salvage

The brother of Tomaso came back. Mary V, cannily watching the wide waste behind her as she rode homeward, saw him and made sure of him through her glasses. The brother of Tomaso seemed to be in a hurry, and he seemed to have been waiting in some convenient covert until she had left. His horse was trotting too nimbly through the sage to have come far at that pace. Mary V could tell a tired horse as far as she could tell that it was a horse.

She did not turn back, for the simple reason that she knew very well her mother would have all the boys out hunting her if she failed to reach home by sundown. That would have meant deep humiliation for Mary V and a curtailment of future freedom. So she put up her glasses and went her way, talking to herself by way of comforting her thwarted curiosity, and accusing Johnny Jewel of all sorts of intrigues; and never dreaming the truth, of course.

"Me, I'm willing to sell, all right. What you pay me?" Tomaso's brother was sitting in Johnny's doorway where he could watch the trail, and he was smoking a cigarette made with Johnny's tobacco.

"She's no good to nobody, setting there in the sand, but she's all right, you bet, for fly. Them fellers, they get lost, I think. They get away off there, and no gas to fly back. No place to buy none, you bet." He grinned sardonically up at Johnny who was leaning against the adobe wall. "They get the big scare, you bet. They take all the water, and they walk and walk, drink the water and walk and walk and walk-loco, that's what. Don't know where they go, don't know where they come from, don't know nothin' no more atall. So that flyin' machine, that's lost. Me, I find out. It don't belong to nobody no more only just the feller that finds. Me, I take you there, I show you. You see I'm telling the truth, all right. You pay me half. I help you drag it over here to your camp, all right. You pay me other half. That's right way to fix him-yes?"

"Sounds fair enough, far as that goes." Johnny's voice had the huskiness of suppressed excitement. The cigarette he was studying so critically quivered in his fingers like a twig in the wind. "But the thing must belong to *somebody*."

"No, I'm find out from lawyer. Only I'm say maybe it's automobile. Cos' me fi' dollar, which is hold-up, you bet. Some day I get even that fi' dollar. That flyin' machine goes into Mexico, that's los' by law. Sal-what you call-oh!" He snapped his fingers as men do when trying to recall a word. "She cos' me fi' dollar, that word! Jus' minute-it's like wreck on ocean, that is left and somebody brings it —"

"Salvage?" Johnny jerked the word out abruptly.

"That's him! Salvage. Belongs anybody that finds. Mexico, she's foreign countree. She could take; it's hers if she want. But what she wants? Nobody can make it go. No Mexicans can fly, you bet. Me, I don't know damn t'ing about flyin' nothin' but monee. Monee, I make it fly, yes." He chuckled at his little joke, but Johnny did not even hear it.

Johnny was seeing a real, military airplane in his possession, cached away in some niche in the lava wall to the west of Sinkhole —a wall that featured queer niches and caverns and clefts. He was seeing-what wonderful things was Johnny not seeing?

"Like them buried treasure," Tomaso's brother went on purring comfortably to Johnny's doubts. "The *hombre* what finds, it belongs to him, you bet. What you say? You pay me —" The eyes of Tomaso's brother dwelt calculatingly upon Johnny's half-averted face. "You pay me fifty dollar when I show you I don't lie. I help you drag him back home, you —"

"Nothing doing." Johnny pulled himself from his dreams to bargain for his heart's desire-because he knew Mexicans. "I ain't sure I want the thing, anyway. It's probably broke, and it takes *money* to fix a busted plane, let me tell you. And there might be complications; and besides, I've got to ride this range. I can't go rambling around all over Mexico hunting an airplane that probably wouldn't be any good when I found it."

Tomaso's brother rose from the doorsill to gesticulate while he argued those points and others which Johnny thought of later. It was a beautiful flying machine. By every object impressive enough to make oath upon, Tomaso's brother swore that it was as he said. Look! Not one peso would he accept until Johnny had seen. And the range? Would it run off in two days, perhaps? Look, then! Tomaso's brother would make the bet. He would agree. They would go for the airship, and they would return with it, and of the fifty pesos that was the full price he asked, not one centavo would he accept until the señor had seen that all was as he had left it. Look! That very night they would go, and by noon to-morrow they would be there. And under the great wings would they rest. And they would return in two more days-such a little while it would take —

Johnny's jaw lengthened. Making due allowance for the lying tongue of Tomaso's brother, it would take a week to get the thing home. And that would mean that Johnny would have no job when he returned; which would mean that he would have no fifty dollars a month coming in; which would mean that he would be broke and would have to hunt another job. And you couldn't pack a government airplane around under your arm. Not once did it occur to Johnny that he might sell it for more money than he had ever possessed in his life, for more than what a full course in aviation would cost him. As his own precious plane he saw it. His to keep. His to fly, his to worship-but never to sell.

He looked away to the southward where the land stretched gray and dreary to the low skyline broken here and there with the pale outline of distant hills. A night and half a day of riding to take them there, and an airplane to haul back through brush and rocks, maybe, and across draws and gulches-Good Lord! The thing might almost as well be in Honolulu!

"But the desert places-me, I'm making the plan how it can be brought across the sand, with little brush to cut away." Tomaso's brother began arguing away his unspoken fears. "We fix that, you bet! Two days, that's all. You got strong, good fence; horses, they don't go away in such little time, you bet!"

Johnny stood irresolute, tempted, weakly trying to beat back the temptation while he hugged it to his soul.

"Why don't you —" Johnny was on the point of asking Tomaso's brother why he didn't sell it to the government, but he shut his teeth on the words. Tomaso's brother evidently had not thought of that; and why put the idea into his head? "Why don't you and Tomaso go after it and bring it here? Then if it's all right, I might buy it-for fifty dollars. I can give you a check on the Arizona State Bank in Tucson."

Tomaso's brother shrugged his shoulders in true Mexican eloquence. "That puts me all the troubles for notheeng, maybe. Maybe you say she's no good-what I'm going to do? Not drag it back for notheeng? Not leave her set here for notheeng." He shrugged again with an air of finality that sent a shiver over Johnny's nerves. "Twenty-fi' dollar when you look at her and say she's all right. Twenty-fi' dollar when she's here. That suits me. It don't suit you, *no importa*."

It did matter, though. It mattered a great deal to Johnny, hard as he tried to hide the fact.

"Well, I'll think about it. I'd have to ride fence first, anyway, and make sure everything's all right. And you'd have to tell Tomaso to drift over this way and kinda keep an eye out. I —you come back to-morrow. If I take the offer at all, which I ain't sure of, we can start to-morrow night. But I'm not making any promises. It's a gamble; I've got to think it over first."

In that way did Johnny invite temptation to tarry with him and wax stronger while it fed on his resistance, while thinking that he was being very firm and businesslike and cautious, and that he was in no danger whatever of yielding unless his reason thoroughly approved.

His manner of thinking it over calmly was rather pathetic. It consisted of building anew his air castle, and in riding out to the forbidden lava ridge that rose like a wall out of the sandy plain west of Sinkhole to choose the niche which might best be converted into a secret hangar. Since first he heard of the derelict airplane, his mind had several times strayed toward those deep clefts, but his feet had heretofore refrained from following his thoughts.

Niches there were many, but they were too prone to yawn wide-mouthed at the world so that whatever treasure they might have contained would be revealed to any chance passer-by. These Johnny disdained without a second glance. Others he investigated by riding in a little way, sending a glance around and riding out again.

Just before dusk, as he was returning disappointedly after looking as far as was practicable, his horse Sandy swung into one of the open-mouthed depressions of his own accord. Probably he had become convinced that they were hunting stock, and that every niche must be entered. (Range horses are quick to form opinions of that sort and to act upon them.) Johnny was dreaming along, and let Sandy go back toward the wall, but Sandy, poking along with his head bobbing contentedly at the end of his long neck, swerved to the right, into a nature-built ell that had a fine-sifted sand floor, walls that converged toward the top, and an entrance which no one would suspect, surely, since Johnny himself had passed it by not half an hour before.

Johnny did not say a word. He sat there and gazed, a little awed by the discovery, thrilled with the feeling that this place had been planned especially for him; that Nature had built it and kept it until he needed it-in other words, that luck was with him and that it would be madness to go against his luck.

He got down, went to the left wall and, taking long strides, stepped off the width of the place. Wide enough, plenty; he couldn't have ordered it any better himself. From the mouth he started to step the depth, but stopped when he had gone a third farther than the length of a military type fuselage. He turned and looked back toward the entrance, his hands on his hips, his eyes wide and glowing, his lips trembling and eager. He looked up at the top; with cottonwood poles and brush he could roof it against the sun and the winds. He looked at the fine, hard-packed sand floor that the winds never stirred. He looked at the walls.

But he would put his luck to another test. He would abide by it-so he told himself bravely. He felt in his pocket for a coin, pulled out a half dollar, balanced it on his bent thumb and forefinger. He turned white around the mouth, as he always did when deep emotion gripped him. He hesitated. What if—? But if his luck was any good, it would hold. It had to hold!

"Heads, I go. Tails, I stay." He muttered the fateful six words and snapped his thumb up straight. The half dollar went spinning, clinked against a high projection of rock, fell back to the sand floor.

Johnny stood where he was and stared at it. From where he was he could not see which side was uppermost, and he was afraid to go and look. But he had to look. He had to know, for he was still boy enough to feel solemnly bound by the toss. He walked slowly toward it, stared hard-and pounced like a kid after a hard-won marble.

"Heads, I go! That's the way I flipped 'er; it's a fair throw."

At the sound of his voice ringing in the confined space, Sandy lifted his head and looked at Johnny tolerantly. Johnny came toward him grinning, tossing the half-dollar and catching it, his steps springy. The last few yards he took in a run, and vaulted into the saddle without touching the stirrups at all. Even that did not seem to ease him quite. So he gave a whoop that echoed and re-echoed from the rock walls and made Sandy squat, lay back his ears, and shake his head violently.

At the mouth of the hidden nook Johnny turned to take a last, gloating survey of the place in the deepening dusk. "She sure will make one bird of a hangar!" he told Sandy glowingly. "Golly! Oh, good *golly*!"

Chapter Seven. Finder, Keeper

From the crest of a low, sandy ridge that had on it a giant cactus standing with four spiney, knobbed fingers uplifted like a warning hand, Johnny surveyed with wide, red-rimmed eyes the hidden basin that held his heart's desire. Tomaso's brother sat his sweaty horse beside Johnny and eyed both the gazer and the object of his gaze. A smile split whitely the swarthiness of Tomaso's brother's face.

"She's settin' there jus' like I told," he pointed out with a wilted kind of triumph, for the day was hot.

"Unh-hunh," Johnny conceded absent-mindedly. He was trying to make the thing look real to him after all the visions he had had of it.

He had had his spells of doubting the probity of Tomaso's brother; of secretly wondering whether the story of the plane might not be a ruse to lure him away from Sinkhole. But then, how would Tomaso or his brother know that Johnny would care anything about whether an airplane "sat" over in Mexico within riding distance of the Border? Johnny did not think of Tex as a possible factor in the proposition.

Well, there it was, anyway, not a quarter of a mile away. Between him and the object of his quest the sand lay wrinkled in tiny drifts, with here and there a ragged gray bush leaning forlornly from the wind. One wing of the machine was tilted, as though it had careened a little in the winds, but from that distance Johnny could not tell what damage had been done. He kicked Sandy in the ribs and led the way down the hill. Tomaso's brother, still grinning, followed close behind.

"It's going to be some sweet job getting the thing home," Johnny growled, trying to disguise his excitement. "I expect I've had my trip for nothing. She don't look to be in very good condition."

The grin of Tomaso's brother changed its expression a bit, but he did not trouble to answer. Tomaso's brother knew far better than did Johnny all the rules of commerce. Johnny's clumsy attempt to depreciate what he wanted very much to buy merely convinced Tomaso's brother of the extreme youthfulness of Johnny.

"Well, I might as well give her the once-over, now I'm here," Johnny added with a fine air of indifference, and urged Sandy into a trot.

Now Sandy had discovered the secret hangar for Johnny without having the slightest imagining of the use which Johnny hoped to make of it. That he should ever have to face a thing like this was beyond his most fevered imagination. He had been a tired, sweaty, head-hanging horse when he started down the slope. He had trotted along with his half-closed eyes on the ground before him, picking the smoothest path for his desert-weary feet. He did not look up until Johnny pulled sharply on the reins and gave a startling whoop built around the word "Whoa."

Sandy's bulging eyes got a full-front, close-up view of the "thing what set." He saw a wicked nose with a feeler about twice as high as he was. He saw great, terrible, outspread wings and a long slim body. It looked poised, ready to come at him and snatch him with one frightful swoop, as he had seen prairie hawks snatch little birds from the grass.

Sandy forgot that he was a tired, sweaty, head-hanging horse. He forgot everything except the four unbroken legs under him. He wheeled half away and went lunging up the far side of the little basin as if he felt the horrible creature close behind him.

Johnny's mind had been so absorbed by the airplane that it took him a few seconds to comprehend that Sandy was actually running away with him. It took him a few seconds longer to realize that Sandy's jaw was set like iron, with the bit gripped tight in his teeth. By the time he was thoroughly convinced that Sandy was going to be hard to stop, Sandy had topped the rise and was streaking it across an expanse of barrenness that rose gently in spite of the fact that it looked perfectly level. A sliding streak of gray dust rising into the heat waves marked his passing.

Nearly a mile he ran before the slight grade and a rocky strip slowed him down to a heavy gallop. Johnny had been in the mind to let the fool run himself down just for punishment, but the rocks and an eagerness to return to the stranded plane urged him to forego the discipline.

He stopped just where the scattered rocks ended abruptly in a wall that rimmed a sunken, green valley, narrowing near where Johnny stood looking down, but broadening farther along, and seeming to extend southward with many twistings and windings. Johnny viewed the place with a passing surprise, familiar though he was with the freakish topography of Arizona. It was the greenness, and the little winding creek, and the huddle of adobe buildings among the cottonwoods that struck him oddly. The creek might be a continuation of Sinkhole Creek, that disappeared into the sands away back there near his camp. There was nothing particularly strange about that, or the green growth that water made possible wherever the soil held latent fertility. It was the fact that those poor devils who lost the airplane-and themselves-should have wandered on and on, crazed with hunger and thirst when food and water and perhaps a guide were to be found within a mile or so of where they landed.

It was a pity, thought Johnny. But, being very human, he also thought that if the airmen had found this place, that plane would not be sitting back there waiting his grave if inexpert inspection. So with his pity cooled a little with self-interest, Johnny turned the puffing Sandy upon the backward trail and followed his tracks across the apparently level stretch of barrenness to the basin where waited the plane and Tomaso's brother. Only for Sandy's tracks, Johnny knew he might have had a little trouble in finding the place again, the country looked so unbroken and monotonous.

However, he found it too soon for Sandy's comfort. There it sat-the giant bird that had seemed ready to swoop and rise. But now its back was turned toward him, and it did not look quite so fearsome. He circled and plunged awhile, and even made shift to pitch a little, tired as he was. But man's mastery prevailed, just as it had always done, and Sandy found himself edging closer and closer to the thing. The horse of Tomaso's brother, standing quiet in the very shade of a great wing, reassured him further, so that presently he stood subdued but wall-eyed still, where Johnny could dismount and hand the reins to the brother of Tomaso while he examined the prize.

His manner was impressive, and the brother of Tomaso stopped grinning to himself and began to look somewhat worried. He watched Johnny's face-and I assure you that Johnny's face would have been worth any one's watching. A cigarette slanted from the corner of his boyish lips, and the eye on that side was squinted to keep out the smoke; which was merely an impressive bit of byplay, because there was no smoke. The cigarette was not burning, though Johnny had made a hasty dab at it with a lighted match. The other eye was as coldly critical as was humanly possible when the whole heart of Johnny was swelling with ecstasy. His head was tilted a little, his hands were on his hips except when he used them to push and test and try some reachable part.

Johnny thrust out a foot and gently kicked the flattened tire on one wheel. "Umh-humh," he muttered to himself. "Flat tire." Never in his life had Johnny enjoyed the privilege of kicking a wheel on the landing gear of an airplane, but you would have thought that this was his business, and that it bored him intensely to do so. He took one hand off his hip long enough to lift the drooping wing that canted toward the south. "Mhm-hmh —busted skid," he observed, in a tone which, to the brother of Tomaso, shaved several dollars off the coveted fifty. Close behind Johnny he stayed, following him around the plane in a secret agony of apprehension.

Johnny, primed by the two rides he had taken-for a price-the fall before, stepped nimbly up and straddled into the pilot's seat. He found out, by actual experimentation, what wires tilted the ailerons, which ones operated the elevators. "Mhm-hmh —dep control here," he commented; whereupon the brother of Tomaso squirmed, thinking Johnny had discovered a fatal flaw somewhere.

With one eye still squinted against cigarette smoke that did not rise, Johnny climbed out and walked back along the fuselage to the tail. "Mhm-hmh —I thought so!" he ejaculated, staring severely at the elevators. "This is bad-pret-ty darn bad! They musta done a tail-slide and pancaked. That's ba-ad." He removed the smokeless cigarette from his lips, looked at it, felt for a match, and shook his head slowly while he drew the match across a hot rock at his feet.

"Jus' broke little small," Tomaso's brother's voice came pleadingly from behind Johnny. "You can feex him easy. She's fine airship, you bet!"

Johnny turned and looked at him pityingly. "Say, where do you get that stuff?" he inquired. "A hell of a lot *you* know about airships-bringing me off down here to see *this*! Say! where's the fuselage at?" he abruptly demanded.

Tomaso's brother gazed at the machine with tragic eyes. "Me, I'm seen it here ontil this time I come," he declared virtuously. "I'm not touch notheeng. That fuz'lawge, she's right here las' time I'm here. I'm not touch notheeng but one little small hammer, one pliers. You find him up there, I bet." Tomaso's brother pointed to the pilot's seat.

"Hunh! a lot you know about it!" snorted Johnny, and turned and walked away to the other side of the machine where Tomaso's brother could not see him grin.

"No matter what kind of a cheese you are, you must know an airplane can't fly without a fuselage," he grumbled to the unhappy brother of Tomaso. "Without that the plane's no good to me or anybody else. You better get busy and hunt it up."

Tomaso's brother tied the horses to the nearest bush and got busy, volubly protesting all the while that he had not touched a thing, and that if Tomaso really had carried off the fuz'lawge, he would presently make that young devil wish he had never been born.

"Maybe the aviators dropped it back there on the edge of the basin when they were coming down," Johnny suggested, and laid himself down in the shade of the plane to smoke and dream and gloat. He felt that he would burst into insane and costly whoops if he attempted another minute's repression. And he knew that Tomaso's brother would bleed him of his last dollar if he guessed one half of Johnny's exultation; wherefore the ruse to send Tomaso's brother off on a senseless quest.

"Oh, golly! Oh-h, good golly!" he murmured ecstatically, his eyes taking in the full sweep of the great wings. "It's too good to be true. No, it ain't; it's too good *not* to be true! You wait. I'll show the Rolling R bunch-you wait!"

He rolled to an elbow and looked back along the fuselage to the tail, his eyes dwelling fondly on the clean lines of her, the perfect symmetry, the glossy, unharmed covering. His glance went farther, to where the brother of Tomaso plodded toward the basin's rim, peering here and there, pausing to look under a bush, swerving to make sure the lost fuselage was not behind a rock.

Johnny's grin widened. Presently it exploded into a laugh, which he smothered with both hands clapped over his mouth. He writhed and kicked and rolled in the sand. His round, blue eyes grew moist with the tears of a boy's exuberant mirth. From behind his palms came muffled *who-who-who-oo-oos* of laughter.

He believed that he was laughing at the trick he had played on Tomaso's brother. He was doing more than that: he was making up for all the sober longing, for all the fears and the discouragements of his barren life. There had been so much hoping and sighing and futile wishing-it had been so long since Johnny Jewel had really laughed-and he was young, and youth is the time of carefree laughter. Now nature was striking a balance for him.

Tomaso's brother went up over the rim of the basin, disappeared, and then came plodding back through the heat. Johnny had laughed all that while; laughed until his sides were sore; until his eyes were red with the tears he had shed; until he was so weak he staggered when he first crawled out from under the plane and stood up. But it did him good, for all that, to have laughed so hard and so long over an impish trick that came from the boy in him.

"Me, I don't find him that damn fuz'lawge," said the brother of Tomaso, wiping his swarthy countenance that was beaded with sweat. "That Tomaso, he has took, I bet. He brings it to you queeck when I'm through with him." He looked at Johnny expectantly. "I'm promise you it comes back all right, if perhaps Tomaso has take. Perhaps now you pay twenty-fi' dollar?"

"No, I don't; I pay you ten dollars now." Johnny, remember, had a full two days' acquaintance with the brother of Tomaso. He was taking a certain precaution, rather than an unfair advantage. He honestly believed that the brother of Tomaso was best dealt with cautiously.

"When this airplane is safe at Sinkhole, and you've brought me every darned thing that's been packed off, I'll pay you the rest of the fifty. There's more," he added meaningly, "that's missing. The fuselage ain't all."

The brother of Tomaso seemed unhappy. He took the ten dollars with a sigh, promised himself much unpleasantness for Tomaso, and wearily set about making camp, too dispirited to care that Johnny spent the time in fussing around the machine, making a thin pretense of looking it over for breakages and defects when all the while he was simply adoring it.

"At daybreak," Johnny announced with a new dignity in his voice-the dignity of one having valuable possessions and a potential power —"we'll start back. But I don't think much of your idea that we can drag this machine home with our saddle horses. We can't —not and have anything but a bundle of junk when we get there. There's a ranch over south here, a mile or so. Better see if you can't get a wagon and team. We'll have to haul it home somehow."

The brother of Tomaso started perceptibly. "A rancho? But that is not possible, señor!"

"Oh, ain't it? I'll show yuh, then."

"Oh, no! *No importa.* If it is a rancho in this countree, me, I'm find it without trobles for you."

Even Johnny's absorption in his treasure-trove could not altogether blind him to the fact that Tomaso's brother was perturbed. He wondered a little. But after all, there was only one thing now that really interested him, and he straightway returned to it, leaving the Mexican to find the ranch and hire a team. He was not afraid that the brother of Tomaso would fail him in that detail. Thirty American dollars look big to a Mexican.

He knew when Tomaso's brother mounted and rode away in the direction of the ranch, and he knew when he returned. But he failed to observe that the brother of Tomaso was gone long enough to have crawled there and back on his hands and knees, and that he returned in a much better humor than when he had left.

"The wagon and mules, it will come at daytime," was his brief report. He crawled into his blankets and left Johnny perched up in the pilot's seat, planning and dreaming in the moonlight. The brother of Tomaso lifted his head once and looked at Johnny's head and shoulders, which was all of him that showed. Through half-closed lids he studied Johnny's profile and the look of exaltation in his wide-open eyes.

"Tex, he's one smart *hombre*," Tomaso's brother paid tribute. "The plan it works aw-right, I bet."

Chapter Eight. Over the Telephone

That night Johnny spread his blankets in a spot where he could lie and look at his airplane with the moon shining full upon it and throwing a shadow like a great, black bird with outstretched wings on the sand. He had to lie where he could look at it, else he could not have lain there at all. He was like a child that falls asleep with a new, long-coveted toy clasped tight in its two hands. He worried himself into a headache over the difficulties of transporting it unharmed over the miles of untracked desert country to Sinkhole. He was afraid the mules would run away with it, or upset it somehow. It looked so fragile, so easily broken. Already the tail was broken, where the flyers in landing had swerved against a rock. He pictured mishaps and disasters enough to fill a journey of five times that length over country twice as rough. He wished that he could fly it home. Picturing that, his lips softened into a smile, and the pucker eased out of his forehead.

But he couldn't fly it. He didn't know how, though I honestly believe he would have tried it anyway, had there been even a gallon of gasoline in the tank. But the tank was bone dry, and the tail was knocked askew, so Johnny had to give up thinking about it.

When he slept, the airplane filled his dreams so that he talked in his sleep and wakened the brother of Tomaso, who sat up in his blankets to listen.

"That plan, she's work fine, I bet!" grinned the brother of Tomaso when Johnny had droned off into mumbling and then silence. "That Tex, she's smart *hombre*." He laid himself down to sleep again.

Speaking of Tex; that same night he lay awake for a long while, staring at the moon-lighted window and wishing that his eyesight could follow his thoughts and show him what he wanted to see. His thoughts took the trail to Sinkhole, dwelt there for a space in anxious speculation, drifted on to the Border and beyond and sought out Johnny Jewel, dwelling upon his quest with even more anxious speculation. Then, when sleep had dulled somewhat his reasoning faculties, Tex began to vision himself in Tucson-well, perhaps in Los Angeles, that Mecca of pleasure lovers-spending money freely, living for a little while the life of ease and idleness gemmed with the smiles of those beautiful women who hover gaily around the money pots in any country, in any clime.

For a hard-working cowpuncher with no visible assets save his riding gear and his skill with horses, the half-waking dreams of Tex were florid and as impossible, in the cold light of reason, as had been the dreams of Johnny Jewel in that bunk house.

That night others were awake in the moonlight. Down at Sinkhole camp five or six riders were driving a bunch of Rolling R horses into the corral where Johnny kept his riding horse overnight. They were not dreaming vaguely of the future, these riders. Instead they were very much awake to the present and the risks thereof. On the nearest ridge that gave an outlook to the north, a sentinel was stationed in the shade of a rocky out-cropping, ready to wheel and gallop back with a warning if any rode that way.

When the horses were corralled and the gate closed, one man climbed upon the fence and gave orders. This horse was to be turned outside-and the gate-tender swung open the barrier to let it through. That horse could go, and that and that.

"A dozen or so is about as many as we better take," he said to one who worked near him. "No-turn that one back. I know-he's a good one, but his mane and tail, and them white stockings behind, they're too easy reco'nized. That long-legged bay, over there-he's got wind; look at the chest on 'im! Forequarters like a lion. Haze him out, boys." He turned himself on the fence and squinted over the bewildered little group of freed horses. He swung back and squinted over the bunch in the corral, weighing a delicate problem in his mind, to judge by the look of him.

"All right, boys. We kain't afford to be hawgs, this trip. Straddle your hosses and take 'em over to that far corner where we laid the fence down. Remember what I said about keepin' to the rocky draws. I'll wait here and turn these loose, and foller along and set up the fence after yuh. And keep agoin'—only don't swing over toward Baptista's place, mind. Keep to the left all you can. And keep a lookout ahead. Yuh don't want that kid to get a squint at yuh."

One answered him in Mexican while they slipped out and mounted. They rode away, driving the horses they had chosen. Unobtrusive horses as to color; bays and browns, mostly, of the commonplace type that would not easily be missed from the herd. The man on the fence smoked a cigarette and studied the horses milling restlessly below him in the corral.

From the adobe cabin squatting in the moonlight came the shrill, insistent jingling of a bell. The man looked that way thoughtfully, climbed down and went to the cabin, keeping carefully in the beaten trail.

The door was not locked. A rawhide thong tied it fast to a staple in the door jamb. With the bell shrilling its summons inside, the man paused long enough to study the knotting of the thong before he untied it and stepped inside. He went to the telephone slowly, thoughtfully, his cigarette held between two fingers, his forehead drawn down so that his eyebrows were pinched together. He hesitated perceptibly before he took down the receiver. Then he grinned.

"Hello!" His voice was hoarse, slightly muffled. He grinned again when he caught the mildly querulous tones of Sudden Selmer, sharpened a little by the transmitter.

"Where the dickens have you been? I've been trying all evening to get you," Sudden complained.

"Huh? Oh, I just got in. I been fixing fence over west of here. Took me till dark-No, the stock's all in-wind had blowed down a couple of them rotten posts-well, they was rotten enough to sag over, so I had to reset them-Had to reset them, I said! Dig new holes!" He turned his face a little away from the transmitter and coughed, then grinned while he listened.

"Oh, nothing-just a cold I caught-Don't amount to anything. I'm doctoring it. I always get hoarse when I catch a little cold-Sure, everything's all right. I'm going to ride fence to-morrow —That so? It blowed to beat the cars, down here all night-Why, they're lookin' fine-No, ain't saw a soul. I guess they know better than to bother our stock-All right, Mr. Selmer, I will-and say! I might be late in getting in to-morrow, but everything's fine as silk-All right —G' bye!"

He hung up the receiver before he started to laugh, but once he did start, he laughed all the time he was re-tying the door in the same kind of knot Johnny had used, and all the while he was returning to the corral.

"Fell for it, all right. Nothing can beat having a cold right handy," he chuckled when he had turned out the stock, whistled for the sentinel, and mounted his horse. "Guess I better happen around to-morrow evening. They won't be back-not if they bring it with 'em."

While he waited for the guard to come in, he eyed the corral and its immediate neighborhood, and afterward inspected the cloud-flecked sky. "Corral shows a bunch of stock has been penned here," he muttered. "But the wind'll raise before sun-up. I guess it'll be all right."

The sentinel came trotting around the corner. "How many?" he asked, riding alongside the other.

"Fifteen, all told. To-morrow night we'll cull that bunch that ranges west of here. Won't do to trim out too many at a time, and they may be back here to-morrow night. They will if they can't get it over. I don't much expect they will, at that-unless they bring it in pieces. Still, yuh can't tell what a crazy kid'll take a notion to do; not when he's got a bug like Tex says this one has got."

"Tex is pretty cute, aw-right. Me, I'd never a thought of that."

The boss grunted. "Tex is paid for being cute. He's on the inside, where he's got a chance to know these things. He wouldn't be worth a nickel to us if he wasn't cute."

"And it's us that takes the chances," readily agreed the guard.

"Yeah-look at the chance I took jus' now! Talked to old Sudden over the 'phone, stalling along like I was the kid. Got away with it, at that. I'd like to see Tex —"

"Aw, Tex ain't in it with *you*. When it comes right down to fine work —" So, feeding the vanity of the boss with tidbits of crude flattery, which the boss swallowed greedily as nine tenths of us would do, they jogged along down the pebbly bottom of Sinkhole Creek where it had gone dry, turned into the first rocky draw that pointed southeastward, and so passed on and away from the camp where Tex's thoughts were clinging anxiously.

When they had carefully mended the fence that had been opened, and had obliterated all traces of horses passing through, they rode home to their beds perfectly satisfied with the night's work, and looking forward to the next night.

A hot, windy day went over the arid range; a day filled with contented labor for some, strenuous activity for some others-Johnny Jewel among these-and more or less anxious waiting for a very few.

That day the fifteen stolen horses, urged forward by grimy, swearing Mexicans and a white man or two, trotted heavily southward, keeping always to the sheltered draws and never showing upon a ridge until after a lookout had waved that all was well.

That day Mary V rode aimlessly to the western hills, because she saw three of the boys hiking off toward the south and she did not know where they were going.

That day Johnny Jewel suffered chronic heart jumpings, lest the four wide-blinkered mules look around again and, seeing themselves still pursued by the great, ungainly contraption on the lengthened wagon they drew, run away and upset their precariously balanced load.

That day the man who had so obligingly answered the telephone for Johnny busied himself with various plans and preparations for the night, and retraced the trail down the rocky draws to the fence where horses and riders had crossed, to make sure, by daylight, that no trace had been left of their passing, and met Tex over by Snake Ridge for a brief and very satisfactory conference.

So the day blew itself red in the face, and then purple, with a tender, rose-violet haze under its one crimson, lazily drooping eye. And at last it wrapped itself in its royal, gemmed robe, and settled quietly down to sleep. Night came stepping softly across the hills and the sandy plains, carrying her full-lighted lantern that painted black shadows beside every rock and bush and cut-bank.

With the deepening of the shadows and the rising drone of night sounds and the whispering of the breeze which was all that was left of the wind, the man came riding cautiously up through a draw to the willow growth just below Sinkhole watering place. He tied his horse there and went on afoot, stepping on rocks and grass tufts and gravelly spots as easily as though he had practiced that mode of travel.

Sinkhole cabin was dark and quiet and lonesome, but still he waited for awhile in the shadow and watched the place before he ventured forth. He did not go at once to the cabin, but always treading carefully where imprints would be lightest, he made a further inspection of the corral. The wind had done its work there, and hoofprints were practically obliterated. Satisfied, he returned to the cabin and sat down on the bench beside the door, where he could watch the trail while he waited.

The telephone rang. The man untied the door, went in, and answered it hoarsely. Everything was all right, he reported. He had ridden the fence and tightened one or two loose wires. Yes, the water was holding out all right, and the horses came to water every night about sundown, or else early in the morning before the flies got too bad. His cold was better, and he didn't need a thing that he knew of. And good-bye, Mr. Selmer.

He went out, very well satisfied with himself; re-tied the door carefully with Johnny's own peculiar kind of hitch, stooped and felt the hard-packed earth to make sure he had not inadvertently dropped a cigarette butt that might possibly betray him, and rolled a fresh smoke before leaving for home. He had just lighted it and was moving away toward the creek when the telephone jingled a second summons. He would have to answer it, of course. Old Sudden knew he couldn't be far away, and would ring until he did answer. He unfastened the door again, cursing to himself and wondering if the Rolling R people were in the habit of calling Johnny Jewel every ten minutes or so. He stumbled over a box that he had missed before, swore, and called a gruff hello.

"Oh, hello, cowboy!" Unmistakably feminine, that voice; unmistakably provocative, too-subdued, demure, on guard, as though it were ready to adopt any one of several tones when it spoke again.

"Oh-er-hello! That you, Mr. Selmer?" The man did not forget his hoarseness. He even coughed discreetly.

"Why, *no*! This is Venus speaking. May I ask if you expected Miss Selmer to call you up?" Raised eyebrows would harmonize perfectly with that tone, which was sugary, icily gracious.

"Oh-er-hello! That you, Miss Selmer? Beg your pardon-my mistake. Er-ah-how are yuh this evenin'?"

"Oh-lonesome." A sigh seemed to waft over the wire. "You see, I have quarreled with Mars again. He *would* drink out of your big dipper in spite of me! I knew you wouldn't like that —"

"Oh-why no, of course not!" The hoarseness broke slightly, here and there. A worried tone was faintly manifesting itself.

"And I was wondering when you are coming to take me for another ride!"

"Why-ah-just as soon as I can, Miss Venus. You know my time ain't my own-but maybe Sunday I could git off."

"How nice! What a bad cold you have! How did you catch, it?" Sweetly solicitous now, that voice.

"Why, I dunno —"

"Was it from going without your coat when we were riding last time?"

"I—yes, I guess it was; but that don't matter. I'd be willing to ketch a dozen colds riding with you. It don't matter at all."

"Oh, but it does! It matters a great deal-Dearie! Did you really think I was that nasty Mary V Selmer calling you up?"

"Why, no, I—I was just talking to her father-but as soon as I—I was thinking maybe the old man had forgot something, and had her-uh course I knowed your voice right away-sweetheart." That was very daring. The man's forehead was all beaded with perspiration by this time, and it was not the heat that caused it. "You know I wouldn't talk to her if I didn't have to." It is very difficult to speak in honeyed accents that would still carry a bullfrog hoarseness, but the man tried it, nevertheless.

"Dearie! Honest?"

"You know it!" He was bolder now that he knew endearing terms were accepted as a matter of course.

"OO-oo! I believe you're fibbing. You kept calling me *Miss* Venus just as if-you-liked somebody else better. Just for that, I'm not going to talk another minute. And you needn't call up, either-for I shall not answer!"

She hung up the receiver, and the man, once he was sure of it, did likewise. He wiped his forehead, damned all women impartially as a thus-and-so nuisance that would queer a man's game every time if he wasn't sharp enough to meet their plays, and went outside. He still felt very well satisfied with himself, but his satisfaction was tempered with thankfulness that he was clever enough to fool that confounded girl. All the way back to his horse he was trying to "place" the voice and the name.

Some one within riding distance, it must be-some one visiting in the country. He sure didn't know of any ranch girl named Venus. After awhile he felt he could afford to grin over the incident. "Never knowed the difference," he boasted as he rode away. "Nine men outa ten woulda overplayed their hand, right there."

Just how far he had overplayed his hand, that man never knew. Far enough to send Mary V to her room rather white and scared; shaking, too, with excitement. She stood by the window, looking out at the moon-lighted yard with its wind-beaten flowers. To save her life she could not help recalling the story of Little Red Riding Hood, nor could she rid herself of the odd sensation of having talked with the Wolf. Though she did not, of course, carry the simile so far as to liken Johnny Jewel to the Grandmother.

She did not know what to do —a strange sensation for Mary V, I assure you. Once she got as far as the door, meaning to go out on the porch and tell her dad that somebody was down at Sinkhole Camp pretending that he was Johnny Jewel when he was nothing of the sort, and that the boys had better go right straight down there and see what was the matter.

She did not get farther than the door, however, and for what would seem a very trifling reason; she did not want her dad to know that she had been trying to talk to Johnny over the 'phone.

She went back to the window. *Who* was down there pretending to be Johnny Jewel? And what, in heaven's name, was he doing it for? She remembered the Mexican who had ridden up that day and pretended that he wanted matches, and how he had returned to the camp almost as soon as she had left. But the man who had talked with her was not a Mexican. No one but a white man-and a range man, she added to herself-would say, "Uh course I knowed yore voice." And he had not really had a cold. Mary V's ears were sharper than her dad's, for she had caught the make-believe in the hoarseness. She knew perfectly well that Johnny Jewel might be hoarse as a crow and never talk that way. Johnny never said "Uh course I knowed," and Johnny would choke before he'd ever call her sweetheart. He wouldn't have let that man do it, either, had Johnny been present in the cabin, she suspected shrewdly.

Being an impulsive young person who acted first and did her thinking afterwards, Mary V did exactly what she should not have done. She decided forthwith that she would take a long moonlight ride.

Chapter Nine. A Midnight Ride

”Mary V, what are you doing in the kitchen? Remember, I told you you shouldn't make any more fudge for a week. I don't want any more sessions with Bedelia like I had last time you left the kitchen all messed up with your candy. What are you *doing*?”

Mary V licked a dab of loganberry jelly from her left thumb and answered with her face turned toward the open window nearest the porch where her mother sat rocking peacefully.

”Oh, for gracious *sake*, mom! I'm only putting up a little lunch before I go to bed. I'm going to take my rides earlier, after this, and it wouldn't be kind for me to wake the whole house up at daybreak, getting my lunch ready —”

“If you're going at daybreak, why do you need a lunch? If you think I'll permit you to stay out in the heat all day without any breakfast —”

”Well, mom! I can't take pictures at daybreak, can I? I've *got* to stay out till the light is strong enough. And there's a special place I want, and if I go early, I can get back early; before lunch, at the very latest. Do you *want* me to go without anything to eat?”

“Seems to me you're running them 'Desert Glimpses' into the ground,” her mother grumbled comfortably. “You've got a stack higher than your head, now. And some of these days you'll get bit with a snake or a centipede or —”

”Centipedes don't bite. They grab with their toes. My goodness, mom! A person's got to do *something*! I don't see what harm there is in my riding horseback in the early morning. It's a healthful form of exercise —”

“It's a darn fad, and you'll go back to school looking like a squaw-and serve you right. It's getting along towards the time when snakes go blind. You want to be careful, Mary V —”

”Oh, piffle! I've lived here all my life, just about, and I never *saw* a person bitten with a snake. And neither did you, mom, and you know it. But, of course, if you insist on making me sit in the house day in and day out —” Mary V cut two more slices of bread and began spreading them liberally with butter. She looked very grieved, and very determined.

“Oh, nobody ever made you sit in the house yet. They'd have to tie you hand and foot to do it,” came the placid retort. “Don't you go helping yourself to that new jelly, Mary V. The old has got to be used up first. And you wipe off the sink when you're through messing around. Bedelia's hinting that she's going to quit when her month is up. It don't help me a mite to keep her calmed down when you leave a mess for her every time you go near the kitchen. She says she's sick and tired of cleaning up after you. You know what'll happen if she does quit, Mary V. You'll be getting your 'Desert Glimpses' out the kitchen window for a month or so, washing dishes while we scurrup around after another cook. Bedelia —”

”Oh, plague *take* Bedelia!” snapped Mary V. But she nevertheless spent precious minutes wiping the butcher knife on Bedelia's clean dish towel, and putting away the butter and the bread, and mopping up the splatters of loganberry jam. Getting her “Desert Glimpses” through the kitchen window formed no part of Mary V's plans or desires.

They seemed to Mary V to be precious minutes, although they would otherwise have been spent in the wearisome task of waiting until the ranch was asleep. She took her jam sandwiches and pickles and cake to her room, chirping a blithe good-night to her unsuspecting parents. Then, instead of going to bed as she very plainly indicated to those guileless parents that she meant to do, she clothed herself in her riding breeches, shirt, and coat, and was getting her riding shoes and puttees out of the closet when she heard her mother coming.

A girl can do a good deal in a minute, if she really bestirs herself. Her mother found Mary V sitting before her dressing table with her hair hanging down her back. She was enfolded in a very pretty pink silk kimono, and she was leisurely dabbing cold cream on her chin and cheeks with her finger tips.

“Be sure you take your goggles with you, Mary V. I notice your eyelids are all red and inflamed lately when you come in from your rides. And do put them on and wear them if the wind comes up. It's easier to take a little trouble preventing sore eyes and sunburn than it is to cure them. And don't stay out late in the heat."

"All right, mommie." Drawing her kimono closer about her, Mary V put her face up to be kissed. Her mother hesitated, looking dubiously at the cream dabs, compromised with a peck on Mary V's forehead, and went away. Mary V braided her hair, put on a pair of beaded moccasins, buckled on her six-shooter and gathered together her other paraphernalia. She waited an hour by her wrist watch, but even that sixty minutes of inaction did not bring her better judgment to the rescue.

Sober judgment had no place in her thoughts. Instead, she spent the time in wondering if Tango would let her catch him in the corral; in fretting because she must wait at all, when there was no telling what might have happened at Sinkhole; and in giving audience to a temptation that came with the lagging minutes and began persuading her that Tango was too slow for the trip she had before her; and in climbing into bed, turning over three times and climbing out again, leaving the light covering in its usual heap in the middle.

It was half-past nine when she climbed out of her window with her riding shoes and puttees, her lunch and her camera and her field glasses, in a bundle under one arm. She went in her moccasins until she had passed the bunk house and reached the shed where she kept her saddle.

A dozen horses were dozing over by the feed rack in the corral, and Mary V's eyes strayed often that way while she was clothing her feet for the ride. Tango was a good little horse, but he was not the horse for a heroine to ride when she went out across the desert at midnight to rescue-er—a good-for-nothing, conceited, quarrelsome, altogether unbearable young man whom she thoroughly hated, but who was, after all, a human being and therefore to be rescued when necessary.

Would she dare —? Mary V hurried the last puttee buckle, picked up her bridle and a battered feed pan, and went quietly across the corral. Wondering if she would dare made her daring.

Most of the horses sidled off from her approach and began to circle slowly to the far side of the corral. Tango lifted his head and looked at her reproachfully, moved his feet as though tempted to retreat, and thought better of it. What was the use? Mary V always did what she wanted to do; if not in one way, then in another. Knowing her so well, Tango stood still.

Mary V smiled. Just beyond him another horse also stood still. A tall, big-chested, brilliant-eyed brown, with a crinkly mane, forelock, and tail, and with a reputation that made his name familiar to men in other counties. His official name was Messenger, but the boys called him Jake for short. They also asserted pridefully that he had "good blood in him." He belonged to Bill Hayden, really, but the whole Rolling R outfit felt a proprietary interest in him because he had "cleaned up" every horse in southern Arizona outside the professional class.

Ordinarily Mary V would never have thought of such a thing as riding Jake. She would have considered it as much as her life was worth to put her saddle on him without first asking Bill. Once she had asked Bill, and Bill had looked as if she had asked for his toothbrush; shocked, incredulous, as though he could not believe his ears. "Well, I should sa-ay not!" Bill had replied when she had made it plain that she expected an answer.

Ordinarily that would be accepted as final, even by Mary V. But ordinarily Mary V did not climb out of her bedroom window to ride all night, even though there was a perfectly intoxicating moon. Certainly not to a far line-camp where a young man lived alone, just to ask him why some one else answered his telephone for him.

To-night was her night for extraordinary behavior, evidently. She certainly showed that she had designs on Jake. She held out the feed pan, and gritted her teeth when Tango gratefully ducked his nose into it. She let him have one quivery-lipped nibble, and pushed the pan in-gratiatingly toward the black muzzle beyond.

Jake was not a bronk. Having "good blood" he was tame to a degree. He knew Mary V very well by sight, and, if horses can talk, he had no doubt learned a good deal about her from his friend Tango, who usually came home with a grievance. Jake accepted the feed pan graciously, and he did not shy off when Mary V pushed Tango out of her way and began to smooth Jake's crinkly mane and coax him with endearing words. After a little he permitted her to slip the bridle reins over his head, and to press the bit gently into his mouth. She set the pan on the ground and so managed to tuck his stiff, brown ears under the headstall, and to pull out his forelock comfortably while he nosed the pan. The bridge was too small for Jake, but Mary V thought it would do, since she was in a great hurry and the buckles would be stiff and hard to open. The throat latch would not fasten where Tango always wore it, but went down three holes farther. Jake was bigger than she had thought.

But she led him over to the shed door and adjusted the saddle blanket and, standing on her tip-toes, managed to heave her saddle into place. The cinch had to be let out too. Mary V was trembling with impatience to be gone, now that she had two heinous sins loaded upon her conscience instead of one, but she knew better than to start off before her saddle was right. And, impressed now with the size of Jake, she stood on a box and let out the headstall two holes.

Jake did not seem to approve of her camera and canteen and field glasses and rifle, and stepped restlessly away from her when she went to tie them on. So she compromised on the canteen and field glasses, and hid camera and rifle under some sacks in the shed. It seemed to her that she would never get started; as though daylight-and Bill Hayden-would come and find her still in a nightmare struggle with the details of departure. Back of all that the thought of that strange, disguised voice talking for Johnny Jewel nagged at her nerves as something sinister and mysterious.

She led Jake by a somewhat roundabout way to the gate, opened it and closed it behind them before she attempted to mount. Jake was very tall-much taller than he had ever before seemed to be. She had to hunt a high spot and coax him to stand on the lower ground beside it before she could feel confidence enough to lift her toe to the stirrup. Bill Hayden always danced around a good deal on one foot, she remembered, before he essayed to swing up. Standing on an ant hill did not permit much of the preliminary dancing around to which Jake was accustomed, so Mary V caught reins and saddle horn and made a desperate, flying leap.

She landed in the saddle, found the stirrups and cried, "You, Jake!" in a not altogether convincing tone. Jake was walking on his hind feet by way of intimating that he objected to so tight a rein. After that he danced sidewise, fought for his head, munched the strange bit angrily, snorted and made what the boys called Jake's chain-lightnin' gitaway.

Mary V knew that Jake was running away with her, but since he was running along the trail to Sinkhole camp she did not mind so much as you might think. At the worst he would fall down and she would get a "spill." She knew the sensation, having been spilled several times. So she gripped him tightly with her strong young knees and let him run. And after the first shock of dismay, she thrilled to the swift flight, with a guilty exultation in what she had done.

Jake ran a couple of miles before he showed any symptom of slowing. After that he straightened out in a long, easy lope that was a sheer delight to Mary V, though she knew it must not be permitted for very long, because Jake had a good many miles to cover before daylight. She brought him down gradually to a swinging, "running walk" that would have kept any ordinary saddle horse trotting to match for speed, and although he still mouthed the strange bit pettishly, he carried Mary V over the trail with a kingly graciousness that instilled a deep respect into that arrogant young lady.

Tango, I think, would have been amazed to see how Mary V refrained from bullying her mount that night. There was no mane-pulling, no little, nipping pinches of the neck to imitate the bite of a fly, no scolding-nothing that Tango had come to take for granted when Mary V bestrode him.

It was only a little after one o'clock when Mary V, holding Jake down to a walk, nervously passed the empty corral at Sinkhole Camp. She paused awhile in the shadows, wondering what she had better do next. After all, it would be awkward to investigate the interior of the little cabin that squatted there so silently under the moon. She hesitated to dismount. Frankly, Mary V felt much safer with a fleet horse under her, and she was afraid that she might not be so lucky next time in mounting. So she began to reconnoiter warily on horseback.

She rode up to the window of the little shed, and saw that it was empty. She rode inside the corral and made a complete circuit of the fence, and saw nothing whatever of Johnny's saddle and bridle. They would be somewhere around, surely, if he were here. She avoided the cabin, but rode down to the pasture in the creek bottom where Johnny's extra horse would be feeding. The horse was there, and came trotting lonesomely up to the fence when he saw Jake. But there was only the one horse, which seemed to prove that the other horse was with the saddle and bridle-wherever they were.

Mary V returned to the corral, still keeping far enough away from the cabin to hide the sound of Jake's hoof beats from any one within. She tied the horse to a corral post and went on foot to the cabin. She carried her six-shooter in her hand, and she carried in her throat a nervous fluttering.

First she sidled up to a window and listened, then peered in. She could see nothing, for the moon had slid over toward the west, and the room was a blur of shade. But it was also silent, depressingly silent. She crept around to the door, and found that it was fastened on the outside.

That heartened her a little. She undid the rawhide string and pushed the door open a little way. Nothing happened. She pushed it a little farther, listened, grew bolder-yet frightened with a new fear-and stepped inside.

It was very quiet. It was so quiet that Mary V held her breath and was tempted to turn and run away. She waited for a minute, her nostrils widened to the pent odor of stale cigarette smoke that clings to a bachelor's cabin in warm weather. She tiptoed across the room to where Johnny's cot stood and timidly passed her hands above the covers. Emboldened by its flat emptiness, Mary V turned and felt along the window ledge where she had seen that Johnny kept his matches, found the box, and lighted a match.

The flare showed her the empty room. Oddly, she stared at the telephone as though she expected it to reveal something. Some one had stood there and had talked with her. And Johnny was not at camp at all; had not been, since —

With a truly feminine instinct she turned to the crude cupboard and looked in. She inspected a dish of brown beans, sniffed and wrinkled her nose. They were sour, and the ones on top were dried with long standing. Johnny's biscuits, on a tin plate, were hard and dry. Not a thing in that cupboard looked as though it had been cooked later than two or three days before.

A reaction of rage seized Mary V. She went out, tied the door shut with two spitefully hard-drawn knots, mounted Jake without a thought of his height or his dancing accomplishments, and headed for home at a gallop.

She hated Johnny Jewel every step of the way. I suppose it is exasperating to ride a forbidden, treasured horse on a forbidden, possibly dangerous night journey to rescue a man from some unknown peril, and discover that the young man is not at hand to be rescued. Mary V seemed to find it so. She decided that Johnny Jewel was up to some devilment, and had probably hired that man to answer the 'phone for him so her dad would not know he was gone. He thought he was very clever, of course-putting the man up to pretending he had a cold, just to fool her dad. Well, he had fooled her dad, all right, but there happened to be a person on the ranch he could not fool. That person *hoped* she was smarter than Johnny Jewel, and to prove it she would find out what it was he was trying to be so secret about. And then she would confront him with the proof, and then where would he be?

She certainly owed it to the outfit-to her dad-to find out what was going on. There was no use, she told herself virtuously, in worrying her dad about it until she knew just exactly what that miserable Johnny Jewel was up to. Poor dad had enough to worry about without filling his mind with suspicious and mysterious men with fake colds, and things like that.

Mary V unsaddled a very sweaty Jake before the sky was reddening with the dawn; before even the earliest of little brown birds were a-chirp or a rooster had lifted his head to crow.

She wakened Tango with the bridle, slapped her saddle on him and tightened it with petulant jerks, got her rifle and her camera out from under the sacks, mounted and rode away again before even the cook had crawled out of his blankets.

Chapter Ten. Signs, and no One to Read Them

Bill Hayden's mouth was pinched into a straight line across his desert-scarred face. He shortened his hold on the rope that held Jake and passed the flat of his hand down Jake's neck under the heavy mane. He held up a moistened palm and looked at it needlessly. He stepped back and surveyed the drawn-in flanks, and with his eye he measured the length and depth of the saddle marks, as though he half hoped thereby to identify the saddle that had made them. His eyes were hard with the cold fury that lumped the muscles on his jaw.

He turned his head and surveyed the scattered group of boys busy with ropes, bridles and saddles-making ready for the day's work, which happened to be the gathering of more horses to break, for the war across the water used up horses at an amazing rate, and Sudden was not the man to let good prices go to waste. The horse herd would be culled of its likeliest saddle horses while the market was best.

To-day, and for several days, the boys would ride north and west, combing the rough country that held two broad-bottomed streams and therefore fair grazing for horses. Bill had meant to ride Jake, but he was changing his mind. Jake, from the look of him, had lately received exercise enough to last him for one day, at least. Suspicion dwelt in Bill's eyes as they rested on each man in turn. They halted at Tex, who was standing with his head up, staring at Jake with more interest than Bill believed an innocent man had any right to feel. Tex caught his glance and came over, trailing his loop behind him.

"What yo' all been doing to Jake, gantin' him up like that, Bill?" Tex inquired, his black eyes taking in the various marks of hard riding that had infuriated Bill.

Bill hesitated, spat into the dust, and turned half away, stroking Jake's roughened shoulder. "Me, I been workin' him out, mebby. What's it *to* yuh?"

"Me? It ain't nothin' a-tall to me, Bill. Only-yo' all shore done it thorough," grinned Tex, and passed on to where a horse he wanted was standing with his head against the fence, hoping to dodge the loop he felt sure would presently come hissing his way.

Bill watched him from under his eyebrows, and he observed that Tex sent more than one glance toward Jake. Bill interpreted those glances to suit himself, and while he unobtrusively led Jake into a shed to give him a hurried grooming before saddling another horse, Bill did some hard thinking.

"Shore is a night-rider in this outfit," he summed up. "He shore did pick himself a top hoss, and he shore rode the tail off'n 'im just about. Me, I'm crazy to know who done it."

Bill had to hurry, so he left the matter to simmer for the present. But that did not mean that Bill would wear "blinders," or that he would sleep with his head under his tarp for fear of finding out what black-hearted renegade had sacrilegiously borrowed Jake. Black-hearted renegade, by the way, was but the dwindling to mild epithets after Bill's more colorful vocabulary had been worn to rags by repetition.

All unconsciously Mary V had set another man in the outfit to sweating his brain and swearing to himself. Tex would not sleep sound again until he knew who had taken to night-riding —on a horse of Jake's quality. Tex would have believed that Bill himself was the man, had he not read the look on Bill's face while he studied the marks of hard riding. Tex was no fool, else his income would have been restricted to what he could earn by the sweat of his skin. Bill had been unconscious of scrutiny when Tex had caught that look, and Bill had furthermore betrayed suspicion when Tex spoke to him about the horse. Bill was mad, which Tex took as proof that Bill had lain in his bed all night. Besides, Bill would hardly have left Jake in the corral where he could have free access to the water trough after such a ride as that must have been. Some one had brought Jake home in such a hurry that he had merely pulled his saddle and bridle off and-hustled back to bed, perhaps.

Tex was worried, and for a very good reason. He had been abroad the night before, dodging off down the draw to the west until he could circle the ridge and ride south. He had been too shrewd to ride a fagged horse home and leave him in the corral to tell the tale of night prowling, however. He had taken the time to catch a fresh horse from the pasture, tie his own horse in a secluded place until his return, and re-saddle it to ride back to the ranch, careful not to moisten a hair. He felt a certain contempt for the stupidity that would leave such evidence as Jake, but for all that he was worried. Being the scoundrel he was, he jumped to the conclusion that some one had been spying on him. It was a mystery that bred watchfulness and much cogitation.

"What's that about some geeser riding Jake las' night?" Bud, riding slowly until Bill overtook him, asked curiously, with the freedom of close friendship. "Tex was saying something about it to Curley when they rode past me, but I didn't ketch it all. Anything in it?"

Bill cleared his mind again with blistering epithets before he answered Bud directly. "Jake was rode, and he was rode hard. It was a cool night-and I know what it takes to put that hawse in a lather. I wisht I'd a got to feel a few saddle blankets this morning! The —" Bill cussed himself out of breath.

When he stopped, Bud took up the refrain. It was not his horse, of course, but an unwritten law of the range had been broken, and that was any honest rider's affair. Besides, Bill was a pal of Bud's. "Hangin"s too good for 'im, whoever done it," he finished vindictively. "I'd lay low, if I was you, Bill. Mebby he'll git into the habit, and you kin ketch 'im at it."

"I aim to lay low, all right. And I aim to come up a-shootin' if the —"

"Yore dead right, Bill. Night-ridin' 's bad enough when a feller rides his own hawse. It'd need some darn smooth explainin' then. But when a man takes an' saddles up another feller's hawse —"

"I kin see his objeck in that," Bill said. "He had a long trail to foller, an' he tuk the hawse that'd git 'im there and back the quickest. Now what I'd admire to know is, who was the rider, an' where was he goin' to? D' you happen to miss anybody las' night, Bud?"

"Me? Thunder! Bill, you know damn well I wouldn't miss my own beddin' roll if it was drug out from under me!"

"Same here," mourned Bill. "Ridin' bronks shore does make a feller ready for the hay. Me, I died soon as my head hit my piller."

"Mary V, she musta hit out plumb early this morning," Bud observed gropingly. "She was saddled and gone when I come to the c'rel at sun-up. Yuh might ast her if she seen anybody, Bill. Chances is she wouldn't, but they's no harm askin'."

"I will," Bill said sourly. "Any devilment that's goin' on around this outfit, Mary V's either doin' it er gettin' next to it so's she kin hold a club over whoever done it. She mebby mighta saw him-if she was a mind to tell."

"Yeah-that shore is Mary V," Bud agreed heartily. "Bawl yuh out quick enough if they's anything yuh want kep' under cover, and then turnin' right around and makin' a clam ashamed of itself for a mouthy cuss if yuh want to know anything right bad. Bound she'd go with us getherin' hosses when she wasn't needed nor wanted, and now when we're short-handed, she ain't able to see us no more a-tall when we start off. You'll have to git upon 'er blind side some way, Bill, er she won't tell, if she does know who rode Jake."

"Blind side?" Bill snorted. "Mary V ain't got no blind side 't I ever seen."

"And that's right too. Ain't it the truth! I don't guess, Bill, yuh better let on to Mary V nothin' about it. Then they's a chance she may tell yuh jest to spite the other feller, if she does happen to know. A slim chance-but still she might."

"Slim chance is right!" Bill stated with feeling.

During this colloquy Mary V's ears might have burned, had Mary V not been too thoroughly engrossed with her own emotions to be sensitive to the emotions of others.

Mary V was pounding along toward Black Ridge-or Snake Ridge, as some preferred to call it. She was tired, of course. Her head ached, and more than once she slowed Tango to a walk while she debated with herself whether it was really worth while to wear herself completely out in the cause of righteousness.

Mary V did not in the least suspect just how righteous was the cause. How could she know, for instance, that Rolling R horses were being selected just as carefully on the southern range as they were to the north, since even that shrewd range man, her father, certainly had no suspicion that the revolutionists farther to the east in Mexico would presently begin to ride fresh mounts with freshly blotched brands? He had vaguely feared a raid, perhaps, but even that fear was not strong enough to impel him to keep more than one man at Sinkhole.

Sudden was not the man to overlook a sure profit while he guarded against a possible danger. He needed all the riders he had, or could get, to break horses for the buyers that were beginning to make regular trips through the country. He knew, too, that it would take more than two or three men at Sinkhole to stand off a raid, and that one man with a telephone and a rifle and six-shooter could do as much to protect his herds as three or four men, and with less personal risk. Sudden banked rather heavily on that telephone. He was prepared, at any alarming silence, to send the boys down there posthaste to investigate. But so long as Johnny reported every evening that all was well, the horse-breaking would go on.

It is a pity that he had not impressed these facts more deeply upon Johnny. A pity, too, that he had not confided in Mary V. Because Mary V might have had a little information for her dad, if she had understood the situation more thoroughly. As thoroughly as Tex understood it, for instance.

Tex knew that any suspicion on the part of the line rider at Sinkhole, or any failure on his part to report every evening, would be the signal for Sudden to sweep the Sinkhole range clean of Rolling R horses. He had worried a good deal because he had forgotten to tell his confederates that they must remember to take care of the telephone somehow, in case Johnny was lured away after the airplane. It had been that worry which had sent him out in the night to find them and tell them-and to learn just what was taking place, and how many horses they had got. When a man is supposed to receive a commission on each horse that is stolen successfully, he may be expected to exhibit some anxiety over the truth of the tally. You will see why it was necessary to the peace and prosperity of Tex that the surface should be kept very smooth and unruffled.

Tex, of course, overlooked one detail. He should have worried over Mary V and her industrious gathering of "Desert Glimpses," lest she glimpse something she was not wanted to see. I suppose it never occurred to Tex that Mary V's peregrinations would take her within sight of Sinkhole, or that she would recognize a suspicious circumstance if she met it face to face. Mary V was still looked upon as a spoiled kid by the Rolling R boys, and she had not attained the distinction of being taken seriously by anyone save Johnny Jewel. Which may explain, in a roundabout way, why her interest had settled upon him, though Johnny's good looks and his peppery disposition may have had something to do with it too.

Mary V, having climbed to the top of Black Ridge, adjusted her field glasses and swept every bit of Sinkhole country that lay in sight. Almost immediately she saw a suspicious circumstance, and she straightway recognized it as such. Away over to the east of Sinkhole camp she saw two horsemen jogging along, just as the Rolling R boys jogged homeward after a hard day's work at the round-up. She could not recognize them, the distance was so great. She therefore believed that one of them might be Johnny Jewel, and the suspicion made her head ache worse than before. He had no business to be away at night, and then to go riding off somewhere with someone else so early in the morning, and she stamped her foot at him and declared that she would like to *shake* him.

She watched those two until they were hidden in one of the million or so of little "draws" or arroyos that wrinkle the face of the range west. When she finally gave up hope of seeing them again, she moved the glasses slowly to the west. Midway of the arc, she saw something that was more than suspicious; it was out-and-out mysterious.

She saw something-what it was she could not guess-moving slowly in the direction of Sinkhole Camp, —something wide and queer looking, with a horseman on either side and with a team pulling. Here again the distance was too great to reveal details. She strained her eyes, changed the focus hopefully, blurred the image, and slowly turned the little focusing wheel back again. She had just one more clear glimpse of the thing before it, too, disappeared.

Mary V waited and waited, and watched the place. If it was crossing a gully, it would climb out again, of course. When it did not do so she lost all patience and was putting the glasses in their case when she saw a speck crawling along a level bit, half a mile or so to the left of where she had been watching.

"Darn!" said Mary V, and hastened to readjust the glasses. But she had no more than seen that it was the very same mysterious object, only now it was not wide at all, but very long-when it crawled behind a ridge like a caterpillar disappearing behind a rock. Mary V waited awhile, but it did not show itself. So she cried with vexation and nervous exhaustion, stamped her foot, and made the emphatic assertion that she felt like *shooting* Johnny Jewel for making her come all this long way to be driven raving distracted.

After a little, when the mysterious thing still failed to reappear anywhere on the face of the gray-mottled plain, she ate what was left of her lunch and rode home, too tired to sit up straight in the saddle.

Chapter Eleven. Thieves Ride Boldly

Johnny Jewel heaved his weary bones off his bed and went stiffly to answer the 'phone. Reluctantly as well, for he had not yet succeeded in formulating an excuse for his absence that he dared try on old Sudden Selmer. Excuses had seemed so much less important when temptation was plucking at his sleeve that almost any reason had seemed good enough. But now when the bell was jingling at him, no excuse seemed worth the breath to utter it. So Johnny's face was doleful, and Johnny's red-rimmed eyes were big and solemn.

And then, when he had braced himself for the news that he was jobless, all he heard was this: "Hello! How's everything?"

"All right," he answered dully to that. So far as he knew, everything was all right-save himself.

"Feed holding out all right in the pasture?" came next. And when Johnny said that it was: "Well, say! If you get time, you might ride up and get one or two of these half-broke bronks and ride 'em a little. The boys have got a few here now that's pretty well gentled, and they're workin' on a fresh bunch. The quieter they are, the better price they'll bring, and they won't have time to ride 'em all. You can handle one or two all right, can't yuh?"

"Yes, I guess I can," said Johnny, still waiting for the blow to fall.

"Well, how many will the pasture feed, do yuh think? You can turn out one of the couple you've got."

"Oh, there's food enough for three, all right, I guess —"

"Well, all right-there's a couple of good ones I'd like to have gentled down. Cold's better, ay?"

"I —why, I guess so." Johnny just said that from force of habit. His mind refused to react to a question which to him was meaningless. Johnny could not remember when he had last had a cold.

"Well, all right-to-morrow or next day, maybe. I'll have the boys keep up the two I want rode regular. If everything's running along smooth, you better come up and get 'em. And when they're bridlewise and all, you can bring 'em in and get more. These boys won't have time to get more 'n the rough edge off...."

When he had hung up the receiver, Johnny sat down on a box, took his jaws between his two capable palms and thought, staring fixedly at the floor while he did so.

It took him a full twenty minutes to settle two obvious facts comfortably in his brain, but he did it at last and crawled into his bed with a long sigh of thankfulness, though his conscience hovered dubiously over those facts like a hen that has hatched out goslings and doesn't know what to do about them. One fact-the big, important one-was that Johnny still had his job, and that it looked as secure and permanent as any job can look in this uncertain world. The other fact-the little, teasingly mysterious one-was that Sudden evidently did not know of Johnny's two-day absence from camp, and foolishly believed Johnny the victim of a cold.

But Johnny's conscience was too much a boy's resilient fear of consequences to cluck very long over what was, on the face of it, a piece of good luck. It permitted Johnny to sleep and to dream happily all night, and it did not pester him when he awoke at daylight.

Just because it became a habit with him, I shall tell you what was the first thing Johnny did after he crawled into his clothes. He went out hastily and saddled his horse and rode to the rock-faced bluff, turned into a niche and rode back to the farther end, then swung sharply to the left.

It was there. Dusty, desert-whipped, one wing drooping sharply at the end, the flat tire accentuating the tilt; with its tail perked sidewise like a fish frozen in the act of flipping; reared up on its landing gear with its little, radiatored nose crossed rakishly by the gravel-scarred propeller, that looked as though mice had nibbled the edges of its blades, it thrilled him as it had never thrilled him before.

It was his own, bought and paid for in money, and the sweat of long, toil-filled miles. It looked bigger in that niche than it had looked out on the desert with nothing but the immensity of earth and sky to measure it by. It looked bigger, more powerful —a mechanical miracle which still seemed more dream than reality. And it was his, absolutely the sole property of Johnny Jewel, who had retrieved it from a foreign country-his prize.

"Boy! I sure do wish she was ready to take the air," Johnny said under his breath to Sandy, who merely threw up his head and stared at the thing with sophisticated disapproval.

Johnny got down and went up to it, laid a hand on the propeller, where its varnish was still smooth. Through a rift in the rock wall a bright yellow beam of sunlight slid kindly along the padded rim of the pilot's pit; touched Johnny's face, too, in passing.

Johnny sighed, stood back and looked long at the whole great sweep of the planes, pulled the smile out of his lips and went back to the cabin. He wouldn't have time to work on her to-day, he told himself very firmly. He would have to ride the fences like a son-of-a-gun to make up for lost time. And look over the horses, too, and ride past that boggy place in the willows. It would keep him on the jump until sundown. He wouldn't even have a chance to go over his lessons and blue prints, to see just what he'd have to send for to repair the plane. He didn't even know the name of some of the parts, he confessed to himself.

He hated to leave the place unguarded while he made his long tour of the fence and the range within. He did not trust the brother of Tomaso, who had been too easily jewed down in his price, Johnny thought. He believed old Sudden was right in having nothing to do with Mexicans, in forbidding them free access to his domain. Johnny thought it would be a good idea to do likewise. Tomaso was to bring back the pliers, hammer, and whatever other tools they had taken, but after that they would have to keep off. He would tell Tomaso so very plainly. The prejudices of the Rolling R were well enough known to need no explanation, surely.

So Johnny ate a hurried breakfast, caught his fresh horse out of the pasture, and rode off to do in one day enough work to atone for the two he had filched from the Rolling R. He covered a good deal of ground, so far as that went. He rode to the very spot where fifteen Rolling R horses had been driven through the fence and across the border, but since his thoughts were given to the fine art of repairing a somewhat battered airplane, he did not observe where the staples had been pulled from three posts, the wires laid flat and weighted down with rocks, so that the horses and several horsemen could pass, and the wires afterward fastened in place with new staples. It is true that the signs were not glaring, yet he might have noticed that the wires there were nailed too high on the posts. And if he had noticed that, he could not have failed to see where the old staples had been drawn and new ones substituted. The significance of that would have pried Johnny's mind loose from even so fascinating a subject as the amount of fabric and "dope" he would need to buy, and what would be their probable cost, "laid down" in Agua Dulce, which was the nearest railroad point.

As it was, he rode over tracks and traces and bits of sinister evidence here and there, and because the fence did not lie flat on the ground, and because many horses were scattered in the creek bottom and the draws and dry arroyos, he returned to camp satisfied that all was well on the Sinkhole range. He passed the cabin by and headed straight for his secret hangar, gloated and touched and patted and planned until the shadows crept in so thick he could not see, and then remembered how hungry he was. He returned to the cabin, turned his tired horse loose in the pasture, with Sandy standing disconsolately beside the wire gate, his haltered head drooping in the dusk and his mind visioning heat and sand and sweaty saddle blankets for the morrow.

Dark had painted out the opal tints of the afterglow. The desert lay quiet, empty, lonesome under the first stars. Johnny's eyes strained to see the ridge that held close his treasure. He had a nervous fear that something might happen to it in the night, and he fought a desire to take his blankets and sleep over there in that niche. Tomaso's brother knew where it was, and the Mexican who had driven the mules that hauled it there. What if they tried to steal it, or something?

That night, before he went to bed, he saddled Sandy and rode over to make sure that the airplane was still there. He carried a lantern because he feared the moon would not shine in where it was. It was there, just as he had placed it, but Johnny could not convince himself that it was safe. He had an uneasy feeling that thieves were abroad that night, and he stayed on guard for an hour or more before he finally consoled himself with the remembrance of the difficulties to be surmounted before even the most persistent of thieves could despoil him.

After that he rode back to the cabin and studied his blue prints and his typed lessons, and made a tentative list of the materials for repairs, and hunted diligently through certain magazine advertisements, hoping to find some firm to which he might logically address the order.

Obstacles loomed large in the path of research. The Instructions for Repairing an Airplane (Lesson XVII) were vague as to costs and quantities and such details, and Johnny's judgment and experience were even more vague than the instructions. He gnawed all the rubber off his pencil before he hit upon the happy expedient of sending a check for all he could afford to spend for repairs, explaining just what damage had been wrought to his plane, and casting himself upon the experience, honesty and mercy of the supply house. Remained only the problem of discovering the name and address of the firm to be so trusted, but that took him far past midnight.

He was just finishing his somewhat lengthy letter of explanations and directions and a passable diagram of the impertinent twist to the tail of his machine. The moon was up, wallowing through a bank of clouds that made weird shadows on the plain, sweeping across greasewood and sage and barren sand like great, ungainly troops of horsemen; filling the arroyos and the little, deep washes with inky blackness.

Up from one deep washout a close-gathered troop of shadows came thrusting forward toward the lighter slope beyond. These did not travel in one easterly direction as did those other scudding, wind-driven night wraiths. They climbed straight across the wind to a bare level which they crossed, then swerved to the north, dipped into a black hollow and emerged, swinging back toward the south. A mile away a light twinkled steadily-the light before which Johnny Jewel was bending his brown, deeply cogitating head while he drew carefully the sketch of his new airplane's tail, using the back of a steel table knife for a rule and guessing at the general proportions.

"Midnight an' after-and he's still up and at it," chuckled one of the dim shapes, waving an arm toward the light. "Must a took it into the shack with 'm!"

Another one laughed rather loudly. Too loudly for a thief who did not feel perfectly secure in his thieving.

"Betcher we c'ud taken his saddle hoss out the pen an' ride 'im off, and he wouldn't miss 'im till he jest happened to look down and see where his boots was wore through the bottom hoofin' it!" continued the speaker contentedly. "Me, I wisht we c'd git hold of some of them bronks they're bustin' now at the ranch. Tex was tellin' me they's shore some good ones."

"What's the good of wishin'?" a man behind him growled. "We ain't doing so worse."

"No-but broke hosses beats broomtails. Ain't no harm in wishin' they'd turn loose and bust some for us; save us that much work."

The one who had laughed broke again into a high cackle. "What we'd oughta do," he chortled, "is send 'em word to hereafter turn in lead ropes with every hoss we take off'n their hands. And by rights we'd oughta *stip*-ilate that all hosses must be broke to lead. It ain't right-them a gentlin' down everything that goes to army buyers, and us, here, havin' to take what we can git. It ain't right!"

"The kid, he'll maybe help us out on that there. I wisht Sudden'd take a notion to turn 'em all over to this-here sky-ridin' fool —"

And the "sky-ridin' fool," at that moment carefully reading his order over the third time, honestly believed that he was watching over the interests of the Rolling R, and was respected and would presently be envied by all who heard his name. I wish he could have heard those night-riders talking about him, jeering even at the Rolling R for trusting him to guard their property. This chapter would have ended with a glorious fight out there under the moon, because Johnny would not have stopped to count noses before he started in on them.

But even though horse thieves are riding boldly and laughing as they ride, you cannot expect the bullets to fly when honest men have not yet discovered that they are being robbed. Johnny never dreamed that duty called him out on the range that night. He went to bed with his brain a whirligig in which airplanes revolved dizzily, and the marauders rode unhindered to wherever they were going. Thus do dramatic possibilities go to waste in real life.

On the shady side of the depot at Agua Dulce, Johnny sat himself down on a truck whose iron parts were still hot from the sun that had lately shone full upon it. With lips puckered into a soundless whistle, and fingers that trembled a little with eagerness, he proceeded to unwrap one of the parcels he had just taken from the express office. On another truck that had stood longer in the shade, a young tramp in greasy overalls and cap inhaled the last precious wisps of smoke from a cigarette burned down to an inch of stub, and watched Johnny with a glum kind of speculation. Johnny sensed his presence and the speculative interest, and read the latter as the preparation for a "touch." And Johnny was not feeling particularly charitable after having to pay a seven-dollar C.O.D. besides the express charges. He showed all the interest he felt in his packages and refused to encourage the hobo by so much as a glance.

He examined the slender ribs, bending them and slipping them through his fingers with the pleasurable feeling that he was inspecting and testing as an expert would have done. He read the label on a tin of "dope," unwrapped a coil of wire cable and felt it, went at a parcel of unbleached linen, found the end and held a corner up to the light and squinted at it with his head perked sidewise.

Whereupon the hobo gave a limber twist of his lank body that inclined him closer to Johnny. "Say, if it's any of my business, how much did Abe Smith tax yuh for that linen?" His tone was languid, tinged with a chronic resentment against circumstance.

Johnny turned a startled stare upon him, seemed on the point of telling him that it was not any of his business, and with the next breath yielded to his hunger for speech with a human being, however lowly, whose intelligence was able to grasp so exalted a subject as aircraft.

"Dunno yet —I'll have to look it up on the bill," he said with a cheerful indifference that implied long familiarity with such matters.

"Looks to me like some of the same lot he stung me with last fall, is why I asked. Abe will sting you every time the clock ticks. Why don't yuh send to the Pacific Supply Company? They're real people. Got better stuff, and they'll treat you right whether you send or go yourself. Take it from me, bo, when you trade with Abe Smith you want a cop along."

Johnny fingered the linen, his face gone sober. "I told him to send the best he had in stock," he said.

"Well, maybe he done it, at that," the hobo conceded. "His stock's rotten, that's all."

"I was looking the bunch over so I could shoot it back to him if it wasn't all right," Johnny explained with dignity. "They sure can't work off any punk stuff on me, not if I know it."

The hobo flipped his cigarette stub into the sand and stared out across the depressing huddle of adobe huts and raw, double-roofed shacks that comprised Agua Dulce. His pale eyes blinked at the glare, his mouth drooped sourly at the corners.

"Believe me, bo, if you're stranded in *this* hole with a busted plane, yuh better not take on any contract of arguing with Abe Smith. He'll stall yuh off till you forget how to fly." He turned his pale stare to Johnny with a new interest. "You aren't making a transcontinental, are you?"

"Well —n-no. Not yet, anyway. I —live here." You may not believe it, but Johnny was beginning to feel apologetic-and before a hobo, of all men.

"The deuce you do!" The tramp hitched himself up on another vertebra of his limp spine. "Why, I thought you were probably just making a cross-country flight, and had a wreck. I was going to bone yuh for a lift, in case you were alone. You *live* here! Why, for cat's sake?"

"Gawd knows," said Johnny. Then added impulsively, "I don't expect to go on living here always. I'm going to beat it, soon as I get my airplane repaired, and —" He was on the point of saying, "when I learn to fly it." But pride and his experience with the Rolling R boys checked him in time.

The hobo looked hungrily at the "makin's" Johnny was pulling from the pocket of his shirt. "At that you're lucky," he said. "Having a plane *to* repair. Mine's junk, and I'm just outa the hospital myself. I was a fool to ever go east, anyway. They are sure a cold proposition, believe me. Long as you're lousy with money, and making pretty flights, you're all right. But let bad luck hit yuh once-say, they don't know you any more a-tall. I was doing fine on the Coast, too, but a fellow's never satisfied with what he's got. The game looked bigger back East, and I went. Now look at me! Bumming my way back when I planned to make a record flight! Kicked off the train in this flyspeck on the desert; nothing to eat since yesterday, not even a smoke left on me, nor the price of one!" He accepted with a nod the tobacco and papers Johnny held out to him, and proceeded languidly to roll a cigarette.

"Down to straight bumming-when I ought to be making my little old thousand dollars a flight. Maybe you've kept in touch with things on the Coast. I'm known there, well enough. Bland Halliday's my name. Here's my pilot's license-about all them sharks didn't pry off me in the hospital! I sure do wish I had of let well enough alone! But no, I had to go get gay with myself and try and beat a sure thing."

Johnny was gazing reverently upon the pilot's license which he held in his hand, and he did not hear the last two or three sentences of the hobo's lament. He was busy breaking one of the ten commandments; the one which says, "Thou shalt not covet." That he had never heard of Bland Halliday did not disturb him, for in Arizona's wide spaces one does not hear of all that goes on in the world. He was sufficiently impressed by the license and what it implied, and he was thinking very fast. Here was a man, down on his luck it is true, but a man who actually knew how to fly; a fellow who spoke of Smith Brothers Supply Factory with the contempt of familiarity; a fellow who had used some of the very same linen.

Johnny Jewel forgot his pose of expert aviator. He forgot that Bland Halliday was absolutely unknown to him and that his personality was not altogether prepossessing. As a rule Johnny did not like pale eyes that seemed always to wear a veiled, opaque look. Heretofore he had not liked those new-fangled little mustaches which the Rolling R boys had dubbed slipped eyebrows. And ordinarily he would have objected to a mouth drawn at the corners in a permanent whine. To offset these objectionable features there were the greasy, brown overalls and the cap which certainly looked bird-mannish enough for any one, and there was the pilot's license-no fake about that-and the fact that the fellow had known all about Abe Smith and the linen.

Johnny threw away his cigarette and his caution together. "Say, I might be able to take you to Los Angeles, all right-provided you will take a hand on the little old boat and help me put her in shape again. It oughtn't to take long, if we go right after it. I —er-to tell the truth, it's hard to get hold of any one around here that knows anything about it. Why, I had one fellow working for me, Mr. Halliday, and just for a josh I asked him where the fuselage was. And he went hunting all over the place and finally brought me a monkey wrench! He —"

"No brains-that's the main trouble with the game," commented Bland Halliday, after he had exhaled a long, thin wreath of smoke which he watched dreamily. "What you got?"

"Hunh? What kind of a plane? Why, it's a tractor. A military —"

"Unh-huh. Dual dep control, or have you monkeyed with it and —?"

"It's a regular military type tractor. It-well, it has been in government service before —"

"You an army flier? Then what 'n hell you doing here? Say, put over something I can take, bo. You don't look the part. Only for that stuff you unwrapped, I'd tag you for a wild and woolly cowboy."

His tone was not flattering, and his very frank skepticism ill became a tramp. But Johnny had plunged, and he swallowed his indignation and explained with sufficient truth to be convincing. He even confessed that he could not fly-yet. There was something pathetic in his eagerness and his trustfulness, though Bland Halliday seemed to miss altogether the pathos, in his greed for technical details of the damage to the plane, and a crafty inquisitiveness as to distance and location.

He smoked another of Johnny's cigarettes, stared opaquely at the sweltering little village and meditated, while Johnny wrapped his parcels and tied them securely, and waited nervously for the decision.

"I wish I'd happened along before you sent for that stuff," Halliday remarked at last, flicking Johnny's face with a glance. "I've got a dope of my own that beats that, any way you take it-and don't cost a quarter as much. And that linen —I sure would love to cram it down old Abe Smith's gullet. Say! You got tacks and hammer, and varnish and brushes? If you're away off from the railroad, as you say you are, all these things must be laid in before we start work. And what about your oil and gas? And how's the propeller? Does she show any crack anywhere? How far is it, anyway? I'd like to look 'er over before I do anything about it. From all I can see, you don't know what condition the motor's in. How far is it, anyway? I might go and take a look."

"When you take a look," said Johnny, with a flash of his old spirit, "it will be with your sleeves rolled up. If you think I'm running a sight-seeing bus, you'd better tie a can to the thought. My time ain't my own-yet. I can get by, this trip, because the bronk I'm riding needed the exercise; or I can say he did, and it will get over. But I don't expect to be riding in to the railroad every day or so. If I get another chance in a month, I'll say I'm lucky."

"Well, I'd like to help you out all right. I can see where you're going to need it, and need it bad. Tell you what I will do, providing it suits you. I'll go over with you, and take a look at the plane. If it can be repaired without shipping it into a shop, all right! I'll help you repair it. You'll learn to fly, all right, on the way to the Coast. That is, if you've got it in you.

"And the other side of it is, if the plane can't be repaired at your camp, and you don't want to trust me to get it to a shop where I can repair it, all right. You stake me to a ticket to Los Angeles and money to eat on. It's going to be worth that to you, to know just what shape your plane's in, and what it will cost to fix it. And without handing myself any flowers, I'll say I'm as well qualified as anybody. I've built fifteen of 'em, myself. I can tell you down to the last two-bit piece what it's going to stand you to put her in shipshape condition, ready to take the air. And believe me, old top, you can throw good money away faster on an airplane than you can on a jamboree. I've tried both ways; I know." He leaned back on the truck and clasped his hands around one bent knee, as though, having stated his terms and his opinion, there remained nothing further for him to say or to do about it.

Johnny looked at him dubiously, did some further rapid thinking, and went to inquire of the station agent the price of a ticket to Los Angeles.

"All right, that goes," he said when he returned. "Come on and eat. We've got to do some hustling to get back before sundown. You make out a list of what we've got to have besides this-you said hammer and tacks-and I'll see if the hardware store has got it. Lucky I brought an extra horse along to pack this stuff on. You can ride him out."

"Ride a *horse? Me?*" the spine of the expert stiffened with horror, so that he sat up straight.

"Sure, ride a horse. You. Think you were going out on the street car?" Johnny's lips puckered. "Say, it won't prove fatal. He's a nice, gentle horse. And," he added meaningly, "you'll learn to ride, all right, on the way to camp. That is, if you've got it in you."

Chapter Thirteen. Mary V Confronts Johnny

Johnny was in one of his hurry-up moods now. He had the material to repair his plane, he had the aviator who could help him far, far better than could his cold-blooded, printed instructions. Remained only the small matter of annihilating time and distance so that the work could start.

In his zeal Johnny nearly annihilated the aviator as well. He rode fast for two reasons: He was in a great hurry to get back to camp, and he had a long way to go: and the long-legged, half-broken bronk he was riding was in a greater hurry than Johnny, and did not care how far he had to go. So far as they two were concerned, the pace suited. But Sandy refused to be left behind, and he also objected to a rider that rode soggily, ka-lump, ka-lump, like a bag of meal tied to the horn with one saddle string. Sandy pounded along with his ears laid flat against his skull, for spite keeping to the roughest gait he knew, short of pitching. Bland Halliday pounded along in the saddle, tears of pain in his opaque eyes, caused by having bitten his tongue twice.

"For cat's sake, is this the only way of getting to your camp?" he gasped, when Johnny and the bronk mercifully slowed to climb a steep arroyo bank.

"Unless yuh fly," Johnny assured him happily, hugging the thought that, however awkward he might be when he first essayed to fly, it would be humanly impossible to surpass the awkwardness of Bland Halliday in the saddle.

"Believe me, bo, we'll fly, then, if I have to *build* a plane!" Halliday let go the saddle horn just long enough to draw the back of his grimy wrist across his perspiring face. "And I've heard folks claim they *liked* to ride on a horse!" he added perplexedly.

Johnny grinned and turned off the road to ride straight across the country. It would be rough going for the aviator, but it would shorten the journey ten or twelve miles, which meant a good deal to Johnny's peace of mind.

He did not feel it necessary to inform his expert assistant that Sinkhole Camp was accessible to wagons, carts, buckboards-automobiles, even, if one was lucky in dodging rocks, and the tires held out. It had occurred to him that it might be very good policy to make this a trip of unpleasant memories for Bland Halliday. He would work on that plane with more interest in the job. The alternative of a ticket and "eating money" to Los Angeles had been altogether too easy, Johnny thought. There should be certain obstacles placed between Sinkhole and the ticket.

So he placed them there with a thoroughness that lathered the horses, tough as they were. Johnny Jewel knew his Arizona-let it go at that.

"Say, bo, do we have to ride down in there?" came a wail from behind when Johnny's horse paused to choose the likeliest place to jump off a three-foot rim of rock that fenced a deep gash.

"Yep-ride or fly. Why? This ain't bad," Johnny chirped, never looking around.

"Honest to Pete, I'm ready to croak right now! I can loop and I can write my initials in fire on a still night-but damned if I do a nose-dive with nothing but a horse under me. He-his control's on the blink! He don't balance to suit me. Aw, say! Lemme walk! Honest —"

"And get snake-bit?" Johnny glanced back and waved his hand airily just as his horse went over like a cat jumping off a fence. "Come on! Let your horse have his head. He'll make it."

"Me? I ain't got his head! Sa-ay, where's —" He trailed off into a mumble, speaking always from the viewpoint of a flyer. Johnny, listening while he led the way down a blind trail to the bottom, caught a word now and then and decided that Bland Halliday must surely be what he claimed to be, or he would choose different terms for his troubles. He would not, for instance, be wondering all the while what would happen if Sandy did a side-slip; nor would he have openly feared a "pancake" at the landing.

Johnny let the horses drink at a water hole, permitted the fellow five minutes or so in which to make sure that he was alive and that aches did not necessarily mean broken bones, and led the way on down that small cañon and out across the level toward another gulch, heading straight for Sinkhole much as a burdened ant goes through, over, or under whatever lies in its path.

It was a very good way to reach home quickly, but it had one drawback which Johnny could not possibly have foreseen. It brought him face to face with Mary V without any chance at all of retreating unseen or making a detour.

The three horses stopped, as range horses have a habit of doing when they meet like that. The riders stared for a space. Then Bland Halliday turned his attention to certain raw places on his person, trying to ease them by putting all his weight on what he termed the foot-controls. Even a pretty girl could not interest him very much just then, and Mary V, I must confess, was not looking as pretty as she sometimes looked.

"Well, Johnny Jewel!" said Mary V disapprovingly. "*What* have you there?"

"Well, Mary V! *What* are you doing here?" Johnny echoed promptly, choosing to ignore her question.

"What is that to you, may I ask?" Mary V challenged him.

"What is the other to you, may I ask?" Johnny retorted.

Deadlocked, they looked at each other and tried not to let their eyes smile.

"You're all over your cold, I see," said Mary V meaningly. "You didn't come after all to ride with me last Sunday, although you promised to come."

"Promised? I did? Well, what did you expect? Not me —I'll bet on it." Johnny had been nearly caught, but he recovered himself in time, he believed.

"I expected you wouldn't know the first thing about it-which you didn't. Oh, there's something here I want to show you." She tilted her head backward, and gave him a warning scowl, and rode slowly away.

Johnny followed, uncomfortably mystified. She did not go more than fifty yards-just out of the hearing of the stranger. She stopped and pointed her finger at a rock which was like any other rock in that locality.

"What is that fellow doing here? He can't ride. I saw you, when you came out of the cañon, so he isn't a new hand. And why did somebody answer your telephone for you, and pretend he had a cold so dad wouldn't know he was a stranger? Dad didn't, for that matter, but *I* knew, the very first words he spoke. And what are you up to, Johnny Jewel? You better tell me, because I shall find out anyway."

"Go to it!" Johnny defied her. "If you're going to find out anyway, what's the use of me telling yuh?"

"Who was it answered your 'phone? You better tell me that, because if I were to just *hint* to dad —"

"What would you hint? I've been answering the 'phone pretty regularly, seems to me. And can't I have a cold and get over it if I want to? And can't I fool you with my voice? You'd pine away if you didn't have some mystery to mill over. You ought to be glad —"

"You weren't at Sinkhole camp that night I 'phoned." Mary V looked at him accusingly.

"Oh, *weren't* I?" Johnny took refuge in mockery. "How do you know?"

Naturally, Mary V disliked to tell him how she knew. She shied from the subject. "You're the most *secretive* thing; you are doing something dad doesn't know about, but you ought to know better than to think you can fool *me*. Really, I should not like to see you get into trouble with my father, even though —"

"Even though I am merely your father's hired man. I get you, perfectly. Why not let papa's hired man take care of himself?"

Mary V flushed angrily. Johnny was reminding her of the very beginning of their serial quarrel, when he had overheard her telling a girl guest at the ranch that Johnny Jewel was "only one of my father's hired men." Mary V had not been able to explain to Johnny that the girl guest had exhibited altogether too great an interest in his youth and his good looks, and had frankly threatened a flirtation. The girl guest was something of the snob, and Mary V had taken the simplest, surest way of squelching her romantic interest. She had done that effectually, but she had also given Johnny Jewel a mortal wound in the very vitals of his young egotism.

"We are so short-handed this season!" Mary V explained sweetly. "And dad is so stubborn, he'd fire the last man on the ranch if he caught him doing things he didn't like. And if he doesn't get all the horses broken and sold that he has set his heart on selling, he says he won't be able to buy me a new car this fall. There's the *dearest* little sport Norman that I want —"

"Hope you get it, I'm sure. I'll take an airplane for mine. In the meantime, you're holding up a hired hand when he's in a hurry to get on the job again. That won't get you any sport Normans, nor buy gas for the one you've got."

"That man —" Mary V lowered her voice worriedly. "I know something nasty and unpleasant about him. I can't remember what it is, but I shall. I've seen him somewhere. What is he doing here? You might tell me that much."

"Why, he's going to stay over night with me. Maybe a little longer. I'm willing to pay for all he eats, if that —"

"Shame on you! Why *must* you be so perfectly intolerable? I hope he stays long enough to steal the coat off your back. He's a crook. He couldn't be anything else, with those eyes."

"Poor devil can't change the color of his eyes; but that's a girl's reason, every time. You better be fanning for home, Mary V. You've no business out this far alone. I think I'll have to put your dad wise to the way you drift around promiscuous. You can't tell when a stray greaser might happen along. No, I mean it! You're always kicking about my doing things I shouldn't; well, you've got to quit riding around alone the way you do. What if I had been somebody else —a greaser, maybe?"

Mary V had seen Johnny angry, often enough, but she had never seen just that look in his eyes; a stern anxiety that rather pleased her.

"Why, I should have said 'Como esta Vd,' and ridden right along. If he had been half as disagreeable as you have been, I expect maybe I'd have shot him. Go on home to Sinkhole, why don't you? I'm sure *I* don't enjoy this continual bickering." She rode five steps away from him, and pulled up again. "Of course you want me to tell dad you have a —a guest at Sinkhole camp?"

Johnny gave a little start, opened his lips and closed them. Opened them again and said, "You'll suit yourself about that-as usual." If she thought he would beg her to keep this secret or any other, she was mistaken.

"Oh, thank you so much. I shall tell him, then-of course."

She gave her head a little tilt that Johnny knew of old, and rode away at as brisk a trot as Tango could manage on that rough ground.

"Some chicken!" Bland Halliday grinned wryly when Johnny waved him to come on. "Great place to keep a date, I must say."

Johnny turned upon him furiously. "You cut that out-quick! Or hoof it back to the railroad after I've licked the stuffin' outa you. That girl is a real girl. You don't need to speak to her or about her. She ain't your kind."

Bland Halliday objected to rising with the sun. In fact, he objected to rising at all. He groaned a great deal, and he swore with great fluency and complained of excruciating pains here and there. The only thing to which he did not object was eating the breakfast that Johnny had cooked. And since Johnny could not remember the time when riding had been really painful, and therefore discounted the misery of his guest, he refused to concede the point of Bland Halliday's inability to get up and go about the business for which he had come so far.

"Aw, you'll be all right when you stir around a little," was the scant comfort he gave. "It's a good big half mile over to where I've got it cached. A ride'll limber you up —"

"Ride? On a horse? Not on your life! Honest, old top, I'm all in; I couldn't walk if you was to pay me a million a step. On the square, bo —"

"Say, I wish you'd cut out that 'bo' and 'old top' and call me Johnny. That's my name. And I wish you'd cut out the misery talk too. Why, good golly! What do you think I brought yuh down here for? Just to give you a ride? I've got an airplane to repair, and you claimed you could repair it. If you do, I promised to take you to the Coast with it. That's the understanding, and she still rides that way. Get up and come eat. We've got to get busy. I ain't taking summer boarders."

"Aw, have a heart, bo —"

Johnny's code was simple and direct, and therefore effective. He had brought this fellow to Sinkhole for a purpose, and he did not intend to be thwarted in that purpose just because the man happened to be a whiner. Johnny went over to the bunk, grabbed Bland Halliday by a shoulder and a leg, and hauled him into the middle of the cabin.

"Maybe you can fly; you sure don't hit me as being good for anything else," he said in deep disgust. "And I wouldn't be surprised right now to hear you swiped that pilot's license. If you did, and if you don't know airplanes, the Lord help yuh-that's all I got to say. Get into your pants. I'm in a hurry this morning."

Bland Halliday nearly cried, but he managed to insert his aching limbs into his trousers, and somehow he managed to move to the washbasin, and afterwards to hobble to the table. He let himself down by slow and painful degrees into a chair, swore that he'd lie on the track and let a train run over him before he would sit again on the back of a horse, and began to eat voraciously.

Johnny listened, watched the food disappear, gave a snort, and fried more bacon for himself. His mood was not optimistic that morning. He was not even hopeful. He had held an exalted respect for aviators, believing them all supermen, gifted beyond the common herd and certainly owning a fine valor, a gameness that surpassed the best courage of men content to remain close to earth. He had brought Bland Halliday away down here only to find that he lacked all the fine qualities which Johnny had taken for granted he possessed.

"Say! On the square, did you ever get any farther away from the ground than an elevator could take you?" he asked bluntly, when he was finishing his coffee after a heavy silence.

"Ten thousand feet-well, once I went twelve, but I didn't stay up. There was a heavy cross-current up there, and I didn't stay. Why?"

Johnny looked him over with round, unfriendly eyes. "I was just wondering," he said. "You seem so scared about getting on the back of a horse —"

"You ain't doing me justice," the aviator protested. "Every fellow to his own game. I never was on a horse's back before, and I'll say I hope I never get on one again. But that ain't saying I can't fly, because I can, and I'll prove it if you lead me to something I can fly with."

"I'll lead you-right now. You can ride that far, can't you?"

Bland Halliday thought he would prefer to walk, which he did, slowly and with much groaning complaint. Earth and sky were wonderful with the blush of sunrise, but he never gave the miracle a thought.

Nor did Johnny, for that matter. Johnny was leading Sandy, packed with the repair stuff and a makeshift camp outfit for the aviator. He had decided, during breakfast, to put Bland

Halliday in the niche with the airplane, and leave him there. He had three very good reasons for doing that, and ridding himself of Bland's incessant whining was not the smallest, though the necessity of keeping Bland's presence a secret from the Rolling R loomed rather large, as did Johnny's desire to have some one always with the plane. He had no fear that Halliday would do anything but his level best at the repairing. He also reasoned that he would prove a faithful, if none too courageous watchdog. That airplane was Bland's one hope of escape from the country, since riding horseback was so unpopular a mode of travel with him.

Thinking these things, Johnny looked back at the unhappily plodding birdman and grinned.

He was not grinning when he rode away from the niche more than an hour later, though he had reason for feeling encouraged. Bland Halliday did know airplanes. He had proved that almost with his first comment when he limped around the plane, looking her over. His whole manner had changed; his personality, even. He was no longer the spineless, whining hobo; he was a man, alert, critical, sure of himself and his ability to handle the job before him. Johnny's manner toward him changed perceptibly. He even caught himself addressing him as Mr. Halliday, and wanting to apologize for his treatment of the aviator that morning.

"We'll have to have a new strut here. You didn't get one in that outfit. And by rights we need a new propeller. There ain't the same thrust when it's gravel-chewed like that. But maybe you can't stand the expense, so we'll try and make this do for awhile. Say," he added abruptly, turning his pale stare upon Johnny, "for cat's sake, how d'yuh figure I'm going to replace them broken cables without a brazing outfit?"

Johnny didn't know, of course. "I guess we can manage somehow," he hazarded loftily.

"A hell of a lot you know about flying!" Bland Halliday snorted. "A lot of cable to fit, and no blowtorch, and you tell me we can manage!"

"Every fellow to his own game," Johnny retorted, feeling himself slipping from his sure footing of superiority. "I can ride, anyway."

"Well, I'll say I can fly. Don't you forget that. And here's where you take orders from me, bo. I took 'em from you yesterday. Got pencil and paper? I'll just make you out a list of what's needed here. And you get it here quick as possible."

"Well, I can't ride in to town for a week, anyway. I've got to —"

"That's your funeral, what you got to do. I've got to have the stuff to work with, and I've got to have it right off. At that, there's two weeks' work here, even if the motor's all right. I haven't looked 'er over yet-but seeing the gas tank is empty, I'm guessing she run as long as she had anything to run on, and that they landed for lack of gas. If that's the case, the motor's probably all right. I'll turn 'er over and see, soon as you get gas and oil down here. And that better be right off. I can be working on the tail in the meantime. But believe me, it's going to be fierce, working without half tools enough." Then he added, fixing Johnny with his unpleasant stare, "You'll have to hustle that stuff along. I'll be ready for it before it gets here, best you can do. Send to the Pacific Supply Company. Here, I'll write down the address. Better send 'em-lessee, a minute. Gimme the list again. You send 'em thirty bucks; what's left, if there is any, they'll return. Some of that stuff may have gone up since I bought last. War's boosting everything. All right-get a move on yuh, bo. This is going to be some job, believe me!"

"All right. There's grub and blankets for you. You'll have to camp right here, I guess. I don't aim to let the whole country know I've got an airplane-and besides, it will save the walk back and forth from your work. I'll see you again this evening."

Bland Halliday looked around him at the blank rock walls and opened his mouth for protest. But Johnny was in the saddle and gone, and even when Halliday cried, "Aw, say!" after him he did not look back. He followed Johnny to the mouth of the cleft and stood there looking after him with a long face until Johnny disappeared into a slight depression, loped out again and presently became, to the aviator's eyes, an indistinguishable, wavering object against the sky line. Whereupon Bland gazed no more, but went thoughtfully back to his task.

It was some time after that when Mary V, riding up on a ridge a mile or so north of the stage road that linked a tiny village in the foothills with the railroad, stopped to reconnoiter before going farther. Reconnoitering had come to be so much of a habit with Mary V that every little height meant merely a vantage point from which she might gaze out over the country to see what she could see.

She gazed now, and she saw Johnny Jewel-or so she named the rider to herself-hover briefly beside the Sinkhole mail box nailed to a post beside the stage road, and then go loping back toward the south as though he were in a great hurry. Mary V watched him for a minute, turned to survey the country to the southwest, and discerned far off on the horizon a wavering speck which she rightly guessed was the stage.

She rode straight down the ridge to the mail box, grimly determined to let no little clue to Johnny Jewel's insufferable behavior escape her. Johnny was up to something, and it might be that the mail box was worth inspecting that morning. So Mary V rode up and inspected it.

There was not much, to be sure; merely a letter addressed to the Pacific Supply Company at Los Angeles. Mary V held it to the sun and learned nothing further, so she flipped the letter back into the box and rode on, following the tracks Johnny's horse had made in the loose soil. She was so busy wondering what Johnny was ordering, and why he was ordering it, that she had almost reached Sinkhole Camp before it occurred to her that Johnny had that unpleasant stranger with him, and that it might be awkward meeting the two of them without any real excuse. Johnny himself knew enough not to expect any excuse for her behavior. Strangers were different.

But she need not have worried, for the cabin was empty. Since Johnny had not washed the dishes, Mary V observed that two persons had breakfasted. She observed also that Johnny had been in so great a hurry to get that letter to the mail box ahead of the stage that he had unceremoniously pushed all the dishes to one side of the table to make space for writing. She picked up a paper on which an address that matched the letter in the mail box and various items were scribbled, in a handwriting unlike Johnny's, and she studied those items curiously. It was like a riddle. She could not see what possible use Johnny could have for a quart of cabinet glue, for instance, or for a blowtorch, or soldering iron, or brass wire, or for any of the other things named in the list. She saw that the amount totaled a little over twenty-five dollars, and she considered that a very extravagant sum for a boy in Johnny's humble circumstances to spend for a lot of junk which she could see no sense in at all.

Having set herself to the solving of a mystery, she examined carefully the blue print laid uppermost on a thin pile of his lessons and circulars. There were pencil markings here and there which seemed to indicate a special interest in certain parts of an airplane. There was a letter, too, from Smith Brothers Supply Factory. She hesitated before she withdrew the letter from the envelope, for reading another's mail was going rather far, even for Mary V in her ruthless quest of clues. But it was not a personal letter, which of course made a difference. She finally read it; twice, to be exact.

Its meaning was not clear to Mary V, but she saw that it had to do with airplanes, or at least with certain parts of an airplane. She wondered if Johnny Jewel was crazy enough to try and make himself a flying machine, away down here miles and miles from any place, and when he did not know the first thing about it. Perhaps that horrid man he had brought was going to help.

"Bland Halliday!" she said abruptly, memory flashing the name that fitted the personality she so disliked. "I *knew* I had seen him. That-whatever made Johnny Jewel take up with *him*, for gracious sake? I suppose he's persuaded Johnny to build a flying machine-the silly idiot! Well!"

She waited as long as she dared, meaning to give Johnny some much-needed advice and a warning or two. She planned exactly what she would say, and how she would for once avoid quarreling with him. It would be a good plan, she thought, to appeal to his conscience-if he had one, which she rather doubted. She would point out to him, in a kind, firm tone, that his first duty, indeed, his only duty, lay in serving the Rolling R faithfully. Trying to build flying machines on the sly was not serving the Rolling R, and Johnny could not fail to see it once she pointed it out to him.

But Johnny was far afield, appeasing his conscience by riding the range and locating the horse herds. He did not return to camp at noon, for he found it physically impossible to ride past the rock wall without turning into the niche to see what Bland Halliday was doing, and to make sure that the airplane was a reality and not one of his dreams.

Bland was down under the corner of the damaged wing, swearing to himself and tacking linen to mend the jagged hole broken through the covering by the skid. He ducked his head and peered out at Johnny morosely.

"Get down here and I'll show yuh how to do this, so I can go at that tail. I just wanted to get it started, so I could turn it over to you-in case you ever showed up again!"

"I haven't time now to help," Johnny demurred. "I've got a big strip of country to ride, this afternoon. The horses are scattered —"

"Say, listen here, bo. You've got a big strip of linen to tack this afternoon, and don't overlook that fact. Fast as we can, I want to get it on so the dope can be hardening. I've figured out how we can save time, so if the motor's all right, we can maybe get outa this damn country in ten days. If you don't lay down on the job, that is, and make me do it all." He crawled out and got stiffly to his feet, rubbing a cramped elbow and eying Johnny sourly.

"Can't help it, Bland; I've got other work to-day. Boss'll fire me if I don't make —"

"For cat's sake, what do I care about the boss? You're going to quit anyway, ain't you, soon as we're ready to fly?"

"We-ell, yes, of course. But I'd have to give him time to get some one in my place. They're working short-handed as it is. I couldn't just —"

"You're laying down on me; that's what you're doing. Look how I've sweat all forenoon on that darned wing! Got the frame fixed, all ready for the linen to go back on; I've *worked* to-day, if anybody should ask you! Oughta have that glue, but I'm making out with what little old Abe sent. And you ain't lifted a hand. It ain't right. I can't do it *all*, and you ride around once in awhile to stall me off with how busy you are. You better can that stuff, and take a hand here."

"Well, don't cry about it. I'll tack that linen on, if that's all that's worrying you. But I can't stay long; I've spent too much time already away from my work. I oughta been riding yesterday, by rights."

Bland Halliday looked at him queerly. "Me, I'd call that riding, what we done," he retorted grimly. "I'm so sore I can hear my muscles squeak. Well, get down here and I'll show yuh how to stretch as yuh tack. And be sure you don't leave a hair's breadth of slack anywheres, or it'll all have to come off and be done over again."

So that is where Johnny was, while Mary V waited for him at the cabin and puzzled her brain over his mysterious actions, and composed her speech-and afterwards lost her temper.

It was three o'clock before Johnny finally finished to the aviator's grudging satisfaction what had looked to be a scant half hour's work. Mary V had gone home, and it was too late for Johnny to catch a fresh mount and make the ride he had intended to make. He made coffee and fried bacon and ate a belated lunch with Halliday, and then, since the afternoon was half gone, he let himself be persuaded-badgered would be a better word-into spending the rest of the daylight helping Bland.

If his conscience buzzed nagging little reminders of his real duty, Johnny's imagination and his ambition were fed a full meal of anticipation, and he had the joy of being actually at work on an airplane that he could proudly speak of as "my plane."

But conscience nagged all the evening. He really must get out on the range to-morrow, no matter how urgent Bland Halliday made the work appear. He really must look over that other bunch of horses, and ride the west fence. Ab-so-lutely without fail, that must be done.

Mary V, watching from that convenient ridge which commanded the Sinkhole mail box and the faint trail leading from it to the camp, saw the home-coming stage stop there. Through her glasses she saw the horses stretching their sweaty necks away from their burdensome collars, and then stand hipshot, thankful for the brief rest. She saw the driver descend stiffly from the seat, walk around to the back of the vehicle and, with some straining, draw out what appeared to be a box the size and shape of a case of tinned kerosene. He carried it with some labor to the mail box, tilted it on end behind the post, and returned to the rig for two other boxes exactly like the first one. He fumbled for Johnny's canvas mail sack —a new luxury of Johnny's —and stuffed it into the mail box. Then, climbing wearily back to the driver's seat, he picked up the lines, released the brake, and started on.

Mary V gave the stage no further attention. She was wondering what in the world Johnny Jewel wanted with three whole cases of coal oil-if that was what the boxes contained. Mary V was not, of course, disposed to stand long on a hill and wonder. The stage was not out of sight before she was riding down the ridge.

"Gasoline!" she ejaculated, kicking a box tentatively with a booted foot. "For gracious sake, what does that boy want with five-ten-with *thirty* gallons of gas? Why that's enough to drive a car from here to Yuma, just about. Surely to goodness Johnny hasn't —"

Tango lifted his head, pointed both ears forward and nickered a languid howdy to another horse. Mary V turned quickly, a bit guiltily, and confronted Johnny himself, riding up with something dragging rigidly from the saddle to the ground behind Sandy's heels. The confusion in Johnny's face served to restore somewhat the poise which Mary V had felt slipping.

"Hello, Skyrider," she greeted him chirpily. "Unless Venus has a filling station, you'll need more gas than this, won't you, for the round trip? Or-isn't it to be a round trip?"

Johnny's eyes flew wide open. Then he laughed to cover his embarrassment. "You're not up on sky-riding, are you, Mary V? I'll have to train you a little. I expect to 'vollup, bank and la-and,' coming back."

"Poor Bud isn't singing to-day. A bronk slammed him against the fence and hurt his leg so he's going around with a limp. What is that contraption, for gracious sake?"

"That? Why, that's a travois. You ask Sandy what it is, though, and he'll give you a different name, I reckon. Sandy's beginning to think life is just one thing after another. But he's getting educated."

Surreptitiously they eyed each other.

"Why do you buy your gas that way?" Mary V inquired with extreme casualness. "It's a lot cheaper if you get a drum, the way we do."

"I know; but it's a lot harder to handle a drum too. Besides —" Johnny broke his speech abruptly, hiding his confusion by straining to carry a case over to the travois.

Mary V studied his reply carefully, keeping silence until Johnny had loaded the other cases and was roping them to the travois frame.

"Is that Bland Halliday with you yet?" she asked him suddenly.

"Yeh-er-how do *you* know anything about Bl —" Johnny was plainly swept off his guard.

"Why, why shouldn't I know about BL?" Mary V's smile was exasperating. "I've seen Bland Halliday fly-and fall, too, once. Because he was drunk, they said. I've seen him drunk, and trying to do figure eights with a car on Wilshire Boulevard. He almost put me in the ditch, trying to dodge him. He was arrested for that, and his car was taken away from him. And I've heard-oh, all kinds of scandal about him. I was awfully surprised at your taking up with him. You ought to be ashamed of yourself, Johnny Jewel."

"He sure knows airplanes," Johnny blurted unwisely.

"Yours must be ready to fly-the amount of gas you're taking to camp."

"She goes in the air-say, good golly, Mary V! How do *you* know anything about my-er —"

"I hope," said Mary V very mildly, "that I have *some* brains. At any rate, I have brains enough to wonder how in the world you can afford to build yourself an aeroplane; I haven't heard a word about any rich uncle dying and leaving you a fortune. And I know it takes a tremendous lot of money to build and fly aeroplanes."

"Didn't set me back so much," Johnny bragged. "I didn't have to build one, you see."

Mary V needed time enough to study that statement also. She mounted Tango and waited until Johnny was ready to start with his queer load. "How did you get it-if I may ask?" she began then. "Did Bland Halliday happen along and have a wreck, and sell you the pieces? You want to be careful, because I know he's an awful grafter, and he'll cheat you, just as sure as you live, Skyrider."

"He can't," Johnny declared with confidence. "He's working for his passage-er —"

"Er-yes?" Mary V smiled demurely. "You may just as well tell me the whole thing, now. *Have* you got an aeroplane? Really truly? I mean, where did you get it? I know, of course, you must have one, or you wouldn't buy all that gas."

"Some deductionist," grinned Johnny, tickled with the very human interest he had roused in himself and his doings. "Where I got it is a secret-but I've got it, all right!"

"Johnny Jewel! You didn't let that Bland Halliday sell you —"

"I picked Bland Halliday up at the station in Agua Dulce," Johnny explained tolerantly. "He'd wrecked his plane back East somewhere. He was beating his way to the Coast, and was waiting to hit a freight. They'd dumped him off there. It was just pure luck. I had some stuff for repairing mine, and he saw me undo it and started talking. I saw he knew the game" (Johnny's tone would have amused the birdman!) "and when he showed me his pilot's license, I got him to help me. That's where Bland Halliday comes in-just helping me get 'er ready to fly. And he's going to teach me. You say you've seen him fly, so —"

"Oh, he can fly," Mary V admitted slightingly. "But he's so tricky, so-so absolutely impossible! A girl friend of mine has a brother that goes in for that sort of thing. I think he invented something that goes on a motor, or something. And I know he was terribly cheated by Bland Halliday. I think Bland borrowed a lot of money, or used a lot that was intended for something else-anyway, Jerry just hates the *name* of Bland Halliday. I didn't know him that day I met him with you, because they look so different all togged up to fly. But I remembered him afterwards, and I was going to warn you, only," she looked at Johnny sidelong, "you're a very difficult person to warn, or to do anything with. You are always so-so pugnacious!"

"I like that," said Johnny, in a tone that meant he did not like it at all.

"Well, you always argue and disagree with a person. Besides," she added vaguely, "you weren't there. And I can't be riding every day to Sinkhole."

"You could have seen me when I took those last horses back the other day," Johnny reminded her. "You did see me, only you pretended to be blind. Deaf, too, for I hollered hello when I passed, and you never looked around!"

"Did you?" Mary V smiled innocently. "Well, I'm here now; and I came just on purpose to warn you about that fellow. And you haven't told me the stingiest little bit about your aeroplane yet, or where you got it, or what you're going to do with it, or anything."

Johnny's lips twitched humorously. "I got it where it was setting like a hawk —a broken-winged hawk-on the burning sands of Mexico. I hauled it over here with four of the orneriest mules that ever flapped an ear at white men. It cost me just sixty dollars, all told-not counting repairs. And I'm going to ride the sky, and part the clouds like foam —"

"'And brand each star with the Rolling R,

An-d lead the Great Bear ho-ome,'"

Mary V chanted promptly. "Oh, Skyrider, won't you take me along too? I've always been just *dying* to fly!"

"You'll have to stave off death till I learn how-and then maybe you'll wish you hadn't."

”Oh, won't the boys be just *wild*! Where have you got it, Johnny? I've looked every place I could think of, the last two weeks, and I couldn't —"

”Oh —*hoh!*" cried Johnny. "So it was you I've been trailing, was it? I wondered who was doing so much riding down this way. You had me guessing, and that's a fact."

”Well, you've had me; now 'fess up the whole mystery of it, Johnny. You *know* that wasn't you, telephoning with a cold, that night. You know very well you weren't at camp at all; not for a couple of days, anyway. Probably that was while you went to the burning sands of Mexico. I don't understand that part, either; how you found out, and all. But who was it 'phoned for you? There were things he said —"

"Huh? What things? On the square, I don't know, Mary V. I never told anybody to 'phone-nobody knew I was going, except a greaser that told me about the plane, and went with me to see it."

"Well, I don't understand it at all. He certainly pretended he was you, and he must have 'phoned from Sinkhole, because there's no other 'phone on that wire. And the way he talked —"

"Oh, I think I know who it could have been," Johnny interposed hastily, thinking of Tomaso. "He —"

Just then the travois hung itself on a lava out-cropping which Sandy himself had dodged with his feet, and Johnny had a few busy minutes. By the time they were again moving forward, Mary V's curiosity had seized upon something else. She wanted to know if Johnny wasn't afraid Bland Halliday might steal his aeroplane and fly off with it in the night.

"Well, he might, at that-if he got a chance," Johnny admitted. "Which he won't —take it from me."

"Which he will-take it from you, if you don't keep an eye on him. From all Jerry said about him, he couldn't be honest to save his life. And I'm sure Jerry —"

”Good golly! You sure do seem to bank a lot on this Jerry person. At that, he may be wrong. Bland Halliday is all right if you treat him right. I ought to know; I've worked right alongside him for over two weeks now. And I'll say, he has *worked*! I'd have been all summer doing what he's done in a couple of weeks; and then it wouldn't have been done right. This said Jerry is welcome to his opinions, and you're welcome to swallow them whole, but me, I've got to hand it to Bland Halliday for sticking right on the job and doing his level best. Why, he couldn't have gone after the job any harder if it was his own plane."

"Which he probably intends that it shall be," Mary V retorted. "Before he does fly off with it, I might like to take a look at it-and a picture. May I, if you please, Mr. Jewel?"

"On one condition only, Miss Selmer. You must promise that you won't show the picture to a living soul till I give the word."

"Well, for gracious sake! How is the photographer going to develop and print it without seeing it?"

"I mean-you know what I mean. Come on, we'll swing over this way. I've got it cached in a secret hangar, over in that ledge. I've got to haul the gas over there, anyway, and you may go along if you like."

With a surprising docility Mary V accepted the somewhat patronizing invitation. Perhaps she really appreciated the fact that Johnny was proving how much confidence he had in her. Presently she urged that confidence to further disclosures. What did he really and truly intend to do with his aeroplane, after he had learned to fly?

”Well, I promised Bland I'd take him to the Coast. I intend to make aviation my real pro-fession, of course. You surely didn't think, Mary V, that I'd be satisfied to bog down in a job that just barely pays living wages? It's all right for fellows like Bud and Curley and Bill, maybe; but I couldn't go on all my life riding bronks and mending fence and such as that. I've just got to ride the sky, and that's all there is to it. Luck happened to come my way, so I can do it a little sooner than I expected; but I'd have done it anyway, soon as the way was clear.

"Aviation is the coming game, Mary V, and it's my game. Why, look what they're doing over in France! And if this country should get let in for a fight, wouldn't they need flyers? I'm not like Bland: I don't just look at it as furnishing thrills to a crowd that is watching to see you break your neck. Exhibition flying is all right, for a side line. But me, I'm going to go after something bigger than the amusement end. I —" his eyes grew round and dreamy, his lips quivering with all the wonderful future he saw before him, "I've thought maybe France or England might want me and my plane-to help lick those Germans. Honest, Mary V, their work is awful raw-blowing up passenger ships and killing children and women-and, of course, we aren't doing anything much about it; but if my little old boat could maybe bring down just one of those raiders that fly over England and drop bombs on houses where there's kids and women, I'd be willing to call it a day!"

"B-but that's dangerous, Johnny! You-you'd be killed, and-and it's so much finer to go on living and doing a little good right along every day. It would count up more-in the long run. And we're neutral. I —I don't think you ought to!"

"Why not? That's the biggest thing the world has ever seen or will see. The men that are in it-look what they're doing! It's tremendous, Mary V! It would be hitting a wallop for civilization."

"It would be getting yourself killed! And then what? What good is civilization to you after you're all smashed to pieces? You-you wouldn't be a drop in the bucket, Johnny Jewel! If it was our war-but to go and butt in on something away over there is absolutely foolish. What if you got one? You couldn't get them all, and there'd be a dozen to take its place.

"But that's the way it goes. You get a streak of perfectly unbelievable good luck, and have an aeroplane just practically drop into your hands, and then you spoil it all by wanting to do some crazy thing that is absolutely idiotic. I should think you'd be contented with what you've got; but no, you must take your aeroplane right straight over to Europe and let the Germans smash it all to pieces and kill you and everything. Why, I never *heard* of anything so absolutely imbecile as that!"

"Well, I haven't gone yet," Johnny reminded her. "Maybe the thing won't fly at all, and maybe I'll break my neck learning to run it. So it's kinda early in the day to get excited about my going to France."

"The idea! I'm not a bit excited. It really doesn't concern me at all, personally, whether you go or not. But it does look to me like a terribly silly idea. Any person with fair reasoning faculties would argue against such idiocy, just as a matter of-of —"

"Of course. Let it ride that way. Would you think, just to look along this ledge, Mary V, that a real military tractor was cached away in it? Talk about luck! You wait till you see the place I've got for it."

Mary V seemed unimpressed. "If I might venture to advise you on a subject that has no personal interest for me," she countered primly, "I would suggest that you hide most of that gas in one of these niches, and take only one can at a time to wherever your aeroplane is. I tell you, Bland Halliday is *not* to be trusted. You say he was broke and had lost his machine in a wreck or something, and was beating his way to the Coast. The truth probably is that he lost it some other way-maybe borrowed money on it and couldn't pay it back. That's what he always does, and then gets drunk and spends it all. But just as sure as you live, he'll steal your machine if he gets a chance. And once he's in the air-you can't chase him up there, you know. And you couldn't *prove* it was your aeroplane afterwards, could you? You haven't any papers or anything; you said it was 'finders, keepers.' And he could claim that he found it himself, couldn't he?"

She looked at Johnny's sobering face, with the pursed lips and the crease between his eyes that told of worry. Bland Halliday, once he was in the air, would be master of the situation. Johnny saw that.

"But you see, Skyrider, he can't fly without gas, and if you just have a little bit-just enough to practice with —"

"Mary V, when you aren't on the fight you're the best little pal in the world!" cried Johnny impulsively, and leaned and caught her hand and held it tight for a minute.

Chapter Sixteen. Let's Go

From a crooked willow branch thrust upright into the hard-packed sand to mark the entrance to the secret niche, a ripped flour sack hung limp in the cool, still air of a red dawn. From the niche itself came the vibrant buzzing of a high-powered motor to which Sandy listened with head up and ears perked anxiously, his staring eyes rolling toward a feasible line of retreat should panic overwhelm his present astonished disapproval.

The buzzing drew steadily nearer the yawning mouth of the cleft. The air swirled with a fine, rushing cloud of sand, against which Johnny blinked and pressed tight his lips while he dug his toes deep to guide and help propel the airplane through the opening. Followed Mary V, walking on her toes with excitement, swallowing dust without a murmur, her camera ready for action when they emerged into a better light. In the pilot's seat Bland Halliday, goggled and capped for flying, tested the controls before he eased the motor into its work.

Johnny, with his head bent low against the backwash of dust, looked at Mary V. Words were useless, worse than inadequate.

Well out from the mouth of the cleft, on the barren strip before the sage growth began, Bland swung the plane so that it pointed to the west. He lifted a hand in signal, and Johnny leaned backward, digging in his heels instead of his toes. The huge man-made dragon fly stopped, buzzing vibrantly. Bland Halliday beckoned imperiously, and Johnny went up to where he could hear.

"I'm going to try her out on a straightaway first, before I take you in," Bland leaned to shout. "Tell the girl she can be ready to snap me when I come back. I've got to test out the controls, and I want you ready to grab 'er if she don't stop right along here somewhere. All right-outa the way!"

Johnny ran back, away from the wing, and stood beside Mary V. He saw Bland turn his head and glance out along the right wing, then to the left. He caught a sense of Bland's tightening nerves, a mental and muscular poising for the flight. The thrumming jumped to a throbbing roar. The plane ran forward like a plover, gathering speed as it went. Fifty yards —a hundred-the little wheels left the sand, the tail sagged, the nose pointed slightly upward. The throb accelerated as distance dimmed the roar, until once more the droning thrum dominated.

"Oh-h-h!" gasped Mary V, and caught Johnny's arm and gripped it.

Johnny did not hear, did not feel her fingers pressing hard upon his biceps. Johnny stood like a man hypnotized; wide-eyed, the white line around his mouth, all his young soul straining after the airplane that went sailing away like a hawk balancing on outstretched wings.

"Oh-h-h-h!" gasped Mary V again, and squeezed his arm without knowing that she did so. "O-h —he's coming back! See-see how he circles-oh-h —he's doing an S, Johnny! Oh, Johnny, you lucky, lucky boy! Oh, and it's yours! Johnny Jewel, you've simply *got* to let me fly! Oh-h, I'm going to learn too! Oh-h-Skyrider! You wooden image, you, why don't you *say* something?"

Johnny looked at her, and there were tears pushing up to the edge of his eyelids. He looked away quickly and blinked them back.

Mary V bit her lip, abashed at the revelation of what this meant to Johnny. And then the drone was a roar again, and the airplane was skimming down to them. A *pop-pop-pop —pop*, and the motor stilled suddenly. The little wheels touched the ground, spurned it, touched again and came spinning toward them, reminding Johnny again of a lighting plover. The propeller revolved slower and slower, stopped at a rakish angle. Mary V felt the trembling of Johnny's arm as he pulled loose from her and went up to steady the machine to its final stand.

Bland Halliday pushed up his goggles. "She's runnin' like a new watch," he announced. "Juh get a picture?" This last to Mary V.

She shook her head, refusing to explain the omission. Bland turned to Johnny.

"She's O.K., old man. All we gotta do now is load up and start. You sure have balled things up by not getting enough gas, though. How far is it to that tank station-or some other that's closer?"

"There isn't any closer. I don't know exactly, but —"

"It's fifty-seven miles," Mary V fibbed hastily, and reached back a foot to kick Johnny into silence.

"Not air-line?"

"Certainly, air-line. Do you realize that you rode *seventy-five miles*, the way you came? And it's pretty rough country to land on, if you ran out of gas." She gave Johnny another kick, which Bland could not observe because of the wing they were leaning against.

Bland's mouth pulled down at the corners. "I *told* yuh we needed more gas," he complained. "Where'd you git the idea of packing gas in a tin cup to run an airplane on?"

"Where'd you get the idea we could pack a fifty-gallon drum on horseback?" Johnny retorted. "Believe me, you're lucky to get any at all!"

"I'll say this is some country!" Bland observed sourly. "Here we are-all ready to go-and not enough gas to take us to the railroad, even! Well, get in. I'll joy-ride yuh up and down this damn' scenery till the gas gives out."

"You'll teach me to fly. There's enough gas for one good lesson, anyway."

"Oh, all right. Sure, I'll teach you, if you're able to learn. But you hustle more gas down here, see? I'm all fed up on this country, and I ain't denying it. First off, we'll do a straightaway. I spotted a good level strip of ground over there a ways; that'll do to teach you how to land. Then we'll come back and fly straight off east for a ways, and circle and come back. How does that suit?"

"Fine and dandy. Hold my hat, Mary V." Johnny went to the front, reached high and caught the propeller blade. "All ready?" he cried, with the air of a veteran.

"A'right!" answered Bland, and Johnny put his weight into the pull, failed to "turn 'er over," took a deep breath and tried it again. The third attempt set the propeller whirling in a blurred circle. The motor woke to throbbing life again.

"Help me turn 'er first," called Bland, with a gesture to make his meaning clear.

"'Bye, Mary V! Now's your chance to get a picture-but you'll have to hurry!"

Johnny climbed up, straddled into the seat ahead of Bland. He placed his feet, pulled down his goggles, grasped the wheel and felt himself balanced-poised, with a drumming beat in his throat, a suffocating fulness in his chest. His moment had come, he thought swiftly, as one thinks when facing a sudden, whelming event. The biggest moment in his life-the moment that he had dreamed of-the culmination of all his hopes while he studied and worked-the moment when he took flight in an airplane of his own!

"Easy on the controls, bo, till you get the feel of it." Bland leaned to shout in his ear. "You can over-control, if yuh don't watch out. You feel my control. Don't try to do anything yourself at first. You'll come into it gradual."

He sat back, and Johnny waited, breathing unevenly. He had meant to wave a hand nonchalantly to Mary V, but when the time came he forgot.

The motor drummed to a steady roar. The plane started, ran along the sand for a shorter distance than before, smoothed suddenly as it left the ground, climbed insidiously. The beat in Johnny's throat lessened. He forgot the suffocated feeling in his chest. He glanced to the right and looked down on the ridge that held the hangar in its rocky face. A perfect assurance, a tranquil exaltation possessed him. Godlike he was riding the air-and it was as though he had done it always.

He frowned. The earth, that had flattened to a gray smoothness, roughened again, neared him swiftly. Ahead was a bare, yellow patch-they were pointed toward it at a slackened speed. They were just over it-the wheels touched, ran for ten feet or so, bounced away and returned again. They were circling slowly, just skimming the surface of the ground. They slowed and stopped, the plane quivering like a scared horse.

"Fine!" Bland shouted above the eased thrum of the motor. "You done fine, but seems like you showed a tendency to freeze onto the wheel when we were coming down; yuh don't wanta do that, bo. Keep your control easy-flexible, like. Now we'll go back where the girl is and make a landing there. And then we'll make a flight-as far as is safe on our teacup of gas!"

"I brought five gallons; that ought to run us a ways," Johnny pointed out. "I didn't want to land, that is why I froze to the wheel, as you call it. I wanted to keep a-goin'!"

"You get me the gas, and we'll keep a-goin', all right, all right! I got a hunch, bo, you're holding out on me."

"Forget it! Let's go!"

Again the short run, the smooth, upward flight, the slower descent, the bouncing along to a stop.

"You done better, bo. I guess this ain't the first time you ever flew, if you told it all. I hardly touched the controls. Now, say! On the square-where's that gas at? She's working perfect, and now's the time we oughta beat it outa here, before something goes wrong. I *know* you've got more gas than what you claim you've got."

"You know a lot you just think. I'll send for some, right off. Let's go. No use burning gas standing still!"

Mary V, her camera sagging in her two hands so that the lens looked at the wheels, gazed wistfully after them as they rose and went humming away toward the rising sun, that had just cleared the jagged rim of mountains and was gilding the ledge behind her. They climbed and swerved a little to the south, evidently to avoid looking straight into the sun.

Sandy stamped and snorted, tugging at the rope that tied him. Mary V looked down, away from the diminishing airplane, and gave a shrill cry of dismay.

"Jake! You come back here —*Whoa!*"

She stood with her mouth partly open, staring down along the ledge to where Jake, whom she had daringly borrowed again because of his strength and his speed that could bring her to Sinkhole in time to watch the trial flight, was clattering away with broken bridle reins snapping. Sandy wanted to follow. When she ran toward him to catch him before he broke loose, he, too, snapped a rein and went racing away after Jake.

Mary V stamped her foot, and cried a little, and blamed Bland Halliday for flying down that way where Jake could see him and get scared. She had been very careful to tie Jake back out of sight of the strip of sand where Johnny had told her they would make their start and their landing. It wasn't her fault that she was set afoot-but Bland Halliday just *knew* Jake would be scared stiff if he went down past where he was, and he had done it deliberately. And now Sandy was gone, too-and Johnny only had a couple of bronks in the little pasture-and she would just like to know what she was going to *do?* She should think that the least Johnny and Bland could do would be to come back and-do *something* about the horses. They surely must have seen Jake running away, and Johnny would have sense enough to know what that meant.

But Johnny, as it happened, was wholly absorbed in other things. He was not thinking of horses, nor of Mary V, nor of anything except flying. He was crowding into a few precious minutes all the pent emotions of his dearest dreams. He was getting the "feel" of the controls, putting his theoretical learning to the test, finding just how much and how little it took to guide, to climb, to dip. Bland Halliday was a good flyer, and he was doing his best, showing off his skill before Johnny.

He shut off the motor for a minute and volplaned. "Great way to see the country!" he shouted, and climbed back in an easy spiral.

Johnny looked down. They were still within the lines of the Rolling R range, he could tell by a certain red hill that, from that height, looked small and insignificant, but red still and perfect in its contour. Beyond he could see the small thread stretched across a half-barren slope-the fence he meant to inspect that day. Between the red hill and the fence were four moving dots, following behind several other smaller dots, which his range-trained eyes recognized as horses driven by men on horseback.

The airplane circled hawklike, climbed higher, and disported itself in an S or two and a "figure eight," all of which Johnny absorbed as a sponge absorbs water. Then, pointing, flew straight.

They were going back to the ledge. Johnny's heart sank at thought of once more creeping along on the surface of the earth like a worm, toiling over the humps and the hollows that looked so tiny from away up there. He wanted to implore Bland to turn and go back, but he did not know how long the gasoline would last, and he was afraid they might be compelled to land in some spot a long way from his rock hangar. He said nothing, therefore, but strove to squeeze what bliss remained for him in the next minutes, distressingly few though they were.

As it happened, Bland did not know the topography of Sinkhole as did Johnny, and in the still air the flour sack did not flutter. Bland was in a fair way to fly too far. Johnny knew they were much too high to land at the cleft unless they did an abrupt dive, and he did not quite like the prospect. He let Bland go on, then daringly banked and circled. Bland had done it, half a dozen times-so why not Johnny? Luck was with him-or perhaps his sense of balance was true. He did not side-slip, and he made the turn on a downward incline, which brought them closer to earth. He sought out the place where Mary V, a tiny wisp of a figure, stood beside the cleft, and flattened out as the ground came rushing up to meet him.

To all intents Johnny made that landing alone, for if Bland helped he did not say so. Johnny was positive that he had made it himself, and his sense of certainty propelled him whooping to where Mary V stood, her camera once more slanted uselessly in her two hands, her lips set in a line that usually meant trouble for somebody.

"How's that-hunh? Say, there's nothing like it! Did you get a picture of that landing I made? Say —"

"It seems to me that you are doing all the saying, yourself," Mary V interrupted him unenthusiastically. "It may be all very nice for you, Johnny Jewel, to go sailing around in an aeroplane. I suppose it *is* very nice for you. I grant that without argument. But as for me —" Sympathy for herself pushed her lips into a trembling, forced a quiver into her voice.

"As for *me*, you went and stampeded Jake so he broke loose and went off like a —a bullet! And Bill Hayden will just about *murder* me for taking him; I was going to sneak him back while the boys were out after more horses, and sneak out again with Tango so Bill wouldn't know. And now *look* what a mess you've got me into! Of course *you* don't care-you and your darned old flying machine! I wish it had busted itself all to pieces! And you too! And Sandy's stampeded after Jake, and I'm just glad of it!" She gulped, forced back further angry-little-girl storming, and recovered her young-lady sarcasm.

"But please don't let me interrupt your very fascinating new pastime. Of course, since you are a young man of leisure, playing with your new toy must seem far more important than the fact that I have about twenty miles to walk-through the sand and the heat, and not even a canteen of water to save me from parching with thirst. I —I must ask you to pardon me for-for thrusting my merely personal affairs upon your notice. Well, what are you grinning about? Do you think it's *funny*?"

"I could take her home, old top-if I had the gas." Bland turned his pale stare significantly from Mary V to Johnny. "Come through, bo. You know you've got more gas hid out on me somewhere. I got a slant at the bill of it, so I *know*. It wouldn't be polite to let the young lady walk home."

Johnny stilled him to silence with a round-eyed stare.

"Thank you, I'd much prefer to walk-if it was forty miles instead of twenty!" Mary V chilled him further. "What are we going to do, Johnny? I don't know *what* will happen if Bill Hayden finds out that I borrowed Jake. And then letting him get away, like that —"

"Sandy's at the pasture fence, I'd be willing to bet; but at that it's going to be the devil's own job to catch him, me afoot. And he wouldn't let you on him if I did. I guess it's a case of ride the sky or walk, Mary V."

"Then we better be stepping, bo, before the wind comes up, as I've noticed it's liable to, late in the forenoon. You dig up the gas, and I'll take her home."

"Thank you, I do not wish to trouble you, Mr. Halliday. Johnny can take me, if anybody —"

"Who-him?" Bland Halliday's smile was twisted far to the left. "Say, where do you get that idea-him flyin' after one lesson? Gee, you must think flyin' is like driving a Ford!"

"You could go to the shack and 'phone home for some one to come after you," Johnny suggested uncertainly.

"And let them know where I am? You must be absolutely crazy, if you think I'd consider such a thing. I'm supposed to be getting 'Desert Glimpses' —"

"Well, you sure got your glimpse," tittered Bland.

Mary V turned her back on him, took Johnny by the arm, and walked him away for private conference.

"You better let him take you home, Mary V. He's all right-for flying. I've got to hand it to him there."

"And give him a chance to steal your aeroplane? He'd never bring it back. I know he wouldn't."

"He'd have to. I'd only give him gas enough to make the trip on, and —"

"And if he had enough to come back with, he'd have enough to get to the railroad with. Don't be stupid. You can take me; couldn't you, now, honest?"

"Well, —I feel as if I could, all right. But a fellow's supposed to practice a lot with an instructor before he gets gay and goes to flying alone. Bland says —"

"Oh, plague take Bland! What would you have done if you hadn't run across him at all? Would you have tried to fly?"

"You know it!" Johnny laughed. "I've sat in that seat and worked the controls every day since I got it. I know 'em by heart. I've studied the theory of flying till I'll bet I could stick Bland himself on some of the principles. And I've been flying in my sleep for months and months. Sure, I'd have tackled it. But I wouldn't have had you along when I started in."

"You know how the thing works, then. Well, come on back and work it! Unless you're scared."

"Me scared? Of an airplane? It's you I'm thinking about. I'd go alone, quick enough. Maybe we could both crowd into the front seat, and let Bland pilot the machine. Then —"

"I abso-*lutely* will not-fly with-Bland Halliday! If you won't take me home, I'll walk!" Mary V pinched in her lips, which meant stubbornness.

Johnny heaved a sigh. "Oh, shoot! I'm game to tackle it if you are. Far as I'm personally concerned, *I know I can fly*." His lips, too, set themselves in the line of stubbornness. And he added with perfect seriousness, "It ain't half as hard as topping a bronk."

He glanced back, saw that Bland had gone into the cleft, and hurried on to where he had buried the gasoline in the sand behind a jagged splinter of rock in a shallow niche.

"Well, the Jane changed her mind, did she?" Bland commented when Johnny arrived at the plane with the gas. "Thought she would. Walking twenty miles ain't no sunshine, if you ask me. Better have the tank full-up, bo. It's always safer."

A suppressed jubilance such as had seized and held him when he first beheld the disabled airplane in the desert valley, filled Johnny now. As he climbed up and filled the tank his lips were pursed into a soundless whistle, his eyes were wide and shining, his whole tanned face glowed. Bland Halliday regarded him curiously, his opaque blue eyes shifting inquiringly to Mary V, halted at a sufficient distance to take a picture. They were very young, these two-wholly inexperienced in the byways of life, confident, with the supreme assurance of ignorance. It had been a queer idea, hiding the gasoline; and threatened to be awkward, since Bland was practically helpless out here in the sand and rocks. But things always turned out the right way, give them time enough. The kid was filling the tank-at present Bland asked no more of the gods than that. His sour lips drew up at the corners, as they had done when Johnny had made him the proposition in Agua Dulce. Mary V closed her camera and came toward them, walking springily through the sand, looking more than ever like a slim boy in her riding breeches and boots.

"All right. You lend Miss Selmer your goggles and cap, Bland. You won't need 'em yourself till I get back."

"Till you-what?"

"Till I get back. I aim to take Miss Selmer home." Johnny's lips were still puckered; his face still held the glow of elation. But his eyes looked down sidelong, searching Bland's face for his inmost thought.

Bland was staring, loose-lipped, incredulous. "Aw, say! D'yuh think I'll swallow that?" There was a threatening note beneath the whine of his voice.

"If you don't choke. Come on, Mary V; 'hop in, and we'll take a spin,' and all the rest of it. Venus'll have nothing on you. Here's my goggles; put 'em on. I'm going to borrow Bland's." It had occurred to Johnny that Mary V would probably shrink from wearing anything belonging to Bland Halliday; girls were queer that way.

Bland stepped pugnaciously forward; his pale eyes were unpleasantly filmed with anger. "Aw, I see your game, bo; but you can't get away with it. Not for a minute, you can't. You think I'm such a mark as that? Come down here and work like a dog to get the plane ready to fly, and then kiss yuh good-bye and watch yuh go off with it-and leave me here to rot with the snakes and lizards? Oh, no! I'll take the young lady —"

"Give me a hand up, Johnny. The front seat? How perfectly *ducky* to ride home in an aeroplane! Oh, Johnny wants your goggles, Mr. Halliday." Mary V reached down quickly and lifted them off the irate aviator's head before he knew what she was after. "Here they are, Johnny. Sit down, and Mr. Halliday will crank up-or whatever you call it. I'll send him right back, Mr. Halliday, just as quick as ever he can make the trip!"

Mr. Halliday gave her a venomous glance, and a sneer which included them both.

"Ain't it a shame she ain't equipped with a self-starter?" he fleered. "You two look cute, settin' there; but I don't seem to see yuh making any quick getaway, at that." He spread his legs and stood arrogantly, arms folded, the sneer looking perfectly at home on his face.

"Don't be a darned boob!" Johnny snapped impatiently. "Turn 'er over. Miss Selmer wants me to pilot her home, and I'm going to tackle it. You needn't be scared, though; I'll come back."

"I don't think so," said Bland, teetering a little as he stood.

"I will, unless I bust something. And it's my machine, so I'm sure going to be right careful that nothing busts." What Johnny wanted to do was get out and lick Bland Halliday till he howled, but since the gratification of that desire was neither politic nor convenient, he promised himself a settlement later on, when Mary V was not present. Just now he must humor Bland along.

"I don't think you'll come back," Bland repeated, "because I don't think you'll start. There's a little detail to be looked after first —a little swingin' on the propeller to be done. I don't see anybody doin' it. And I never did hear of anybody flying without their motor running." He tittered malevolently.

"Cut out the comedy, bo, and let me in there. You start 'er for me, and *I'll* take Miss Selmer home for you. You ain't got your pilot's license yet-by a long ways. I never heard of a flyer getting his license on a thirty or forty minute course. It ain't done, bo-take it from me." He spat into the sand with an air of patient tolerance.

"Are you all ready, Johnny?" Mary V's voice was rather alarmingly sweet. "I'm not going to *touch* this ducky little wheel. I'm afraid I might think it was my car and do something queer. I shall let you drive-if you *call* it driving. Now if Mr. Halliday will crank up for us, we'll go."

"Mr. Halliday will let you set there till you get enough," Bland grinned sourly. "I'm thinking of your safety, sister. I'm thinkin' more of you than that piece of cheese in the pilot's seat."

"Mr. Halliday, won't you *please* start the motor?" There was a remarkable stress upon the "please," considering the gun in Mary V's steady little right hand. She peered down owl-eyed at Bland through the big goggles. "This is Arizona-where guns are not loaded with blanks, Mr. Halliday. I'll prove it if you like. I'd just *love* to shoot you!"

Bland Halliday drew his feet together as though he intended to run. Mary V, still peering down through the goggles, shot a spurt of sand over the toe of one scuffed shoe. Bland stepped aside hastily.

"I can't see well enough to be sure of missing you next time," Mary V assured him. "Generally I can shoot awfully close and miss, but —I'd *like* to shoot you, really. You'd better crank the motor."

Bland saw the hammer lift again, ominously deliberate. He sidled hurriedly down to the propeller. His pale stare never left the gun, which kept him inexorably before its muzzle.

Johnny's eyes looked as big as his goggles, but he did not say a word. And presently, after three rather hysterical attempts, Bland set the propeller whirring, and ran out to one side, his hands up as though he feared for his life if he lowered them. The motor's hum increased to the steady roar which Johnny's ear recognized as the sound Bland got from it when he started. And with an erratic wabbling the plane moved forward jerkily, steadied a bit as Johnny set his teeth and all his stubbornness to the work, and gradually-very gradually-lifted and went whirring away through the sunlight.

They say that Providence protects children and fools. Johnny Jewel, I think, could justly claim protection on both grounds. He was certainly attempting a foolhardy feat, and he was doing it with a childlike confidence in himself. As for Mary V —oh, well, Mary V was very young and a woman, and therefore not to be held accountable for her rash faith that the man would take care of her. Mary V had centuries of dependent womanhood behind her, and must be excused.

Johnny wished that he had warned her about the peculiar tendency of the air currents to follow the contour of the ground. He climbed as high as Bland had climbed at first, hoping to escape the abruptness of the waves such as he had studied patiently from charts, and which he had felt when they flew over arroyos and rough ground. He did not want Mary V to be alarmed, but the noise of the motor made speech impossible, so he let the explanation go for the present. Mary V was sitting exactly in the center, grasping rather tightly the edges of the pit as a timid person holds fast to the sides of a canoe. Sitting so, she did not look in the least like a young woman who has just compelled a man at the point of a revolver to do her bidding. More like a child who is having its first boat ride, and who is holding its breath, mentally balanced between howls of fear and shrieks of glee. But Johnny did not believe she was scared.

Johnny was keyed up to the point of working miracles, of accomplishing the impossible. Johnny was happy, a little awed at his own temerity, wholly absorbed in his determination to handle that airplane just as well as Bland or any other living man could handle it. He kept reminding himself that it was simple enough, if you only had the nerve to go ahead and *do* it; if you just forgot that there was such a thing as falling; and, of course, if you knew what it was you ought to do, and how you ought to do it. Johnny knew-theoretically. And it did not seem possible to him that he could fall. He was master of a machine that was master of the air. He was riding the sky-and Mary V was there, riding with him, absolutely confident that he would not let her be hurt.

He did not attempt any "fancy stunts," such as Bland had done. He merely climbed to where he dared circle, then circled deliberately, carefully. When he came about so that the sun was warming his right shoulder, he flew straight for the Rolling R ranch, like a homing pigeon at sunset.

It was exhilarating-it was wonderful! Johnny, knowing the country so well, avoided passing over the roughest places, keeping well out from the hills, and into the smoother flow over the broad levels. The drone of the motor was a triumphal song. The flattening wind against his cheeks was sweeter than kisses. Supreme confidence in himself and in the machine stimulated him, made him ready to dare anything, do anything. Once more he was a god, skimming godlike through space, gazing down on the little world and the little, crawling things of the world with pity.

Ahead of him, Mary V never moved. Her little fingers never loosened their grip of the padded leather. Wisps of her brown hair, caught in the terrific air-pressure, stood back from her head like small pennants.

Black Ridge they passed, and it looked squatty and insignificant. Johnny swerved a little to the westward, to avoid a series of washes and deep gullies and small ridges between that might affect the smooth flight of the plane. On and on and on, boring steadily through the air that rushed to meet them-or so it seemed.

Far ahead, lumped on a brushless level which Johnny knew of old, a little, milling cluster of antlike creatures attracted Johnny's eye.

He watched it a minute, knew it for a horse round-up, and chuckled to himself. The Rolling R boys-and revenge for the sneers and the fleers they had given him when he had only dared to *dream* of flying. He wanted to tell Mary V, but then he thought that Mary V's eyes were as sharp as his. Yes, her fingers reluctantly loosened their hold and she tried to point-and had her hand swept backward by the wind. She tried again, and Johnny nodded, though Mary V could not see him without turning her head, which she seemed to think she must not do.

The Rolling R boys-Tex and Bill Hayden and Curley and Aleck and one or two more whom this story has not met-were driving a small herd of horses from which they meant to cut out a few chosen ones for breaking. Away up toward where the sun would be at two o'clock, a little droning dragonfly thing coming swiftly, and a little imp of mischief whispering into the willing ear of one who felt that he had suffered much and patiently. Mary V, hanging on tight, with her lips pressed together and her eyes big and bright behind her goggles, watched how swiftly the antlike creatures grew larger and took the form of horses and men.

Johnny dared a volplane, slanting steeply down at the herd. He wanted to get close enough so that they could see who he was, and he wanted to fill his lungs and then shout down to them something that would make them squirm. He meant to flatten out a hundred feet or so above them and shout, *"For I'm a rider of the sky!"* and then give a range yell and climb up away from them with arrogant indifference to their stunned amazement.

Well, Johnny did it. That is, he volplaned, banked as much as he thought wise, and flattened out and yelled, *"I'm a rider of the sky!"* just as he had planned.

It happened that no one heard him, though Johnny did not know that. Horses and men tilted heads comically and stared up at the great, swooping thing that came buzzing like a monstrous bumblebee that has learned to stutter. Then the horses squatted cowering away from it, and scattered like drops of water when a stone is thrown into a pond.

Johnny did not see any more of it, for Johnny was busy. Which was a pity, for the horse of Tex bolted a hundred yards and began to pitch so terrifically that Tex was catapulted from the saddle and had to walk home with a sprained ankle. Little Curley's horse took to the hills, and little Curley did not return in time for his dinner. Aleck and Bill Hayden went careening away toward the north, and one of the two strangers went so far west that he got lost. Since that day no horse that was present can see a hawk fly overhead without suffering convulsions of terror.

Johnny flew to a certain grassy spot he knew, not half a mile from the house, and landed. I cannot say that he landed smoothly or expertly, but he landed with no worse mishap than a bent axle on the landing gear, and a squeal from Mary V, who thought they were going to keep on bouncing until they landed in a gully farther on. Johnny climbed down and turned the plane around by hand, and Mary V helped him. Then she took a picture of him and the plane, and climbed back and let Johnny take a picture of her in the plane. It was rather tame, for by all the laws of logic they should have broken their necks.

Before he started back, Johnny leaned over and shouted to Mary V: "You can tell the boys they can sing that Skyrider thing all they want to, now."

"They won't want to-now," Mary V yelled back.

Chapter Eighteen. Flying Comes High

Johnny Jewel reined his horse on a low ridge and stared dully down into the little valley where a scattered herd of horses fed restlessly, their uneven progress toward Sinkhole Creek vaguely indicated by the general direction of their grazing. The pendulum of his spirits had swung farther and farther away from his ecstasy of the morning, until now he had plumbed the deepest well of gloom. That he had flown to the Rolling R ranch and back without wrecking his airplane or killing himself did not cheer him. He was in the mood to wish that he had broken his neck instead of coming safely to earth.

Johnny was like a sleeper who has dreamed pleasantly and has awakened to find the house falling on him-or something like that. He had dreamed great things, he had lulled his con- science with promises and reassurances that all was well, and that he was not shirking any really important duty. And now he was awake, and the reality was of the full flavor of bitter herbs long steeped.

The forenoon had been full of achievement. Johnny had, for safety's sake, removed the propeller from his airplane and carried it home with him, in the face of Bland Halliday's bitter whining and vituperation, which reminded Johnny of a snake that coils and hisses and yet does not strike. It had been an awkward job, because he had been compelled to thrash Bland first, and then tie his hands behind him to prevent some treacherous blow from behind while he worked. Johnny had hated to do that, but he felt obliged to do it, because Bland had found the buried gasoline and had taken away the full cans and hidden them, replacing them with the empty cans. If Bland had not shown a town man's ignorance of the tale a man's tracks will tell, Johnny would never have suspected anything.

Bland had also threatened to wreck the plane for revenge, but Johnny did not worry about that. He had retaliated with a threat to starve Bland until he repaired whatever damage he wrought-and Bland had seen the point, and had subsided into his self-pitying whine.

Johnny felt perfectly easy in his mind so far as the airplane was concerned. He had explained to Bland that he meant to keep his promise as soon as he could and be square with his boss, and Bland had at the last resigned himself to the delay-no doubt comforting himself with some cunning plan of revenge later, when he had gotten Johnny into the city, where Bland felt more at home and where Johnny would have all the odds against him, being a stranger and-in Bland's opinion —a "hick."

The forenoon, therefore, had been all triumph for Johnny. All triumph and all glowing with the rose tints of promise. The afternoon was a different matter.

Johnny had ridden out on the recaptured Sandy. When he had time to think of it, that glimpse of the horsemen and the loose horses over beyond the red hill nagged him with a warning that all was not well on the Rolling R range. He had headed straight for the red hill, and he had noticed many little, betraying signs that had long escaped him in his preoccupation with his own dreams and ambitions.

The horses were wild, and ducked into whatever cover was nearest when he approached. Johnny knew that they had lately been chased and frightened, and that there was only one logical reason for that, because none of the Rolling R boys had been down on the Sinkhole range since the colts were branded and these horses driven down for the summer grazing.

Johnny rode to where he had seen the horseman, picked up the tracks of shod hoofs and followed them to the fence. Saw where two panels of wire had been loosened and afterwards refastened. Some one had dropped a couple of new staples beside one post, and there were fresh hammer dents in the wood. Johnny had not done it; there was only one other answer to the question of the fence-mender's reason. There was no mystery whatever. Johnny looked, and he knew.

He looked out across the fence and knew, too, how helpless he was. He had not even brought his rifle, as Sudden had told him to do. The rifle had been a nuisance, and Johnny conveniently forgot it once or twice, and then had told himself that it was just a notion of old Sudden's —and what was the use of packing something you never would need? He had not carried it with him for more than three weeks. But if he had it now, he knew that it would not help him any. The thieves had hours the start of him. It had been just after sunrise that he had seen them-he, a Rolling R man, sailing foolishly around in an airplane and actually *seeing* a bunch of Rolling R horses being stolen, without caring enough to think what the fellows were up to! Self-disgust seized him nauseatingly. It was there at the fence he first wished he had fallen and broken his neck.

He turned back, rode until he had located a bunch of horses, made a rough count, and went on, heavy-hearted, steeped in self-condemnation. He located other horses, scattered here and there in little groups, and kept a mental tally of their numbers. Now, while the sun dipped low toward the western hills, he watched this last herd dismally, knowing how completely he had failed in his trust.

Square with his boss! He, Johnny Jewel, had presumed to prate of it that day, with half the horses stolen from Sinkhole. For so did conscience magnify the catastrophe. He had dared to assume that his presence there at Sinkhole was necessary to the welfare of the Rolling R! Johnny laughed, but tears would have been less bitter than his laughter.

He had been proud of himself, arrogantly sure of his ability, his nerve, his general superiority. He, who had shirked his duty, the work that won him his food and clothes and money to spend, he had blandly considered himself master of himself, master of his destiny! He had fatuously believed that, had belittled his work and thought it unworthy his time and thought and ability-and he had let himself be hoodwinked and robbed in broad daylight!

He remembered the days when he had compromised with his work, had ridden to a certain pinnacle that commanded a wide view of the range, and had looked out over the country from the top-and had hurried back to the niche to work on the airplane, calling his duty to the Rolling R done for that day. He might better have stolen those horses himself, Johnny thought. He would at least have the satisfaction of knowing that he had accomplished what he had set out to do; he would not have to bear this sickening feeling of failure along with his guilt.

But staring at the horses the thieves had left would not bring back the ones they had stolen, so Johnny rode back to camp, caught the gentlest of his two bronks and turned Sandy loose in the pasture. He had formed the habit of riding over to the airplane before he cooked his supper; sometimes eating with Bland so that he might the longer gaze upon his treasure. But to-night he neither rode to the niche nor cooked supper. He did not want to eat, and he did not want to see his airplane, that had tempted him to such criminal carelessness.

The telephone called him, and Johnny went dismally to answer. It was old Sudden, of course; the full, smooth voice that could speak harsh commands or criticisms and make them sound like pleasantries. Johnny thought the voice was a little smoother, a little fuller than usual.

"Hello. The boys tell me that they had quite a lot of-excitement-this morning when they were rounding up a bunch of horses. An aeroplane swooped down on them with-er-somewhat unpleasant results. Yes. The horses stampeded, and-er-the boys were compelled to do some hard riding. Yes. Tex was thrown-that makes two of the boys that are laid up for repairs. They haven't succeeded in gathering the horses so far. Know anything about it, Johnny?"

"Yes, sir." Johnny's voice was apathetic. What did a little thing like a stampede amount to, in the face of what Sudden had yet to hear?

"Oh, you do?" Sudden was plainly expectant. He did not, however, sound particularly reassuring. "Where did that aeroplane come from? Do you know?"

"Yes, sir. It's one I —salvaged from Mexico. I —was trying it out."

"Oh. You were? Trying it out on the stock. Well, I don't believe I care to work my stock with flying machines. Aviators-come high. I prefer just plain, old-fashioned riders."

He paused, quite evidently waiting to hear what Johnny had to say. But Johnny did not seem to have anything at all to say, so Sudden spoke again.

"How about the horses down at Sinkhole? Are they broken to aeroplane herding, or have they all stampeded like these up here?"

Here was escape, reprieve, an excuse that might save him. Johnny hesitated just long enough to draw his breath deeply, as a man does before diving into cold water.

"They haven't stampeded. I never had the plane in the air till this morning, and then I flew-toward the ranch. These horses down here have been stolen. About half of them, I should say. I was gone for nearly three days, getting that airplane from across the line. A greaser told me about it, and took me where it was. And when I got back I didn't ride the range the way I should have done-the way I did do, at first. I was working on the airplane, all the time I possibly could. I ran across a fellow that's been an aviator, and brought him down here, and he helped. And so the horses were stolen —a few at a time, I think. I believe I'd have missed them if they had gone all at once."

Johnny could feel the silence at the other end of the line. It lasted so long that he wondered dully if Sudden were waiting for more, but Johnny felt as though there was nothing more to add. Of what use would it be to protest that he was sorry? Bad enough to rob a man, without insulting him with puerile regrets.

"Now-let's get this thing straight." Sudden's voice when it came was fuller than ever, smoother than ever. It was a bad sign. "You say-about half of the horses on that range have been stolen? Have you counted them?"

"No. I'm just guessing. I don't think I've lost more than half. I just made a rough tally of what I found to-day."

"You say not *more* than half, then. But you're guessing. Now, when did you first miss them?"

"To-day. I was all taken up with that damned airplane before, and I didn't pay much attention. This morning the fellow here took me for a flight, and we went east. Beyond the red hill I happened to see four riders driving a few horses. They were inside our fence. I didn't think what it meant then, because Bland was climbing in a spiral and my mind was on that. But I rode over there this afternoon, and I saw where they'd let down the fence and then put it back up again. And they'd tried to cover up the tracks of horses going through. So I rode all afternoon, making a sort of tally of what horses ranged over that way. A lot of 'em's gone. I missed some of the best ones-some big geldings that I think I'd know anywhere."

"You say they went through the fence on the east line?"

"Yes, sir. It was just after sunrise that I saw them."

"And it was afternoon, you say, before it occurred to you that they might possibly have been stealing my horses. In the meantime, you were up this way, playing hell with the round-up."

"Yes, sir, that's about the way it stacks up."

"What are you going to do?"

"I don't know. Try and get back what horses I can, I guess." Johnny did not speak as though he had much faith.

"Going to go out and round them up with your flying machine, I suppose! That sounds practical, perfectly plausible. As much so as the rest of the story."

Johnny was too utterly miserable and hopeless to squirm at the sarcasm.

"Well, we don't want to be hasty. In fact, you have not been hasty so far, from what I can gather. Except in the matter of indulging yourself in aircraft at my expense. Don't leave the cabin. I shall probably want to talk about this again to-night."

That was all. It was enough. It was like Sudden to withhold condemnation until after he had digested the crime. Johnny did not think much about what Sudden would do, but he had a settled conviction that condemnation was merely postponed for a little while. It would come. But Johnny sat already condemned by the harshest judge a man may have-the harshness of his own youthful conscience.

He sat brooding, his palms holding his jaws, his eyes staring at the floor. What was he going to do? Sudden had asked him that. Johnny had asked himself the same question; indeed, it had drummed insistently in his brain since he had inspected the fence that afternoon and had known just what had befallen him. The bell rang-Sudden was calling again. He got up stolidly to answer more questions.

"Oh-Skyrider! I can only talk a minute. Mom's in the kitchen, and dad's gone to hunt up Bill Hayden. Is it true, Johnny, that a lot of horses have been stolen?"

"Yes."

"I heard dad talking. Oh, I wish I could help hunt them, but I'm in an awful mess, Skyrider! Bill Hayden knew I'd taken Jake, because my saddle was gone, and none of the other horses were. I never *saw* any one so mean and suspicious! And he knows Jake got away from me, too, because I was trying to catch him when Bill rode up, just perfectly furious over the horses stampeding. And Bill told dad-he certainly is the *meanest* thing! And now dad won't let me go out of sight of the house unless he or mom are with me. And mommie never goes anywhere, it's so hot. And dad only goes to town. But they don't know it was us in the aeroplane-and I'm just glad of it if we did scatter their old herd for them. Everybody's so mean to me! And I was planning how you'd teach me to fly, and we'd have the duckiest times-and now —"

She hung up so abruptly that Johnny knew as well as though he had been in the room with her, what had happened. She had heard her dad coming. Before Johnny had sat down again to his brooding, Sudden called him.

"You spoke about a greaser telling you about an aeroplane, and that you went with him and got it." Sudden's voice was cool and even-an inexorable voice. "Do you remember my telling you not to let a greaser on the Rolling R range if you could help it?"

"Yes, sir. This one's brother came first. He was just a kid, and he wanted —a drink." It struck Johnny quite suddenly that Tomaso's reason for coming had been a very poor one indeed. For there was water much nearer Tucker Bly's range, which was to the east of Sinkhole. And Tomaso should have had no occasion whatever to be riding to Sinkhole.

"Oh. He wanted a drink, did he? Where did he come from?"

"He works for Tucker Bly. So he said. And he told me about the airplane that had been lost, across the line. His brother had found it."

"And you went to see his brother?"

"His brother came to see me. The kid told him I was-interested."

"You went after the flying machine when? Over two weeks ago, eh? And you were gone —I see. Approximately two days and two nights-nearer three days. Who answered the telephone while you were gone? It happens that I have not missed calling you every night; did the man have a cold?"

"I —I don't know. I didn't know anybody —" Johnny frowned. It would be just as well, he felt, to keep Mary V out of it.

"You didn't know the 'phone was answered in your absence. Well, it was. By a man with a bad cold, who represented himself to be you. Did you notice any signs of any one being there while you were gone?"

"N-no, I can't say I did. Well, the string was tied different on the door, but I didn't think much about that."

"No-you wouldn't think much about that." Sudden's tone made a mental lash of the words. "You had your own affairs to think about. You were merely being —*paid* to think of my affairs."

"Yes, sir-that's the kind of a hound I've been."

Johnny's abject tone-he who had been so high-chested in the past-may have had its effect upon the boss. When Sudden spoke again his voice was almost kind, which is unusual, surely, for a man who has been robbed.

"Well, I shall have to investigate those greasers, I think. It looks to me as though they had used that flying machine for a bait to get you out of the way, and that looks to me too clever for greasers. It looks to me as though some one knew what bait you would jump at the quickest, young man. Do some thinking along those lines, will you? The horses are gone; but there might be some slight satisfaction in catching the thieves."

"Yes, sir. What shall I do to-morrow? Am I fired, or what?"

"You are —*what!*" Sudden was sarcastic again. "I believe, since you have been doing pretty much as you please down there, I shall expect you to go on doing as you please. I don't see how you are going to do any more damage than you have already done. On the other hand, I don't see how you are going to do much good-unless I could take those horses out of your hide!"

Johnny stared round-eyed at the 'phone, even after Sudden had hung up his receiver.

"Good golly!" he muttered, with a faint return of his normal spirit. "Old Sudden oughta been a lawyer." Then he went back to holding his jaws in two spread palms, and brooding over the trouble he was in.

Chapter Nineteen. "We Fly South"

Johnny did a great deal of thinking along the line suggested by old Sudden. At first he thought merely how groundless was any suspicion that the airplane was in any way connected with the horse-stealing, except that it might justly be accused of contributing to his negligence. Even so, Johnny could not see how one man could possibly protect the whole of Sinkhole range from thieves. He could have been on his guard, could have noticed when the first horses were missing, and notified Sudden at once. That, of course, was what had been expected of him.

But as to Tomaso and his oily brother, Johnny did not at first see any possible connection between them and his present trouble, save that they also had innocently contributed to his neglect. But Sudden had told him to think about it, and the suggestion kept swinging his thoughts that way. Finally, for want of something better, he went back to the very beginning and reconstructed his first meeting with Tomaso. Sudden had hinted that they must have known how deeply he was interested in aviation. But Johnny did not see how that could be. He had not talked much about his ambition, even at the Rolling R, he remembered; not enough to set him apart from the others as one who dreamed day and night of flying. Until the boys got hold of that doggerel he wrote, Johnny was sure they had not paid any attention to his occasional vague rhapsodies on the subject.

Tomaso had seen the letterhead of that correspondence school, and had just accidentally mentioned it. Or was it accidental? To make sure, Johnny got out the circular which Tomaso had seen, laid it where he remembered it to have been that day, and sat down at the table where Tomaso had been sitting. He placed the lamp where the light fell full upon the paper and studied the letterhead for several minutes, scowling.

Tomaso, he decided, had remarkably sharp eyes. Seen from that angle, the letterhead was not conspicuous. The volplaning machine was not at all striking to the eye. Unless a person knew beforehand what it represented, or was looking for something of the sort, Johnny was forced to admit that he would be likely to pass it over without a second glance.

Tomaso, then, must have come there with the intention of leading adroitly to the subject of airplanes. He must have brought those little, steel pliers purposely. And after all, he really had no business on the Rolling R range, if he was riding for the Forty-seven. He had come a good five miles inside the line. And when you looked at it that way, how had he got inside the line? There was no gate on the east side of the fence.

It looked rather far-fetched, improbable. Johnny was slow to accept the theory that he had been led to that airplane just as a toy is given to a child, to keep its attention engrossed with a harmless pastime while other business is afoot. It hurt his self-esteem to believe that-wherefore he prospected his memory for some other theory to take its place.

"Well! If that's why they did it-it sure worked like a charm," he summed up his cogitations disgustedly. "I'll say I swallowed the bait whole!" And he added grimly: "I wish I knew who put them wise."

Youth began to make its demands. He started a fire, boiled coffee, fried bacon, made fresh bread, and ate a belated supper. Sudden had told him to do as he pleased. "Well," Johnny muttered, "I will take him at his word." He did not know just what he would please to do, but he realized that fasting would not help him any; nor would sleeplessness. He ate, therefore, washed his few dishes and went straight to bed. And although he lay for a long while looking at his trouble through the magnifying glass of worry, he did sleep finally-and without one definite plan for the morrow.

Half an hour before dawn, Johnny went stumbling along the ledge to the cleft. On his broad shoulder was balanced the propeller. On his face was a look of fixed determination. He scared Bland Halliday out of a sleep in which his dreams were all of a certain cabaret in Los Angeles-dreams which made Bland's waking all the more disagreeable. Johnny tilted the propeller carefully against the rock wall, lighted a match, and cupped the blaze in his palms so that the light shone on Bland.

"Where's the lantern? You better get up-it's most daylight."

"Aw, f'r cat's sake! What more new meanness you got on your mind? Me, I come down here in good faith to help fix a plane that's to take me back home-and I work like a dog —"

"Yeah —I know that song by heart, Bland. You in your faith and your innocence, how you were basely betrayed. I can sing it backward. Lay off it now for a few minutes. I want to talk to yuh."

He lighted the lantern, and Bland lay blinking at it lugubriously. "And me —I dreamed I was in to Lemare's just after a big exhibition flight, and a bunch of movie queens was givin' me the glad eye."

"Yes, I've done some dreaming myself," Johnny interposed dryly. "I'm awake now. Listen here, Bland. I've been playing square with you, all along. I want you to get that. I can see how you being so darn crooked yourself, you may always be looking for some one to do you, so I ain't kicking at the stand you take. You've got no call, either, to kick against my opinion of you. I'm satisfied you'd steal my airplane and make your getaway, and lie till your tongue wore out, proving it was yours. You'd do it if you got a chance. That's why I hid the gas on you. That's why you couldn't take Miss Selmer home. I knew darn well you wouldn't come back. And that's why I took off the propeller and hid it. It ain't why I licked you yesterday-that was for what you said about Miss —"

"Aw, f'r cat's sake! Did yuh have to come and wake me up in the middle of the night just to —"

"No-oh, no. I'm merely explaining to you that I don't trust you for one holy minute. I don't want you to think you can put anything over on me by getting on my blind side. I haven't got any, so far as you're concerned. Now listen. I meant, and if possible I still mean, to keep my promise and take you to the Coast in the plane; but something's come up that is going to hold up the trip for a few days, maybe —"

"Aw, yes! I had a hunch you'd —"

"Shut up! I told you I'd go as soon as I could without leaving the boss in the hole. Well, it happens that-well, some horses were stolen off this range, and I'm the one that's responsible. So —"

"Say, bo, you don't, f'r cat's sake, think *I* stole your damn horses? Why, honest, bo, I wouldn't have a horse on a bet! I—"

"Oh, shut *up!*" thundered the distracted Johnny above the other's whine. "Of course I know you didn't steal 'em. Horses ain't in your line, or I wouldn't be so sure. The point is this. I've got to get out and get 'em back, or get a line on who did it. I can't go off without doing something about it. This range was in my charge. I was supposed to report anything that looked suspicious, and I —well, the point is this —"

"So you said," Bland cut in, with something of his natural venom.

"Shut up. There's just a chance I can find out where those horses were taken. We'll go in the plane. You'll have to go along to handle it, because I'm liable to be busy, if I run across anybody. I'm going to pack a rifle and a six-shooter, and I don't want my hands full of controls right at the critical minute. Besides," he added ingenuously, "some of these darned air currents nearly got the best of me yesterday, coming back. You can handle the machine, and I'll do the look-see."

"Aw, sa-ay! I —"

"I know it's against my promise to a certain extent," Johnny went on. "I know I've got you in a corner, too, where you can't help yourself. You couldn't walk to the railroad, or even to the closest ranch, if you knew the way-which you don't. You'd wander around in the heat and the sand-well, you're pretty helpless without me, all right, or the plane. I sabe that better than you do. You've got to do about as I say, because you haven't got the nerve to kill me, even if I gave you the chance. Sneaking off with the plane is about as much as you're game for.

"Well, the point is this: I don't want to take any mean advantage of you. I can't afford to pay you what your services are really worth, as pilot-and there's no reason why I should. But-well, I ain't quite broke yet. I'll give you twenty-five dollars for helping me out, in case what I want to do only takes a day or two days. If it takes more, I'll give you ten dollars a day. It isn't much, but it helps when you're broke."

Bland permitted the sour droop of his lips to ease into a grin. "Now you're coming somewhere near the point, bo," he said. "But ten dollars-say! Ten dollars ain't street-car fare. Not in little old L.A. Make it twenty, bo, and you're on."

"I'll make it nothing if ten dollars a day don't suit you!" Johnny declared hotly. "Why, damn your dirty hide, that's as much as I make in a *week*! And listen! I expect to sit in the back seat-and I'll have two guns on me."

"Aw, ferget them two guns!" Bland surrendered. "This is sure the gunniest country I ever stopped in. Even the Janes —"

"Shut up!"

"Oh, well, I'll sign up for ten, bo. It ain't eatin' money, but it'll maybe help buy me the makin's of a smoke now and then."

"Well, get up, then. I'll get us some breakfast, and we'll go. It's going to be still to-day —and hot, I think. You better get up."

"Aw, that's right! You've got the upper hand, and so you can go ahead and abuse me like a dog-and I ain't got any come-back. It was Bland this and that, when you wanted the plane repaired. Now you've got it, and it's git-ta-hell and git busy. Pull a gun on me, beat me up-accuse me of things I never done-drag me outa bed before daylight —" His self-pitying whine droned on monotonously, but he nevertheless got into his clothes and pottered around the plane by the light of the lantern and the flaring fire Johnny started.

The one praiseworthy thing he could do he did conscientiously. He inspected carefully the control wires, went over the motor and filled the radiator and the gas tank, and made sure that he had plenty of oil. His grumbling did not in the least impair his efficiency. He replaced the propeller, cursing under his breath because Johnny had taken it off. He was up in the forward seat testing the control when Johnny called him to come and eat.

In the narrow strip of sky that showed over the niche the stars were paling. A faint flush tinged the blue as Johnny looked up anxiously.

"We'll take a little grub and my two canteens full of water," he said, with a shade of uneasiness in his voice. "We don't want to get caught like those poor devils did that lost the plane. But, of course —"

"Say, where you going, f'r cat's sake?" Bland looked over his cup in alarm. "Not down where them —"

"We're going to find out where those horses went. You needn't be scared, Bland. I ain't organizing any suicide club. You tend to the flying part, and I'll tend to my end of the deal. Air-line, it ain't so far. We ought to make there and back easy."

He bestirred himself, not exultantly as he had done the day before, but with a certain air of determination that impressed Bland more than his old boyish eagerness had done. This was not to be a joy-ride. Johnny did not feel in the least godlike. Indeed, he would like to have been able to take Sandy along as a substantial substitute in case anything went wrong with the plane. He was taking a risk, and he knew it, and faced it because he had a good deal at stake. He did not consider, however, that it was necessary to tell Bland just how great a risk he was taking. He had not even considered it necessary to telephone the Rolling R and tell Sudden what it was he meant to do. Time enough afterwards-if he succeeded in doing it.

He was anxious about the gas, and about water, but he did not say anything about his anxiety. He made sure that the tank would not hold another pint of gas, and he was careful not to forget the canteens. Then, when he had taken every precaution possible for their welfare, he climbed into his place and told Bland to start the motor. He was taking precautions with Bland, also.

"We fly south," he yelled, when Bland climbed into the front seat. "Make it southeast for ten miles or so-and then swing south. I'll tap you on the shoulder when I want you to turn. Whichever shoulder I tap, turn that way. Middle of your back, go straight ahead; two taps will mean fly low; three taps, land. You got that?"

Bland, pulling down his cap and adjusting his goggles, nodded. He drew on his gloves and slid down into the seat-alert, efficient, the Bland Halliday which the general public knew and admired without a thought for his personal traits.

"About how high?" he leaned back to ask. "High enough so the hum won't be noticed on the ground? Or do you want to fly lower?"

"Top of your head means high, and on the neck, low," Johnny promptly finished his code. Having thus made a code keyboard of Bland's person, he settled himself with his guns beside him.

Bland eased on the power, glancing unconsciously to the right and left ailerons, as he always did when he started.

The buzz of the motor grew louder and louder, the big plane quivered, started down the barren strip toward the reddening east, skimmed lighter and lighter the ground, rose straight and true, and went whirring away into the barbaric splendor of the dawn.

Chapter Twenty. Men are Stupid

Into that same dawn light filed the riders of the Rolling R, driving before them a small *remuda*. Behind them clucked the loaded chuck wagon, the leathery-faced cook braced upon the front seat, his booted feet far spread upon the scarred dashboard, his arms swaying stiffly to the pull of the four-horse team. Behind him still came the hoodlum wagon with its water barrels joggling sloppily behind the seat. Little Curley drove that, and little Curley's face was sober. It had been whispered in the bunk house that Skyrider was deep in disgrace, and Curley was worried.

On the porch of the bungalow Sudden stood with his morning cigar unlighted in his fingers, watching the little cavaleade swing past to the gate. He waved his cigar beckoningly to Bill Hayden, turned his head to shake it at something Mary V had said from the doorway, and waited for Bill to ride close.

Mary V, camouflaged in her blue negligee worn over her riding clothes, came out and stood insistently, her two hands clasped around Sudden's unwilling arm.

"No, sir, dad, I'm not going back to bed. I'm going to say every little thing I want to say, and you and Bill have both got to listen. Get off that horse, Bill. He makes me nervous, dancing around like that. Heaven knows I'm just about raving distracted, as it is. Dad, give Bill that cigar so he won't look quite so disagreeable."

Bill looked inquiringly at Sudden. It did not seem to him that even so spoiled an offspring as Mary V should be permitted to delay him now, when minutes counted for a good deal. He wished briefly that Mary V belonged to him; Bill mistakenly believed that he would know how to handle her. Still, he took the cigar which Sudden obediently surrendered, and he got down off his horse and stood with one spurred foot lifted to the second step of the porch while he felt in his pocket for a match.

"Well, now, Bill's in a hurry, Mary V. We haven't got time —"

"You'd better take time, then! What's the use of Bill going off to Sinkhole unless he listens to me first? Do you think, for gracious sake, I've been riding around all over the country with my eyes shut? Or do I look nearsighted, or *what*? What do you suppose I laid awake all night for, piecing things that I know together, if you're not going to pay attention? Do you think, for gracious sake —"

"There, now, we don't want to get all excited, Mary V. Sit down here and stop for-gracious-saking, and tell dad and Bill what it is you've seen. If it's anything that'll help run down them horse thieves, you'll get that Norman car, kitten, if I have to pawn my watch." Sudden gave Bill a lightened look of hope, and pulled Mary V down beside him on the striped porch swing. Then he snorted at something he saw. "What's the riding breeches and boots for? Didn't I tell you —"

"Well, Bill's going to lend me Jake, and I'll be in a hurry."

"Like h —" Bill began explosively, and stopped himself in time.

"Just like that," Mary V told him calmly. "Dad, if Bill doesn't let me ride Jake, I don't believe I can remember some things I saw down on Sinkhole range-through the field glasses, from Snake Ridge. I shall feel so badly I'll just have to go into my room, and lock the door and cry-all-day-long!" To prove it, Mary V's lips began to quiver and droop at the corners. To prepare for the deluge, Mary V got out her handkerchief.

Bill looked unhappy. "That horse ain't safe for yuh to ride," he temporized. "He's liable to run away and kill yuh. He —"

"I've ridden him twice, and he didn't," Mary V stopped quivering her lips long enough to retort. "I don't see why people want to be so mean to me, when I am trying my best to help about those horse thieves, and when I know things no other person on this ranch suspects, and if they did, they would simply be stunned at knowing there is a thief on their own pay roll. And when I just want Jake so I can hel-lp —and Tango is getting so lazy I simply *can't* get anywhere with him in a month —" Mary V did it. She actually was crying real tears, that slipped down her cheeks and made little dark spots on her blue kimono.

Bill Hayden looked at Sudden with harassed eyes. Sudden looked at Bill, and smoothed Mary V's hair-figuratively speaking; in reality he drew his fingers over a silk-and-lace cap.

"H—well, it's up to your dad. You can ride Jake if he's willin' to take the chance of you getting your neck broke. I shore won't be responsible." Bill looked more unhappy than ever, not at all as though he gloried in his martyrdom to the Rolling R.

"Why, Jake's as gentle as a ki-kitten!" Mary V sobbed.

"Like hell he's gentle!" muttered Bill, so far under his breath that he did not feel called upon to apologize.

"Well, now, we'll talk about Jake later on. Tell dad and Bill what it was you saw, and what you mean by a thief on the pay roll. I don't promise I'll be simply stunned with surprise; that story young Jewel told last night does seem to have some awful weak points in it —"

"Why dad *Selmer*! You know perfectly well that Johnny Jewel is the soul of honor! Why you owe an *apology* to Johnny for ever *thinking* such a thing about him! Why, for gracious sake, must everybody on this ranch be so blind and stupid?" Mary V asked the glorious sunrise that question, and straightway hid her face behind her handkerchief.

"Well, now, we're wasting time. I apologize to the soul of honor, and you may ride Jake-when Bill or I are with you to see how he behaves. Now tell us what you know. This is a serious matter, Mary V. Far too serious —"

"I should think *I* am the person who knows how serious it is," Mary V came from behind her handkerchief to remind him.

"Just who or what did you see, through your field glasses, when you looked from the top of Snake Ridge?" Sudden wisely chose to waive any irrelevant arguments.

"Why," said Mary V, "I first saw one of your men dodging along down a draw, to a place where there were some cottonwood trees. I saw him get off his horse and wait there for a few minutes, and then I saw another man riding along the gully from the other direction. And so I saw them meet, and talk a few minutes, and ride back. And-your man was in a great hurry, and the other man was a Mexican."

"H-m-m. And who was my —"

"And so I thought I'd ride a little farther, and see what they were waving their hands toward the south for. And so I did. And it was very hot," said Mary V pensively, "and I was so tired that when I found I was close to Sinkhole camp I went on and rested there. And before I left, that same Mexican came to the cabin, and Johnny didn't know him at all, because the Mexican said right away, 'I am the brother of Tomaso,' which, of course, was to introduce himself. And then he saw me, and he said he had come to borrow some matches, and Johnny gave him some and he beat it. And after I left, I had gone perhaps a mile when I happened to look back, and the same Mexican was riding in a hurry to the cabin. So, of course, he had waited until I left. And that was the man," she finished with some attention to the dramatic effect, "who told Johnny he would take him to where the airplane was sitting like a hawk —a broken-winged hawk-on the burning sands of Mexico."

"Jerusalem!" Sudden paid tribute to the tale. But Bill said a shorter word. "And which one of my —"

"And it was right after that," Mary V went on calmly, "that you found your man at Sinkhole talking with a very bad cold. The second night, I —I was curious. And so after you had called him up, I called him. I had to wait a few minutes, as though he had to come into the house to answer. And *I* knew perfectly well that it was not Johnny speaking. I —tested him to make sure. I spoke of things that were perfectly ridiculous, and he was afraid to seem not to understand. I said I was Venus speaking, and so he called me Miss Venus. And it was *not* that Mexican," she added quickly, seeing the guess in her dad's face. "He was a white man-an American. I can *almost* recognize the voice, in spite of his pretended cold. I jarred him away from that once or twice. He said, 'Uh course I knowed yer voice,' and no Mexican would say that."

"So then I was *very* curious. I —I knew Johnny would never permit things to be said that were said. So it was a beautiful moonlight evening, and I wanted —I shall be expected to describe our Arizona plains by moonlight. So I decided that I would solve a mystery and collect my material that evening, and I—went riding."

"The deuce you—"

"So I had quite a distance to go, and I did not want to worry any one by being gone long. So I—er-didn't like to wake Bill up—"

"Hunh!" from Bill, this time.

"I really intended to take Tango as usual," Mary V explained with dignity. "I had no thought of intruding on a person's piggishness with their old race horse, but Jake came right up and put his nose in the feed pan, and-and acted so-sort of eager-and I knew he just suffers for exercise, standing in that old corral, so it was very wrong, but I yielded to him. I rode him down to Sinkhole, and I found him a perfectly gentle lady's horse. So there now, Mr. Bill. You just—"

"And what did you find at Sinkhole?" Sudden led her firmly back to the subject.

"I found that the beans were sour, and the bread was hard as a rock, and there wasn't one thing to show that a meal had been cooked in that camp for two days, at least. And Johnny's bedding was gone-or some of it, anyway. And so was Sandy. So I came back, and changed horses, and took Tango. I knew, of course, how stingy a person can be about a horse. And as I was riding away, behind that line of rocks so Mr. Stingy wouldn't see me, I saw a certain person come sneaking up to the corral and turn his horse inside. It was just barely daylight then, but it was the same person I saw meet the Mexican.

"And I hurried hack to Snake Ridge, so I got there quite early in the morning. And I saw two men ride off toward the eastern line of Sinkhole range, and they were not Johnny Jewel at all, which would be perfectly impossible. Because soon afterwards I saw something very queer being hauled by mules, and that was Johnny bringing home his airplane, perfectly innocent."

"Who's the fellow—" Sudden and Bill spoke together, the question which harried the minds of both.

"Of course," said Mary V, "I understand that some one from the ranch would have to put them up to distracting Johnny's attention by letting him have that airplane. I can see that they would want to keep him busy so he wouldn't pay so much attention to the horses down there, and would not notice a few horses gone now and then. So somebody had heard about the airplane, and told them that Johnny was perfectly mad about aviation, and—"

Sudden turned, and took her by the shoulders. "Mary V, who was that man? Don't try to shield him, because I shall—"

"The very idea! I don't want to shield him at all. I merely want Jake, without any strings on him whatever. Because he can go like the very dickens, and I want to keep an eye on Tex myself. He won't pay any attention—"

"Tex! Good Lord! Bill, you—"

"Listen, dad, I think I *deserve* to have Jake. You *know* I can ride him, and you're so short-handed, and I can watch Tex—"

"Go saddle him up for her, Bill, will you? I guess the kid's done enough to put her on a par with the rest of us."

"I'll say she has," Bill surrendered, a grin splitting his leathery face straight across the middle. "I been watchin' Tex myself, but I didn't know it was horses he was after. I thought it was some woman."

"I can't see what *makes* men so stupid!" Mary V observed pensively. "I never did like Tex. I don't like his eyes."

"I see," said her dad. "You ought to 've told me before." And he added disapprovingly, "There's a good deal you ought to 've told your dad. It would have saved the Rolling R some mighty fine horses, I reckon. I don't know what your mother's going to say about me letting you go—"

But Mary V had whisked into the house to complete her preparations for the day's ride. Also to escape whatever her dad would have to say in that particular tone. She saw him leave the porch and follow Bill to the corral, whereupon she immediately tried to call Johnny on the telephone. Failing in that, she proceeded to powder her nose.

Old Sudden in the ranch Ford, and Bill and Mary V on horseback, overtook the jogging caval-cade of riders and loose horses. Sudden looked pained and full of determination, as he always did when necessity called him forth upon the range in a lurching mechanical conveyance where once he had ridden with the best of them. Too many winters had been spent luxuriously in the towns; a mile or two, at a comfortable trail trot, was all that Sudden cared to attempt nowadays on horseback. But that did not lessen his dislike of negotiating sand and rocks and washes and rough slopes with an automobile. Every mile that he traveled added something to his condemnation of that young reprobate, Johnny Jewel, who had let the Rolling R in for all this trouble.

A bend in the trail brought him close to the boys, who had ridden straight across country. Mary V and Bill had just joined the group, and Sudden gave a snort when he saw Mary V maneuver Jake so that he sidled in alongside Tex, who rode a little apart with his hat pulled over his eyes, evidently in deep thought. Sudden had all the arrogance of a strong man who has managed his life and his business successfully. He wanted to attend to Tex himself, without any meddling from Mary V.

He squawked the horn to attract her attention, and caused a wave of turbulence among the horses that made more than one of his men say unpleasant things about him. Mary V looked back, and he beckoned with one sweeping gesture that could scarcely be mistaken. Mary V turned to ride up to him, advanced a rod or two and abruptly retreated, bolting straight through the group of riders and careening away across the level, with Bill and Tex tearing after her. Presently they slowed, and later Bill was seen to lag behind. Tex and Mary V kept straight on, a furlong in advance of the others.

The road swung away to the right, to avoid a rough stretch of rocks and gullies, and Sudden perforce followed it, feelingly speaking his mind upon the subjects of spoiled daughters and good-for-nothing employees, and horses and the men that bestrode them, and Fords, and the roads of Arizona, and the curse of being too well fed and growing a paunch that made riding a martyrdom. He would put that girl in a convent, and he would see that she stayed there till she was old enough to have some sense. He would have that young hound at Sinkhole arrested as an accomplice of the horse thieves. He would put a bullet through that fool of a horse, Jake, and he would lynch Tex if he ever got his hands on him. He would sell out, by glory, and buy himself a prune orchard.

And then he had a blow-out while he was down in a hollow a mile from the outfit. And some darned fool had lost the handle to the jack, and the best of the two extra tires was a darn poor excuse and wouldn't last a mile, probably, and he got hold of a tube that had a leaky valve, and had to hunt out another one after he had worked half an hour trying to pump up the first one. And what in the blinkety blink did any darn fool want to live in such a country for, anyway?

Thus it happened that Mary V was not forbidden to ride with Tex. And, not being forbidden, Mary V carried out her own ideas of diplomacy and tact. Her idea was to make Tex believe that she liked him better than the other boys. Just what she would gain by that, Mary V did not stop to wonder. It was the approved form of diplomacy, employed by all the leading heroines of ancient and modern fiction and of film drama, and was warranted to produce results in the way of information, guilty secrets, stolen wills, plots and plans and papers.

Tex was inclined to eye her askance, just at first. He was also very curious about her riding Jake, and he seemed inquisitive about whether that was the first time she had ever ridden him. He was, too, very absent-minded at times, and would go off into vacant-eyed reveries that sealed his ears against her artfully artless chatter.

Some girls would have been discouraged. Mary V was merely stimulated to further efforts. Tex did not mention the stealing of any horses at Sinkhole. He seemed to take it for granted that they were going to work the range to get horses for breaking, and Mary V wondered if perhaps her dad had not thought it best to confine the knowledge of horse-stealing to himself and Bill-at least until he had made an investigation. That would be like dad-and also like Bill Hayden. Mary V was glad that she had not said anything about it. She thought she would try Tex out first on the subject of airplanes. None of the boys knew that Johnny had one, and she was perfectly sure that she would detect any guilty knowledge of it in the mind of Tex. She had just read a long article in a magazine about "How our Faces Betray our Thoughts," and this seemed a splendid chance to put it to the test.

"Bill says an aeroplane came and stampeded all you boys yesterday," she began with much innocence.

"Yeah. One did fly over our haids. I didn't git to see much of it. My fool hawse, he started in pitchin' right away, soon as he seen it."

Mary V paused, meditating upon the significance of his words, his tone, his profile. That there was no particular significance did not in the least affect her deliberate intention.

"I wonder who it could have been!" she said, stealing a glance from under her lashes.

"Hunh? Who? The flyin' machine? Search me!" This time his tone was surely significant. It signified, more than anything else, that the mind of Tex was busy with other matters. Contrary to the magazine article, his face did not betray his thoughts. "Yore dad buy Jake off'n Bill for yo' all to ride?" he asked suddenly.

"No. Bill just lent him to me."

"Hnh! Bill, he shore is generous-hearted to lend yuh Jake."

"Yes," said Mary V, smiling at Tex innocently. "Yes, isn't he?"

But Tex did not reiterate, as pleasant converse demanded. He went off again into meditation so deep that it quite excluded Mary V.

"Yo' all going to help round up?" Tex asked her suddenly. "You shore can ride the ridges, with that hawse. I guess yo' all can bring in more hawses than what any two of us kin."

"That's exactly what I mean to do," Mary V assured him promptly. "You'll see me riding the ridges almost exclusively."

Tex looked at her and grinned, which did not enhance his good looks, because his teeth were badly stained with tobacco.

"Yo' all don't want to ride away over in them breaks toward the southeast corner," he advised. "That's a long, hard ride to make. It's too much for a girl to tackle-combin' the hawses outa them little brushy draws. They like to git in there away from the flies, in the heat uh the day. But yo' all better not tackle it, even if Bill lets yuh. I don't guess he would, though."

"Bill," said Mary V with a little tilt to her chin, "does not enjoy the privilege of 'letting' me do things. I shall ride wherever I please. And it is possible that I may please to bring in what horses are in the red-hill end of the range. I'm sure I don't see why I shouldn't, if I like."

"Well," said Tex, "that country's plumb hard to ride. It takes real work to bring in hawses from there. I wouldn't tackle that, if I was you; I'd ride out where it's easier."

"Oh, would you? Well, thank you very much for the advice, I'm sure." Mary V looked back, saw the other boys jogging closer, and held Jake in to wait for them. She did not want to tell Tex that she certainly would make it a point to ride the red-hill side of the range. There was probably some sly, secret reason Tex did not want her to go over that way. She remembered that she had seen the Mexican coming from that direction both times. Certainly, there must be some secret reason. Tex was afraid she might find out something.

Mary V waited for the boys, and talked to them prettily, and wondered aloud where her dad was all this time, and hoped he had not had a puncture or anything. Because, she said, it was bad enough for his temper to have to drive the flivver, without any bad luck to make it worse.

She was particularly nice to Bill, and forced him to confess that she really got along perfectly all right with Jake. She comported herself so agreeably, in fact, that Bill was reconciled to her coming and paid no attention when she presently swung off to the southeast, saying that she wanted to get a picture of a perfectly ducky giant cactus which she had seen through her glasses one day. Indeed, the dismal honking of the machine called Bill back to the trail, where

Sudden came jouncing along like a little, leaky boat laboring through a choppy sea. Bill rode off without noticing Mary V at all.

It was a little after noon, and the boys were eating dinner at the camp set up close to the creek at Sinkhole cabin. Sudden, sprawled in the shade of the wagon, was staring glumly at the sluggish little stream, smoking his after-dinner cigar and trying to formulate some plan that would promise results where results were most vital to his bank account. It would, of course, take two or three days to gather in all the horses on Sinkhole range, and the restless lot in the corral yonder might be a large or a small part of the entire number down there. Sudden was not worrying so much over those that were left, as he was over what had been stolen. It seemed to him that there ought to be some way of getting those horses back. He was trying to think of the way.

"Oh, Bill!" he called, getting stiffly to his feet. "Let's get into the cabin and go over those tally books." Which was merely a subterfuge to get Bill away from the wagon without letting the boys know something was wrong. Bill got up, brushed the dirt off his trousers with a flick of his fingers, lighted the cigarette he had just rolled and followed the boss.

"Bill, what's your idea about this horse-stealing, anyway? If they were going to steal horses, why didn't they run off a whole herd and be done with it?"

Bill seated himself on Johnny's bunk, spat toward the stove, pulled a splinter off the rough board of the bunk's side, and began carefully nipping off tiny shreds with his finger nails. Bill, by all these signs and tokens, was limbering up his keen old range-bred wits for action.

"Well, I'll tell yuh. The way to get at the thing is to figger out why you'd do it, s'posin' you was in their place. Now if it was *me* that was stealin' these hawses-say, s'posin' I was aimin' to sell 'em over across the line —I'd aim to take the best I could git holt of, because I'd be wanting 'em for good, all-round, tough saddle hawses. Them greasers, the way they're hellin' around over the country shootin' and fightin', they got to have good hawses under 'em. Er they want good hawses, if they can git 'em.

"Well, s'posin' 't I was out to furnish what I could. Chances is I wouldn't have a very big bunch in with me-say five or six of us, jest enough to handle a few head at a time. I'd aim to git 'em over acrost the line first shot. Anybody would do that. Well, s'posin' I didn't have a place that'd take care of very many at a time. Feed's pore, over there, and a hawse has got to eat. These here hawses are in purty fair condition, and I'd aim to keep 'em in flesh whilst I was breakin' 'em —I'd git better prices. And then again, mebby I wouldn't want too many on hand at once, in case some party come along with the gall to loot 'em instead of buy 'em.

"I figger I'd be plumb content if I could take over a few at a time, and let the rest go ahead eatin' grass here till I was ready for 'em. The longer I could keep that up, the better I'd like it. Same as we been doin' at the home ranch, y' see. We didn't go t' work and haze in the hull bunch and keep 'em up, eatin' their heads off, waitin' till we got ready for 'em. No, sir, we go out and bring in half a dozen, or a dozen at most and cut out what we want. We bust them, and git more.

"I figger, Mr. Selmer, that these geezers down here have been doin' that very same way. They had the kid baited with that flyin' machine, so he wouldn't have no eyes for anything else. And he was *here*, so you wouldn't be worryin' none about the stock. And they've been helpin' theirselves at their own convenience-like Mary V would put it. I dunno, but that's the way I figger it. And I don't guess, Mr. Selmer, you'll see none of yore hawses again, unless mebby it's the last ones they took. And I don't guess there's very much chance of gittin' them back, either, because we don't know whereabouts they took 'em to. Way I look at it, you're doin' about the only thing that can be did-cleanin' out this range and drivin' the hawses all up on the north range. That kinda leaves the jam pot empty when they come lickin' their lips for more of the same."

"Well, I guess you're right, Bill. And how do you figure young Jewel not being here? His saddle is out there in the shed, and all his horses are here."

"Him?" Bill laughed a little. "Me, I don't aim to do no figgerin' about Skyrider. He's got his flyin' machine workin', though, accordin' to Mary V. I guess Skyrider has mebby flew the country. He'd likely think it was about time-way he gummed things up around here."

Sudden permitted himself a snort, probably in agreement with Bill's statement that things were "gummed up" at Sinkhole. He went to the door and stood looking out, his face sour as one may expect a face to be when thoughts of loss are behind it.

"Where's Mary V?" he turned abruptly to ask of Bill.

"Mary V? Why, I guess she went home. Said something about takin' a picture of some darn thing; she never come on with the boys to camp, anyhow."

"She didn't go foolin' off with Tex, did she?"

"Tex? No, Tex rode after stock. Had some trouble with his hawse. I heard him tellin' the boys. Said his hawse run away with him. Come in all lathered up."

Sudden turned back, went to the telephone, changed his mind. No use worrying her mother by asking if she had got home, he thought.

"You're sure she went home?" his eyes dwelt rather sharply upon Bill's lean, leathery face. Bill looked up from the slow disintegration of the splinter. He spat toward the stove again, looked down at the splinter, and then got up quite unexpectedly.

"Hell, no! I ain't shore, but I can quick enough find out." He brushed past Sudden and took long steps toward the camp. Sudden followed him.

The boys were standing in a group, holding their hat brims down to shield their eyes from the bitter glare of the sun while they gazed up into the sky, their faces turned towards the south. A speck was scudding across the blue —a speck that rapidly grew larger, circled downward in a great, easy spiral. Sudden and Bill perforce turned and held their own hat brims while they looked.

"Sa-ay, if that there's Skyrider sailin' around in an airship, he's shore got the laugh on us fellers," Aleck observed, squinting his nose until his gums showed red above his teeth. "Look at 'im come down, would yuh!"

"Wonder where he got it?" little Curley hazarded. "I always told you fellers —"

"Does anybody know where Mary V went?" Sudden's voice brought them all facing him. They looked at him uncomprehendingly for a minute, then uncertainly at one another.

"Why-she was going to take a picture of a cactus. I dunno where she went after that." This was Bud, a shade of uneasiness creeping into his face.

"Which way did she go? Toward home?"

"She started that way-back toward Snake Ridge —"

"I seen her riding east," Curley broke in. "Jake shore was pickin' 'em up and layin' 'em down too. I thought at first he was running off with her, but he wasn't. He slowed down, climbin' that lava slope-and after that I didn't see no more of 'er."

Sudden looked at his watch, frowning a little. Mary V probably was all right; there was nothing unusual in her absence. But this country south of Snake Ridge was closer to the lawless land across the boundary than he liked. Their very errand down there gave proof enough of its character. North of Snake Ridge, Sudden would merely have stored away a lecture for Mary V. Down here at Sinkhole —

"You boys get out and hunt her up!" he snapped, almost as though they were to blame for her absence. "I didn't tell you before, but I'm telling you now that rustlers have been at work down here, and that's why we're taking the horses off this range. This is no place for Mary V to be riding around by herself."

"It's a wonder he wouldn't of woke up to that fact before," Bud grumbled to Aleck, while he went limping to the corral. "If she was a girl uh mine, she'd be home with her maw, where she belongs!"

"Rustlers-that sounds like greasers had been at work here. Runnin' hawses acrost the line. For Lord sake, git a faster wiggle on than that limp, Bud! If that poor little kid meets up with a bunch of them damn renegades —"

Bud swore and increased his pace in spite of the pain. Others were before him. Already Tex had his loop over the head of a speedy horse, and was leading it toward his saddle. Curley, the quickest of them all, was giving frantic tugs to his latigo. Bill was in the saddle ready to direct the search, and Sudden was standing by his car, wondering whether it would be possible to negotiate that rough country to the eastward with a "mechanical bronk."

Nothing much was said. You would have thought, to look at them, that they were merely in a hurry to get back to the work. Nevertheless, if it should happen that Mary V was being annoyed or in any danger, it would go hard with the miscreants if the Rolling R boys once came within sight of them.

Chapter Twenty-Two. Luck Turns Traitor

Johnny Jewel, carrying the propeller balanced on his shoulder and his rifle in the other hand-and perspiring freely with the task-came hurrying through the sage brush, following the faint trail his own eager feet had worn in the sand. His eyes were turned frowning upon the ground, his lips were set together in the line of stubbornness.

He tilted the propeller against the adobe wall of the cabin, and went in without noticing that the door was open instead of closed as he had left it. He was at the telephone when Sudden stepped in after him. Johnny looked over his shoulder with wide, startled eyes.

"Oh. I was just going to call up the ranch," he said with the brusqueness of a man whose mind is concentrated on one thing.

"What you want of the ranch?" Sudden's tone was noncommittal. Here was the fellow that had caused all this trouble and worry and loss. Sudden meant to deal with him as he deserved, but that did not mean he would fly into a passion and handicap his judgment.

"I want the boys, if you can get hold of them. I've located the ranch where they've been taking those horses to that they stole. There's some there now-or there was. I went down and let down the fence of the little field they had 'em in, and headed 'em for the gap. There wasn't anybody around but two women-an old one and a young one-and some kids. They spluttered a lot, but I went ahead anyway. There's about a dozen Rolling R horses I turned loose. The brands were blotched, but I knew 'em anyway.

"So I got 'em outa the field, and then we went back to the plane and circled around and come up on 'em from the south, and flew low enough to scare 'em good, but not enough to scatter 'em like that bunch up at the ranch scattered. They high-tailed it this way, and I guess they'll keep coming, all right, if they aren't turned back again. The boys can pick 'em up.

"If the boys could come down I think they could get a whack at the rustlers themselves. I got a sight of 'em, with a little bunch of horses, as I was coming back. Far as I could see, they didn't notice the plane-we were high, and soon as I saw 'em I had Bland shut off the motor and glide. They must have camped just across the line till they got a bunch together, or something. They were taking their time, and if the boys could get down here right away, I believe we could get 'em. If not, I'll go back and stampede the horses this way, and see if I can't get me a greaser or two. We had to come back and fill up the tank again, anyway. I didn't want to get caught the way those other fellows did. Is Bill at the ranch, Mr. Selmer?"

It speaks well for Sudden Selmer that he could listen to this amazing statement without looking dazed. As it was, his first bewildered stare subsided into mere astonishment. Later other emotions crept in. By the time Johnny had finished his headlong report, Sudden had recovered his mental poise and was able to speak coherently.

"Been hunting horses with a flying machine, eh? I must say you're right up to date, young man. No, Bill isn't at the ranch. If you'd keep your eyes open here at home, same as you do when you're flying around next the clouds, you'd see the chuck wagon down there by the creek. I moved 'em down here to save what horses are left. The boys are out now hunting up Mary V. She had to go larruping off by herself on Bill's horse Jake, and she hasn't come back yet. I guess she's all right; but the boys went after her so as not to take any chances. I'm kinda hoping the kid went home. I don't like to scare her mother, though, by calling up to see."

Johnny's eyes had widened and grown round, just as they always did when something stirred him unexpectedly. "I could call up, Mr. Selmer, and ask if I can speak to Mary V. That wouldn't scare her mother."

"Sure, you can find out; only don't you say anything about the wagons being camped here. If she asks, say you haven't seen us yet. She'll think we made camp somewhere else. Go ahead."

It did not take long, and when Johnny turned to Selmer he had the white line around his mouth. "She says Mary V went out with you and the boys, to a round-up somewhere down this way."

"Well, maybe she just rode farther than she intended. But she was on Jake; she deviled us into letting her take him. Bill thinks Jake isn't very safe. I don't think he is, either. You say the rustlers were away down across the line, driving a bunch of horses, so there's no danger —"

"I didn't say all of them were down that way. I don't know how many there are. They were just little dots crawling along-but I guessed there were about four riders." Johnny started for the door, picking up his rifle from the table where he had placed it. "I wish I'd got after 'em as I wanted to, but Bland kept hollering about gas —" He balanced the propeller on his shoulder again, and turned to Sudden.

"Don't you worry, Mr. Selmer, we'll get right out after her. Which way did she go? There's times when an airplane comes in kinda handy, after all!"

"You young hound, there wouldn't be all this hell a-poppin' if it wasn't for you and your bederned airplane! Don't overlook that fact. You've managed to hold up all my plans, and lose me Lord-knows-how-many horses that are probably the pick of the herds; and you've got the gall to crow because your flying machine will fly! And if that girl of mine's in any trouble, it'll be your fault more than anybody's. If you'd stuck to your job and done what I've been paying you wages to do —"

"You don't have to rub all that in, Mr. Selmer. I guess I know it better than you do. Just because I don't come crying around you with a lot of please-forgive-me stuff, you think I don't give a cuss! Which way did Mary V go? That's more important right now than naming over all the kinds of damn fools I've been. I can sing that song backwards. Which way —"

"She went east. Damn yuh, don't yuh stand there talking back to me, or I'll —"

"Oh, go to-war," said Johnny sullenly, and hitched the propeller to a better balance on his shoulder, and went striding back whence he had come.

He had not meant to crow. He knew perfectly well what harm he had wrought. He was doing what he could to undo that harm, and he was at that high pitch of self-torment when the lash of another was unbearable. He did not want to quarrel with the boss, but no human being could have reproached Johnny then without receiving some of the bitterness which filled Johnny's soul.

He routed Bland out of nap and commanded him to make ready for another flight. Bland protested, with his usual whine against extra work, and got a look from Johnny that sent him hurrying around the plane to make his regular before-flying inspection.

Fifteen minutes after Johnny's arrival the plane was quivering outside on the flying field, and Bland was pulling down his goggles while Johnny kicked a small rock away from a wheel and climbed up to straddle into the rear seat, carrying his rifle with him-to the manifest discomfort of Bland, who was "gun-shy."

"Fly a kinda zigzag course east till I tell yuh to swing south," Johnny called, close to Bland's ear. "Miss Selmer's off that way somewhere. If you see her, don't fly low enough to scare her horse-keep away a little and hunt a landing. I'll tell yuh when to land, same as before."

He settled back, and Bland nodded, glanced right and left, eased the motor on and started. They took the air and climbed steadily, circling until they had the altitude Johnny wanted. Then, swinging away toward Snake Ridge, they worked eastward. Johnny did not use the controls at all. He wanted all his mind for scanning the country spread out below them.

Ridges, arroyos, brushy flats-Johnny's eyes went over them all. Almost before they had completed the first circle he spied a rider, then two-and over to the right a couple more, scattered out and riding eastward. Johnny wished that he could have speech with the boys, could tell them what he meant to do. But he knew too well how the horses would feel about the plane, so he kept on, skimming high over their heads like a great, humming dragon fly. He saw them crane necks to watch him, saw the horses plunge and try to bolt. Then they were far behind, and his eyes were searching anxiously the landscape below.

Mary V, it occurred to him suddenly, might be lying hurt. Jake might have thrown her-though on second thought that was not likely, for Mary V was too good a rider to be thrown unless a horse pitched rather viciously. Jake would run away, would rear and plunge and sidle when fear gripped him or his temper was up, but Johnny had never heard of his pitching. Jake was not a range-bred horse, and if there was a buck-jump in his system, it had never betrayed itself. After all, Mary V's chance of lying hurt was minimized by the very fact that she rode Jake.

Red hill came sliding rapidly toward them. Now it was beneath, and the plane had risen sharply to the air current that flowed steadily over the hill. It swooped down again-they were over the flat where he had seen the riders. The line of fence showed like knotted thread drawn across the land. And within it was no Mary V.

Johnny tapped Bland's shoulder for a circle to the north, hoping that she might be riding back that way. He strained his eyes, and saw tiny dots of horses feeding quietly, but no rider moving anywhere. He sent Bland swinging southward, while he leaned a little and watched the swift-sliding panorama of arid land beneath. It was a rough country, as Tex had said. To look for one little moving speck in all that veined network of little ridges and draws was enough to tax quicker, keener eyes than Johnny Jewel's.

But Johnny would not think of failure. Somewhere he would see her; he would circle and seek until he did find her-if she were there.

Twice they sailed round, keeping within the boundaries of the east and south fences. Then, flying as low as was safe, Johnny turned south, along the course which he believed the horse thieves to have followed. It did not seem possible-rather, he did not want to think it possible-that they should have met Mary V. But Mexico is always Mexico, and sinister things do happen along its border. The boys were coming on horseback, and they would scatter and comb the draws which Johnny had looked down into as he passed over. He would leave that closer search to the boys, while he himself went farther-as far as Jake could travel in half a day.

They reached the south fence, left it dwindling behind them. Minutes brought them over the invisible line which divides lawful country from lawless. They went on, until Johnny spied again the group of stolen horses being herded loosely in a shallow arroyo where there was a little sparse grass. The men he did not at first see, save the one on herd. Then he thought he could detect them sprawled in the shade of a few stunted trees.

Apparently they felt safe, close though they were to the line. Indeed, they were safe enough-from horsemen riding down from the Rolling R. So far they had thieved at their leisure and with impunity. The element of risk had been discounted until they no longer considered it at all, except when they were actually within the Rolling R Boundaries. Now, in the heat of the day, they slept as was their habit. Even the herder was probably dozing in the saddle and leaving watchfulness to his cow-pony. Certainly he did not give any sign that he saw the airplane as it glided silently over so that they could come back from the south.

"What I want, Bland, is to scare these horses back toward home," Johnny said. "We'll come at 'em first from the south, and if they don't run straight, we'll have to circle round till they do. But I want to come within shooting distance of them hombres under the trees. See? So fly as low as yuh dare, when we come back."

Bland threw on the motor, circled and came volplaning back. He did not complain; he left that for times when he was not flying. Johnny braced himself, rifle ready. He was sorry then that he was not an expert shot; but he hoped that luck would be with him and make up for what he lacked in skill.

The horses stampeded, carrying the herder with them. They ran north, in a panic that would keep them going for some time. As they raced clattering past the camp, Johnny saw four men rise up hastily, their faces turned up to the sky. He leaned, took what aim was possible, and fired four shots as the plane swept over.

He did not hit any one, so far as he could see, but he saw them duck and run close to the tree trunks, which gave him some satisfaction. Moreover, they were afoot. Not a single horse remained within sight or hearing of that camp.

Johnny did not go back for another try at them, though he was tempted to land and fight it out with them. There was Mary V to think of, and there were the horses. They went on, shying off from the fleeing animals lest they drive them back instead of forward. Bland spiraled upward, waiting to see what Johnny wanted next. Whatever it might be, Bland would do it-with two guns and a headstrong young man just behind him.

The thrum of the motor stuttered a little on the last upward turn. Bland straightened out the plane, fussed with the spark and the gas, banked cautiously around and headed for home. Like a heart that skips a beat now and then, an odd little pause, scarcely to be distinguished except when the ear has become accustomed to the rhythm of perfect firing, manifested itself. Bland turned his head sidewise, listening. The pause became more marked. The steady, forward thrust slackened a little. Johnny was aware that the monotonous waste below did not slip behind them quite so fast; not quite.

Bland was nursing the motor along, Johnny could tell by his slight movements. It seemed to him that a tenseness had crept into the set of Bland's head. Johnny braced himself for something-just what, he did not know. His knowledge of motors was superficial. Something was wrong with the ignition, he guessed, but he had no idea what it could be.

A sick feeling of thwarted purpose came over him. He knew it was not fear. He felt as though he could not possibly be afraid in an airplane, however much reason he might have for fear. He felt betrayed, as though this wonderful piece of mechanism, for which he had paid so dear a price and which he worshiped in proportion, had suddenly turned traitor. It was failing him, just when his need of it was so vital. Just when he had so much to retrieve, just when he had counted on its help in re-establishing his self-respect.

Bland turned his head, and gave Johnny a fleeting glance from the corner of one eye. Bland's face was a sallow white.

Johnny laid down his rifle and carefully placed feet and hands on the controls. Bland might get scared and lose his head, and if he did, Johnny did not want to be altogether at his mercy. Anyway, Bland did not know the country.

"How far will she glide?" Johnny shouted above the sputtering cough of the motor. But Bland only shook his head slowly from right to left and back again. Bland's ears were a waxy white now, and the line of his jaw had sharpened. Johnny believed that Bland would fail him too.

They were gliding down an invisible incline, and it was a long way to Sinkhole. Johnny began to think feverishly of certain sandy patches, bare of brush and rocks, and to estimate distances. Now they crossed the line fence and were over the rough country below Red Hill and the plane was lifting and falling to the uneven currents like a boat riding the waves. Gliding parallel with a dry tributary of Sinkhole Creek, the plane side-slipped and came perilously close to disaster. Bland righted it, but Johnny held his breath at the way the ground had jumped up at them.

Ahead, and a little to one side, three riders went creeping up a slope. They seemed to be heading toward Sinkhole Camp, and Johnny signaled Bland to keep off, and so avoid scaring the horses. But the slight detour cost them precious feet of altitude while the nearest sandy stretch was yet far off.

The earth was rising with incredible swiftness to meet them. The nearest landing Johnny could think of was farther over, across Sinkhole Creek. He did not believe they could make it, but he headed for it desperately, and felt Bland yielding to his control.

Rocks, brush, furrowed ditches; rocks, brush. Ahead, they could see the irregular patch of yellow that was sand. But the brush seemed fairly to leap at them, the rocks grew malignantly larger while they looked, the ditches deepened ominously. Over these the frail thing of cloth and little strips of wood and wire and the delicate, dumb motor, skimmed like a weary-winged bird. Bland flattened it out, coaxed it to keep the air. Lower, lower —a high bush was flicked by a wheel in passing. On a little farther, and yet a little.

She landed just at the edge of the goal. The loose sand dragged at the wheels, flipped the plane on its nose so suddenly that Johnny never did know just how it happened. Bland had feared that sand, and braced himself. But Johnny did not know. His head had snapped forward against the rim of the cowl —a terrible blow that sent him sagging inertly against the strap that held him. Bland got out, took one look at Johnny, and sank down weakly upon the sand.

Johnny dreamed two separate dreams. The first dream was confused and fragmentary. He seemed to hear certain sentences spoken while he was whirling through space with the Milky Way flinging stars at him. As nearly as he could remember afterwards, this is what he heard.

Mary V's voice: "Don't be so stupid! If a girl happens to bring in two perfectly bandittish outlaws that imagine they are kidnaping her, why must she be lectured, pray tell? If a man had done it —"

Mumble, mumble, and a buzzing in Johnny's head.

Bland's voice: "I don't know as I could tell. He could, if he should come to. We got 'em headed this way —"

Bill's voice: " —and I seen him hittin' for the line and headed him off —"

More mumbling.

Mary V's voice: "I can't see why he doesn't hurry! Why, for gracious sake, must a person lie forever out in the sun when he's all smashed —"

Bland's voice: " —not as much as yuh might think, in all this brush. I ain't gone over it yet —" (mumble) " —short circuit —" (mumble, buzz-buzz) "went past me so close I could feel the wind —" (mumble) " —I dunno. I've seen 'em hurt worse and get over it, and I've seen 'em die when you'd think —"

After that it was all mumble and buzz, and then more stars, and blackness and silence.

Piecing together the fragments, as Johnny could not do, here is the interpretation.

The three riders whom Johnny had seen as the plane was dipping to its final fall were Mary V, Tomaso, and Tomaso's brother. Mary V had gone off to ride the country which Tex had said was too difficult for her —"and it was *not* too difficult for a person who had any brains or any gumption and who did not lose all the sense a person had," etc. She had gone some distance toward the southeast boundary, and Jake was behaving like a perfect dear. She had seen a few horses, and they had all run every which way when they got sight of her, so she was keeping right along and planning to just gently urge them toward Sinkhole as she came back.

Well, and on the way back she had seen the young Mexican riding along, and he had looked perfectly harmless and innocent, and he had a rag tied around his head besides, and kept putting his hand up, and wabbling in the saddle exactly as though he was just about ready to fall off his horse. And how, for gracious sake, was a person going to know he was only pretending and not sick or hurt a speck, but merely taking a low and mean advantage of a person's kindness of heart?

Well, and so she had let him come up to her, and he had asked her if she had any water with her. And she had, and so she twisted around in the saddle to untie the canteen, and Jake kept stepping around, so the young Mexican just reached out and held Jake by the bridle while she got the water-and how was a person to know that he was not trying to help but was kidnaping a person's horse and herself in the most treacherous manner ever heard of?

Just when she had got the canteen untied, and was unscrewing the cap to give it to the boy, another Mexican rode up behind, and he had the most insipid smile on his face, and a detestable way of trying to be polite. And he said it was a nice horse she was riding, and he would like to show that horse to his brother, if she would be so kind to come with him. It would not be far, he said, and they would show her the way. And they went on talking in the most detestable manner, and actually forced her to go along with them. They had guns, and they said they would shoot her in a perfectly polite way.

So Mary V had gone back with them toward the line fence, because the fat one rode behind her with a gun and the boy had a gun, too, and they said they would not tie her hands if she would be good, because there was a swarm of gnats and little flies that kept pestering so, and she had to brush them away from her face.

They kept down in hollows, and mostly they had to go single file, with the boy in front and the detestable one behind. But after awhile they had to climb over a ridge, and the horses were picking their own way, and the horrid one got off to one side, where Mary V could see him out of the corner of her eye. And he was not watching her very closely, and the gun was not pointing at her as she naturally supposed it would be, from what he said.

So Mary V very carefully turned in her heel, and watched her chance, and gave Jake a kick in the ribs. And Jake did exactly as a person expected, and gave a big jump against the horse of the boy. And the fat one did not shoot after all, because he thought it was Jake that did it himself.

So Mary V, having reached into her riding shirt and got her gun, whirled Jake around and took a shot at the fat one before he saw what she meant to do. And she hit him in the hand where he was holding the gun across the saddle horn, which was careless of him, but, of course, he never *dreamed* that Mary V had a gun and would use it.

So the gun dropped on the ground, and the man tried to grab his hand and his side at the same time, because the bullet hit his side too. And then Mary V got Jake down off his hind feet where he had stood with surprise, and made the boy drop his gun. And they were there on the ground yet, just where they dropped them, because Mary V thought they were safer there than being picked up by any one present.

So that was all there was to it. The fat one was all wilted down in the saddle, and their ponies were used to shooting and just stopped and stood there thankful that they had an excuse, because the poor things were terribly hot and sweaty and tired. And Mary V made the boy get off and back up to her, which was some trouble on account of Jake and the gun she had to hold ready to shoot, so she only had one hand for Jake, really. And she was going to take the rag off his head to tie his hands the best she could under the circumstances, but the boy would not do as she said, but instead tried to run away and duck into the bushes. And that was how the boy got shot in the leg. It seemed a pity to do it, still a person couldn't surely be expected to tie outlaws and hold a gun and hold Jake and everything, and not mess them up any. He seemed a kind of nice boy, and his tricky ways were no doubt because he had not been raised properly.

So she made him get on his horse, which was difficult on account of being shot in the leg, and then it seemed cruel and unnecessary to tie him, because they had both been sufficiently shot by her to know what they might expect if they did it again. And that was how it happened that she drove them both ahead of her without being tied or anything, as a person would naturally expect outlaws and horse thieves and kidnapers would be. But Mary V would like to know how, for gracious sake, a person could do *everything* right, with a horse to manage and a gun to hold, and only two hands to their name?

What Bill had said was that he had kept an eye on Tex, because it looked to him like Tex was at the bottom of the whole business. He had seen Tex working away from the others, innocent as a hen turkey with a nest hid out in the weeds. Bill had done some innocent kinda sidlin' off himself, and he had seen Tex suddenly duck into a narrow wash and disappear.

Wherefore, knowing the country even better than did Tex, Bill had ducked into another draw that would intercept Tex, if Tex was going where Bill guessed he was aiming to go. Tex must have aimed that way, because Bill got him and brought him back with his hands tied behind him and his gun riding in Bill's holster, and with no bullet holes in his person such as Mary V's captives carried.

Johnny did not know that the other boys had been signaled back with shots, and that the prisoners had been turned over to them while Bill, Bland, and Mary V stayed with Johnny and waited for Sudden to negotiate that rough stretch of country with the Ford. That was what Mary V's voice referred to when she couldn't see why he didn't hurry.

Between times, Bland told their side of the adventure, as far as Bland understood it. He told of the horses they had scared back, and of the horse thieves left afoot several miles across the line. He did not know just where, however. He told of the rancho they had flown to that morning, the rancho Johnny had discovered a short mile from where he had got the plane in the first place.

The horses which they had turned loose from the field would probably make their way back, Bill said. So would the last little bunch. But he would send the boys down after them just as soon as they had put the three prisoners away in the cabin with a guard until the sheriff could come and get them. Which would be easy, Bill said. They'd telephone to the ranch and have the message repeated on the town line.

Everything was easy, Bill said, except getting Skyrider to a doctor quick, without shaking him up too much. And getting the flying machine outa there-though he guessed mebby Skyrider wouldn't want no more flyin' in his. He guessed mebby Skyrider would aim to keep one foot on solid ground hereafter-if he didn't go clean under it. That shore was a bad lookin' head he had on 'im.

Which brought forth questions from Mary V, and the somewhat qualified comfort of Bland's experience.

Johnny's next dream was a nightmare of pain and jolting. He did not know where he was, but it seemed to him that something kept pounding him on the head; something very hot and very heavy-something he could not escape because his head was being held in a vice of some sort. The pain and the jolting seemed to have no relation to this steady beating. The dream lasted a long, long while. And after that there was darkness and silence.

That came when he had been put to bed at the Rolling R ranch house, in a guest room that faced north. A doctor was there, waiting for them when they arrived, because Sudden had telephoned him when he had finished calling for the sheriff. The boys had told him soberly that Skyrider was bad off, and that his whole head was smashed, and that the flyin' machine was busted all to pieces. They didn't hardly think it would be worth while getting a doctor to the ranch, because they didn't see how Skyrider was goin' to last long enough for a doctor to git to work on him. It was a damn shame. Skyrider was one fine boy-and did anybody know where his folks lived?

But the doctor was sent for just the same, and he was ready to do what could be done. It looked at first as though that was not much. Mary V had kept cold cloths on Johnny's head during the whole drive, and the doctor told her that she had made it a little more possible to pull the young man through. He certainly had received a terrible blow, and-well, the doctor refused to predict anything at all. Johnny was a strong-looking, healthy young man-it took a lot to kill a youngster like that. He advised a nurse, and gave the name of a young woman who was very good, he said.

Sudden telephoned straightway for the nurse, and Mary V locked herself into her room to cry about it.

The nurse came that night, and went briskly in and out of the guest room. She wore her hair parted and slicked back from her face, and rubber heels; and she smiled reassuringly whenever she saw Mary V or Mrs. Selmer or any one else who looked anxious. And she never once failed to close the door of the guest room gently but firmly behind her. Mary V hated that nurse with a vindictiveness wholly out of proportion to the cause.

None of these things did Johnny know. Johnny lay quietly on his back with a neat, white bandage around his head. His eyes were closed, his face was placid with the inscrutable calm of death or deep unconsciousness. The next day it was the same, and the day after that-except that his cheeks began to hollow a little, and his eye sockets to deepen and darken.

And that pesky nurse wouldn't let Mary V stay in the room two minutes! She just shooed her out with that encouraging smile of hers, that Mary V wanted to slap. Did she think, for gracious sake, that Mary V was going to murder Johnny? Mary V was just going to tell the doctor that she had learned all about nursing, in her "Useful Knowledge" class at school. She should think she was just exactly as well qualified to moisten that bandage with whatever it was they put on it, and keep the flies out of the room, and little things like that, as any old tow-headed nurse that ever shook down a thermometer.

But when the doctor came he looked so sort of sober that Mary V was afraid to ask him anything at all. She went out into the hammock on the porch, where she could see the curtains flapping gently in the open window of Johnny's room. And after awhile the doctor came out and looked at her and smiled a little, and said, "Well, have we captured any more bandits? By

George, I'd hate to be one and run across you, young lady. I had the honor of repairing the damage you did to 'em; and I will say, you are so-ome bone smasher!"

Which was all very well-but what did Mary V care about the damage done to those Mexicans? She looked at the open window with the flapping curtains, and then she looked at the doctor. She did not ask a single question, and I don't think she dreamed how wistful her eyes were.

"Well, our young aviator seems to be-holding on," the doctor observed very, very casually, seeming not to see the question Mary V's eyes were asking because her lips would not form it in words. "Better, on the whole, than I expected."

"Then you think —"

"I think we won't worry about it until we have to. They're tough, these young devils."

Mary V tried and tried to wring encouragement from the words, but it was very hard, with Johnny lying like that and never moving.

They brought the airplane to the ranch, much as Johnny had brought it up from "the burning sands of Mexico." Mary V went out to look at it, but it seemed too terrible to think of how high Johnny's hopes had been, how he had worshiped that thing-and what it had done to him. She went to her ledge on the bluff, and sat there and cried heart-brokenly.

There it stood, reared up on its silly little wheels, with its broken propeller still pointing straight up at the sky. Its tail was broken too-and served it right for thrashing around like that in the brush.

She had not known her dad was having it brought in, until she saw them coming with it. Little Curley had driven the team, and he had looked as though he was driving a hearse. She did not even know what her dad was going to do with it. He hadn't said a word to anybody, about anything. He just went ahead as if taking care of Johnny and Johnny's airplane was part of the regular work on the ranch. Even Bill did not appear to know, nor Bland. Perhaps Sudden himself did not know. It seemed to Mary V that the whole ranch was just waiting, minute by minute, for Johnny to open his eyes, or stop breathing. The unbearable part of it was, no one said anything much about it. They just waited.

The doctor came again, and he did not say anything at all to Mary V. He stayed at the ranch all night, mostly in the room with Johnny. The next day another doctor came, and the nurse went in and out of the room sterilizing things and looking very mysterious and important-but always with that intolerably reassuring smile. Mary V gritted her teeth every time she saw that nurse.

They were going to operate, the nurse said, when Mary V simply could not stand it another minute. She went and sat all curled up in the hammock, not letting it swing, but just keeping very, very still, and listening. There were voices in there mumbling sentences she could not catch. After awhile a sickly odor came drifting through the window, and more muttering between the two doctors. Sudden came wandering up, tiptoed to his chair on the porch, and sat down rather heavily and twirled a cigar in his fingers without lighting it. Mary V pulled a magazine toward her and began turning the leaves idly, her lips pressed tight together, her ears strained and listening still.

Ages passed. Twice Mary V placed her fingers over her lips to stifle an impulse to scream. Then —

"We can't make it. Damn that brush," said a new voice-Johnny's voice-quite clearly.

Mary V dropped the magazine and went and put her arms around her dad's neck and pressed her face hard against his shoulder. Her dad held her tight, and swallowed fast, and said never a word.

Chapter Twenty-Four. Johnny's Dilemma

"Well, thank heavens she's gone! Perhaps a person can have a minute or two of peace and comfort on this ranch now. I don't know when I have ever disliked a person so much. I don't see how you stood her. For my part, that creature would *make* me sick, just having her around!" As a final venting of her animosity, Mary V made faces at the car that carried the nurse back to town.

Johnny looked at Mary V, looked after the nurse, and looked at Mary V again. He had thought the nurse a very nice nurse, with a quiet kind of efficiency that soothed a fellow without any fuss or frills. It was queer Mary V did not like her, but then —

"I know I've been a darned nuisance," he apologized so meekly that he did not sound in the least like Johnny Jewel. "But I'm getting well fast. I'll be able to beat it in a few days now."

"Why, for gracious sake? Haven't we-er-made you *comfortable?*"

"Sure, you have. Only you shouldn't have put yourselves out, this way. I ought to have gone to a hospital or some place." Johnny looked so distressed that Mary V could have cried. Only she was afraid that would distress him still more, and the doctor had said he must not be worried about anything.

"It wasn't any trouble. You are being absolutely silly, so I guess you are getting well, all right. I —I didn't see any sense of having that nurse in the first place. Because I can take temperature and count pulse and everything. I've really been crazy for a chance to practice nursing on somebody. And then when I had the chance, they wouldn't let me do a thing."

Johnny grinned, which was rather pathetic-he was so thin and so white. "Why didn't you practice on the greasers?" he taunted her. "Bill says you sure made some dandy work for the hospitals."

"Well, I couldn't help that. I didn't have any way of tying them, or anything, and —"

"Brag, girl! For Lord's sake don't apologize; it doesn't come natural to you. What gets me is that I was ripping the atmosphere wide open, trying to rescue you, and all the while you were making a whole sheriff's posse of yourself-and it was you that rescued me. I should think —"

"I did not! I —did Bill tell you the latest, Johnny? You know how dad is-about making people tell things he wants to know, and keeping them right to the point —"

"I know." Johnny's tone was eloquent.

"Well, he got at those Mexicans, and they told everything they knew-and some besides. And who do you think was the real leader of that gang, Johnny? And I know now it was his voice that I couldn't quite recognize over the 'phone. They've arrested him and two or three of his men, and you wouldn't *believe* a neighbor could be so tricky and mean as that Tucker Bly. Stealing *our* horses to sell to the Mexicans, if you please, and selling his own to the government mostly-but some to the Mexicans, too, I suppose. And nobody suspecting a thing all the while, and Tex in with them and all. And if you hadn't stampeded the horses so they came back to the line, and the boys rounded them up, dad would have lost a lot more than he did. But now the whole thing is out, and really, if I hadn't caught those two greasers, there wouldn't be any evidence against the Tucker Bly outfit, or Tex either. And I just think it's awful, the way —"

She stopped abruptly. Johnny's bandaged head was leaning against the back of his big chair, and his eyes were closed. His face looked whiter than it had a few minutes ago. Mary V was scared. She should have known better than to talk of those things.

"Shall-would you like a drink, or-or something?" she asked in a small, contrite voice.

Johnny opened his eyes and looked at her.

"No, I don't want a drink; I just want somebody to give me another knock on the head that will finish me." And before Mary V could think of anything soothing to say, Johnny spoke again. "I think I'll go back and lie down awhile. I —don't feel very good."

He would not let Mary V help him at all, but walked slowly, steadying himself by the chairs, the wall, by anything solid within reach. He did not look much like the very self-assured, healthy specimen of young manhood whom Mary V could bully and tease and talk to without constraint. She felt as though she scarcely knew this thin, pale young man with the bandaged head and the somber eyes. He seemed so aloof, as though his spirit walked alone in dark places where she could not follow.

After that she did not mention stolen horses, nor thieves, nor airplanes, nor anything that could possibly lead his thoughts to those taboo subjects. Under that heavy handicap conversation lagged. There seemed to be so little that she dared mention! She would sit and prattle of school and shows and such things, and tell him about the girls she knew; and half the time she knew perfectly well that Johnny was not listening. But she could not bear his moody silences, and he sat out on the porch a good deal of the time, so she had to go on talking, whether she bored him to death or not.

Then one day, when the bandage had dwindled to a small patch held in place by strips of adhesive plaster, Johnny broke into her detailed description of a silly Western picture she had seen.

"What's become of Bland?" he asked, just when she was describing a thrilling scene.

"Bland? Oh, why-Bland's gone." Mary V was very innocent as to eyes and voice, and very uneasy as to her mind.

"Gone where? He was broke. I didn't get a chance to pay him —"

"Oh, well, as to that —I suppose dad fixed him up with a ticket and so on. And so this girl, Inez, overhears them plotting —"

"Where's your dad?"

"Dad? Why, dad's in Tucson, I believe, at the trial. What *makes* you so rude when I'm telling you the most thrill —"

"When's he coming back?"

"For gracious *sake*, Johnny! What do you want of dad all at once? Am I not entertaining —"

"You are. As entertaining as a meadow lark. I love meadow larks, but I never could put in all my time listening to 'em sing. I generally had something else I had to do."

"Well, you've nothing else to do now, so listen to this meadow lark, will you? Though I must say —"

"I'd like to, but I can't. There are things I've got to do."

"There are not! Not a single thing but be a nice boy and get well. And to get well you must —"

"A lot you know about it-you, with nothing to worry you, any more than a meadow lark. Not as much, because they do have to rustle their own worms and watch out for hawks and things, and you —"

"I suppose you would imply that I have about as much brains as a meadow lark, perhaps!" Mary V rose valiantly to the argument. If Johnny would rather quarrel than talk about things that didn't interest either of them a bit, why, a quarrel he should have.

But Johnny would not quarrel. He made no reply whatever to the tentative charge. When Mary V stopped scolding, she became aware that Johnny had not heard a word of what she had said.

"How many horses did your dad figure had been stolen? I mean, besides the ones he got back."

"Why-er-you'll have to ask dad. I don't see what that can have to do with meadow larks' brains."

"It hasn't a thing to do with brains. I was merely wondering."

"Well," Mary V retorted flippantly, "I believe the wondering is very good to-day. Help yourself, Johnny."

Johnny looked at her unsmilingly. "That," he told her bitterly, "is what I'm trying to do."

He did not explain that somewhat cryptical remark, and presently he left her and went to his room. Mary V felt that she was not being trusted by a person who surely ought to know by this time that he needn't be so secretive about his thoughts and intentions. If she had not proved her loyalty and her friendship by this time, what did a person want her to do, for gracious sake?

Mary V had rather an unhappy time of it, the next week or so. She had, for some reason, lost all interest in collecting "Desert Glimpses"; so much so that when her mother told her she must stay close to the ranch lest she meet more of those terrible Mexican bandits, Mary V was very sweet about it and did not argue with her mother at all. She seldom went farther than the ledge, these days, and she could not keep her mind off Johnny Jewel, even when there was no doubt at all that he was nearly as well as ever.

Of course, it did not really matter-but why was Johnny so glum with her? Why wouldn't he talk, or at least quarrel the way he used to do? He did not seem angry about anything. He simply did not seem to care whether she was with him or not. She might as well be a stick or a stone, she told herself viciously, for all the attention Johnny Jewel ever paid to her. She did not mind in the least; but it did seem perfectly silly and unaccountable; she wondered merely because she hated mysteries.

It really should not have been mysterious. Mary V made the mistake of not putting herself in Johnny's place and from that angle interpreting his preoccupation. Had she done that she would have seen at once that Johnny was fighting a battle within himself. All his ideas, his plans, and his hopes had been turned bottom up, and Johnny was working over the wreck.

She sat and watched him from the ledge one day, and wondered why he did not act more pleased when he walked down toward the corral and discovered his airplane all repaired, just exactly as good as it had been before. He stood there looking at it with the same apathetic gloom in his bearing that had marked him ever since he was able to be out of bed. Mary V thought he might at least show a little gratitude-not to herself, but toward her dad, because he had kept Bland and had paid him to repair the machine for Johnny, when Johnny was too sick to know anything about it-too sick even to hear the noise of it when Bland tried out the motor-and the nurse was so afraid it would disturb "her patient."

She saw her dad stroll down that way, and stop and look at the airplane with Johnny. Johnny seemed to be asking a few questions. But they did not talk five minutes until Johnny went off by himself to the bunk house, and stayed there. He did not even come back to the house for supper, but ate with the boys.

Mary V would have died before she would ask Johnny what was the matter, but she took what measures she could to find out, nevertheless. She asked her dad, that evening, what Johnny thought about his aeroplane being all fixed up again.

Sudden smoked for a minute or two before he answered. "Well, I don't know, kitten. He didn't say." Sudden's tone was drawling and comfortable, but Mary V somehow got the notion that her dad, too, was rather disappointed in Johnny's lack of appreciation.

"Well, but what's he going to do with it, dad?"

"He didn't say, kitten."

"Well, but dad, he was looking at it, and you were with him, and didn't he say *anything*, for gracious sake?" Mary V could not have kept the exasperation out of her voice if she had tried.

Sudden's lips quirked with the beginning of a smile. He looked at the end of his cigar, looked toward the bunk house, scraped off the cigar's ash collar on the porch rail, looked at Mary V.

"Well, he asked me how it got here to the ranch, and I told him with a wagon and team and so on. And he said, 'Mh-hum, I see.' Then he asked me who repaired it, and I told him that buttermilk-eyed aviator he'd had with him. He replied, 'I —see.' Then he asked me what the repairing had cost, and the fellow's wages or whatever he had got, and I told him, 'Dam-fi recollect, Johnny.' And he didn't say a word. Just strolled off as if he'd talked himself tired-which I guess maybe he had."

"Well, but dad, what do you *suppose* he's going to do? He-he's awfully queer since he was hurt. Do you suppose —?"

"Kitten," said her dad quietly, "when you're breaking a high-strung colt he sometimes sorta resents his schooling and sulks. Then you've just got to wait till he figures things out for himself a little. If you force him you're liable to spoil him and make him mean. Johnny's like that. He's just a high-strung human colt that life is breaking. I guess, kitten, we better not crowd him right now."

"Well, I don't see why he should act that way with *me*," Mary V complained, and thereby proved herself altogether human and feminine in her point of view.

Chapter Twenty-Five. Skyrider "Has Flew"!

Just at dawn the humming of the airplane motor woke Mary V. She sat up in bed and listened, a little fear gripping at her heart; a fear which she fought with her reason, her hopes, and all her natural optimism. Surely Johnny would not be foolish enough to attempt a flight that morning. He must be just trying put the motor. He would know he was not yet in condition to bear any physical or nervous strain, sick as he had been. Of course he wouldn't be so selfish as to make a flight without so much as asking her if she would like to go with him. He knew she was simply crazy over flying.

By that time she was out on the porch, where she was immediately joined by her father and mother, also awakened by the motor. They were just in time. From the neighborhood of the corral came an increasing roar. A sudden rush of cool morning wind brought dust and bits of hay and gravel flying in a cloud. A great, wide-winged, teetering bird-thing went racing out into sight, spurned the earth and lifted, climbed steadily, circling like a hungry hawk over a meadow full of mice.

"By heck, the boy can fly, all right!" Sudden paid tribute to Johnny's skill in one unpremeditated ejaculation. "An airplane using our very dooryard for a flying field, mommie! Times are certainly changing."

Mary V bit her lip and blinked very fast while she watched the plane go circling up and up, the motor droning its monotonous song like a hive of honey bees at work. It was pure madness for Johnny to attempt flying so soon again. He would be killed; anything could happen that was terrible. She shut her eyes for a minute, trying to rout a swift vision of Johnny crumpled down limp in the pilot's seat as she had seen him that day-nearly a month ago-with Bland, white-faced and helpless, walking aimlessly around the crippled plane, so sure Johnny was dead that he would not touch him to find out. If anything like that should happen again, Mary V believed that she would go crazy. She simply couldn't stand it to go through such a horror again.

The plane was circling around once more and flew straight northeast. They watched it until they could not hear the humming; until it looked like a bird against the glow of sunrise.

"Hm-mm, I wonder where —" Sudden began, but Mary V did not stay to hear the rest of the sentence.

She went back and crept into her bed, sick at heart with an unnamed fear and a hurt that went deep into her soul. She gave a little, dry sob or two and lay very still, her face crushed into a pillow.

But Mary V was not born to take life's hurts passively. Presently she dressed and went straight down to the bunk house, where she knew the boys would be at their breakfast-unless they had finished and gone to the corral. She walked into the old-fashioned, low-ceiled living room where she had first learned to walk, and stood just inside the door, smiling a little.

Bud had just finished eating, and was rolling a cigarette before he got up from the long table. The others were finishing their coffee and hot biscuits, and they said hello to Mary V and went on undisturbed.

"Hello-what's all that racket I heard as I was getting up?" Mary V inquired lightly. "My good gracious, I thought you boys had started a sawmill-or maybe somebody had overslept down here and was snoring. It sounded like Aleck."

They laughed, and Curley spoke. "That there was Skyrider. He has flew —"

Bud, fumbling for a match, had a fit of genius. He grinned, cleared his throat, and began to warble unexpectedly.

> "Skyrider-r has flew into-o the blew
>
> Ta-da, da-da, da-daa-a-a —
>
> No-obody knew what he aimed to do

Till he went and said adieu.

"Says he, 'Good-bye, I aim to fly

To foreign lands, ta da-a —'"

"Oh, for gracious *sake*, Bud! I always knew you were queer at times, but I really didn't know you had fits. So it was Skyrider riding off to call on Venus, was it? I wish I had seen him start; but that's just my luck, of course. Er —*where* was he going? Or didn't he say?"

"He didn't say. But he shook hands with us and told us we had treated him white at times, and that some day he'd write —"

"Oh, say! I got a letter he left for your father," Curley broke in. "I'll git it and you can take it up to the house." He gave Mary V a mysterious look and went into the room where he slept.

Mary V followed him as far as the door, and saw Curley take two letters from under his pillow. Her heart gave a jump at that, and it began to beat very fast when he turned and put them into her hand with another mysterious look. She thanked him and hurried out on the porch and straight to her pet ledge. Her dad's letter could wait.

On the ledge she sat down, and with fingers that shook she tore open, an envelope addressed to "Miss Mary V. Selmer, care of Curley." It had been sealed very tightly, as though it contained secrets. Which it did.

Mary V read that letter through from beginning to end five times before she left the ledge. It was not exactly a love letter, either, though Mary V squeezed it between her palms and then kissed it before she put it away out of sight. After that she cried lonesomely and stared away into that part of the sky where Johnny and his airplane had last been a disappearing speck.

"*Dear Mary V,*" (Johnny had written) "I'm not going to tell anybody good-bye. Not even you, or I might say especially not you. It's hard enough to go as it is.

"Maybe you won't care much, but I am a hopeful cuss, and I'm going to build air castles about you till I come back, which I hope to do when I have made good. I made an awful mess of things here, and it's up to me to make good now before I say anything to you about air castles and so on.

"I told you once that they need flyers in France, and that's where I'm going if they will have me. I've got to fly and that's all there is to it, and I can't fly and be a stock hand at one and the same time because the two don't go together worth a cent, and I have sure found that out, and so has your dad, I guess.

"Well, I can't ask you to wait till I have made good, because that wouldn't be square, but I can say that when I have made good I am coming back, and then if some other fellow has got the start of me he will sure have to go some to keep his start. Because I am going to have you some day, if I have anything to say about it. I'll teach you to fly, and we will sure part the clouds like foam and all the rest of it. You've got more nerve than any other girl I ever saw, and, anyway, I'd like you just the same if you was a coward, because I couldn't help it no matter what you was, just so you were Mary V.

"So good-bye, and look for me back with my chest all dolled up with medals, because I am sure coming if you will let me. When I get to Tucson, I'll call you up on long distance, and then if your folks ain't in the room, I wish you'd tell me if it's all right with you, my loving you the way I do. Or if they are in the room, you can just say 'all right,' and I'll know what you mean. And anyway I'll write to you and I hope you'll write to me, because I am sure going to miss you till I come back. I wish I had the nerve to go right up to the house and tell you all this instead of writing, but I know I couldn't do it, so I won't try. But you be sure and let me know some way over the 'phone. So good-bye for the present. Always your faithful Skyrider, Johnny."

His letter to her father was not so long, and it was more coherent. To Sudden he had written:

Mr. Selmer.

Dear Sir, —I have decided to fly my airplane to where I can sell it, and will turn the money over to you to help pay for the expense you have been under of having your horses stole. I can't find out how many you lost all told, but whatever I can get for the plane will not cover it, I am afraid, so I will make up the balance as soon as possible.

I want to thank you for all the kindness of yourself and family while I was sick, and before and afterwards. You have certainly treated me white, and much better than I deserve, and I certainly appreciate it all, and some day I will refund every nickel you are out on account of having me in your employ. The doctor's bill I intend to pay and the nurse, too, and whatever you were out on getting the plane repaired.

I am thinking of enlisting somewhere as an aviator, as that seems to be my chosen field. I am leaving early in the morning if the weather is all right for flying, and one of the boys will give you this letter so you will know why I went and not think I sneaked off. I am fully determined to make good, and when I have done so I will come back and finish squaring up for your trouble and expense in having the horses stole. I feel that I balled things up bad, and it is my desire to square everything up.

I feel that it is merely the square thing to tell you I love your daughter Mary V, and I hope you will not object to having me marry her when I have made good. Of course, I would not want to until I had done so. And I hope that will be all right with you; but if it isn't, it is only fair to tell you that you won't be able to stop me if she is willing, and I hope she is. So I am merely telling you, and not asking, because that ain't my style; when I have made good I will do my asking to Mary V. And I hope you will not think I have got my gall, because I am very grateful for all you have done for me and your family also. I will write when I have made some deal to turn the plane so I can send you whatever it brings.

Yours truly,

John Ivan Jewel.

Old Sudden did not say anything when he had read that letter-read it twice, to be exact. He folded it carefully and gave it to his wife to read, and sat smoothing down his face with his hand while she studied it, reading slowly, sometimes going back to get the full meaning out of a somewhat involved sentence.

"Johnny's a dear boy," she observed meditatively, after they had sat for a little while in silence. "I hope he doesn't enlist in that terrible war; it's so dangerous!"

Sudden turned in his chair and looked in through a window to where Mary V was sitting very quietly within three feet of the telephone, her album of "Desert Glimpses" in her lap. Undoubtedly Mary V was listening, but she was also undoubtedly waiting for something. He looked at his wife, and his wife also glanced into the room and caught the significance of Mary V's position and attitude.

The telephone rang, and Mary V dropped the album in her haste to answer the call. She glanced out at them while she announced, "Yes, this is Mary V —it's *all right* —right on the porch, but it's all right —"

Dad and mommie took the hint and withdrew.

THE END

The Thunder Bird

Chapter One. Johnny Assumes a Debt of Honor

Since Life is no more than a series of achievements and failures, this story is going to begin exactly where the teller of tales usually stops. It is going to begin with Johnny Jewel an accepted lover and with one of his dearest ambitions realized. It is going to begin there because Johnny himself was just beginning to climb, and the top of his desires was still a long way off, and the higher you go the harder is the climbing. Even love does not rest at peace with the slipping on of the engagement ring. I leave it to Life, the supreme judge, to bear me out in the statement that Love must straightway gird himself for a life struggle when he has passed the flowered gateway of a woman's tremulous yes.

To Johnny Jewel the achievement of possessing himself of so coveted a piece of mechanism as an airplane, and of flying it with rapidly increasing skill, began to lose a little of its power to thrill. The getting had filled his thoughts waking and sleeping, had brought him some danger, many thrills, a good deal of reproach and much self-condemnation. Now he had it-that episode was diminishing rapidly in importance as it slid into the past, and Johnny was facing a problem quite as great, was harboring ambitions quite as dazzling, as when he rode a sweaty horse across the barren stretches of the Rolling R Ranch and dreamed the while of soaring far above the barrenness.

Well, he had soared high above many miles of barrenness. That dream could be dreamed no more, since its magic vapors had been dissipated in the bright sun of reality. He could no longer dream of flying, any more than he could build air castles over riding a horse. Neither could he rack his soul with thoughts of Mary V Selmer, wondering whether she would ever get to caring much for a fellow. Mary V had demonstrated with much frankness that she cared. He knew the feel of her arms around his neck, the look of her face close to his own, the sweet thrill of her warm young lips against his. He had bought her a modest little ring, and had watched the shine of it on the third finger of her tanned left hand when she left him-going gloveless that the ring might shine up at her.

The first episode of her life thus happily finished, Johnny was looking with round, boyish, troubled eyes upon the second.

"Long-distance call for you, Mr. Jewel," the clerk announced, when Johnny strolled into the Argonaut hotel in Tucson for his mail. "Just came in. The girl at the switchboard will connect you with the party."

Johnny glanced into his empty key box and went on to the telephone desk. It was Mary V, he guessed. He had promised to call her up, but there hadn't been any news to tell, nothing but the flat monotony of inaction, which meant failure, and Johnny Jewel never liked talking of his failures, even to Mary V.

"Oh, Johnny, is that you? I've been waiting and *waiting*, and I just wondered if you had enlisted and gone off to war without even calling up to say good-by. I've been perfectly *frantic*. There's something —"

"You needn't worry about me enlisting," Johnny broke in, his voice the essence of gloom. "They won't have me."

"Won't *have* —why, Johnny Jewel! How *can* the United States Army be so stupid? Why, I should think they would be glad to get —"

"They don't look at me from your point of view, Mary V." Johnny's lips softened into a smile. She was a great little girl, all right. If it were left to her, the world would get down on its marrow bones and worship Johnny Jewel. "Why? Well, they won't take me and my airplane as a gift. Won't have us around. They'll take me on as a common buck trooper, and that's all. And I can't afford —"

"Well, but Johnny! Don't they know what a perfectly wonderful flyer you are? Why, I should think —"

"They won't have me in aviation at all, even without the plane," said Johnny. "The papers came back to-day. I was turned down-flat on my face! Gol darn 'em, they can do without me now!"

"Well, I should say so!" cried Mary V's thin, indignant voice in his ear. "How perfectly idiotic! I didn't want you to go, anyway. Now you'll come back to the ranch, won't you, Johnny?" The voice had turned wheedling. "We can have the duckiest times, flying around! Dad'll give you a tremendously good —"

"You seem to forget I owe your dad three or four thousand dollars," Johnny cut in. "I'll come back to the ranch when that's paid, and not before."

"Well, but listen, Johnny! Dad doesn't look at it that way at all. He knows you didn't mean to let those horses be stolen. He doesn't feel you owe him anything at all, Johnny. Now we're engaged, he'll give you a good —"

"You don't get me, Mary V. I don't care what your father thinks. It's what I think that counts. This airplane of mine cost your dad a lot of good horses, and I've got to make that good to him. If I can't sell the darned thing and pay him up, I'll have to —"

"I suppose what I think doesn't count anything at all! I say you don't owe dad a cent. Now that you are going to marry me —"

"You talk as if you was an encumbrance your dad had to pay me to take off his hands," blurted Johnny distractedly. "Our being engaged doesn't make any difference —"

"Oh, doesn't it? I'm tremendously glad to know you feel that way about it. Since it doesn't make any difference whatever —"

"Aw, cut it out, Mary V! You know darn well what I meant."

"Why, certainly. You mean that our being engaged doesn't make a particle —"

"Say, *listen* a minute, will you! I'm going to pay your dad for those horses that were run off right under my nose while I was tinkering with this airplane. I don't care what you think, or what old Sudden thinks, or what anybody on earth thinks! I know what I think, and that's a plenty. I'm going to make good before I marry you, or come back to the ranch.

"Why, good golly! Do you think I'm going to be pointed out as a joke on the Rolling R? Do you think I'm going to walk around as a living curiosity, the only thing Sudden Selmer ever got stung on? Oh —h, no! Not little Johnny! They can't say I got into the old man for a bunch of horses and the girl, and that old Sudden had to stand for it! I told your dad I'd pay him back, and I'm going to do it if it takes a lifetime.

"I'm calling that debt three thousand dollars-and I consider at that I'm giving him the worst of it. He's out more than that, I guess-but I'm calling it three thousand. So," he added with an extreme cheerfulness that proved how heavy was his load, "I guess I won't be out to supper, Mary V. It's going to take me a day or two to raise three thousand-unless I can sell the plane. I'm sticking here trying, but there ain't much hope. About three or four a day kid me into giving 'em a trial flight-and to-morrow I'm going to start charging 'em five dollars a throw. I can't burn gas giving away joy rides to fellows that haven't any intention of buying me out. They'll have to dig up the coin, after this —I can let it go on the purchase price if they do buy, you see. That's fair enough —"

"Then you won't even listen to dad's proposition?" Mary V's tone proved how she was clinging to the real issue. "It's a perfectly wonderful one, Johnny, and really, for your own good-and not because we are engaged in the least-you should at least consider it. If you insist on owing him money, why, I suppose you could pay him back a little at a time out of the salary he'll pay you. He will pay you a good enough salary so you can do it nicely —"

Johnny laughed impatiently. "Let your dad jump up my wages to a point where he can pay himself back, you mean," he retorted. "Oh —h, no, Mary V. You can't kid me out of this, so why keep on arguing? You don't seem to take me seriously. You seem to think this is just a whim of mine. Why, good golly! I should think it would be plain enough to you that I've got to do it if I want to hold up my head and look men in the face. It's —why, it's an insult to my self-respect and my honesty to even hint that I could do anything but what I'm going to do. The very fact that your dad ain't going to force the debt makes it all the more necessary that I should pay it.

"Why, good golly, Mary V! I'd feel better toward your father if he had me arrested for being an accomplice with those horse thieves, or slapped an attachment on the plane or something, than wave the whole thing off the way he's doing. It'd show he looked on me as a man, anyway.

"I'll be darned if I appreciate this way he's got of treating it like a spoiled kid's prank. I'm going to make him recognize the fact that I'm a *man*, by golly, and that I look at things like a man. He's got to be proud to have me in the family, before I come into the family. He ain't going to take me in as one more kid to look after. I'll come in as his equal in honesty and business ability, —instead of just a new fad of Mary V's —"

"Well, for gracious sake, Johnny! If you feel that way about it, why didn't you say so? You don't seem to care what I think, or how I feel about it. You don't seem to care whether you ever get married or not. And I'm sure I wasn't the one that did the proposing. Why, it will take years and *years* to square up with dad, if you insist on doing it in a regular business way —"

Johnny's harsh laugh stopped her. "You see, you do know where I stand, after all. If I let it slide, the way you want me to, that's exactly what you'd be thinking after awhile-that I never had squared up with your dad. You'd look down on me, and so would your father and your mother. They'd always be afraid I'd do some fool thing and sting your dad again for a few thousand."

"Well, of all the crazy talk! And I've gone to the trouble of coaxing dad to give you a share in the Rolling R instead of putting it in his will for me. And dad's going to do it —"

"Oh, no, he isn't. I don't want any share in the Rolling R. I'd go to jail before I'd take it."

Mary V produced woman's final argument. "If you cared anything at all for me, Johnny, when I ask you to come back and do what dad is willing to have you do, you'd do it. I don't see how you can be stubborn enough to refuse such a perfectly wonderful offer. You wouldn't, if you cared a snap about me. You act just as if you were sorry —"

"Aw, lay off that don't-care stuff!" Johnny growled indignantly. "Caring for you has got nothing to do with it, I tell you. It's just simply a question of what kinda mark I am. You know I care!"

"Well, then, if you do you'll come right over here. If you start now you can be here by sundown, and it's nice and quiet and no wind at all. You've absolutely no excuse, Johnny, and you know it. When dad's willing to forget about those horses —"

"When I come, your dad won't have anything to forget about," Johnny reiterated obstinately. "I do wish you'd look at the thing right!"

Mary V changed her tactics, relying now upon intimidation. "I shall begin to look for you in about an hour," she said sweetly. "I shall keep on looking till you come, or till it gets too dark. If you care anything about me, Johnny, you'll be here. I'll have dinner all ready, so you needn't wait to eat." Then she hung up.

Johnny rattled the hook impatiently, called hello with irritated insistence, and finally succeeded in raising Central's impersonal: "Number, please?" Whereupon he flung himself angrily out of the booth.

"Do you want to pay at this end?" The girl at the desk looked up at him with a gleam of curiosity. Mentally Johnny accused her of "listening in." He snapped an affirmative at her and waited until "long distance" told her the amount.

"Four dollars and eighty-five cents," she announced, giving him a pert little smile. Johnny flipped a small gold piece to the desk and marched off, scorning his fifteen cents change with the air of a millionaire.

Johnny was angry, grieved, disappointed, worried-and would have been wholly miserable had not his anger so dominated his other emotions that he could continue mentally his argument against the attitude of Mary V and the Rolling R.

They refused to take him seriously, which hurt Johnny's self-esteem terribly. Were he older, were he a property owner, Sudden Selmer would not so lightly wave aside that debt. He would pay Johnny the respect of fighting for his just rights. But no-just because he was barely of age, just because he was Johnny Jewel, they all acted as though-why, darn 'em, they acted as though he was a kid offering to earn money to pay for a broken plate! And Mary V —

Well, Mary V was a great little girl, but she would have to learn some day that Johnny was master. He considered this as good a day as any for the lesson. Better, because he was really upholding his principles by not going to the ranch meekly submissive, because Mary V had announced that she would be looking for him. Johnny winced from the thought of Mary V, out on the porch, watching the sky toward Tucson for the black speck that would be his airplane; listening for the high, strident drone that would herald his coming. She would cry herself to sleep.

But she had deliberately sentenced herself to tears and disappointment, he told himself sternly. She must have known he was in earnest about not coming. She had no right to think she could kid him out of something big and vital to his honor. She ought to know him by this time.

Briefly he considered returning to the hotel and calling up the ranch, just to tell her not to look for him because he was not coming. But the small matter of paying the toll deterred him. It was humiliating to admit, even to himself, that he could not afford another long-distance conversation with Mary V, but he had come to the point in his finances where a two-bit piece looked large as a dollar. He would miss that small gold piece.

Since the government had refused to consider accepting his services and paying him a bonus for his plane, he would have to sell it-if he could.

There it sat, reared up on its two little wheels, its nose poked rakishly out of an old shed that had been remodelled to accommodate it, its tail sticking out at the other side so that it slightly resembled a turtle with its shell not quite covering its extremities. The Mexican boy whom Johnny had hired to watch the plane in his absence lay asleep under one wing. A faint odor of varnish testified to the heat of the day that was waning toward a sultry night.

Without disturbing the boy Johnny rolled a smoke and stood, as he had stood many and many a time, staring at his prize and wondering what to do with it. He had to have money. That was flat, final, admitting no argument. At a reasonable estimate, three thousand dollars were tied up in that machine. He could not afford to sell it for any less. Yet there did not seem to be a man in the country willing to pay three thousand dollars for it. It was a curiosity, a thing to come out and stare at, a thing to admire; but not to buy, even though Johnny had as an added inducement offered to teach the buyer to fly before the purchase price was taken from the bank.

The stalking shadow of a man moving slowly warned Johnny of an approaching visitor. He did not trouble to turn his head; he even moved farther into the shed, to tighten a turnbuckle that was letting a cable sag a little.

"Hello, old top-how they using yuh?" greeted a voice that had in it a familiar, whining note.

Johnny's muscles stiffened. Hostility, suspicion, surprise surged confusingly through his brain. He turned as one who was bracing himself to meet an enemy, with a primitive prickling where the bristles used to rise on the necks of our cavemen ancestors.

Chapter Two. And the Cat Came Back

"Why, hello, Bland," Johnny exclaimed after the first blank silence. "I thought you was tied up in a sack and throwed into the pond long ago!"

The visitor grinned with a sour droop to his mouth, a droop which Johnny knew of old. "But the cat came back," he followed the simile, blinking at Johnny with his pale, opaque blue eyes. "What yuh doing here? Starting an aviation school?"

"Yeah. Free instruction. Want a lesson?" Johnny retorted, only half the sarcasm intended for Bland; the rest going to the town that had failed to disgorge a buyer for what he had to sell.

"Aw, I suppose you think you could give me lessons, now you've learned to do a little straight-away flying without landing on your tail," Bland fleered, with the impatience of the seasoned flyer for the novice who thinks well of himself and his newly acquired skill. "Say, that was some bump you give yourself on the dome when we lit over there in that sand patch. I tried to tell yuh that sand looked loose —"

"Yes, you did-not! You was scared stiff. Your face looked like the inside of a raw bacon rind!"

"Sure, I was scared. So would you of been if you'd a known as much about it as I knew. I knew we was due to pile up, when you grabbed the control away from me. You'll make a flyer, all right-and a good one, if yuh last long enough. But you can't learn it all in a day, bo-take it from me. Anyway, I got no kick to make. It was you and the plane that got the bumps. All I done was bite my tongue half off!"

Boy that he was, Johnny laughed over this. The idea of Bland biting his tongue tickled him and served to blur his antagonism for the tricky aviator who had played so large a part in his salvaging of this very airplane.

"Uh course you'll laugh-but you wasn't laughing then. I'll say you wasn't. I thought you was croaked. Cost something to repair the plane, too. I'm saying it did. Had to have a new propeller, and a new crank-case for the motor-cost the old man at the ranch close to three hundred dollars before I turned her over to him, ready to take the air again. That's including what he paid me, of course. But I guess you know what it cost, when he handed you the bill."

This was news to Johnny, news that made his soul squirm. Lying there sick at the Rolling R ranch, he had not known what was taking place. He had found his airplane ready to fly, when he was at last able to walk out to the corrals, but no one seemed to know how much the repairing had cost. Certainly Sudden Selmer himself had suffered a lapse of memory on the subject. All the more reason then why Johnny should repay his debt.

"What I'm wondering about is why you aren't in Los Angeles," he evaded the unpleasant subject awkwardly. "Old Sudden gave you money to go, and dumped you at the depot, didn't he? That's what Mary V told me."

"He did-and I missed my train. And while I was waiting for the next I must 'a' et something poison. I was awful sick. I guess it was ten days or so before I come to enough to know where I was. I've had hard luck, bo —I'll say I have. I was robbed while I was sick, and only for a tambourine queen I got acquainted with, I guess I'd 'a' died. They're treacherous as hell, though. Long as she thought I had money-oh, well, they's no use expecting kindness in this world. Or gratitude. I'm always helpin' folks out and gittin' kicked and cussed for my pay. Lookit the way I lived with snakes and lizards-lived in a cave, like a coyote! —to help you git this plane in shape. You was to take me to Los for pay-but I ain't there yet. I'm stuck here, sick and hungry —I ain't et a mouthful since last night, and then I only had a dish of sour beans that damn' Mex. hussy handed out to me through a window! Me, Bland Halliday, a flyer that has made his hundreds doing exhibition work; that has had his picture on the front page of big city papers, and folks followin' him down the street just to get a look at him! Me-why, a yellow dawg has got the edge on me for luck! I might better be dead —" His loose lips quivered. Tears of self-pity welled up into his pale blue eyes. He turned away and stared across the barren calf lot that Johnny used for a flying field.

Johnny began to have premonitory qualms of a sympathy which he knew was undeserved. Bland Halliday had got a square deal-more than a square deal; for Sudden, Johnny knew, had paid him generously for repairing the plane while Johnny was sick. Bland had undoubtedly squandered the money in one long debauch, and there was no doubt in Johnny's mind of Bland's reason for missing his train. He was a bum by nature and he would double-cross his own mother, Johnny firmly believed. Yet, there was Johnny's boyish sympathy that never failed sundry stray dogs and cats that came in his way. It impelled him now to befriend Bland Halliday.

"Well, since the cat's come back, I suppose it must have its saucer of milk," he grinned, by way of hiding the fact that the lip-quiver had touched him. "I haven't taken any nourishment myself for quite some time. Come on and eat."

He started back toward town, and Bland Halliday followed him like a lonesome pup.

On the way, Johnny took stock of Bland in little quick glances from the corner of his eyes. Bland had been shabby when Johnny discovered him one day on the depot platform of a tiny town farther down the line. He had been shabbier after three weeks in Johnny's camp, working on the airplane in hope of a free trip to the Coast. But his shabbiness now surpassed anything Johnny had known, because Bland had evidently made pitiful attempts to hide it. That, Johnny guessed, was because of the hussy Bland had mentioned.

Bland's shoes were worn through on the sides, and he had blackened his ragged socks to hide the holes. Somewhere he had got a blue serge coat, from which the lining sagged in frayed wrinkles. His pockets were torn down at the corners; buttons were gone, grease spots and beer stains patterned the cloth. Under the coat he wore a pink-and-white silk shirt, much soiled and with the neck frankly open, imitating sport style because of missing buttons. He looked what he was by nature; what he was by training, —a really skilful birdman, —did not show at all.

He begged a smoke from Johnny and slouched along, with an aimless garrulity talking of his hard luck, now curiously shot with hope. Which irritated Johnny vaguely, since instinct told him whence that hope had sprung. Still, sympathy made him kind to Bland just because Bland was so worthless and so miserable.

At a dingy, fly-infested place called "Red's Quick Lunch" whither Johnny, mindful of his low finances, piloted him, Bland ordered largely and complained because his "T bone" was too rare, and afterwards because it was tough. Johnny dined on "coffee and sinkers" so that he could afford Bland's steak and "French fried" and hot biscuits and pie and two cups of coffee. The cat, he told himself grimly, was not content with a saucer of milk. It was on the top shelf of the pantry, lapping all the cream off the pan!

Afterwards he took Bland to the hotel where his room was paid for until the end of the week, led him up there, produced an old suit of clothes that had not seemed to wear a sufficiently prosperous air for the owner of an airplane, and suggestively opened the door to the bathroom.

Bland took the clothes and went in, mumbling a fear that he would do himself mortal injury if he took a bath right after a meal.

"If you die, you'll die clean, anyway," Johnny told him grimly. So Bland took a bath and emerged looking almost respectable.

Johnny had brought his second-best shoes out, and Bland put them on, pursing his loose lips because the shoes were a size too small. But Johnny had thrown Bland's shoes out of the window, so Bland had to bear the pinching.

Johnny sat on the edge of the dresser smoking and fanning the smoke away from his round, meditative eyes while he looked Bland over. Bland caught the look, and in spite of the shoes he grinned amiably.

"I take it back, bo, what I said about gratitude. You got it, after all."

"Huh!" Johnny grunted. "Gratitude, huh?"

"I knowed you wouldn't throw down a friend, old top. I was in the dumps. A feller'll talk most any way when he's feeling the after effects, and is hungry and broke. Now I'm my own man again. What next? Name it, bo —I'm game."

"Next," said Johnny, "is bed, I guess. You're clean, now-you can sleep here."

Bland showed that he could feel the sentiment called compunction.

"Much obliged, bo-but I don't want to crowd you —"

"You won't crowd me," said Johnny drily, "I aim to sleep with the plane." Bland may have read Johnny's reason for sleeping with his airplane, but beyond one quick look he made no sign. "Still nuts over it —I'll say you are," he grunted. "You wait till you've been in the game long as I have, bo."

With a blanket and pillow bought on his way through the town, Johnny disposed himself for the night under the nose of the plane with the wheels of the landing gear at his back. He was not by nature a suspicious young man, but he knew Bland Halliday; and to know Bland was to distrust him.

He felt that he was taking a necessary precaution, now that he knew Bland was in Tucson. With the landing gear behind him, no one could move the airplane in the night without first moving him.

Now that he thought of it, Bland had been left fifty miles farther down the line, to catch his train. Tucson was a perfectly illogical place for him to be in, even for the purpose of carousing. One would certainly expect him to hurry to the city of his desires and take his pleasure there. Johnny decided that Bland must still have an eye on the plane.

That he was secretly envious of Bland as an aviator did not add to his mental comfort. Bland could speak with slighting familiarity of "the game," and assume a boredom not altogether a pose. Bland had drunk deep and satisfyingly of the cup which Johnny, to save his honor, must put away from him after a tantalising sip or two. Not until Bland had said, "Wait till you've been in the game as long as I have," had Johnny realized to the full just what it would mean to him to part with his airplane without being accepted by the government as an aviator.

At the Rolling R, when his conscience debt to Sudden pressed so heavily, he had figured very nicely and had found the answer to his problem without much trouble. To enlist as an aviator with his airplane, or to sell the plane in Tucson, turn the proceeds over to Sudden to pay his debt and enlist as an aviator without the machine, had seemed perfectly simple. Either way would be making good the mistakes of his past and paving the way for future achievements. Parting with the plane had not promised to so wrench the very heart out of him when he fully expected to fly faster and farther in airplanes owned by the government; faster and farther toward the goal of all red-blooded young males: glory or wealth, the hero's wreath of laurel or the smile of dame Fortune.

Mary V stood on the heights waiting for him, as Johnny had planned and dreamed. He would come back to her a captain, maybe-perhaps even a major, in these hot times of swift achievement. They would all be proud to shake his hand, those jeering ones who called him Skyrider for a joke. Captain Jewel would not have sounded bad at all. But —

There is no dodging the finality of Uncle Sam's no. They had not wanted Johnny Jewel to fly for fame and his country's honor. And if he sold his own airplane, how then would he fly? How could he ever hope to be in the game as long as Bland had been? How could he do anything but go back meekly to the Rolling R Ranch and ride bronks for Mary V's father, and be hailed as Skyrider still, who had no more any hope of riding the sky?

Gloom at last plumbed the depths of Johnny's soul, and showed him where grew the root of his unalterable determination to combat Mary V's plan to have him at the ranch. Much as he loved Mary V he would hate going back to the dull routine of ranch life. (And after all, a youth like Johnny loves nothing quite so much as his air castles.) As a rider of bronks he was spoiled, he who had ridden triumphant the high air lanes. He had talked of paying his debt to Sudden, he had talked of his self-respect and his honesty and his pride-but above and beyond them all he was fighting to save his castle in the air. Debt or no debt, he could never go back to the Rolling R and be a rancher. Lying there under his airplane and staring up at the starred purple of the night he knew that he could not go back.

Yet he knew too that once he had sold his airplane he would be almost as helpless financially as Bland Halliday, unless he returned to the only trade he knew, the trade of riding bronks and performing the various other duties that would be his portion at the Rolling R.

Johnny pictured himself back at the Rolling R; pictured himself riding out with the boys at dawn after horses, or sweating in the corrals, spitting dust and profanity through long, hot hours. There was a lure, of course; a picturesque, intangible attraction that calls to the wild blood of youth. But not as calls this other life which he had tasted. There was no gainsaying the fact-ranch life had grown too tame, too stale for Johnny Jewel. And there was no gainsaying that other fact-that Mary V would have to reconcile herself to being an aviator's wife, if she would mate with Johnny.

He went to sleep thinking bitterly that neither he nor Mary V need concern themselves at present over that point. It would be some time before the issue need be faced, judging from Johnny's present prospects.

Chapter Three. Johnny Would do Stunts

Bland woke him, just as day was coming. A new Bland, fresh shaven, —with Johnny's razor, — and with a certain languid animation in his manner that was in sharp contrast to his extreme dejection of the night before.

"Thought I'd come out and see if you was going to make a flight this morning," he said. "It's a good morning for it, bo. How's she working, these days? Old man at the ranch wouldn't let me try her out after I'd fixed her up; said you was too sick to have the motor going. So I couldn't be sure I'd made a good job of it. Give you any trouble?"

Johnny sat up and knuckled his eyes, his mouth wide open in a capital O. It seemed to him that Bland had his nerve, and he guessed shrewdly that the aviator was simply making sure of his breakfast. When cats come back they have a fashion of hanging around the kitchen, he remembered. Oh, well, there was nothing to be gained by being nasty and even Bland's company was better than none.

"Hey, ain't yuh awake yet? I asked yuh how the motor's acting."

"O —o —h, aw-righ!" yawned Johnny, blinking around for his boots. "I ain't been flying much. Just flew over here from the ranch, and a little circle now and then when something come along that looked like money. I wanted to keep her in good shape in case the gover'ment —"

"Trying to sell it back to the gover'ment, huh? I coulda told yuh, bo, they wouldn't take it as a gift. She's a back number now —a has-been, from the gover'ment viewpoint. Why don't you keep it? What yuh want to sell it for, f'r cat's sake? She's a gold mine if you know how to work it, bo-take it from me."

"Well, I wish to thunder you'd show me the gold, then," Johnny retorted crossly, pulling on his boots.

"Lend us a smoke, will yuh, old top? The money's here, all right, if yuh just know how to get it out. And flying for the gover'ment ain't the way. I'll say a man's got to be his own boss if he wants to pull down real money. Long as you're workin' for somebody else, he's getting the velvet. You ain't, believe me. And the gover'ment as a boss —"

"Well, good golly, come to the point!" snapped Johnny. "How can I make money with this plane?" He gave it a disgruntled look, and turned to Bland. "She's a bird of a millionaire's toy, if you ask me," he said. "She's a fiend for gas and oil, and every time you turn 'er around there's some darned thing to be fixed or replaced. I'm about broke, trying to keep her up till I can sell out. It's coffee and sinkers for you, old timer, if you're going to eat on me. Another meal like you had last night, and we'll both have to skip a few in order to buy gas to joy-ride some cheap sport that lets on he's thinking of buying. I suppose your idea is —"

"F'r cat's sake give me a chance to tell yuh! Course you'll go broke trying to support the plane. You're goin' at it backwards. Make the plane support you. That's my idea. And you do it by exhibition flying for money-not sailin' around giving the whole damn country a free treat.

"I know-you think I'm a bum and all that; maybe you think I'm a crook, fer all I know. And you turn up your nose at anything I say. But lemme tell yuh, old top, I ain't a D. and O. because I never made any money flyin'. It's because I blowed what I made. And it's because I made so damn' much it went to my head and made a fool outa me. Listen here, bo: I bought me a Stutz outa what I earned flyin' in one season-and I blowed money right and left and smashed the car and like to of broke my neck, and had to pay damages to the other feller that peeled my roll down to the size of a pencil. The point is, it took *money* to do them things, didn't it? And I made it flyin' my own plane. That's what you want to soak into your system. *I made big money flying.* What I done with the money don't need to worry you-you ain't copyin' me for morals.

"Now what you want to do is learn some stunts, first off. You learn to loop and tail-slide and the fallin' leaf, and to write your name, and them things. It ain't so hard-not for a guy like you that ain't got sense enough to be afraid of nothing. The way you went off in that plane with the girl made my hair stand on end, and that's no kiddin', neither. If you'd had a fear germ in your system you wouldn't 'a' done that. But you done it, and got away with it, is the point.

And you been gittin' away with it right along-and you not knowin' your motor any more'n I know ridin' on a horse!"

"Aw, say! That's goin' too far," protested Johnny, but Bland gave him no heed.

"You learn the stunts-early in the morning when there ain't the hull town out to rubber-and then pull off an exhibition or two. Seventy-five dollars is the least you ever need to expect. Don't go in the air for less. From that up-depends on how spectacular you are. The public loves to watch for the death fall. That's what they pay to see-not hopin' you get killed, but not wantin' to miss seeing it in case yuh do. And with this the only airplane around here-why, say, bo, it's a cinch!"

Johnny fanned the smoke away from his face and eyed Bland with lofty tolerance. "And where do you expect to come in? You needn't kid yourself into hoping I'll take you for a self-forgetful martyr person. What's the little joker, Bland?"

Bland turned his pale, opaque stare upon Johnny for a minute. "Aw, for cat's sake, gimme the doubt, bo! I'm human in more ways than tryin' to see how much booze I kin lap up. It's a chance I want to start fresh. This bumming around ain't getting me anything. I'm sick of it. You gotta be learnt to do exhibition stuff, and I'm the guy that can learn yuh. You'll want a mechanician to keep your motor in shape. I can *make* a motor, gimme the tools. You want somebody that knows the game to kinda manage things. You're Skyrider Johnny, same as the boys at the ranch calls yuh. You gotta have a flunkey, ain't yuh? I'm willin' to be it. I'll change my name, so nobody needs to know it's Bland Halliday. Or you can gimme a share in the net profits, and I'll keep the name and make it pull things our way. They's no use talking, bo, I've got the goods! The name Bland Halliday is a trademark for flyin' —and never mind if it also stands for damfool. I'll brace up and give yuh the best I got. Honest, that's what I want —a chance to get on my feet agin. I'd ruther help you fly your plane than fly one of my own. I'd run amuck agin if I owned anything I could raise money on.

"If you think I tried to do you dirt, back there in the desert, bo, you're wrong. Ab-so-lutely. I thought you was fixing to double-cross me, and git away with the plane and leave me there. It got my goat —I'll say it did-that desert stuff. So I hid the gas, so you couldn't go off and leave me. But that's behind us. You can give me a chance now to straighten up, and I can put you in the way to make big money. You think it over, bo. They's no great hurry, and we can make a flight now and see how she stacks up. Be a sport-go fill up the tank and let's go."

Johnny ground the cigarette stub under his heel in the dirt, shrugged his shoulders with a fine imitation of perfect indifference, and yawned. He would think over Bland's idea. He did not, of course, intend to fall for anything that did not look like good business, and he was not at all anxious to have Bland for a partner. Indeed, having Bland for a partner was about the last thing Johnny would ever expect himself to do. Still, there was no harm in letting Bland down easy. A flight or two, maybe, would give Johnny some good pointers. He had learned much from Bland, in a very short time, he admitted readily to himself. He could learn more, and he could let Bland go over the motor. By that time he would maybe have a buyer. If not, he would have time to decide about exhibition flying.

Johnny did not know that as he went after gas his step was springier than it had been for a long, long while. He did not know why it was that he whistled while he filled the torpedo-shaped tank-indeed, Johnny did not even know that he whistled, nor that it was the first time since he had worked over his plane down at Sinkhole Camp when all his dreams were bright, and bad luck had not knocked at his door. Yet he did whistle while he made ready for flight, and his eyes were big and round and eager, said he moved with the impatient energy of a youth going to his favorite game. These signs Mary V would have recognized immediately; Johnny did not know the signs existed.

Bland helped himself to a pair of new coveralls of Johnny's and tinkered with the motor. Johnny went around the plane, testing cables and trying to conceal even from himself his new hope of keeping it.

"All right, bo," Bland announced at last. "Kick the block away and let's run her out. She sounds pretty fair-better than I expected."

It pleased Johnny that Bland seemed to take it as a matter of course that he should occupy the front seat. The last time they had flown together, Bland had occupied it perforce, with Johnny and two guns behind him. After all, Johnny reflected, he would not have been so suspicious of Bland if Mary V had not influenced him. And every one knows that girls take notions with very little reason for the foundation. Bland was a bum, but the little cuss seemed to want to make good, and a man would be pretty poor stuff that wouldn't help a fellow reform.

With that comfortable readjustment of his mental attitude toward the birdman, Johnny strapped himself in, pulled down his goggles while Bland eased in the motor. He saw Bland glance to right and left with the old vigilance. He felt the testing of controls, the unconscious tensing of nerves for the start. They raced down the calf pasture, nosed upward and went whirring away from a dwindling earth, straight toward the heart of the dawn.

It was like drinking of some heady wine that blurs one's troubles and pushes them far down over the horizon. Johnny forgot that he had problems to solve or worries that nagged at him incessantly. He forgot that Mary V, away off there to the southwest, had probably cried herself to sleep the night before because he had disappointed her. He was flying up and away from all that. He was soaring free as a bird, and the rush of a strong, clean wind was in his face. The roar of the motor was a great, throbbing harmony in his ears. For a little while the world would hold nothing else.

They were climbing, climbing, writing an invisible spiral in the air. Bland half turned his head, and Johnny caught his meaning with telepathic keenness. They were going to loop, and Bland wanted him to yield the control and to watch closely how the thing was done.

They swooped like a hawk that has seen a meadow mouse amongst the grass. They climbed steeply, swung clean over, so that the earth was oddly slipping past far above their heads; swung down, flattened out and flew straight. It was glorious.

A second time Bland looped, and yet again. It was exactly as Johnny had known it would be. He who had flown so long in his day-dreaming, who had performed wonderful acrobatics in his imagination, felt the sensation old, accustomed, milder even than in his dreams.

Once more, and he did the loop himself, hardly conscious of Bland's presence. Bland turned his head, signalling, and did a flop, righted, and was flying straight in the opposite direction. Again, and flew southeast by the sun. They practised that manoeuver again and again before Johnny felt fairly sure of himself, but once he did it he was one proud young man!

All this while the familiar landmarks were slipping behind them. Tucson was out of sight, had they thought to look for it. And all this while the sturdy motor was humming its song of force triumphant. Subsequently it stuttered faintly in expressing itself. Triumph was there, but it was not so joyously sure of itself. Bland glided, cocking an anxious ear to listen while he slowed the motor. It was there, the stutter-more pronounced than before; and once that pulsing power begins to flag a little and grow uncertain, there is but one thing to do.

They glided another ten miles or so before Bland picked a spot that looked safe for landing. They had one ill-chosen landing still vivid in their memory, and Johnny carried a long, white scar along the side of his head and a tenderness of the scalp to assist him in remembering.

Wherefore they came down circumspectly in a flat little field beside a flat little stream, with a huddle of flat dwellings drawn back shyly behind a thin group of willows. They came down gently, bouncing toward the willows as though they meant to drive up to the very doorway of the nearest hut. As they came on, their great wings out-spread rigidly, the propeller whirring at slackened speed, the motor sputtering unevenly, the doorway spewed forth three fat squaws and some naked papooses who fled shrieking into the brush behind the willows.

Chapter Four. Mary V to the Rescue

Mary V Selmer was a young woman of quick impulses, a complete disdain for consequences as yet unseen, and a disposition to have her own way, to override obstacles man-made or sent by fate to thwart her desires. Ask any man on the Rolling R Ranch, where Mary V was born; they will bear witness that this is true.

Mary V had fired the first gun in the battle of wills. She had told Johnny Jewel that she would expect him to fly straight to the ranch-if Johnny loved her. Mary V did not mean to seem dictatorial; she merely wanted Johnny to come back to the Rolling R, and she took what seemed to her to be the surest means of bringing him. So, serenely sure of Johnny's love, she had no misgivings when the sun went down and those wonderful, opal tints of the afterglow filled all the sky.

Johnny would be hungry, of course. She wheedled Bedelia, the cook, into letting her keep the veal roast hot in the oven of the gasoline range. She herself spread one of mommie's cherished lunch cloths on Bedelia's little square table in the kitchen alcove, where she and Johnny could be alone while he ate. She dipped generously into the newest preserves and filled a glass dish full for him. She raided the great refrigerator, closing her eyes to the morrow's reckoning. Johnny would be hungry, Johnny was a sort of prodigal, and the fatted calf should be killed figuratively and the ring placed upon his finger.

She told her mommie and her dad that Johnny was coming, and that everything was all right, and Johnny would be sensible and settle down now, because he was not going to enlist after all. She kissed them both and flew back to the kitchen because she had thought of something else that Johnny would like to eat.

This, you must understand, was while Johnny was feeding Bland, —and himself, —in "Red's Quick Lunch", and worrying because Bland tactlessly chose such expensive fare as T-bone steak and French fried. She was out on the porch, watching the sky toward Tucson and looking rather wistful, while Johnny was generously sorting out clothes for Bland and insisting upon the bath and the change before Bland should sleep in Johnny's bed. Mary V, you will observe, had no telepathic sense at all.

She watched while dark came and brought its star canopy, —and did not bring Johnny. Long after she saw the rim of hills draw back into vague shadows, she remained on the porch and listened for the hum of the airplane speeding toward her. He would come, of course; he loved her.

Johnny did love her more than he had ever loved any one in his life, but a man's love is not like a woman's love, they say.

"He must have had some trouble with his motor," Mary V observed optimistically to her sleepy parents, when their early bedtime arrived. "I'm going to leave the lights all on, so he'll see where to land. It will be tremendously exciting to hear him come buzzing up in the dark. It'll sound exactly like an air raid-only he won't have any bombs to drop."

"He'll have himself to drop," her mother tactlessly pointed out. "I guess he won't do much flying around in the dark, Mary V. Not if he's got sense enough to come in when it rains. You go to bed, and don't be setting out there in the mosquitoes. They're thick, to-night."

"Well, for gracious sake, mom! It's perfectly easy to fly at night. Over in France they *always* —"

"It's the lightin' I'm talking about," her mother interrupted with that terrible logic that insists upon stating unpleasant truths, "And this ain't France, Mary V. You go on to bed. I'm going to turn out the lights."

"And have him bump right into the house? A person would think you wanted Johnny to smash himself all to pieces again! And it isn't going to cost anything so terrible to leave the lights on for another little minute, mom! A few cents' worth of gas will run the dynamo —"

"For land's sake, Mary V, don't go into a tantrum just at bedtime. Who's talking about cost? Your father can't sleep with all the lights turned on in the house, and neither can I. And it ain't a particle of use for you to sit up and wait for Johnny; he won't come to-night, and you needn't look for him."

Mary V did not want to hear a statement of that kind, even if it were a mere argumentative flourish on the part of a selfish, unsympathetic parent who would jeopardize a person's life rather than annoy herself with a light or two burning. Mary V immediately had what her mother called a tantrum. That is, she began to cry and to declaim unreasonably that no one cared whether Johnny smashed himself all to pieces in the dark-that perhaps certain persons wished that Johnny would fall and be killed, just so they could sleep!

Her mother may have been weak in discipline, but now that Mary V was spoiled to the extent of having tantrums, she proved herself a sensible, level-headed sort of woman. She went away to her bed quite unmoved by the tears and self-pity, and left Mary V alone.

"You turn out all the lights except the porch light, Mary V," Old Sudden himself commanded from his bedroom door. "I guess if he comes, one light will be as good as a dozen. You better do as your mother tells you. The kid's got more sense than to tackle flying from Tucson after sundown. If I thought he didn't have, I'd kick him off the ranch!"

This perfectly heartless statement served to distract Mary V's mind from her mother's lack of feeling. She obediently turned out the lights, —all the lights, since they meant to kill Johnny in cold blood! —and wept anew upon the darkened porch, while swarms of mosquitoes hummed just without the screen, sending a slim scout through now and then to torment Mary V, who spatted her chiffon-covered arms viciously and wished that she were dead, since no one had any feelings or any heart or any conscience on that ranch.

It was midnight before healthy youth demanded sleep and dulled her half-feigned agonies of self-pity. It was morning before she began to feel really uneasy about Johnny. After her tantrum she slept late, so that when she awoke it was past time for Johnny's arrival, supposing he had started at sunrise, which she now admitted to herself was the most sensible time for the flight. Eight o'clock-and he must have started, else he would have called her up on the 'phone and told her he was not coming. For that matter, he would have called up the night before if he had not meant to do as she wanted him to do. Of course, Johnny was awfully stubborn sometimes, and he might have waited until morning, just to worry her. But he would have called up if he hadn't intended to come. A little thing like hanging up her receiver would not bother him, she argued, and a little obstacle like long-distance toll never occurred to Mary V, whose idea of poverty was vague indeed.

He must have started this morning, at the latest. And he should have been here before now. To make sure that he had not come while she slept Mary V went to a window overlooking the open space between the house and corrals. It was empty, but to make doubly sure she asked Bedelia. For answer, Bedelia threatened to quit, declaring shrilly that she would not work where nothing was safe under lock and key, and a girl might work her fingers to the bone putting up jell for spoiled, ungrateful, meddlesome Matties to waste, and so forth and so on.

Mary V wisely withdrew from the kitchen without having her question answered. She asked no more questions of any one. In silk kimono and Indian moccasins, one of her pet incongruities, she forthwith explored the yard down by the corrals which the bunk house had hidden from her view. There was no sign of Johnny Jewel's airplane anywhere. Mary V was thorough, even to the point of looking for tracks of the little wheels, but at last she was convinced, and returned to the porch to digest the ominous fact of Johnny's failure to arrive.

He must have started, —she would not admit the possibility that he had deliberately ignored her ultimatum, —but she would make sure. So she called Tucson on the telephone and was presently in conversation with the clerk at Johnny's hotel.

Hotel clerks are usually quite positive that they know what they are supposed to know about their guests. This clerk interviewed somebody while Mary V held the line, and later returned to assure her that Mr. Jewel had been seen leaving the lobby the night before, and had not returned. A strange young gentleman had occupied Mr. Jewel's room. No, Mr. Jewel had not been seen since last evening. The clerk was positive, but since Mary V's voice was young and feminine, he permitted her to hold the line while he called the night clerk to the 'phone. The result was disheartening. Mr. Jewel had brought in a young man, and later had left the hotel. The young man had gone out very early and neither had returned. Could he do anything else for her?

Mary V thanked him coldly and hung up the receiver, mentally calling the clerk names that were not flattering. Why in the world did he keep harping on that one fact that Johnny had gone out and had not come back? Why didn't he know where Johnny had gone? What, for gracious sake, was a hotel clerk for, if not to tell a person what she wanted to know? The strange young man who had slept in Johnny's room meant nothing at all to Mary V just then.

She had a dislike of creating unnecessary excitement, but it did seem as though something ought to be done about Johnny. All her faith was pinned to the fact that he had let her final word stand uncontradicted; he had not told her he would not come. She went outside and stared for awhile in the direction of Tucson, turning with a little start when her mother spoke just behind her.

"Did Johnny tell you he was coming, Mary V?"

"My goodness, mom! Of *course*, he-well, it was just the same as saying he would. I told him he had to come and I'd expect him, and he didn't say he wouldn't. Why, for gracious sake, do you suppose I went and fixed his din-dinner —?" Mary V gulped down a sob she had not suspected was present.

"Well, there, now, don't cry about it. You'll have plenty better reasons to cry after you're married to him. Seems to me the boy's changed considerable, if he comes and goes at the crook of your finger, Mary V. Johnny's most as stubborn as you be, if I'm any judge. If I was in your place, Mary V, I'd 'phone and find out if he's started, before I commenced crying because he was late."

"I did 'phone. And he wasn't at the hotel —"

"Land sakes, child, I heard you! You might as well have asked what the weather was like. If I was you I'd ask if his airplane is there. If it is, there's no sense in you straining your eyes looking for it. If it ain't, he's likely on the way somewhere. But from what I heard of your talk last night, and from what I know about Johnny —"

"For pity's *sake*, mom! If you listened in —"

"There now, Mary V, you shouldn't object to your own mother overhearing anything you've got to say. And if you expect me to clap my hands over my cars and start on a long lope across the desert the minute you begin to 'phone —"

Mary V laughed and gave her mother a bear-hug. Mommie was a plump matron, and the idea of her loping across the desert with her hands over her ears was funny. "You do have tremendously sensible ideas, mommie, though you simply do not understand Johnny as I do. I am perfectly positive that he would not disappoint me. However, I'll just make sure when he started. I'm so afraid of some horrible accident —"

"Well, you 'phone first, before you begin to borrow trouble," her mother advised her shrewdly. "I know if you had laid down the law to me the way you did to Johnny, I'd stay away if it was the last thing I did on earth. And Johnny —"

Mary V called Tucson again, and mommie subsided so as not to interrupt. There was a delay while the hotel clerk obligingly sent a boy over to where Johnny kept his airplane. While she waited for his ring, Mary V went restlessly out to watch the sky toward Tucson. Half an hour slipped away. Mary V was just declaring pettishly that she could walk to Tucson and find out, while she waited for that idiotic clerk, when he called her. Mary V listened, hung up the receiver with trembling fingers, and went to find her mother in the kitchen.

"Mommie, the plane is gone, and they are almost sure he went last night, because he was seen going that way after he left the hotel. So he did start, just as I told him to do-and something awful has happened to him-and where's dad?"

Mary V's father, whom men for some unaccountable reason called "Sudden" when he was not present, crawled out from under the rear end of his battered touring car when Mary V's moccasins and the fluttering hem of blue kimono moved within his range of vision. Sudden's face was smudged with black grease and the dust of the desert, and in his hand was a crescent wrench worn shiny where it had nipped nuts and bolts.

"You musta done some fancy driving the other day," he greeted his anxious-faced daughter. "Didn't you know you was sliding a wheel every time you threw on the brake? Wonder to me is you didn't skid off a grade somewhere!" He hitched himself into a new and uncomfortable pose and set the wrench on a nut, screwing his well-fed face into an agonized grimace while he put his full strength into the turn. "If I could find a man that I'd trust my life with on these roads, I'd have me a chauffeur," he grumbled for the millionth time. "That reformed blacksmith musta welded these nuts on to the bolts," he added, and muttered something savage when the wrench slipped and he barked a knuckle. "Well, what yuh want? Go ahead and have it, or do it-only don't stand watching me when I'm trying to —" He gritted his teeth, threw the wrench away and picked up another. "Go ask your mother," he exclaimed. "Tell her I'll let you if she will."

At another time Mary V would have deeply resented the implication that she never approached her dad save when she wanted something; or more likely she would have stated her want before her dad had time to speak. Just now she was hopefully watching a buzzard that sailed on outstretched, rigid wings, high in the sky. It seemed to be circling toward the ranch, and it looked like an airplane flying very high. Mary V's heart forgot to beat while she watched it. But the buzzard sighted something, flapped its wings and went off in another direction, and the girl winced as though some one had dropped a leaden weight on her chest.

"Dad!" The voice did not sound like Mary V's, and her father ducked his head out where he could look up at her with startled attention. "We must have the car-and all the boys-and get out and find Johnny. He-he started in his airplane, to come to the ranch. And they haven't seen him since last night, and-and you know what happened at Sinkhole!"

Sudden got heavily to his feet and stood looking down at her, his whimsical mouth slack with dismay. But he pulled himself together and took the dominant, cool initiative which was so much a part of his nature.

"You say he started last night. How do you know?"

"The hotel clerk —I 'phoned-oh, don't start cross-questioning, dad! I *know*! His plane is gone, and-he should have been here last night! He was alone, and-oh, get the boys and start them out! There isn't a minute-he may be dead somewhere-or hurt —"

"Now, now, we'll only bungle things by getting excited, Mary V. I'll send the cook after the boys while I fix this brake and fill up the gas tank. You go get some clothes on, and tell your mother to get the emergency box ready, in case he's hurt. And if you can be calm enough, you 'phone to Tucson to the sheriff, and tell him to send out a party from that end, and work this way. Tell them to scatter out, but keep the general airline to the ranch. We'll start in from here. And for Lord's sake, baby, don't look like that! We'll find him-and the chances are he's all right; maybe landed for some little repair or something. Now hurry along, if you expect to go with me, because I won't wait a minute."

Mary V looked at her dad, standing there grease-smudged and calm and capable, and half the terror went out of her eyes to leave room for hope. Her dad had such a way of gathering up the threads of logic and drawing them firmly into coherent action-just as a skilled driver would take the slack reins of a runaway team and pull them down to a steady pace. It seemed to her that Johnny Jewel was half found before ever her dad laid down the wrench and began unscrewing the cap of the gas tank.

Like a fluttering bluebird she flew back to the house to do his bidding. Excited she was, and worried, and more than ever inclined to exclamation points and unfinished sentences; but she was no longer panic-stricken. She was the Mary V who would move heaven and earth and slosh all the water out of our five oceans in her headlong determination to do what she had set out to do.

In two minutes she had her mother and Bedelia rushing around like scared hens, trying to collect the things she wanted to take for Johnny's comfort and welfare. In three she was bullying the long-distance operator. In five she was laying down the law to the sheriff, just as though he were one of her father's cowpunchers.

"Get all the men you can," she commanded, when she had reached the details, "and scatter them like a round-up. You know how, of course. And keep them within sight of each other, and make them keep watch in every hollow and wash and high brush-because an airplane might not show up very plainly if it's all smashed. And 'phone to all the places down this way, and make all the men you can get out and help. It's tremendously important that you find Mr. Jewel immediately, because he may be badly hurt. My father will give a thousand dollars to the man who finds him. You tell that to every one, Mr. Sheriff, will you, please? And say that the Rolling R will pay well for the time of those who aren't lucky enough to win the reward. We will pay every man twenty-five dollars that goes out. And have an automobile follow you, with a doctor in it, to take care of John-Mr. Jewel, when he is found. We will start all our riders out from here, and ride until we meet you. Now hurry! Don't stop for a lot of red tape and orders and things-get right out on the trail. And don't forget the thousand dollars reward." Just when the sheriff was saying "Aw right-goo'by," Mary V thought of something else.

"Be sure and have every man carry an extra canteen for Mr. Jewel. Injured men are always tremendously thirsty. And don't forget that every man will get twenty-five dollars, and the man that finds him —"

The sheriff had hung up, which was rude of him. Mary V had several other little suggestions to make-but men never do want to be told anything, especially by a woman. Mary V was glad she had not been permitted to say that the sheriff would of course receive an especially attractive reward. He could go without, now, just for his smartness.

The Rolling R boys, hastily summoned by the cook who had galloped off without removing his flour-sack apron, came racing in and saddled fresh mounts. In a surprisingly short time they were filling canteens and gathering in a restive circle around the big touring car where the boss sat behind the wheel, and Mary V, fidgeting on the seat beside him, was telling them all for gracious sake to hurry up and get started, and not fool around until dark.

Bill Hayden got his orders, leaning down from his horse so that Mary V's impatient young voice should not submerge her father's in Bill's big, sun-peeled ears. "All right-better scatter out right now, soon as we git past the fence. You foller along about in the middle." He wheeled and was gone, overtaking the boys who were already starting for the gate, which little Curley held open until the last man should pass.

Sudden stepped on the starter, the big car began to gurgle. The search was on. A hundred men were presently combing the desert land and looking for an airplane that had not flown that way-just because Johnny Jewel was true to his supreme purpose in life. And just because Johnny's whole heart and soul were set upon repaying a conscience debt to Mary V's father, Mary V herself was innocently saddling his conscience with a still greater debt. For that is the way Fate loves to set us playing at cross-purposes with each other.

Chapter Five. Gods or Something

"Well, here we are," Johnny announced with more cheerfulness than the occasion warranted. "Now what?"

Bland was staring slack-jawed after the squaws. "Wasn't them Injuns?" he wanted to know, and his voice showed some anxiety. "We want to get outa here, bo, while the gittin's good. You bring any guns?" His pale eyes turned to Johnny's face. "I'll bet they've gone after the rest of the bunch, and we don't want to be here when they git back. I'll say we don't!"

Johnny laughed at him while he climbed down. "We made a dandy landing anyway," he said. "What ails that darned motor? She didn't do that yesterday."

Bland grunted and straddled out over the edge of the cockpit, keeping an eye slanted toward the brush fringe. What Johnny did not know about motors would at any other time have stirred him to acrimonious eloquence. Just now, however, a deeper problem filled his mind. Could he locate the fault and correct it before that brush-fringe belched forth painted warriors bent on massacre? He pushed up his goggles and stepped forward to the motor.

"I put in new spark plugs just the other day," Johnny volunteered helpfully. "Maybe a connection worked loose-or something." He got up on the side opposite Bland, meaning to help, but Bland would have none of his assistance.

"Say, f'r cat's sake, keep a watch out for Injuns and leave me alone! I can locate the trouble all right, if I don't have to hang on to my skelp with both hands. You got a gun?"

"Yeah. Back in Tucson I have," Johnny suppressed a grin. Bland's ignorance, his childlike helplessness away from a town tickled him. "But that's all right, Bland. We'll make 'em think we're gods or something. They might make you a chief, Bland-if they don't take a notion to offer you up as a burnt offering to some other god that's got it in for yuh."

Bland, testing the spark plugs hastily, one after the other, dropped the screwdriver. "Aw, f'r cat's sake, lay off that stuff," he remonstrated nervously. "Fat chance we got of godding over Injuns this close to a town! They're wise to white men. Quit your kiddin', bo, and keep a watch out." And he added glumly, "Spark plugs is O.K. Maybe it's the timer. I'll have to trace it up. Quit turning your back on that brush! You want us both to git killed? Hand me out that small wrench."

"Say, I know what ailed them squaws, Bland. Gods is right. You know what they thought? They took us for their Thunder Bird lighting. I'll bet they're making medicine right now, trying to appease the Bird's wrath. And say, listen here, Bland. If they do come at us, all we've got to do is start up and buzz at 'em. There ain't an Injun on earth could face that."

Bland lifted a pasty face from his work. "Fat chance," he lamented. "You'd oughta brought your gun. Back there at Sinkhole you was damn generous with the artillery-there where you had no use for it. Now you fly into Injun country without so much as a sharp idea. Bo, you give me a pain!"

Johnny spied an Indian peering fearfully out from the branches of a willow. He ducked behind the motor and hissed the news to Bland. Bland nearly fell from his perch.

"Gawd!" he gasped, clinging to a strut while he stared fascinatedly in the direction Johnny had indicated. "Git in, bo, and we'll beat it. She may have power enough to hop us outa this death trap. We can come down somewheres else." He clawed back and climbed in feverishly.

Johnny emitted a convulsive snort. "Death trap" sounded very funny, applied to this particular bit of harmless landscape. Behind him, Bland was imploring him to hurry, and Johnny climbed in.

"You let me pilot the thing," he ordered. "I know Injuns. I still have hopes of saving our lives, Bland. We'll scare 'em to death. We'll be their Thunder Bird for 'em. Now lemme tell yuh, before we start-oh, we're safe for the present. They'll stutter some before they attack us in here-say, good golly, Bland! Is that your teeth chattering? Hold your jaws still, can't yuh, while I tell yuh what we'll do?"

"F'r cat's sake, hurry! I seen another one peekin' around the corner of the house!"

"Now listen, Bland. The Navajos have got a Thunder Bird mixed up in their religion, and I guess maybe these Injuns will have, too. If so, we are reasonably safe. They must not know we're plain human-we've got to be gods come down to earth, and this is the Thunder Bird. Or another kind of bird. We'll make 'em think that. They don't sabe flying machines-see? And we'll find out where they're all at, and fly low over their heads to convince them that didn't see us come down. It'll scare 'em, and work on their superstition, so when we come down again to locate that motor trouble, they'll stand in awe of us long enough to give us time to get in shape. You leave the soaring to me, Bland. I'll pull us through all right. Think she'll lift us off the ground?"

"She's *gotta* lift us!" Bland chattered. "She's runnin' better since we landed. And say, bo, don't go any closer to them —"

Johnny told him to shut up; he was running things. Whereupon he circled and taxied back down the field, thankful that the soil was sun-baked and hard. The motor ran smoothly again — a fact which Bland was too scared to notice. He gasped when Johnny turned back toward the huts, but beyond a protesting look over his shoulder he gave no sign of dissent.

They started to climb, got fifty feet from the ground and the motor began to spit and pop again. Then it stalled completely, and they came down and went bouncing over the uneven surface and stopped again, a rod or so nearer the willows than before.

Several scuttling figures left that particular hiding place like rabbits scared out of a covert, and Bland took heart again. A few minutes he spent crouched down in the cockpit, watching the willows, and when nothing happened he ventured forth, armed with pliers and wrench, and went at the motor.

"Sounds to me like poor contact," he diagnosed the trouble. "Like the breaker-points are roughened, maybe. You'll have to work the gawd stuff, bo, and work it right. Because if I start tearing into the hull ignition system, we ain't going to be able to hop outa here at a minute's notice, nor even start the motor and buzz at 'em."

"Fly at it," said Johnny, eyeing the huts speculatively. He was hungry, and certain odors floated to his nostrils. Something left cooking over a fire was beginning to scorch, if his nose told the truth, and it seemed a shame to let food burn when his stomach clamored to be filled.

With Bland watching him nervously, he crossed the little open space and entered the hut nearest, presently emerging with two flat cakes in his hand. Another hut yielded a pot of stew which he thought it wise not to analyze too closely. It was this which had begun to burn, but it was still fairly palatable. So, with a can of water from a muddy spring, they breakfasted, their hunger charitably covering much distrust and dulling for the time even Bland's fear of the place.

The sun, shining its Arizona fiercest though the season was early fall, brought a cooked-varnish smell from the wings. There was no shade save the scant shadow which the scraggly willows and brush cast over the edge of the parched field, and of that Bland refused to avail himself. He would rather roast, he said.

Johnny conscientiously carried the kettle back to the hut, then set to work helping Bland. Which help consisted mainly of turning the propeller whenever Bland wanted to start the motor; a heartbreaking task in that broiling heat, especially since the motor half the time would not start at all. Crimson, the perspiration streaming down his cheeks like tears, Johnny swung on that propeller until Bland's grating voice singing out "Contact!" stirred murder within his soul and he balked with the motor and crawled under a wing.

"You can start her yourself if you want to start," he growled when Bland expostulated. "I've turned that darned propeller enough to fly from here to New York. Why don't you get in and locate the trouble?"

"There ain't any trouble-not according to the look of things. Acts like water in the gas, or something. F'r cat's sake, don't lay down on the job now, bo! We gotta beat it outa here."

"I'm ready to go any time you are," Johnny retorted, mopping neck and chest while he lay sprawled on his back. "But I'd rather stay here till Christmas than get sun-struck trying to start, I'm all in."

Bland could not budge him and swore voluminously while he worked over the motor. Finally he too gave up and crawled under a wing where the heat was not quite so unendurable, and tried to think of something he had not done but which he might do to correct the motor trouble. No Indians having been sighted since their second landing, he could push his fear of them into the back of his mind until a dark face peered out at him again.

Miles away to the west men were sweating while they rode, searching for this very airplane that sat so placidly in the midst of an Indian corn field. Farther away the news went humming along the wires, of a young aviator lost with his airplane on the desert. The fame of that young aviator was growing apace while he lay there, casually wishing there was a telephone handy so he could call up Mary V and tell her he had a plan which might make him big money without his having to sell his plane.

Not once did it occur to him that any one would be especially concerned over his absence. Not once did he look upon this mishap as anything more serious than an unpleasant incident in the life of a flyer. He went to sleep, lying there under a wing of his plane, and presently Bland himself drifted off into dreams that would have been much less agreeable had he known that a full two dozen Indians had crawled into the willows and were peering timorously out at them.

It was past noon when Bland awoke. Johnny was still sound asleep, snoring a little now and then. Bland grumbled more profanity, sent a questing glance toward the willows and saw nothing to alarm him, crawled out into the searing sunlight and tried to work. But the motor was so hot he could not touch it anywhere. His pliers and wrenches were too hot to hold, and his face felt scorched where the sun fell upon it. So Bland crawled back again and cursed the land that knew such heat, and himself for being in it, and presently slept again.

Hunger woke Johnny at last, and he straight-way woke Bland, politely intimating that it was about time he got busy and did something. Johnny did not propose to settle down for life in that neighborhood, he pointed out. There must be something they could do, if the darned engine wasn't broken anywhere.

Bland, too miserable to argue, sat up and pushed greasy fingers through his lank hair. Having remained alive and unharmed for so long in that neighborhood, his faith in Johnny's knowledge of Indians waxed stronger. He began to think less of his danger and more about the motor.

The thing mystified him, who could tear a motor apart and put it together again. What he felt he ought to do was impossible for lack of the proper tools, Johnny's emergency kit being quite as useless for any real emergency as such kits usually are. Merely as an experiment he removed the needle valve and washed several specks of dirt off it with gasoline. Without hesitation the motor started, and Bland cursed himself quite sincerely for not having sooner thought of the simple expedient. He must be getting feeble-minded, he said, while he adjusted the mixture and made ready to fly.

Once more they taxied down the denuded corn field, turned and ascended buoyantly, boring into the hot breeze that rose as the shadows lengthened into late afternoon. They circled, climbing steadily. Then pop-pop-pop-pop —pop, the motor began to stutter. The earth lifted to them as if pulled up by a string. They could see more huts and tiny figures running like disturbed ants. The field where they had spent most of the day broadened beneath them, like a brown blanket spread to receive them.

They came down with a jolt that bent the axle of the landing gear, sent them bounding into the air, and all but wrecked them. They went ducking and wobbling up to the willow fringe and swung off just in time to escape plunging into a deep little creek. As they stopped they heard a great crackling of brush and glimpsed many forms fleeing wildly, but they were too engrossed in their own trouble to be greatly impressed. One wing had barely escaped damage with the tilting of the machine, and the near-catastrophe chilled them both with the memory of a certain other forced landing which had not ended so harmlessly. They climbed down soberly and inspected the landing gear.

"Well, that can be fixed," Bland stated in the tone of one who is grateful that worse has not befallen. "I'll say it was a close shave, though, bo."

"I'll try and straighten the axle, while you see what ails that cussed motor. Good golly! We'll be here all night at this rate. And if we keep on hopping over this field like a lame crow, we'll be plumb outa gas. For a mechanic that can *make* a motor, Bland, you sure ain't making much of a showing!"

"Aw, f'r cat's sake, lay off the crabbing! Gimme the tools and I'll rip your damn motor apart so quick it'll make your head swim! I'll say I've tied into a sweet mess of trouble when I tied up with you. I mighta knowed I'd git the worst of it. Look at what I was handed the other time I throwed in with you! Got stuck in a cave and had to live like a darned animal, and double-crossed when I'd helped you outa the hole you was in. And now you wish this job on to me and begin to lay the blame on me when this mess of junk fails to act like a motor. Come off down here with a monkey wrench and a can opener and expect me to rebuild a motor that oughta been junked ten year ago!"

"Aw, shut up!" snapped Johnny, and stalked off to find something they could eat. "Monkey wrench and can opener are about as many tools as you know how to use-unless maybe it's a corkscrew."

He went on, muttering because he had ever let himself be imposed upon by Bland Halliday. Muttering too because he had started out that morning to do stunts, instead of trying to find a buyer for the machine as he had first planned. Now the prospect of getting back to Tucson that night looked very remote indeed. And the winning of a fortune doing exhibition work looked even more remote. "Unless we take up a collection amongst the Injuns cached out in the brush," he grinned ruefully to himself. "We're liable to take up a collection all right, if we have to sleep here-but it won't be money."

Chapter Six. Fame Waits Upon Johnny

That day was a terrible one for Mary V. The big car went lurching here and there over roads that never expected an automobile to travel them, and Mary V watched and hoped and would not give up when even her dad showed signs of yielding to heat and discouragement.

Before noon they had met the sheriff and some of his men, and had compared notes and given what information they could. The sheriff, in a desert-scarred Ford loaded mostly with water and some emergency rations, had managed to scatter his men and yet keep in fairly close touch with them, and he seemed very sure that the search had been thorough as far as they had gone. Young Jewel, he asserted, had not so much as dropped a handkerchief on the ground they had covered, or his men would certainly have found it.

This, while it served as a temporary relief from the dread of hearing the worst, merely postponed the full knowledge of a disaster which Mary V could not bear to contemplate. They drove to a rendezvous previously agreed upon with Bill Hayden and gleaned what news the boys had to tell. Which was no news at all. Their search had been as barren of results as the sheriff's, and Mary V's eyes, when they turned from face to face, were hard to meet. Little Curley, who had been Johnny Jewel's especial admirer and champion when that youth was spending his days more or less tumultuously at the Rolling R Ranch, was seen to draw his shirt sleeve hastily across his eyes after he had confronted Mary V for a minute's questioning.

She watched with painful interest a car that came bouncing toward them over the rough trail they had taken. When it arrived their fears might become a terrible certainty. Two men occupied the dusty roadster, and neither was Johnny, and their haste implied great urgency. Mary V weakened to the point of covering her face with her hands as they drew near. But they were merely reporters anxious for news.

That afternoon other reporters appeared, and the next day an enterprising motion-picture concern had a camera man on the job. The mystery of the vanished airplane grew with the passing hours. The desert fairly swarmed with men, and theories were thick as lizards. On the second night beacon fires were burning on every hilltop, and water was being hauled in barrels to certain rest stations where the searchers could come and recuperate. Old Sudden achieved some front-page fame himself as a stalwart Napoleon of the desert-which he profanely resented, by the way.

On the third day Mary V was ordered to stay at home. There were reasons which her father did not care to dwell upon, which made it extremely undesirable that the girl should be present when her lover was discovered. And, since the search had narrowed to a point where discovery was practically certain within a few hours, Sudden was not to be cajoled or bullied.

Mary V was lying on the porch, wondering dully when the nightmare would end and she would wake up and find life just as it had always been, with Johnny alive and full of fun and ready to argue with her over every little thing. It seemed grotesquely impossible that her own innocent command that he come to her should result in all this horror.

Upheld at first by a frenzied hope that they should find him, she now dreaded the finding, and refused to reckon the time since she had last heard his voice over the telephone. Hurt and without water or food on the desert in all that heat-she set her teeth to stifle a groan. A little while ago when he had been so sure that he could enlist as a flyer, she had shrunk from the thought of his going to war. Before that, when he had lain unconscious for so many days there in the bedroom behind her; when a trained nurse had stood guard and would not let Mary V so much as look at Johnny, and the doctor had spoken glibly of hope, when his eyes told her how little hope there was, she had suffered terribly. She had thought that she had touched the depths of worry over Johnny-and she had not begun to know the meaning of the word.

She lay a small, huddled heap of heartache, shrinking from her own thoughts, shrinking from the sight of every one, dazed with terror of what she might hear if any one spoke. Into this nightmare jingled the telephone bell. Mary V gave a faint scream and put her hands over her ears.

"There, there, baby —I'll answer it," her mother's voice came soothingly, and Mary V shrank farther down in the hammock cushions.

"Oh-why-land alive! Just a minute-hold the line," she heard her mother say in a strange, flustered voice. Then she called, "Mary V —I guess you better come and —"

"Oh, I —*can't*, mommie! I'll go crazy if I have to hear —"

"There, there, baby, it's something you want to hear!"

Mary V's knees shook under her as she went to the telephone. Her voice was pinched and feeble when she tried to call the stereotyped hello.

"Oh, hello, Mary V. That you? I just got in, and I thought I'd better call up. I hear they're out looking for me —"

Mary V's eyes turned glassy. She made a faint sound and drooped forward until her forehead rested on the table. The receiver slid soundlessly into her lap and lay there while Johnny Jewel rattled on hurriedly.

"—And so after that happened, we were held up till dark getting the landing gear straightened out. And of course we couldn't fly very well after dark. And then next morning, after Bland had cleaned out the carburetor-say, it was straight mud in there and the screen was packed solid, so of course she didn't get gas half the time, and that's what ailed her-and when we did start, or was going to start, we found out there wasn't enough gas in the tank to take us home. So I had to catch an Injun and make him take a note to the nearest station for gas, and wait till he got back with some. I'd have sent word on to you, but I was in such a darned hurry I forgot-and the Injuns were all scared stiff, and it was only by making them understand I wanted water for the Bird, and nothing else would do."

"Mary V's fainted," mommie interrupted him then. "I guess it was too sudden, hearing you on the wire when she thought you was dead. You better wait and call up after awhile when her mind's more settled. She's had an awful hard time. I'm real glad you're all right, Johnny, but I've got to take care of Mary V now."

Johnny's eyes were very wide open when he came out of the telephone booth in the hotel lobby. That Mary V should faint when she heard his voice sounded rather incredible, but it seemed to confirm the strange intent looks and the flustered manners of every one around that hotel. People seemed to be flocking in from the street and from other parts of the hotel, and that they were gathering to gaze upon him, Johnny Jewel, came with a shock.

Three reporters came at him so impetuously that the foremost man skidded on the polished floor and all but fell. Bland was plucking at his elbow and whispering, "You let me handle the publicity, bo!" The clerk was staring at him, both palms planted firmly on the desk, and men were pushing up and craning for a look at him. Johnny whirled suddenly and retreated to the telephone booth, shutting the door tightly behind him. It was the first time in his life that he had run from any one.

To gain time, he called up the Rolling R Ranch again and managed to get Bedelia, the cook, on the 'phone. Bedelia was perfectly willing to tell all she knew, and she appeared to know a great deal. Johnny held the receiver to his ear until his elbow cramped, and said "uh-huh" once in a while, and wondered how much Bedelia was exaggerating the truth. As a matter of fact Bedelia was giving him a conservative history of the past three days and, indirectly, she was explaining the crowd in the lobby behind him.

Telephone booths are not any too comfortable on a hot day, and Johnny emerged rather limp and sober.

He edged in to where Bland was gesticulating in the center of a group that seemed to be drinking in his words eagerly.

"I'm going on to the ranch, Bland," he said shortly. "Jar loose here and come help get the machine ready."

"In a minute, bo. As I was saying —"

"Ah —I hear you had quite an adventure, Mr. Jewel, down among the Indians with your airplane. Now, just where —"

"I'm in a hurry," Johnny hedged. "I don't know anything about any adventure. We had a little carburetor trouble, and had to wait for gas before we could get back. That's all." He grabbed Bland firmly by one arm and hustled him outside, where men were seemingly waiting far his appearance.

"Oh, Mr. Jewel! I wish you'd tell me —"

"I'm in a hurry! Good golly, folks seem to think talking is all there is to do in this world! Come on, Bland." He hurried on, his mind absorbed in grasping the full significance of Bedelia's excited report of events at the Rolling R and this curious crowd that gaped at him. The thought of Mary V lying unconscious, stricken by the sound of his voice over the telephone, nagged at him persistently and unpleasantly. He had not told Bedelia that he was coming, and now he feared that his unheralded appearance might be another shock to Mary V; but he would not take the time to go back and warn her, for all that. Instead, he walked a little faster to where his plane was waiting.

"I think you're making a bad play, bo-duckin' out when all them newspaper guys are hot after dope on us," Bland expostulated while he drilled along beside his boss. "I give 'em some scarehead stuff, but they'd lap up a lot more. We can get a lot of valuable publicity right now if we play 'em right. I give 'em that gawd stuff for a start-off, and I made —"

"Shut up and save your breath," snapped Johnny. "I'm not chasing up any newspaper notoriety now."

"Well, it'd be better business if yah did, bo —I'll say it would. Why, it's free advertising we couldn't have pulled off on a bet, if we'd tried to frame it. Absolutely not. Well, mebby your duckin' out right now is a good play, too. It'll keep 'em chasin' yuh for more-and I'll say that's about the only way to handle them smart guys. Oncet you chase them, the stuff's off. You can bust your spine in four different places and wreck your machine, and mebby get a four- or five-line notice down in a corner next the dentist ads. It's worse, too, since the war begun. There ain't no more chance, hardly, of getting front-page publicity. Say, a couple of 'em took your picture. D' yuh know that?"

"No, and I don't care," Johnny retorted.

Just now nothing mattered save getting to the Rolling R as soon as possible and stopping that idiotic search for him. He hustled Bland around to such good purpose that by the time the reporters had trailed him to the hangar he was already in his seat and was barking "Contact!" at Bland, who was unhappily turning the propeller at stated intervals and wondering when he would ever again have a square meal, and hoping that no misfortune would delay their arrival at the Rolling R, where he remembered hungrily certain past achievements of the cook.

"Going back to your Indian tribe?" one smiling, sandy-haired fellow called out to Johnny.

"No. I'm going to the Rolling R!" Johnny retorted unguardedly. "Ready, Bland? Contact!"

The motor started, and Bland pulled down his cap. "His best girl lives at the Rolling R. He's goin' to see her," he informed the sandy-haired man as he passed him. "They're engaged." He climbed up and took his place, tickled at the chance to hand out more "dope." The sandy-haired one seemed tickled, too, until he saw that his ears had not been the only ones to drink in Bland's words.

They moved hastily aside as the big plane swung round and went down the field like a running plover. They watched it swing and come back, taking the air easily, thrumming its high, triumphant note. They tilted heads backward and followed it as Johnny circled, getting his altitude. They squinted into the sun to see the plane head straight away toward the Rolling R, its little wheels looking very much like the tucked-up feet of some gigantic bird, until it had dwindled to the rigid, dragon-fly outline.

"He's got nerve, that kid!" the sandy-haired one declared to his fellows. "Didn't care a whoop for publicity-did you fellows get that? I'd been wondering if it wasn't some frame-up, but it's on the level. That boy couldn't frame anything."

"Not with those eyes," a sallow companion agreed. "I seem to know that other bird. He's a crook, if I know faces."

"He's just the mechanic. He don't count. But that kid-say, I like that kid!" And he added enthusiastically, "Great story, that stuff the mechanic doped out for us. We'd never have pulled it out of the kid."

"I wish I could remember that bird. I ought to know him. Leaves a bad taste in my memory, somehow. You're right-it's some story."

Mary V wadded a soft cushion under the nape of her neck, looked again at Johnny sprawled in her dad's pet chair and smoking a cigarette after a very ample meal that had been served him half-way between dinner and supper, and stifled a sigh. Johnny was alive and well and full of enthusiasm as ever. He had just finished telling her all the wonderful things he could do and would do with his airplane, and the earnings he had hopefully mentioned ran into thousands of dollars, and left a nice marrying balance after her father's debt was paid. Yet Mary V felt a heaviness in her heart, and though she listened to all the wonderful things Johnny meant to do, she could not feel that they were really possible.

Something else troubled Mary V, but just now, with Johnny there before her almost like one risen from the grave, she dreaded to recognize the thing that shadowed the back of her mind. Johnny turned his head and looked at her, and she forced a smile that held so little joy that even Johnny was perturbed.

"What's the matter? Don't you believe I can do it?" he challenged her instantly. "There's no reason why I can't. It's being done all the time. Other flyers make as much money as your dad makes here on the ranch. And-you know yourself, Mary V, I couldn't settle down and be just a rider again. Fighting bronks is too tame, now-too slow. I'll have to make a flyer of you, Mary V, and then you'll know —"

Mary V suddenly buried her face in a cushion. Johnny heard a smothered sob and got up, looking very much astonished and perturbed. With a glance over his shoulder to make sure no one saw him, ho put an arm awkwardly around her shaking shoulders.

"If you don't want to fly, you needn't," he reassured her. "I didn't mean you had to. I only meant —"

"It-it isn't that at all," Mary V managed to enunciate more or less clearly. "But we've been simply crazy, worrying about you and thinking all kinds of horrible things, and —"

"Well, but I'm all right, you see, so you don't need to worry any more. I was all right all the time, if you had only known it. You don't want to let that give you a prejudice against flying. It's just as safe as riding bronks."

"It-it isn't the safeness." Mary V choked back a sob and wiped her eyes. "But you don't seem to take it seriously at all!"

"Now, you know I do! It's the most serious thing in my whole life —-except you, of course. And you know —"

"I don't mean that!" Mary Y gave a small stamp with her slipper toe on the porch floor, thereby proving how swiftly her resilient young self was coming back to a normal condition after the strain of the past forty-eight hours. "You ought to know what I mean."

Johnny sat down again and looked at her with his eyebrows pulled together. Mary V had always been more or less puzzling in her swift changes of mood, wherefore this sudden change in her did not greatly surprise him.

"Well, what do you mean, then?" he asked patiently. "Seems to me I've been taking everything too seriously to suit you, till just this minute. I've been pretty serious, let me tell you, about making good, and now I can see my way clear for the first time since all those horses were run off right under my nose, while I was busy with my airplane, getting it in shape to fly. You've been after me all the time because I couldn't let things slide. Don't you think, Mary V, you're kinda changeable?"

Mary V gave him a quick, intent look and bit her lower lip. "I only wish I could change you a little bit," she retorted. "I don't want to be disagreeable, Johnny, after you were given up for lost and everything, and then turned out to be all right. But that's just the trouble! You —"

"The trouble is that I wasn't killed? Good golly!"

"No, I don't mean that at all. But we thought you were, and everybody in the country was simply frantic, and you weren't even —"

"Huh!" Johnny got up, plainly hesitating between dignified retreat and another profitless argument with Mary V. Another, because his acquaintance with her had been one long series of arguments, it seemed to him; and profitless, because Mary V simply would not be logical, or ever stick to one contention, but instead would change her attack in the most bewildering manner.

"I'm very sorry," he said stiffly, "that the whole country was frantic without due cause. But I never asked them to take it upon themselves to get all fussed up because I happened to be late for my meals. I was foolish enough to take it for granted that a man has a right to go about his business without asking permission of the general public. I didn't know the public had my welfare on its mind like that. I'll have to call a meeting after this, I reckon, and put it to vote whether I can please go up in my little airplane. Or maybe the public will pass the hat around and buy a string to tie on to me, so I can't get too far away. Then they can take turns holding the string and pull me down when they think I've been up long enough! Darned boobs-what did they want to get up searching parties for? Couldn't they find anything else to do, for gosh sake?"

"Why, Johnny Jewel!" Righteous indignation brought Mary V to her feet, trembling a little but with the undaunted spirit of her fighting forebears shining in her eyes. "Johnny Jewel, you silly, ungrateful boy! What if you had been hurt somewhere? You'd have been glad enough then for the public to take some interest in you, I guess!"

"Well, but I wasn't hurt," Johnny reiterated with his mouth set stubbornly. "They had to go and worry the life outa you, Mary V —that's what I'm kicking about. They —"

Mary V gazed at him strangely. "But you see, Johnny, it was I who worried the life out of them! When you didn't come, I got dad started, and then I 'phoned the sheriff and offered a reward and big pay and everything, to get men out. All the sheriff's men will get twenty-five dollars a day, Johnny, for hunting you. And there was a reward and everything. So don't blame the public for taking an interest in whether you were killed or not. Blame me, Johnny-and dad, and the boys that have been riding day and night to find you."

Johnny reddened. "Well, I appreciate it, of course, Mary V —but I don't see why you should think —"

"Because, Johnny, you didn't come the next morning after I told you to come. And the hotel clerk found your plane was gone, so —"

"But I never said I'd come. I told you I wouldn't come to the ranch till I had the money to square up with your dad. I meant it-just that. You must have known I wasn't talking just to be using the telephone."

"But you knew I expected you just the same. And how could I know-how could I *dream*, Johnny, that instead of coming or letting me know, or anything, you would take up with that perfectly horrible Bland Halliday again, and go off in the opposite direction, and be gone three whole days without a word? I'm sure I wouldn't have believed it possible you'd do a thing like that, Johnny. I —I can't believe it now. It-it seems almost worse than if you had started for the ranch and —"

"Got killed on the way, I suppose! I like that. I must say, I like that, Mary VI You'd rather have me with my neck broken than not doing exactly as you say. Is that it?"

Mary V set her teeth together until she had herself under control, which, had you known the girl, would have meant a great deal. For Mary V was not much given to guarding her tongue.

"Johnny, tell me this: After knowing Bland Halliday as you do, and after knowing what I think of him, and what he tried to do down there at Sinkhole when he was going to steal your airplane and fly off with it, *why* have you taken up with him again, without one word to me about it? And why didn't you take the time and the trouble to call me up and say what you were going to do, when you knew that I'd be looking for you? I hate to say it, Johnny, but it does look as though you didn't care one bit about me or what I'd think, or anything. You've just gone crazy on the subject of flying, and that Bland Halliday is just working you, Johnny, for an easy mark. You think it's pride that's holding you back from taking dad's offer and staying here and settling down. But it isn't that at all, Johnny. It's just plain conceit and swell-headedness, and I hate to tell you this, but it's the truth.

"That airplane has simply gone to your head and you can't look at anything sensibly any more. If you could, you'd have *kicked* that miserable Bland Halliday when he came sneaking around-wanting money and a square meal, and you needn't deny it, Johnny. But no, instead of taking the chance that's given you to make good, you turn up your nose at it because it isn't spectacular enough to keep you in the limelight as the original Boy Wonder! And you-you take that crook, that tramp, that-that *bum* as a partner, and imagine you're going to do wonderful things and get rich and everything! And you won't do anything except give that tramp a chance to steal you blind!"

"I didn't say I'd taken Bland as a partner. But I may do it, at that-if my judgment approves of the deal."

"Your judgment! Johnny Jewel, you haven't got any more judgment than a cat!"

This was putting it rather strongly, since Mary V had fully intended to guard her tongue, being careful not to antagonize him. That heady young man now stood glaring at her in a thoroughly antagonistic manner. Speech trembled on his lips that would not formulate the scathing rebuke surging within his mind. He had been called conceited, swell-headed, inconsiderate of others, and now this final insult was heaped upon the full measure of his wrongs, just when he had a clear vision of future achievements that should have dazzled any young woman whose life was to be linked with his. But Mary V, he reminded himself, could not look beyond her own little desires and whims. Because she had tried to lay down the law for him and he had failed to obey, she refused to see that he was playing for big stakes and that he could not be expected to throw everything up just because she had been worried over him for a couple of days. The mere fact that he had not been lost on the desert, as every one supposed he was, could not affect his plans for the future, though Mary V seemed to think that it should.

"Well, since that is the way you feel toward me, I may as well drift," he made belated retort in a tone of suppressed wrath. "I guess it would have been better if I'd stayed away, I'll remember —"

"For gracious *sake*, what does make you so horrid?" Mary V now had one arm crooked around his neck, which he stiffened stubbornly. With her other hand she was tweaking his ears rather painfully. "You're going to stay right here and behave yourself till dad comes, and you're going to have a talk with him about your affairs before you go doing anything silly. You know perfectly well that my father's advice is worth something. Everybody in the country thinks he has a wonderful brain when it comes to business or anything like that. He can tell you what you ought to do, Johnny, if you'll only be sensible and listen to him."

"What do I want to listen to him for?" Johnny's eyes looked down at her with no softening of his anger. "Good golly! Do you think your dad's got the only brain in the world? How do men run their affairs, and get rich, that never heard of him, do you suppose? I don't want to mock your dad-he's all right in his own field, and a smart man and all that. But he don't know the flying game, and his advice wouldn't be worth the breath he'd use giving it. Perhaps I am conceited and swell-headed and a few other things, but I am perfectly willing to take a chance on my own judgment for awhile yet, anyway. When I do need advice, I'll know where to go."

"To Bland Halliday, I suppose!" Mary V took away her arm and stood back from him. "You'd take a tramp's advice before you would my father's, would you?" She pressed her lips together, seeming to hold back with difficulty a storm of reproaches.

"I would, where flying is concerned." Johnny's lips spelled anger to match her own. "He knows the game, and your father doesn't. And just because Bland's playing hard luck is no reason why you need call him names. Give the devil his due, anyway."

"I just perfectly ache to do it!" cried Mary V. "He wouldn't be talking you into all kinds of crazy things —"

"Crazy because they don't happen to appeal to you," Johnny flung back. "Oh, well, what's the use of talking? You don't seem to get the right angle on things, is all." He busied himself with a cigarette, his face, that had been so boyishly eager while he told her his plan, gone gloomy with the self-pity of one who feels himself misunderstood.

Mary V had gone back to her hammock and was lying with one arm thrown up across the cushion, her face concealed behind it. She, too, felt miserably misunderstood. Flighty she was, spoiled and impulsive, but beneath it all she had her father's practical strain of hard sense. Mary V had grown older in the past three days. She had faced some bitter possibilities and had done a good deal of sober thinking. She felt now that Johnny was carried away by the fascination of flying, and that Bland's companionship was the worst thing in the world for him. She was hurt at Johnny's lack of consideration for her, at his complete absorption in himself and his own plans. She wanted him to "settle down," and be content with loving her and with being loved-to be satisfied with prosperity that carried no element of danger.

Moreover, that he had not troubled to send her any message but had deliberately gone flying off in the opposite direction with Bland, regardless of what she might think or suffer, filled her with something more bitter than mere girlish resentment. Johnny was like one under a spell, hypnotized by his own air castles and believing them very real.

Mary V had no faith in his dreams, and not even to please Johnny would she pretend that she had. She had nothing but impatience for his plans, nothing but disgust for his partner, nothing but disappointment from his visit. She moved her arm so that she could look at him, and wondered why it should give her no pleasure to see him standing there unharmed, sturdy, alive to his finger tips-him whom she had but a little while ago believed dead. Johnny, I must confess, was cot a cheerful object. He was scowling, with his face turned so that Mary V saw only his sullen profile; with his mouth pinched in at the corners and his chin set in the lines of stubbornness.

As if he felt her eyes upon him, Johnny turned and sent her a look not calculated to be conciliating. If Mary V wanted to sulk, he'd give her a chance. He certainly could not throw up all his plans just on her whim.

"I guess I'll go down and help Bland," he said in the repressed tone of anger forcing itself to be civil. "We ought to be getting back to-night." He opened the screen door, gave her another look, and went off toward the corral, sulks written all over him.

Mary V waited until she was sure he did not mean to turn back, then went off to her room, shut the door with a force that vibrated the whole house, and turned the key in the lock.

Chapter Eight. Sudden Must do Something

"I been thinking, bo, what we better do." Bland climbed down from the motor and approached Johnny eagerly, casting suspicious glances here and there lest eavesdroppers be near. That air of secrecy was a habit with Bland, yet it never quite failed to impress Johnny and lend weight to Bland's utterances. Now, having been put on the defensive by Mary V, he was more than ever inclined to listen.

"Shoot," he said glumly, and sent a resentful glance back at the house. At least, Bland showed some interest in his welfare, he thought, and regretted that it had not occurred to him to tell Mary V that and see how she would take it.

"Well, bo, all this limelight stuff is playing right into your mitt. I didn't spill who I was to them news hounds, and I don't have to. I let you take all the foreground. I was the mechanic-see? So it's you that will have to put this over; and put it over strong, I say.

"Now first off you want some catchy name for the plane, and you've got it ready-made. All yuh need is paint to put it on with. Across the top of the wings you want to paint THE THUNDER BIRD-just like that. Get the idea? And we'll go back to Tucson and clean up a piece of money. While you work into the exhibition stuff we can take up passengers and make good money. Ten minutes of joyride, at ten dollars per joy-you mind the mob that follered us to the hotel just for a look-in? Say one in ten takes a ride, look at the clean-up! You take 'em yourself, bo-do the flunkey work and look wise. I never mentioned the joyridin' at first, because I look on that as side money, and exhibition flyers don't do nothing like that. They think it cheapens 'em, and it does. But right now it means quick money, see. With all this publicity, and the Injun name-say, it's a cinch, bo! They'll fall over theirselves to git a ride.

"My idea is to get the name painted on right now, before we go back. Then we'll circle over town and do a few flops and show our sign. So right away the name'll stick in their minds and make good advertising. Then when we land, the mob'll be there —I'll say they will! And they'll take a ride, too. I wonder is there any lampblack on the place?"

Johnny smoked a cigarette and studied the proposition. It looked feasible. Moreover, it promised ready money, and ready money was Johnny's greatest, most immediate need. Not a little of his captiousness with Mary V was caused by his secret worry over his empty pockets. He grinned ruefully when the thought struck him that, if the bald truth were known, he himself did not have much more than the price of one joyride in his own machine! He had been seriously considering asking Curley for a loan when that staunch little friend returned from the search, but it galled his pride to borrow money from any one. Bland's idea began to look not only feasible but brilliant. It would establish at once his independence and furnish concrete proof to Mary V that his determination to fly was based on sound business principles. Supposing he only took up four or five passengers a day, he would make more money than he could earn in two weeks at any other occupation.

Bland seemed to read this thought. "You can count on an average of ten a day, bo-that's a hundred dollars. Sometimes, like on Sundays, it would run to two and three hundred bones. I guess that will let you throw your feet under the table regular-what?"

"What about you?" Johnny asked, looking up at him studiedly.

"Me? I'll tell yuh, bo. You give me the second ten bucks you take in. You keep the rest until the tenth passenger, and give me that, and then the fifteenth. And you pay all expenses. That's fair enough, ain't it? I'll make good money when you make better. Any exhibition work, you give me half, because it'll really be me that's pulling off the stunts. The public needn't be wise to that. You as Skyrider Johnny, see. I'm just anybody, for the present."

"Why all this modesty to-day? When you first wanted to go in with me, I couldn't call you no violet, Bland. You said then that your name was worth a lot."

Bland's loose lips parted in a crafty grin. "It is worth a lot, bo-to keep it under cover right now. One of them newspaper guys reminded me of somebody. I don't think he remembered me-but it wouldn't do us no good now to jogg-e his memory, bo. I ain't saying he's got anything on me-only —"

"Only he has," Johnny rounded out the sentence dryly. "All right. I'm willing to play that way till I find out more about you. We'll try your scheme out. It can't do any hurt."

He went off to the shed where all sorts of things were stored, looking for lamp black. And Bland, seeing ready money just ahead, overlooked Johnny's blunt distrust of him, and pulled the corners of his mouth out of their habitual whining droop and whistled to himself while he tinkered with the motor.

Johnny was up on a stepladder laboriously painting the R on THUNDER when old Sudden drove into the yard with half the Rolling R boys packed into the big car. They had heard the strident humming of the plane when Johnny made his homing flight, and craning necks backward, had seen him winging away to the Rolling R. They had guessed very close to the truth, and for them the search ended right there. So, after signalling the other searchers, many of the boys had ridden back in the car, leaving patient, obliging little Curley to bring home their horses.

Bud and Aleck, who had ridden uncomplainingly from dawn to dark, looking for Johnny's remains, straightway pulled him, paint-pot and all, from the stepladder and began to maul him affectionately and call him various names to hide their joy and relief. Which Johnny accepted philosophically and with less gratitude than he should have shown.

"What yo' all doin', up there?" Bud wanted to know when the first excitement had subsided. "Writin' poetry for friend Venus to read? I'll bet that there's where Skyrider has been all this while! I'll bet he's been visitin' with Venus and brandin' stars with the Rollin' R whilst we been ridin' the tails off our hawses huntin' his mangled ree-mains. Ain't that right, Eyebrow?"

Bland grinned sourly. "Us, we been gawdin' amongst the Injuns," he stated loftily. "We sure had some time. I'll say we did! Say, we're goin' to be ready to do business now pretty quick. Don't you birds want to fly? Just a little ways-to see how it feels?"

Halfway up the stepladder Johnny stopped. "What's the matter with you, Bland?" he asked sharply. "You crazy?"

"We're out to do business. That's right, boys. Now's your time to fly. All it takes is a little nerve-and ten dollars."

"Shut up!" growled Johnny. "Don't be a darned boob."

The boys looked at one another uncertainly. It might be some obscure joke of Bland's, and they were wary.

"Fly where?" Bud guardedly sought information.

"Anywheres. Just a circle or two, to show yuh how this ranch looks to a chicken hawk, and down again," Bland persisted, in spite of Johnny.

"Yeah-it's that *down again* I wouldn't much hanker for," Aleck put in. "I seen how you and Skyrider come down, once."

"That there was him learnin' not to pick nice, deep, soft sand for a landin'," Bland explained equably, glancing up to where Johnny was painting a somewhat wobbly B. "He ain't done it lately, bo."

"Lemme up there, Skyrider, and see what it is yo'all are paintin' on," Bud pleaded. "If it's po'try, maybe I can sing it."

Johnny relaxed into a grin, but he did not answer the jibe. He was disgusted with Bland for having such bad taste as to drum up trade here on the ranch, among the boys who had ridden hard and long, believing him in dire need. He hoped the boys would not guess that Bland was in earnest; a poor, cheap joke is sometimes better than tactless sincerity. He was even ashamed now of the name he was painting on the wings. That, too, seemed cheap and pointless. He felt nauseated with Bland Halliday and his petty grafting.

A little more and he would have told Bland so and sent him about his business. At that moment of revulsion against Bland he was almost in the mood to give up the whole scheme and do as Mary V wished him to do: settle down there at the ranch and work out his debt where he had made it. Looking down into the grimy, friendly faces of those who had braved desert wind and sun for him, the sallow, shifty-eyed face of Bland Halliday seemed to epitomize the sordid avariciousness of the man and made him wonder if any measure of success would atone for the forced intimacy with the fellow. Mary V, had she known his mood then, might have won her way with him and altered immeasurably the future.

But Mary V knew only that he was staying down there with that unbearable Bland Halliday, fussing around his horrid old airplane instead of coming to the house and telling her he was sorry. Besides, there was her dad, who had gone to all that trouble and expense for him, not so much as getting a word of thanks or appreciation from Johnny. Instead of coming right away to see her dad, he was down there fooling with the boys. What, for gracious sake, ailed Johnny lately? He ought to have a good talking to, she decided. Perhaps her dad could talk some sense into him-she was sure that she couldn't.

So she stopped her dad when he was on the point of going down where Johnny was, and she told him what perfectly crazy ideas Johnny had, and how he had refused to listen to a word she said, but instead had taken up with Bland Halliday again. And wouldn't dad please talk to Johnny?

"He keeps harping on owing you for those horses he lost," she said impatiently. "I've told him and told him that you don't care and would never hold it against him, but he won't listen. He keeps on talking about paying it back, and making good before we can be married and all that. And he simply will not consent to come and make good on the ranch, and pay you out of his salary, if he feels he must pay.

"He says ranching is too tame for him-dad, think of that! Too tame, when he knows very well it would mean — But he doesn't seem to care whether we're together or not. He says he can make a fortune flying, and he said he might go in partnership with Bland Halliday. He says we can't think of being married until he has paid you-and he imagines he can earn the money with that airplane! And I know perfectly well he can't, because if he does make a cent Bland Halliday will cheat him out of it. And dad —" Mary V's voice trembled " —he went off that morning with that fellow, exactly in the opposite direction from the ranch! He never intended to come, and he didn't care enough to tell me, even. He just went as if nothing in the world mattered! And we were all hunting —"

"Well, if you look at it that way it's easy enough to handle him," Sudden observed. "I've been thinking myself the young imp showed mighty little thought for you. Of course you don't want to marry a fellow like that."

"Why, I do too! What, for gracious sake, ever put that idea into your head? But I don't want him to act like a perfectly crazy lunatic. I wish you'd speak to him. He won't listen to me-we just quarrel when I try to reason with him."

Sudden smoothed down his face with his hand. "I expect you do, all right. The dove of peace is going to find mighty poor roosting on your roof, babe, if I'm any judge."

"I suppose you mean I'm quarrelsome, but you simply don't understand. It was Johnny who quarrelled with me because I wanted him to have some sense. I wish you'd speak to him, dad."

"Oh, I'll speak to him," her dad promised grimly.

Still, he did not immediately proceed to speak. Instead, he drove the car down to the garage and put it away, passing rather close to the airplane without giving much attention to Johnny. His casual wave of a hand could have meant almost anything, and Johnny felt a small tremor of apprehension. When he was merely one of the men on the payroll he had stood just a bit in awe of old Sudden, and he could not all at once throw off the feeling, even though Sudden had willingly enough acknowledged him as a prospective son-in-law. He allowed a blob of black paint to place a period where no period should be while he stared after Sudden's bulky form in the dust-covered car.

Sudden busied himself in the garage, turning up grease cups and going over certain squeaky spots with the oil can while he studied the problem before him. He had once before likened Johnny Jewel to a thoroughbred colt that must be given its head lest its temper be spoiled for all time. Just now the human colt seemed inclined to bolt where the bolting threatened disaster to Mary V. The question of using the curb or giving a free rein was a nice one; and the old car was given an astonishing amount of oil before Sudden wiped his hands on a bit of waste with the air of a man who had just made an important decision.

"If you've got time," he said to Johnny, when he approached the group at the plane, "I'd like to have a little talk with you. No hurry, though. Glad to see you got back all right. You had the whole country guessing for a while."

Johnny scowled, for the subject was becoming extremely unpleasant. "I'm sorry-but I don't see what I can do about it, unless I go off and smash things up to carry out the program as expected," he retorted, and it did not occur to him that the words sounded particularly ungracious. The thing was on his nerves so much that it seemed to him even Sudden was taunting him with the trouble he had caused.

"No, the show's over now, and the audience has gone home. No use playing to an empty house," Sudden drawled.

Johnny looked at him quickly, suspiciously. He had an overwhelming wish to know just exactly what Sudden meant. He climbed down and took the ladder back to the shed near by.

"I'm ready for the talk, Mr. Selmer," he said when he came back. Whatever Sudden had in his mind, Johnny wanted it in plain speech. A white line was showing around his mouth —a line brought there by the feeling that his affairs had reached a crisis. One way or the other his future would be decided in the next few minutes.

He followed Sudden to the house and into the office room fronting the corrals and yards. Sudden sat down before his desk and Johnny took the chair opposite him, his spirits still weighted by the impending crisis. He tried to read in Sudden's face what attitude he might expect, but Sudden was wearing what his friends called his poker expression, which was no expression at all. His very impassiveness warned and steadied Johnny.

Chapter Nine. Giving the Colt his Head

"You and Mary V are engaged to be married," Sudden began abruptly. "Have you any particular time set for it, or any plans made?"

Johnny faced him steadily and explained just what his plans were. That Mary V had undoubtedly forestalled him in the telling made no difference to Johnny. Since Sudden had asked him, he should have it straight from headquarters. We all know what Johnny told him; we have heard him state his views on the subject.

"H-mm. And how long do you expect it will take to pay me for the horses?"

Johnny hesitated before he plunged-but when he did he went deep enough in all conscience. "With any kind of luck I expect to be square with you in a year at the latest."

"A year. H-mm! Will you sign a note for that three thousand, with interest at seven per cent., and give your flying machine as security?"

"I will, provided I can pay it any time within the year," Johnny answered, trying to read the poker face and failing as many a man had failed.

Sudden nodded, pulled a book of note blanks from a drawer and calmly drew up a note for three thousand dollars, payable "on or before" one year from date, with interest at seven per cent. per annum, with a bill of sale of Johnny's airplane attached and taking effect automatically upon default of payment of the note.

Johnny read the document slowly, pursing his lips. It was what he had proclaimed to Mary V that he wished to do, but seeing it there in black and white made the debt look bigger, the year shorter, the penalty of failure more severe. It seemed uncompromisingly legal, binding as the death seal placed upon all life. He looked at Mary V's father, and it seemed that he, too, was stern and uncompromising as the agreement he had drawn. Johnny's shoulders went back automatically. He reached across the desk for a pen.

"There will have to be witnesses," said Sudden, and opened a door and called for his wife and Bedelia. Until they came Johnny sat staring at the bill of sale as though he meant to commit it to memory. "One military type tractor biplane . . . ownership vested in me . . . without process of law . . ." He felt a weight in his chest, as though already the document had gone into effect.

When he had signed his name and watched Bedelia's moist hand, reddened from dishwater, laboriously constructing her signature while she breathed hard over the task, the plane seemed irrevocably lost. Mommie, leaning close to his shoulder so that a wisp of her hair tickled his cheek while she wrote, gave him a little cheer by her nearness and her unspoken friendliness. She signed "Mary Amanda Selmer" very precisely, with old-fashioned curls at the end of each word. Then, quite unexpectedly, she slipped an arm around Johnny's neck and kissed him on his tanned cheek where a four-day's growth of beard was no more than a brown fuzz scarcely discernible to the naked eye. She gave his shoulder two little affectionate pats that said plainly, "There, there, don't you worry one bit," and went away without a word. Johnny gulped and winked hard, and wished that Mary V was more like her mother, and hoped that Sudden was not looking at him.

Sudden was folding the paper very carefully and slipping it into an envelope, on the face of which he wrote "John Ivan Jewel, $3000. secured note, due ——" whenever the date said. When he finally looked up at John Ivan Jewel, that young man was rolling a cigarette with a fine assumption of indifference, as though giving a three-thousand-dollar note payable in one year and secured with all he owned in the world save his clothes was a mere bagatelle; an unimportant detail of the day's business.

Sudden smoothed his face down with the palm of his hand, as he sometimes did when Mary V demanded that she be taken seriously, and spoke calmly, with neither pity, blame, nor approval in his voice.

"I have held you accountable for the horses stolen through your neglect while you were in charge of Sinkhole range and therefore responsible for their safety within a reasonable limit. The expenses of your sickness after your fall with your flying machine, I will take care of myself.

You were at that time trying to find Mary V, which naturally I appreciated. More than that, I make it a rule to pay the expenses of any man hurt in my employ.

"The expense I have been under in hiring men, letting my own work go to the devil, and so forth, while we thought you were lost, I shall not expect you to pay. As I understand the matter, you had no intention of coming to the ranch and had not said that you were coming. The expense of looking for you really ought to come out of Mary V —and serve her right for having so much faith in you. I am lucky in one sense —I shan't have to pay the thousand-dollar reward the kid so generously offered in my name for your recovery. The bonus she offered that sheriff's posse will mighty near eat up that new automobile she's been wanting, though. Maybe next time —"

"I'll buy Mary V an automobile if she wants one-when I get the note paid," Johnny stated boyishly, to show his disapproval of Sudden's hardness.

Sudden once more passed his palm thoughtfully over the lower half of his face. "Mary V ought to appreciate that," he said dryly, and Johnny flushed.

"Anyway, it ain't right to make her suffer for being worried about me. That was my fault, in a way. If you'll tell me how much you're out —?"

"That's all right. It's on me, for falling so easy for one of Mary V's spasms. I was led to believe you had actually started for the ranch-in which case I was justified in supposing you had come to grief somewhere en route. We'll let it go." He cleared his throat, glanced at Johnny from under his eyebrows, took a cigar out of a drawer, and bit off the end.

"Now under the circumstances, I think I have a right to know how you expect to pay that note. I realize that if I leave the flying machine in your hands it's going to depreciate in value, and the chances are it'll go smash and I'll be out my security. Don't you think you had better run it under a shed somewhere and go to work? Of course it's nothing to me, so long as I get my money, just how you earn it. Working for me you couldn't earn any three thousand dollars in a year-you ain't worth it to anybody. You're too much a kid. You ain't grown up yet, and I couldn't depend on you like I can on Bill. But I could strain a point, and pay you a thousand dollars a year, and split the debt into three or four yearly payments. In four years," he pointed out relentlessly, "you might come clear-with hard work and good luck."

"On the other hand, when Mary V marries with our consent she gets a third interest in the Rolling R. Her husband will naturally fall into a pretty good layout. So you might fix it with the kid to jump down the four years some. That's between you and —"

"That's an insult! I'll pay you, and it won't be any Rolling R money that does it, either. When I marry Mary V or any other girl it's my money that will support her. I may be a kid, all right-but I ain't that kind of a hound. I don't know the law on such things, but there ain't anything in that Bill of Sale that says I've got to stand my plane in your cow shed till I've paid the note, and I won't do it. The plane ain't yours till I don't pay. Seems to me you better wait till the note's due before you begin to worry, Mr. Selmer. And I'll set your mind at rest on one point, anyway. The plane may go to smash, as you say, but if I don't smash with it, I'll pay you that three thousand. And you don't have to strain any point, either, to give me a job. When I want to work for you I'll sure tell you so. In the meantime, I don't know as it's very businesslike for you to go prying into my plans. You've accepted my note, and you've got your security, and what the hell more do you want?"

Sudden was very much occupied with his cigar just then, and he did not answer the challenge. Moreover, he was having some difficulty with his poker face, which showed odd twitchings around his mouth. But Johnny did not wait for a reply. He was started now, and he went on hotly, relieving his mind of a good many other little grievances.

"You don't go around asking other men how they expect to meet their obligations a year from now, do you? Then why should you think you've got a right to butt in on my private business, I'd like to know? Put my plane in your cow shed and go to work for you! Huh! I've caused you trouble and expense enough, I should think, without saddling myself on you like that. I appreciate all you have done-but I absolutely will not get under your wing and let you pet and humor me along like you do Mary V. Why, good golly! You've spoiled and humored her now until I can't do a thing with her! Why, she harps on my staying here at the ranch-under dad's wing, of course! —instead of getting out and making something of myself. You didn't fool around and let somebody else shoulder your responsibilities, did you? You didn't let somebody plan for you and dictate to you and do all your thinking-no, you bet your life you didn't! And nobody's going to do it for me, either. If I haven't got brains enough and guts enough to make good for myself, I'll blow the top of my head off and be done with it."

He rose and pushed his chair back with a kick that sent it skating against the wall. His stormy blue eyes snapped at Sudden as though he would force some display of emotion into that smooth, impassive, well-fed countenance, the very sight of which lashed his indignation into a kind of fury.

"If you really think I don't amount to any more than to hang around here for you to support, why the devil don't you kick me out and tell Mary V not to marry me? You must think you're going to have a fine boob in the family! And it's to show you-it's —why the hell don't you-what I can't stand for," he blurted desperately, "is your insinuating right to my face that I'd want to marry Mary V to get a third interest in the Rolling R. I want to tell you right now, Mr. Selmer, you couldn't give me any third interest nor any one millionth interest. If I thought Mary V had put you up to that I'd absolutely-but she didn't. She knows where I stand. I've told her straight out. Mary V's got more sense-she knows me better than you do. She knows —"

"There's another thing I neglected to mention," Sudden drawled, blowing smoke with maddening placidity under the tirade. "It's none of my business how you hook up with that tramp flyer out there-but you understand, of course, that flying machine is tied up in a hard knot by this note. I couldn't accept any division of interest in it, you know. You have given it as security, affirming it to be your own property. So whatever kind of deal you make with him or any one else, the flying machine must be kept clear. Selling it or borrowing money on it-anything of that kind would be a penal offence. You probably understand this-but if so, telling you can do no harm; and if you didn't know it, it may prevent you from making a mistake."

"I guess you needn't lay awake nights over my going to the pen," Johnny replied loftily. "I believe our business is finished for the present-so good day to you, Mr. Selmer."

"Good day, Mr. Jewel. I wish you good luck," Sudden made formal reply, and watched Johnny's stiff neck and arrogant shoulders with much secret amusement. "Oh-Mary V's out on the front porch, I believe!"

Johnny turned and glared at him, and stalked off. He had meant to find Mary V and tell her what had happened, and say good-by. But old Sudden had spoiled all that. A donkey engine would have stalled trying to pull Johnny around to the front porch, after that bald hint.

As it happened, Mary V was not taking any chances. She was not on the front porch, but down at the airplane, snubbing Bland most unmercifully and waiting for Johnny. When he appeared she was up in the front seat working the controls and pretending that she was speeding through the air while thousands gaped at her from below.

"I'm doing a make-believe nose dive, Skyrider," she chirped down at him, looking over the edge through Johnny's goggles, and hoping that he would accept her play as a tacit reconciliation, so that they could start all over again without any fussing. No doubt dad had fixed things up with Johnny and everything would be perfectly all right. "Look out below."

"You better do a nose dive outa there," Johnny told her with terrific bluntness. "I'm in a hurry. I want to make Tucson yet this afternoon."

Mary V's mouth fell open in sheer amazement.

"Johnny Jewel! Do you mean to tell me you're going to leave? And I was just waiting a chance to ask you if you won't give me a ride! I'm just dying to fly, Johnny."

Johnny looked at her. He turned and looked back at the house. He looked at the boys and at Bland. He took a deep breath, like a man making ready to dive from some sheer height into very deep water. "All right, stay where you are-but leave those controls alone. Want to show the boys a new stunt, Bland? We'll take Miss Selmer up, and you ride here on the wing.

You can lay down close to the fuselage and hang on to a brace. They've been doubting your nerve, I hear." He climbed in, pulling off his cap for Mary V to wear. "Reach down there on the right-hand side, Mary V, and get me those extra goggles. All right-come on, Bland, let's show 'em something."

Bland hesitated, plainly reluctant to try the stunt Johnny had suggested. But Johnny was urgent. "Aw, come on! What's the matter with you? They do it all the time, over in France! Turn her over. All ready? Retard-contact!"

Bland cranked the motor, but it was plain that his mind was working furiously with some hard problem. Should he refuse to ride on a wing and let Johnny fly off without him? All Bland's hatred of the wilderness, his distrust of men who wore spurs and big hats as part of their daily costume, shrieked no. Where the plane went he should go. Should he consent to ride flat on his stomach on a wing, with the wind sweeping exhaust fumes in his face and the earth a dwindling panorama of monotonous gray landscape far beneath him? His nerves twittered uneasily at the suggestion.

But when the motor was going and the plane quivering and kicking back a trail of dust, and Johnny had his goggles down and was looking at him expectantly, Bland chose the lesser woe and laid himself alongside the fuselage with his head tucked under a wire brace, his hands gripping brace and wing edge, his toes hooked, and his cheek pressed against the sleek covering. He grinned wanly at the boys who watched him, and sent one fervent request up to Johnny.

"F'r cat's sake, bo, don't stay up long-and keep her balanced!"

"Hang on!" Johnny shouted in reply.

The plane veered round, ran down the smooth space alongside the corrals, lifted, and went climbing up toward the lowering sun. Then it wheeled slowly in a wide arc, still climbing steadily, swung farther around, pointed its nose toward Tucson, and went booming away, straight as a laden bee flies to its hive.

Chapter Ten. Lochinvar up to Date

In the Tucson calf pasture adjoining the shed now vested with the dignity of a hangar, the Thunder Bird came to a gentle stand. Bland slid limply down and leaned against the plane, looking rather sick. Mary V pushed up her goggles and looked around curiously, for once finding nothing to say. Johnny unfastened his safety belt and straddled out.

He had done it-the crazy thing he had been tempted to do. That is, he had done so much of it. Unconsciously he repeated to Mary V what he had said to Bland down in the Indiana corn patch.

"Well, here we are."

Mary V unfastened herself from the seat, twisted around and stared at Johnny, still finding nothing to say. A strange experience for Mary V, I assure you.

"Well," said Johnny again, "here we are." His eyes met Mary V's with a certain shyness, a wistfulness and a daring quite unusual. "Get out. I'll help you down."

"Get-out?" Mary V caught her breath. "But we must go back, Johnny! I —I never meant for you to bring me away up here. Why, I only meant a little ride —"

"Now we're here," said Johnny, "we might as well go on with it-get married. That," he blurted desperately, "is why I brought you over here. We'll get married, Mary V, and stop all this fussing about when and how and all that. When it's done it'll be done, and I can go ahead the way I've planned, and have the worry off my mind. There's time yet to get a license if we hurry."

Bland muttered something under his breath and went away to the calf shed and reclined against it disgustedly, too sick from the exhaust in his face all the way to speak his mind.

"But Johnny!" Mary V was gasping. "Why, I'm not ready or anything!"

"You can get ready afterwards. There's just one thing I ought to tell you, Mary V. If you do marry me, you can't take anything from your dad. I can't buy you a new automobile for a while yet, but I'll do the best I can. The point is, your dad is not going to support you or do a thing for you. If you're willing to get along for a while on what I can earn, all right. I guess you won't starve, at that."

"Well, but you said you wouldn't get married, Johnny, until you'd paid —"

"I changed my mind. The best way is to settle the marrying part now. I'll do the paying fast enough. Are you coming?"

Mary V climbed meekly out and permitted her abductor to lift her to the ground, and to kiss her twice before he let her go. Events were moving so swiftly that Mary V was a bit dazed, and she did not argue the point, even when she remembered that a white middy suit was not her idea of the way a bride should be dressed. The very boldness of Johnny's proposition, its reckless disregard of the future, swept her along with him down the sandy side street which already held curious stragglers coming to see what new sensation the airplane could furnish. These they passed without speaking, hurrying along, with Bland, like a footsore dog, trailing dejectedly after.

They passed the hotel and made straight for the county clerk's office, too absorbed in their mission to observe that their passing had brought the three newspaper men from the hotel lobby. Bland fell into step with one of these and gave the news. The three scented a good story and hastened their steps.

In the county clerk's office were two strangers who glanced significantly at each other when Johnny entered the room with Mary V close behind him and with Bland and the three reporters following like a bodyguard.

"Here they are," said a short, fat man whom Mary V recognized vaguely as the sheriff. He gave a little, satisfied, nickering kind of chuckle, and the sound of it irritated Johnny exceedingly. "Old man's a good guesser-or else he knows these young ones pretty well. Ha-ha. Well, son, you can get any kind of license here yuh want, except a marriage license." Place a chuckle at the end of every sentence, and you will wonder with me what held Johnny Jewel from doing murder.

"And who the heck are you?" Johnny inquired with a deadly sort of calm. "You ain't half as funny as you look. Get out." With a jab of his elbow he pushed the sheriff and his chuckle away, guessing that the man with an indoor complexion and a pen behind his ear was the clerk. Him he addressed with businesslike bluntness. He wanted a marriage license, and he could see no reason why he should not have it. The man with the chuckle he chose to ignore, instinct telling him that haste was needful.

The clerk was a slow man who deliberated upon each sentence, each signature. Eager prospective bridegrooms could neither hurry him nor flurry him. He took the pen from behind his ear as a small concession to Johnny's demand, but he made no motion toward using it.

"Are you sure this is the couple?" he cautiously inquired of the sheriff.

"Sure, I am. I knew this kid of Selmer's —have known her by sight ever since she could walk. It's the couple, all right. The girl's eighteen on the twenty-fourth day of next January, at five o'clock in the morning. If you like, Robbins, I'll call up Selmer. I guess I'd better, anyway. He may want to talk to these kids himself."

The clerk put his pen behind his ear again and turned apologetically to Johnny. "We'd better wait," he said mildly. "If the young lady's age is questioned, I have no right —" He waved his hand vaguely.

"You bet it's questioned," chuckled the sheriff. "Her dad 'phoned the office and told us to watch out for 'em. Made their getaway in that flying machine there's been such a hullabaloo about. He had a hunch they'd make for here." He turned to Johnny with a grin. "Pretty cute, young man-but the old man's cuter. Every town within flying distance has been notified to look out for you and stop you. Your wings," he added, "is clipped."

Johnny opened his mouth for bitter retort, but thought better of it. Nothing could be gained by arguing with the law. He whirled instead on Bland and the three reporters, standing just within the open door.

"What the hell are you doing here?" he demanded hotly. "Who asked you to tag around after me? Get out!" Whereupon he bundled Bland out without ceremony or gentleness, and the three scribes with him; slammed the door shut and turned the key which the clerk had left in the lock. "Now," he stated truculently, "I want that marriage license and I want it quick!"

The sheriff was humped over the telephone waiting for his connection. He cocked an eye toward Johnny, looked at his colleague, and jerked his head sidewise. The man immediately stepped up alongside the irate one and tapped him on the arm.

"No rough stuff, see. We can arrest —"

"Don't you *dare* arrest Johnny!" Mary V cried indignantly. "What has he done, for gracious sake? Is it a crime for people to get married? Johnny and I have been engaged for a long, long while. A month, at least! —and dad knows it, and has thought it was perfectly all right. I told him just this afternoon that I intended to marry Johnny. He has no right to tell everybody in the country that I am not old enough. Why didn't he tell me, if he thought I should wait until after my birthday?"

"If that's my father you're talking to," she attacked the sheriff who was attempting to carry on a conversation and listen to Mary V also, "I'd just like to say a few things to him myself!"

The sheriff waved her off and spoke into the mouthpiece. "Your girl, here, says she wants to say a few things . . . What's that? . . . Oh. All right, Mr. Selmer, you're the doctor."

He turned to Mary V with that exasperating chuckle of his. "Your father says he'd rather not talk to you. He says you can't get married, because you're under age, and you can't marry without his consent. So if I was you I'd just wait like a good girl and not make any trouble. Your father is coming after you, and in the meantime I'll take charge of you myself."

"You will like hell," gritted Johnny, and hit the sheriff on the jaw, sending him full tilt against the clerk, who fell over a chair so that the two sprawled on the floor.

For that, the third man, who was a deputy sheriff as it happened, grappled with Johnny from behind, and slipped a pair of handcuffs on his wrists. The deadly finality of the smooth steel against his skin froze Johnny into a semblance of calm. He stood white and very still until the deputy took him away down a corridor into another building and up a steep flight of dirty stairs to a barren, sweltering little room under the roof.

Baffled, stunned with the humiliation of his plight, he had not even spoken a good-by to Mary V, who had looked upon him strangely when he stood manacled before her.

"Now you've made a nice mess of things!" she had exclaimed, half crying. And Johnny had inwardly agreed with her more sweepingly than Mary V suspected. A nice mess he had made of things, truly! Everything was a muddle, and like the fool he was, he went right on muddling things worse. Even Mary V could see it, he told himself bitterly, and forgot that Mary V had said other things, —tender, pitying things, —before they had led him away from her.

He had no delusions regarding the seriousness of his plight. Assaulting an officer was a madness he should have avoided above all else, and because he had yielded to that madness he expected to pay more dearly than he was paying old Sudden for his folly of the early summer. It seemed to him that the rest of his life would be spent in paying for his own blunders. It was like a nightmare that held him struggling futilely to attain some vital object; for how could he ever hope to achieve great things if he were forever atoning for past mistakes?

Now, instead of earning money wherewith to pay his debt to Sudden, he would be sweltering indefinitely in jail. And when they did finally turn him loose, Mary V would be ashamed of her jailbird sweetheart, and his airplane would be-where?

He thought of Bland, having things his own way with the plane. Dissipated, dishonest, with an instinct for petty graft-Johnny would be helpless, caged there under the roof of their jail while Bland made free with his property. It did not occur to him that that he could call the law to his aid and have the airplane stored safe from Bland's pilfering fingers. That little gleam of brightness could not penetrate his gloom; for, once Johnny's indomitable optimism failed him, he fell deep indeed into the black pit of despair.

Strangely, the failure of his impromptu elopement troubled him the least of all. It had been a crazy idea, born of Mary V's presence in the airplane and his angry impulse to spite old Sudden. He had known all along that it was a crazy idea, and that it was likely to breed complications and jeopardize his dearest ambition, though he had never dreamed just what form the complications would take. Even when he landed it was mostly his stubbornness that had sent him on after the marriage license. He simply would not consider taking Mary V back to the ranch. It was much easier for him to face the future with a wife and ten dollars and a mortgaged airplane than to face Sudden's impassive face and maddening sarcasm.

Darkness settled muggily upon him, but he did not move from the cot where he had flung himself when the door closed behind his jailer. He still felt the smooth hardness of the hand-cuffs, though they had been removed before he was left there alone.

He did not sleep that night. He lay face down and thought and thought, until his brain whirled, and his emotions dulled to an apathetic hopelessness. That he was tired with a long day's unpleasant occurrences failed to bring forgetfulness of his plight. Until the morning crept grayly in through his barred window he lay awake, and then slid swiftly down into slumber so deep that it held no dreams to soothe or to torment with their semblance of reality.

Two hours later the jailer tried to shake him awake so that he could have his breakfast and the morning paper, but Johnny swore incoherently and turned over with his face to the wall.

Chapter Eleven. Johnny Will not be a Nice Boy

The jailer reappeared later, and finding Johnny sitting on the edge of the cot with his tousled head between his two palms, scowling moodily at his feet, advised him not unkindly to buck up.

Without moving, Johnny told him to get somewhere out of there.

"Your girl's father is here and wants to talk to you," the jailer informed him, overlooking the snub.

"Tell him to go to hell," Johnny expanded his invitation. "If you bring him up here I'll kick him down-stairs. And that goes, too. Now, get out of here before I —"

"Aw, say, you ain't in any position to get flossy. Look where you are," the jailer reminded him good-naturedly as he closed the door.

He must have repeated Johnny's words verbatim, for Sudden did not insist upon the interview, and no one else came near him. At noon the jailer brought him a note from Mary V, along with his lunch, but Johnny had no heart for either. He had just finished reading the front-page account of his exploits, and his mood was blacker than ever.

No man likes to see his private affairs garbled and exaggerated and dished to the public with the sauce of a heartless reporter's wit. The headlines themselves struck his young dignity a deadly blow:

BIRDMAN FURNISHES NEW SENSATION!

Lochinvar Lands in Jail!

Thunder Bird Carries Maiden Off.

Telephone Halts Flight in County Clerk's Office, Where Couple is Arrested. Abductor Attacks Sheriff Viciously. Is Manacled in Presence of Hysterical Young Heiress Who Faints as Her Lover is Overpowered. Irate Father Hurries to the Scene.

After keeping the country in a turmoil of excitement over his disappearance in an airplane, the Skyrider, young Jewel, flies boldly to Rolling R ranch and abducts beautiful Mary V Selmer, only daughter of the rich rancher who led the search for the missing birdman.

Romance is not dead, though airplanes have taken the place of horses when young Lochinvar goes boldly out to steal himself a bride. Modern inventions cannot cool the hot blood of youth, as young Jewel has once more proven. This sensational young man, apparently not content with the uproar of the country for the past three days, when he was believed to be lost on the desert with his airplane, attempts one adventure too many. When he brazenly carried off his sweetheart in his airplane he forgot to first cut the telephone wire. That oversight cost him dear, for now he languishes in jail, while the young lady, who is under age, is being held by the sheriff —

It was sickening, because in a measure it was true, though he had never thought of emulating Lochinvar or any one else. He had neither thought nor cared about the public and what it would think, and the blatant way in which he had been made to entertain the country at large humiliated him beyond words.

He picked up the square, white envelope tightly sealed and addressed in Mary V's straight, uncompromising chirography, turned it over, reconsidered opening it, and flipped it upon the cot.

"There was an answer expected," the jailer lingered to hint broadly. "The young lady is waiting, and she seemed right anxious."

But Johnny merely walked to the barred window and stared across at the blank wall of another building fifteen feet away, and in a moment the jailer went away and left him alone, which was what Johnny wanted most.

After a while he opened Mary V's letter and read it, scowling and biting his lips. Mary V, it would seem, had read all that the papers had to say, and was considerably upset by the facetious tone of most of the articles.

". . . and I think it's perfectly terrible, the way everybody stares and whispers and grins. What in the world made you act the way you did and get arrested. And those were reporters that you shoved out of the office, too, and that is why they wrote about us in such a horrid way. And I shall never be able to live it down. I shall be considered hysterical and always fainting, which is not true and a perfect libel which they ought to be sent to jail for printing. I shall probably have that horrid Lochinvar piece recited at me the rest of my life, Johnny, and I should think you would be willing to apologize to the sheriff and be nice now and make them let you off easy. And dad blames me for eloping with you and thinks we had it planned before he got home yesterday, and he says there was no excuse and it showed a lack of confidence in his judgment. He says you are a d. fool and take yourself too seriously, and it is a pity you couldn't have some sense knocked into you. But you must not mind him now because he is angry and will get over it. But Johnny, please do be a good boy now and don't make us any more trouble. I am sure I never dreamed what you had in mind, but I would have married you since we started to, but now it is perfectly odious to have it turn out such a fizzle, with you in jail and I being preached at every waking moment by dad and mommie. If you had only kept your temper and waited until dad and mommie got here, I am sure we would be married by now, because I could have made them give their consent and be present at the Wedding and everything go off pleasantly instead of such a horrid mess as this is.

"I want you to promise me now that you will be good, and I will make dad get the judge to let you off. Won't you please see dad and be nice to him? His calling you a d. fool does not mean anything. That is dad's way when he is peeved, and the jailer says you told him dad could go to h. That is why he said it and not on general principles, because he does really like you, Johnny. Of course we could see you anyway, because you couldn't help yourself, but dad won't do it unless you are willing to be good. So please, dear, won't you let us come up and talk nicely together? I am sure the sheriff bears no ill will though his jaw is swelled a little but not much. So we can get you out of this scrape if you will meet us halfway and be a nice sensible boy. Please, Johnny.

"Your loving Mary V."

Johnny read that last paragraph three times, and gave a snort with each reading. If being let off easy involved the intercession of Mary V's father, Johnny would prefer imprisonment for life. At least, that is what he told himself. And if being a nice sensible boy meant that he was to apologize to the sheriff and say pretty please to Sudden, the chance of Johnny's ever being nice and sensible was extremely remote. His loving Mary V had said too much —a common mistake. What she should have done was confine her letter to a ten-word message, and tear the message up. A fellow in Johnny's frame of mind were better left alone for a while.

He sulked until he was taken down into the police court, where his crime was duly presented to the judge and his sentence duly pronounced. Knowing nothing whatever of the seamy side of life, as it is seen inside those dismal houses with barred windows, Johnny thought he was being treated with much severity. As a matter of fact, his offence was being almost forgiven, and the six days' sentence was merely a bit of discipline applied by the judge because Johnny sulked and scowled and scarcely deigned to answer when he was spoken to.

The judge had a boy of his own, and it seemed to him that Johnny needed time to think, and to recover from his sulks. Six days, in his opinion, would be about right. The first two would be spent in revilings; the third and fourth in realizing that he had only himself to blame for his predicament, and the fifth and sixth days would stretch themselves out like months and he would come out a considerably chastened young man.

Another thing Johnny did not know was that, thanks to Mary V's father, he was not herded with the other prisoners, where the air was bad and the company was worse. He went back to his room under the roof, where the jailer presently visited him and brought fruit and magazines and a great box of candy, sent by Mary V with a doleful little note of good-by as tragic as though he were going to be hanged.

Johnny was sulkier than ever, but his stomach ached from fasting. He ate the fruit and the candy and gloomed in comparative comfort for the rest of that day.

The next day, when the jailer invited him down into the jail yard for a half hour or so, Johnny experienced a fresh shock. Somewhere, high in the air, he heard the droning hum of his airplane. Bland was not neglecting the opportunity Johnny had inadvertently given him, then.

Johnny craned his neck, but he could not see the plane in the patch of sky visible from the yard. He listened, and fancied the sound was diminishing with the distance. Bland was probably leaving the country, though Johnny could not quite understand how Bland had managed to get the funds for a trip. Perhaps he had taken up a passenger or two-or if not that, Bland undoubtedly had ways of raising money unknown to the honest.

Oh, well, what did it matter? What did anything matter? All the world was against John Ivan Jewel, and one treachery more or less could not alter greatly the black total. Not one friendly face had he seen in the police court-since he did not call the reporters friendly. Mary V had not been there, as he had half expected; nor Sudden, as he had feared. The sheriff had not been friendly, in spite of his chuckle. Bland had not shown up-the pop-eyed little sneak! —probably because he had already planned this treachery.

He went back to his lonely room too utterly depressed to think. Apathetically he read the paper which his jailer brought him along with the tobacco which Johnny had sent for. Smoke was a dreary comfort-the paper was not. The reporters had lost interest in him. Whereas two columns had been given to his personal affairs the day before, his troubles to-day had been dismissed with a couple of paragraphs. They told him, however, that the "irate father" had taken the weeping maiden out of town and left the "truculent young birdman pining in captivity." It was a sordid end to a most romantic exploit, declared the paper. And in that Johnny agreed. He could not quite visualize Mary V as a weeping maiden, unless she had wept tears of anger. But the fact that her irate father had taken her away without a word to him seemed to Johnny a silent notice served upon him that he was to be banished definitely and forever from her life. So be it, he told himself proudly. They need not think that he would ever attempt to break down the barrier again. He would bide his time. And perhaps some day —

There hope crept in, —a faint, weary-winged, bedraggled hope, it is true, —to comfort him a little. He was not down and out-yet! He could still show them that he had the stuff in him to make good.

He went to the window and listened eagerly. Once more he heard the high, strident droning of the Thunder Bird. He watched, pressing his forehead against the bars. The sound increased steadily, and Johnny, gripping the bars until his fingers cramped afterwards, felt a suffocating beat in his throat. A great revulsion seized him, an overwhelming desire to master a situation that had so far mastered him. What were six days-five days now? Why, already one day had gone, and the Thunder Bird was still in town.

Johnny let go the bars and returned to his cot. The brief spasm of hope had passed. What good would it do him if Bland carried passengers from morning until night, every day of the six? Bland couldn't save a cent. The more he made, the more he would spend. He would simply go on a spree and perhaps wreck the plane before Johnny was free to hold him in check.

Once more the motor's thrumming pulled him to the window. Again he craned and listened, and this time he saw it, flying low so that the landing gear showed plainly and he could even see Bland in the rear seat. He knew him by the drooping shoulders, the set of his head, by that indefinable something which identifies a man to his acquaintances at a distance. In the front seat was a stranger.

He could see the swirl of the propeller, like fine, circular lines drawn in the air. The exhaust trailed a ribbon of bluish white behind the tail. And that indescribable thrumming vibrated through the air and tore the very soul of him with yearning.

There it went, his airplane, that he loved more than he had ever loved anything in his life. There it went, boring through the air, all aquiver with life, a sentient, live thing to be worshipped; a thing to fight for, a thing to cling to as he clung to life itself. And here was he, locked into a hot, bare little room, fed as one feeds a caged beast. Disgraced, abandoned, impotent.

It was in that hour that Johnny found deeper depths of despair than he had dreamed of before. Bedraggled hope limped away, crushed and battered anew by this fresh tragedy.

Chapter Twelve. The Thunder Bird Takes Wing

The days dragged interminably, but they passed somehow, and one morning Johnny was free to go where he would. Where he would go he believed was a matter of little interest to him, but without waiting for his brain to decide, his feet took him down the sandy side street to the calf shed that had held his treasure. He did not expect to see it there. For three days he had not heard the unmistakable hum of its motor, though his ears were always strained to catch the sound that would tell him Bland had not gone. Some stubborn streak in him would not permit him to ask the jailer whether the airplane was still in town. Or perhaps he dreaded to hear that it was gone.

His glance went dismally over the bare stretches he had used for his field. The wind had levelled the loose dirt over the tracks, so that the field looked long deserted and added its mite to his depressed mood. He hesitated, almost minded to turn back. What was the use of tormenting himself further? But then it occurred to him that his whole world lay as forlornly empty before him as this field and hangar, and that one place was like another to him, who had lost his hold on everything worth while. He had a vague notion to invoke the aid of the law to hold Bland and the plane, wherever he might be located, but he was not feeling particularly friendly toward the law just now, and the idea remained nebulous and remote. He went on because there was really nothing to turn back for.

His dull apathy of despair received something in the nature of a shock when he walked around the corner and almost butted into Bland, who had just finished tightening a turnbuckle and stepped back to walk around the end of a wing. Bland's pale, unpleasant eyes watered with welcome—which was even more surprising to Johnny than his actual presence there.

"Why, hello, old top! They told me you'd be let out t'day, but I didn't know just when. You're looking peaked. Didn't they feed yuh good?"

Johnny did not answer. He went up and ran his fingers caressingly along the polished propeller blade that slanted toward him; he fingered the cables and touched the smooth curve of the wing as if he needed more evidence than his eyes could furnish that the Thunder Bird was there, where he had not dared hope he would find it. Bland came up with an eager, apologetic air and stood beside him. He was like a dog that waits to be sure of his mastery mood before he makes any wild demonstrations of joy at the end of a forced separation.

"I been overhauling the motor, bo, and I got her all tuned up and in fine shape for you. She's ready to take the long trail any old time. I flew her for a couple of days, bo; took up passengers fast as they could climb in and out. I knew you said you was about broke, so I went ahead and took in some coin. I'll say I did. Three hundred bones the first day, —how's that? There was a gang around here all day. I didn't get a chance to eat, even. Second day I made a hundred and ninety, and got a flat tire, so I quit. Next day I took in a hundred and thirty. Then I put her in here and went to work on the motor. I figured, the way they had throwed it into you, you'd probably want to beat it soon as you got out, and I was afraid to overwork the motor and maybe have to wait while I sent to Los Angeles for new parts. It was time to quit while the quittin' was good, bo. Here's your money-all except what I spent for gas and oil and a few tools and one thing and another. I kept out my share, and I ain't chargin' you for flying. That goes in the bargain, that I'll fly in an emergency like that. So this is yours." Then he had to add an I-told-you-so sentence. "Goes to prove I was right, don't it? Didn't I say there was big money in flyin'?"

He held out a roll of bills tied with a string; a roll big as Johnny's wrist. Johnny looked at it, looked into Eland's lean, grimy face queerly. "Good golly!" he said in a hushed tone, and that was the first normal, Johnny-Jewel phrase he had spoken for six days.

"Well, there's plenty to see yuh through, if you want to try the Coast," Bland urged, watching Johnny's face avidly. "Way they done yuh dirt here, bo, I couldn't git out quick enough, if it was me. I'll say I couldn't. And out there's where the real money is. Here, I've taken everybody up that's got the nerve and the ten dollars. In Los Angeles you can be taking in money like that every day. F'r cat's sake, bo, let's git outa this. They ain't handed you nothin' but the worst of it."

He had changed his point of view considerably since he painted the picture of easy wealth in Tucson, to be won on the strength of the newspaper publicity Johnny had acquired. He had seen something in Johnny's face that encouraged him to suggest Los Angeles once more as the ultimate goal of all true aviators. Johnny had nothing to hold him, now that Mary V had broken with him-as Bland understood the separation. With Mary V's influence strong upon Johnny's decisions, Bland had bided his time; but there was nothing now to hold him, everything to urge him away from the place. And Bland pined for the gay cafes on Spring Street. (They are not so gay nowadays, but that is beside the point, for Bland remembered them as being gay, and for their gayety he pined.)

Johnny resorted to his old subterfuge of rolling and smoking a cigarette very deliberately while he made up his mind what to do. And Bland watched his face as a hungry dog watches for flung scraps of food.

"Aw, come on, bo! F'r cat's sake let's get to a regular town where we got a chance to make real money! Why-think of it! We can start now, and with luck we can sleep in Los Angeles to-night. And it won't be hot like it is here, and you can git a decent meal and see a decent show while you put yourself outside it. And," he added artfully, giving the propeller a pull, "the Thunder Bird is achin' to fly. Look underneath, bo. I've got her name painted on the under side, too, so she'll holler her name like a honkin' goose as she flies. And you don't want her to go squawking Thunder Bird to these damn' hicks, I guess, and keep 'em rememberin' that you spent six days —"

"That'll be about all," Johnny cut him short. "No, I don't want anything more of this darn country. I'm willing to fly to Los Angeles or Miles City, Montana-just so we get outa here. Come on, if you're ready. We'll make a bee line for the Coast. We'd better take grub and water in case of accidents. You know what happened to the poor devils that lost this plane in the first place, before I got it."

Bland's jaw went slack. Los Angeles, that had seemed so near, wavered and receded like a fading mirage. What had happened to those who had abandoned the plane where Johnny had found it was a horror Bland disliked to contemplate; a horror of thirst and crazed wanderings over hot Band and through parched greasewood, with lizards and snakes for company.

"There can't be any accidents, bo," he said uneasily. "I've went over the motor careful, and we oughta make it with about two stops for gas and oil. If I thought we'd git caught out —"

Johnny threw away his cigarette stub and straightened his shoulders. "Well, we're going to try it," he stated definitely. "You needn't think I'm anxious to get caught out in that damned desert —I know what it's like, a heap better than you do, Bland. There's ways to commit suicide that's quicker and easier than running around in circles on the desert without water. I aim to play safe. You go down town and buy an extra water bag and some grub. And when we start we'll follow the railroad. Beat it-and say! Don't go and load up with sandwiches like a town hick. Get half a dozen small cans of beans, and some salt and pancake flour and matches and a small frying pan and bucket and a hunk of bacon and some coffee. And say!" he called as Bland was hurrying off, "don't forget that water bag!"

Bland nodded to show that he heard, and struck a trot down the street. And Johnny, while he occupied himself with going over the plane and making sure that the gas tank was full and there was plenty of oil, almost whistled until the thought of Mary V pulled his lips down at the corners. He wanted to call up the ranch and see if she were there, and tell her where he was going, but that seemed foolish, after a week of silence from her. He shrank from the possibility of being told that Mary V wished to have nothing to do with him. So pride stiffened his determination to go on and let them think what they pleased of him.

Bland came back with a furtive look in his pale-blue eyes. Johnny gave him a keenly apprais-ing glance, edged close and sniffed, and decided that he was too suspicious and that Bland's sneaking look was merely an outcropping of his nature and had nothing to do with prohibition. Bland had the supplies in a gunny sack and made haste to stow them away to the best advantage.

Bland carried a guilty conscience. The hotel clerk had hailed him as he passed and had inquired for Johnny. "Long distance" had a call for him, and had insisted that Johnny be found at once and put in connection with the "party" who wished to talk with him. Bland had promised to find Johnny and tell him, and had hurried on. A block farther down the street a messenger boy had hailed him and asked him if he knew where Johnny Jewel was. "Long distance" was calling and had orders to search the town and get Johnny on the 'phone at once. The call had come in just after Johnny had left the jail, and no one seemed to know where he had gone.

"It's his girl-the one he tried to elope with," the boy had informed Bland with that uncanny knowledge of state secrets which messenger boys are prone to display. "She'll tear the telephone out by the roots if we don't get him. Is he over to the flying-machine shed?"

Bland lied, and promised again that he would try and find Johnny and tell him to hurry to a telephone. Bland had shaved seconds off every minute thereafter, getting through with his errand and back to the hangar. He had expected to be followed out there, and he was in a secret agony of haste which he betrayed in every move he made.

But Johnny was himself in a hurry to be gone, and excitement over the adventure and a troubled sense of running away occupied his mind so that he gave little heed to Bland. He climbed in, and Bland raised his two arms to the propeller blade and waited with visible impatience for the word. He had that word. And Bland, who had glanced over his shoulder and glimpsed some one coming, —some one who much resembled a messenger boy, —turned the motor over with one mighty pull, and made the cockpit in two jumps and a straddle.

"We're off, bo! Give it to 'er!" he shouted, in a tone quite foreign to his usual languid whine, and fastened his safety belt.

Johnny settled himself, felt out his controls, gave her more gas. A uniformed young fellow, running toward them, shouted something, but Johnny gave no heed. Uniforms did not appeal to him, anyway. He scowled at this one and went taxieing down the field, spurned the earth, and whirred off into the air.

"We want to climb to about ten thousand," Bland shouted over his shoulder, "and f'r cat's sake, don't let's lose sight of the railroad."

Rapidly the earth dropped away. The town shrunk to a handful of toy houses flung carelessly down upon a dingy gray carpet, with a yellow seam stretched across-which was the railroad-and yellow gashes here and there. The toy houses dwindled to mere dots on a relief map of gray with green splotches here and there for groves and orchards not yet denuded of leaves. Their ears were filled with the pulsing roar of the motor, their faces tingled with the keen wind of their passing through the higher spaces.

Away down below, where the dust they had kicked up had not yet settled, the messenger boy stood open-mouthed, with his cap tilted precariously on the bulge of his head, a damp lock of hair straggling down into his right eyebrow, while he craned his neck to stare after the dwindling speck.

He waited, leaning against the shady side of the shed with his feet crossed; but the Thunder Bird did not circle back and prepare to descend the invisible spiral it had climbed so ardently. Two cigarettes he smoked leisurely, now and then tilting back his head and squinting into the silent blue depth above. He drew out his book and looked at the slip saying that Johnny Jewel was being called by the Rolling R Ranch on long-distance telephone. He squinted again at the sky, cocked his ear like a spaniel and got no faint humming, replaced the slip in his book and the book in his torn-down pocket, and presently meandered back to town.

Away off to the west, so high that it looked a mere speck floating swiftly, the Thunder Bird went roaring, steadily boring its way to journey's end. And a little farther to the south, Mary V was making life unpleasant for the telephone operator and for her mother who preached patience and courtesy to those who toil, and for her dad who had ventured to inquire what she wanted to dog that young imp for, anyway, and why didn't she try waiting until he showed interest enough in somebody besides himself to call her up? And where was her pride, anyway?

Then, after what seemed to Mary V sufficient time to call Johnny from the farthest corner of the universe, the telephone jangled. The operator told her, with what Mary V called a perfectly intolerable tone of spite, that her "party" could not be located for her at present, as he had left town.

"And I hope to goodness he stays!" gritted Mary V, slamming the receiver on its hook. "With dad acting the way he did and treating Johnny like a *dog*, and with Johnny acting worse than dad does and treating me as if I were to blame for everything, I just wish men had never been born. I don't see what use they are in the world, except to drive a person raving distracted. Now, dad, just see what you have done!" She confronted Sudden like a small fury. "You wanted to teach Johnny a lesson, and you refused to let me see him while he was in jail, just because he told you to go somewhere. And you know perfectly well that you swore worse about him. And he did not plan to elope. He-he just did it because I was right there and-handy. And now see what you've done! You wouldn't let me go to him, and now he's out, and he has left town, and nobody knows where he is! I should think, for a parent who is responsible to heaven for his offspring's happiness, you'd be ashamed of yourself. You let me be engaged to him, and now you've gone and balled things up until I wish I were dead!"

About that time Johnny turned his head and stared wistfully down at the gray expanse sliding away beneath him. Off there to the left was the Rolling R Ranch-and Mary V. He wondered dully if it would hurt her, this abrupt ending of their dreams. Or had she ever really cared?

Bland, sitting in front with his guilty secret, felt the swing Johnny was unconsciously giving to the plane, and set his control against it. The Thunder Bird veered, hesitated, and came back to the course. Johnny took a long breath and turned his eyes to the front again. The past was past-the future lay all before him. He set his teeth together and drove the Thunder Bird straight into the west.

Fiction would give to the venture a hairbreadth escape or two and many insurmountable obstacles which would, of course, be triumphantly surmounted by the hero. But fact will have it otherwise, and the chronicler of events must not be blamed if the hegira of John Ivan Jewel lacked excitement.

The Thunder Bird flew high, with a steady air current behind which gave the plane more speed than Johnny had hoped for, and brought them close to Yuma before the gas gauge began to worry him. They descended cautiously, circled over the town like a wild duck over a pond, choosing their landing. They alighted without mishap and Johnny hired a decent-looking Mexican to watch the plane and protect it from curious meddlers while he and Bland went into town and ate their fill, and bought gas and oil to be delivered immediately. Before the town had fairly awakened to the fact that an airplane had descended in its immediate vicinity, they were off again, climbing once more to the high air lanes that made smoother going.

The motor worked smoothly, the hand of the tachometer wavering around twelve hundred, and the altometer registering nine thousand feet, save when they dipped and lifted to the uneven currents over the mountains. The Thunder Bird seemed alive, glorying in her native element. The earth slid away like a map unrolled endlessly beneath them. Desert and little towns on the railroad like broken beads strung loosely on a taut wire. Salton Sea was cool and tempting, though the air shimmered all around it with heat. They flew the full length of it and on up the valley. Then they climbed higher and so breasted the currents flowing over the San Jacintos. And over a little town set in level country they wheeled, descending and searching for a field. Again they landed and filled their gas tank and went on. Always it was the distance ahead that called them. Always they grudged the minutes lost, as though they were racing against time and the stakes were high.

After the last stop, exaltation seized Johnny and lifted him high above the sordid things of earth. Trouble dropped away from him; rather, it was left behind as he flew toward the sunset, He lost the sense of weight that clogs the bodies of human creatures plodding over the earth's uneven surface and became as an eagle, soaring high on wings that never tired. Never before had he remained so long in flight, wherefore he had never attained so completely that birdlike feeling of mastery in the air. Falling seemed impossible; as easily could his senses have visualized falling through the earth in the old days of crawling. There was no earth. There was only a sliding relief map far below to guide him in his triumphant flight. Tucson, the Rolling R —they were clouds that hovered far back on the horizon of his mind. Mary V was a dim vision that came and went but never quite took definite form. The roar of the motor he had long ceased to hear. Godlike he floated with wings outspread, straight into the sunset.

The sliding map below took on strange, beautiful colors of purple and gold and rose, with sometimes a wonderful blending of all. Before him the sky was a gorgeous, piled radiance. The earth colors changed, softened, deepened to a mysterious shadowy expanse, with here and there a brightness where the sun touched a hilltop.

"We better drop a little," Bland shouted. "I gotta keep my bearings!"

Swiftly the vague outlines sharpened. Groves and groves and groves appeared beneath them. And small islands of twinkling stars, set in patterns and squares, with here and there a splotch of brightness. And single stars that had somehow strayed and lay twinkling, lost in the great squares of dark green.

"We gotta make it before dark," Bland yelled. "I been away a year. I need daylight —"

They gave her more gas, and Johnny became conscious of the motor's voice. Eighty miles she was doing now, on a gentle incline that lifted the earth a little nearer. The glory before them was deepening to ruby red that glowed and darkened. Beneath the heaped radiance lay a sea of stars-and beyond, a smooth floor of polished purple.

"There's Los Angeles-and over beyond is the ocean!" called Bland, turning his head a little.

Johnny sucked in his breath and nodded, forgetting that Bland could not see the motion.

"Gimme the control—I gotta pick out a landing! I'll head for Inglewood. They's a big field—"

Inglewood meant nothing at all to Johnny, even had he heard the name distinctly, which he did not. It cost him an effort to yield the control, but he pulled hands and feet away and sat passive, breathing quickly, gazing down at the wonders spread beneath him. For this was his first amazed sight of Los Angeles, though he had twice passed through the city in a train that clung to dingy streets and left him an impression of grime and lumbering trucks and clanging street cars and more grime, and Chinese signs painted on shacks, and slinking figures.

But this was a magic city spread beneath him. It glowed and twinkled behind the thin veil of dusk. There seemed no end to the lights which overflowed the lower slopes of the cupped hills at their right and hesitated on the very brink of the purpling ocean before them.

Bland shut off the motor and they glided, the plane silent as a great bat. The city disclosed houses, and streets down which lighted cars seemed to be standing still, so much greater was the speed of the Thunder Bird. They passed the thickest sprinkle of lights and headed for dark slopes midway between the indrawing hills. Many pairs of bright lights crawled along a narrow black pathway. Now the ocean was nearer, so that Johnny could see a fringe of white along its edge where waves lapped up to the lights.

They swooped, flattened out, and glided again while Bland picked up certain landmarks. The motor spoke, its voice increased while they banked in a circle and swooped again. Now a long bare stretch lay just ahead. The motor stopped, and they volplaned steeply; flattened, dipped a little, skimmed close to earth, touched, lifted again.

"F'r cat's sake, what they went and done to this field?" Bland's whining voice complained, and he swung the Thunder Bird away from a long windrow of dried vines, just in time to avoid entangling the wheels. They settled, ran along uneven surface for a space. A small loose pile lay just ahead, and Bland veered sharply away. Another pile to the left caught the wheels just as the tail was settling. The Thunder Bird jerked, staggered drunkenly, wheeled over the pile and then, with a gentle determination quite unexpected in so docile a bird, turned itself up on its nose and with a splintering crash of the propeller tilted on over until it lay flat on its back. Which was a silly ending to so glorious a flight.

Johnny, hanging upside down with the strap strained tight across his loins, with Bland dangling before him, felt even sillier than the Thunder Bird looked. He freed himself after the first paralyzing shock of surprise, dropped on all fours upon the upper wing covering, and crawled out between the front braces. A minute later Bland followed, looking extremely foolish.

"That's a hell of a way to land!" Johnny snorted. "What kinda pilot are you, for gosh sake?"

"Aw, how was I to know they'd went and planted this field to beans? I been away a year, almost. It was a good field when I was here before. Come on and let's turn her back, bo, before all the cylinders is full of oil." Then Bland added with a surprising optimism in one so given to complaining, "We're here, and we ain't hurt, and Los Angeles is just back there a ways. I'm satisfied."

"Yes, and we shelled the beans-that's something more," Johnny sarcastically added to the sum of their blessings.

With some labor they turned the Thunder Bird right side up. It was too dark to estimate the damage, and Bland suggested that they catch a street car and ride into town. He did not inform Johnny then how far they must walk before they would be within catching distance, and Johnny started off willingly enough, after Bland had convinced him that the Thunder Bird would be perfectly safe until morning. It was a quiet neighborhood, he declared, and no one would be likely to come near the place. If they did, they could not fly off with the Thunder Bird unless they happened to be carrying an extra propeller around with them. This, Johnny suspected, was Bland's best attempt at irony.

They walked and they walked, at first along a rough country road that seemed real boulevard to Johnny, who was accustomed to the trails of Arizona. Later they emerged upon asphalt, and trudged along the edge of that for a time, moving aside as swift bars of light bathed them briefly, with the swish of speeding automobiles brushing close. Johnny's head was roaring with the remembered beat of the Thunder Bird's motor. In the silence between automobiles it deafened him so that Bland's drawling voice came to him dully, the words muffled.

"We'll have to get us a car," Bland repeated three times before Johnny understood.

"Oh. I thought you meant we're getting close to a car," Johnny grumbled. "How much farther we got to walk, for gosh sake?"

"About a mile now, bo. It's only —"

"A mile! Good golly! I thought we was flying to Los Angeles! You never said we had to walk half the way from Tucson. What in thunder made you fly forty miles beyond the darned place! Just so you'd have a chance to wreck the plane? A hell of a pilot you are!"

Bland protested, trailing a step behind Johnny, whose stride had lengthened with the bad news. Did Johnny think, f'r cat's sake, he could light in front of the Alexandria and call a bell-hop to take the plane? Did he think they could put the darn thing in an auto park? What about telephone wires and electric light wires and trolley wires? Bland would like to know. Leave it to Johnny, the crowd would now be roped off the spot and the cops fighting to make a gangway for the ambulance, and women would edge up and faint at the ghastly sight. Leave it to Johnny —

"Leave it to me," Johnny cut in acrimoniously, "and we'd have landed right side up, anyway. I wouldn't have lit in the middle of a mess of beans. Beans! Good gosh! For half a cent I'd go back and make camp there. That's what we ought to do, anyway, instead of walking all night, getting to town. We've got grub enough—and there's *beans*!"

"Aw, now, bo, have a heart! You wait till I lead you into the Frolic, and you won't say beans no more. You wait till you git your knees pushed under the mahogany and the head waiter scatters the glasses around your plate, and you lamp the dames —"

He stopped abruptly, his jaw going slack with dismay. "Only we ain't got the scenery for no such place as the Frolic," he mourned. "Lookin' the way we do, we'd be eyed suspicious if we went to grab a tray in Boos Brothers! Some Main Street waffle joint is about our number, unless —"

"A waffle joint sounds good to me," Johnny said. "I didn't come out here to spend money. I'm here to make it."

"That's all right, bo. I ain't going to hit any flowery path either. But listen, old top. We've had a hard day, and before that a bunch of 'em. We've earned one good meal, ain't we? That ain't going to hurt nobody, bo. Just to celebrate our arrival and git the taste of the desert out of our mouths. I'll say we've earned it. And it needn't cost so much. And listen here, bo. I know a place on Main where we can rent the scenery. Lots of fellers do that, and nobody the wiser. I don't mean open-face coats, neither. Just some good clothes that have got class will do fine. And we can git a shave there, and go to the Frolic and have some regular chow, bo, and listen to the tra-la-la girlies warble whilst we eat. Come on. Be a regular guy for oncet!"

"Do regular guys wear borrowed clothes? Not where I come from, they don't."

"Aw, them hicks! Well, you can buy what you want, if that suits you better. I'll take you to a place that keeps open evenings. There'll be time enough. The Frolic don't hardly git woke up till ten or 'leven, anyway."

"At that it will be closed for the night before we arrive," Johnny stated morosely. "It's a wonder to me you let the ocean stop you, Bland.

"Why didn't you go on and light in Japan? We could have caught a boat back then, instead of walking."

Once more Bland protested and explained and defended himself. But Johnny had already drifted off into troubled meditation rendered somewhat vague and inconsequential by his rapid changes of financial condition, moods, environment—the brief ecstasy of his triumphant flight that had so ridiculous a climax. Small wonder that Bland's whining voice failed to register anything but a dreary monotone of meaningless words in Johnny's ears. Small wonder that

Johnny's thoughts dwelt upon little worries that could have no possible bearing upon the big things he meant to do.

How much would a new propeller cost? Would all the barber shops be closed when they reached town? He needed a haircut and a hot bath before he would feel fit to walk the streets. Should he take at once the position he meant to maintain, and stop at the best hotel in town, as an aviator who owned the plane he flew and had a roll of money in his pocket might be expected to do? Or should he go to some cheap rooming house and save a few dollars, and sink into obscurity among the city's strange thousands?

He remembered the headlines concerning him-front-page headlines that crowded Europe's war into second place! He had not seen anything much about himself lately, though the jailer had brought him a paper every morning. Certainly his misfortune had not been given the prominence accorded to his disappearance. If he should go to some good hotel and register as John Ivan Jewel, Tucson, Arizona, the reporters might remember the name. Probably they would, and his arrival would beannounced —

What would they think, if he walked in just as he was; leather coat, aviator's cap with the ear-tabs flapping, corduroy breeches tucked into riding boots that needed a shine and the heels straightened? Would they put him out, or would they think he was so rich and famous he didn't give a darn?

He wondered what Mary V would think, if she knew that he was here in Los Angeles. Would she care whether she ever saw him again? Or could girls forget a fellow all at once? Were they still engaged, so long as she did not return his ring? He wished he knew what was the rule in cases like this. Then it struck him that Mary V could not return the ring now if she wanted to. She would not know where to send it. She might have sent it to him while he was in jail-but probably she feared that the reporters might hear about it. How much would a propeller cost, any way? There would probably be more than that broken-the Thunder Bird had turned over with quite a jolt.

No, certainly he should not spend money on high-priced hotels until he had things moving again. There would be no more money coming in until the plane was repaired-darn it, there was always that big hump in the trail; always something in the way, something to postpone his grasping at success! Now he'd have to sleep in some hot, frowsy little room for about four bits, instead of luxuriating in a suite as he would like to do.

They reached the little suburban village and the street car. Johnny had an impulse to stop there for the night and leave the city to a more propitious time, but Bland was already licking lips in anticipation of the joys of Spring Street, and made such vehement protest that Johnny yielded. If he stayed in Inglewood Bland would go on without him, and Johnny did not want that, for Bland might not come back. And whatever his mental and moral shortcomings, Bland was somebody whom Johnny knew; if not a friend, yet a familiar personality in a city filled with strangers.

Perhaps it was the night that veiled the city's big human workaday side and showed only the cold, blue-white residence streets palm-shaded and remote, and the inhospitable closed stores and shops of the business district, that gave Johnny a lost, lonesome feeling of utter homelessness. For the matter of that, Johnny could not remember when he was not homeless-but he did not often feel depressed by the fact. He followed Bland down the car steps at Fifth Street, walked with him past a delicatessen store whence apartment dwellers were trickling, their hands full of small paper bags and packages. They looked pale and sickly and harassed to Johnny, to whom desert-browned faces were a standard by which he measured all others.

A barber shop reminded him of grime and untrimmed hair, and he halted so abruptly that Bland forged several paces ahead before he missed him. He turned back grumbling, just as Johnny went in at the door, and followed grudgingly. He had wanted a glass of beer first of all, but yielded the point and took his shave resignedly.

Johnny spent a full hour in that shop, and when he emerged he was worth the second glance he got from the girls hurrying homeward. Tubbed, shaven, trimmed, a fresh shine on boots that still showed the marks of spurs worn from dawn to dark when those boots were new, he towered above Bland Halliday, who looked dingier and more down-at-heel than ever by contrast. It would take more than shaven jowls to make a gentleman of Bland.

They went on to Broadway, crossed it precariously, and reached the pavement by what Johnny considered a hair's-breadth of safety as a big car slid past his heels. They passed lighted plate-glass windows wherein silver and gold gleamed richly. Then Bland unwittingly pushed Johnny Jewel from the edge of obscurity into the bright light of notoriety again.

Bland said, "I know a joint where we can git a good room for fifty cents-and no questions asked, bo."

They happened at that moment to be nearing the immaculate white-gloved doorman who stands ward over the entrance to the Alexandria. Johnny looked at him, saw what exclusive hostelry was named upon his cap band, and stopped. "You can go to your joint where they don't ask questions," he said somewhat loftily to Bland. "I'll stop here where they don't have to."

Bland gasped, but Johnny was already turning in past the immaculate white-gloved one who bowed as Johnny brushed him by. Bland had only time enough to mutter, "I'll wait here till you register," before Johnny disappeared into the subdued elegance where Bland would not venture. "Till they throw yuh out, you boob," Bland amended his parting sentence. "Stoppin' at the Alexandria-hnm!"

Johnny, secure in his fresh cleanness and his ignorance of the traditions of the place, strode through the onyx-pillared lobby peopled with well-fed, modish human beings who conversed in modulated voices or bustled in and out, engrossed with affairs which might or might not be of national importance. At the desk a perfectly groomed, worldly wise aristocrat proffered a pen well inked and gave Johnny what Bland would have termed the double O.

Before he had finished pressing blotter upon "John Ivan Jewel, Tucson, Arizona", his brain had registered certain details and his smile had attained a certain quality of deference.

"We are glad to have you with us, Mr. Jewel. Ah —a room and bath, say on the sixth floor? Ah-did you have a good flight, Mr. Jewel?"

Oh, the adaptability of American youth! "Made it in seven hours continuous flight," Johnny informed him carelessly. "Nothing to it. Yes, the sixth floor will be all right. Didn't bring any baggage-didn't want to load the plane down."

And that clerk, to whom baggageless guests are ever objects of suspicion, smiled understandingly and called his favorite boy, and when Johnny's back was turned, immediately whispered the news that that Arizona flyer who had been so much in the public eye lately, was a guest of the hotel, having flown over in five hours.

Chapter Fourteen. Fate Meets Johnny Smiling

Johnny inspected his room and bath on the sixth floor and straightway began to worry about the bill. The shaded reading lamp by the bed impressed him mightily, as did the smoking set on its own little mahogany stand, and the coat-hangers in the closet. Johnny was accustomed to stopping in hotels where the furnishings were all but nailed down, and the little conveniences were conspicuously absent. This, he decided, was a regular place; a home for millionaires. He doubted very much whether the Thunder Bird was worth the furniture in this one room, and wondered at his own temerity in making free with it. To brace his courage he must untie the roll of money Bland had given him in Tucson and count the bank notes twice.

"By golly, I can stand one night here, any way," he reassured himself finally, and took a long breath.

Just then a bell boy tapped discreetly on the door, and when Johnny opened it he slipped in with a pitcher of ice water, which he carried to a table with the air of a loyal henchman serving his king, which means that he was thinking of tips. In the exuberance of his fresh sensation of affluence and his gratitude for the service, Johnny pulled off a five-dollar bill and gave it to the boy. The bell boy said, "Thank you, sir," and added breathlessly, "Gee, I wish I was an aviator, Mr. Jewel!"

Sir and Mister all in one breath, and to be called an aviator besides had a perceptible effect upon Johnny. He swaggered across the room that had a moment ago awed him to the point of wanting to walk on his toes. Of course he was an aviator! Hadn't he been flying in his own plane? What more did it take, for gosh sake? A pilot's license was a mere detail, alongside the night he had made that day. He should say he was an aviator!

The 'phone tinkled. A man from the *Times* wanted to talk with him, it seemed. Johnny gruffly told him over the house 'phone that he didn't care to be interviewed. "You boys get too fresh," he censured. "You don't stick to facts. You're going to get in trouble if you don't let up on me. I hate this publicity stuff, anyway. I wish you'd go off somewhere and die quietly and leave me alone."

"Well, just let me come up and explain," the reporter urged. "All I want is a story of your flight across country. You're mistaken if you think I'm guilty of—"

"Oh, well, if that's all you want. But I'm just about off reporters for life. You'll have to do some apologizing, believe me!"

Johnny was sprawled on the nice, white bed, with his boot heels cocked up on the expensive mahogany footboard. He had the two big, puffy pillows wadded under his head and the reading lamp lighted and throwing a rosy shadow on his tanned countenance. The smoking set was pulled close and he was reaching for a match when the reporter knocked.

"Come in," he called boredly, and fanned the smoke from before his face that he might look upon this unwelcome visitor who was going to apologize for the sins of his colleagues in Arizona.

The reporter, once he was inside, did not look apologetic, nor did he resemble a reporter, as Johnny knew them. He was a slim young man, tall enough to wear his clothes like the Apollos you see pictured in tailors' advertisements. Indeed, he much resembled those young men. He wore light gray, with the coat buttoned at the bottom and loose over his manly chest. He also wore a gray hat tilted over one temple in the approved style for illustrated catalogues. He had gray gloves crumpled in one hand and a cane in the other, and he stood with his immaculately shod feet slightly apart, gently swung the cane, and regarded Johnny with a faint smile of extreme boredom.

Johnny bore the scrutiny in silence, stifling the impulse to rise and offer Apollo a chair. Instead, he turned lazily and knocked the ash collar off his cigarette, and afterward thumped the top pillow before he resettled himself.

"Won't cost anything to sit down," he observed amiably. "Well, where's that apology?"

The slim young man laughed to himself, deposited his cane and gloves on a chair, moved his feet slightly farther apart and produced a small pad. "For the sins I may commit, I humbly apologize. Whatever it was your sagebrush scribes perpetrated I didn't write it, therefore we should not quarrel. A few details on your trip to-day will be of interest, Mr. Jewel."

Johnny grinned. "There ain't any details. We just flew till we got here, and then we lit."

"We?" The gray-clad one lifted a finely formed eyebrow.

"My mechanic and me."

"Ah." The fellow made a mark or two with his pencil and waited for more-until he perceived that more would not be forthcoming.

"And now that you have lit, what do you expect to do, may I ask?"

"Oh-h —" Johnny covered a wide yawn with his palm, "make money. What else is there to do?"

"Go broke," the reporter suggested, smiling again-with less boredom, by the way.

"Old stuff," Johnny grunted. "I aim to be different."

The fashion plate laughed almost humanly. "If half they said of you is true, you've nothing to complain about. By the way-how much of it was true? I mean how you salvaged the plane from Mexico and used it to catch horse thieves, and the Indian god stuff, and the Lochinvar —"

Johnny sat up belligerently. "Say! What are you looking for? Trouble?"

"Merely verifying rumors. A very natural professional caution, I assure you."

"Caution! Hnh! Funny way you've got of being cautious, old-timer. I'd call it a fine way of heading down-stairs without waiting for the elevator."

"I understand-perfectly. So you have no settled plans for the future, I take it? Just ready for whatever turns up that looks promising?"

Johnny grunted and looked at his watch. Hunger, which he had forgotten in the novelty of his surroundings, began to manifest itself again. He got up and gleaned his aviator's helmet from a branch of the mahogany hatrack and looked at it dubiously, wishing that it was his Big Four Stetson instead.

"What I'm ready for right now is chuck," he said pointedly. "I ain't fortune teller enough to give you any line on my future. I wish to heck I could. I'm out here to make good at flying. Money-that's what I want. Lots of it. But right now I want a square meal more than anything. So I'm afraid —"

"All right, Jewel. I cease to be a news hound and become your host, with your permission. Let me take you to a regular place, will you? I haven't had dinner yet myself."

"You ain't? Good golly! What you been doing all day?"

The reporter who had ceased to be a reporter checked a smile while he picked up gloves and cane and opened the door.

"Say! If I told you all I've been doing, old man, you'd think flying from Tucson is a snap! It's a merry life we newspaper men lead. Not."

They were at the elevator before it occurred to Johnny that he was deviating considerably from his intended line of conduct. He remembered that Bland had promised to wait for him outside the door. He was not at all certain that Bland would do so in the face of temptations, —such as hunger and thirst, —but it seemed a shabby trick to play him nevertheless. Instinct warned him that Bland could not be included in the invitation. Bland was indefinably but inexorably out of it. This fellow-and there Johnny remembered that he did not know the name of his host, and that he had but a moment ago all but threatened to throw him down six flights of winding stairs built all of steel or marble or some hard fireproof substance that would make painful tobogganing. He eyed askance the nameless one and was impressed anew by the absolute correctness of his attire. He wondered that the fellow was not ashamed to be seen in public with him.

"My name, by the way, is Lowell. Cliff Lowell." This was in the elevator. "The desk clerk will tell you as much as any one need know about me, if you feel the need of credentials." The elevator halted, and the human automaton who operated it slid open the door. "I don't often yield to these sudden impulses myself. But life is a bore-and you are different. I somehow feel as if we are going to hit it off all right together. At any rate, I am willing to gamble on the acquaintance for one evening. I take it you are in the same boat-eh?"

"Sure," said Johnny, flattered without in the least knowing what it was that warmed him toward Cliff Lowell so suddenly. "I suppose I ought to-my mechanic was to wait outside for me —"

Cliff Lowell lifted an eyebrow and smiled a little smile. "You must have a very well-trained mechanic if he really would wait outside at this time in the evening." He bowed and lifted his hat to an impressive old lady in some glittery, lacy kind of gown, and Johnny bowed also and blushed because a girl just beyond the old lady gave him a slant-eyed glance and the shadow of a smile. Ten steps farther a fierce looking man with a wide, white frontage and a high silk hat slowed his pace and cried, "Why, hello, Cliff!" in a manner not at all fierce. Between there and the entrance Johnny counted seven important looking persons who recognized his host as an acquaintance. He began to wonder at his own presumption in receiving one of Los Angeles' leading citizens as he had received Cliff Lowell. It was with a conscious effort that he maintained his attitude of sturdy independence.

Bland, it transpired, had tired of waiting for Johnny. He was nowhere to be seen, and with a parting salute from the white-gloved doorman they set out briskly for the regular place Cliff Lowell had chosen to honor with his patronage. The regular place was such a very regular place that it had disdained blatant electric signs and portents of its presence. Cliff led Johnny up a flight of narrow stairs and turned sharply to the left through a subdued kind of vestibule that gave no inkling of what lay beyond, except that a chipper young hat boy took their headgear and the cane and gloves before they went on.

Johnny Jewel, desert product that he was, nearly stampeded before Cliff had safely seated him, with the help of the head waiter, who spoke with a full French flavor. The table chosen for them stood before a long divan whereon they sat side by side and faced the room filled to overflowing with small groups of diners who seemed very much at home there and very much pleased with life and with one another. Many of them called greetings to Cliff Lowell, who responded with his bored smile, like a matinee idol who feels he needs a vacation.

Girls with improbable complexions and sophisticated eyes sent Johnny curious glances and provocative smiles when their companions were not looking. "Movie queens," Cliff Lowell explained in an undertone, "coming and going. Some of them dreaming of coronation, others about ready for the axe. It has taken them just about ten seconds to register interest in the strange male person who must be Somebody or he would not be here in high boots and flannel shirt."

Johnny flushed. "You saw the clothes I had on, and you brought me here," he retorted. "The joke's on you."

"No less than seven have given me the high sign to bring you over and introduce you," Cliff Lowell went on imperturbably. "They are frantically searching their memories at the present moment, trying to place you. They are positive that you are some star whom they have not met, and they are trying to remember what picture they ought to mention when the introduction has been successfully accomplished." He paused long enough to murmur an order to a hovering waiter whose English was almost unintelligible to Johnny because of its French.

"Should the crisis have to be met suddenly, do you wish to dodge the publicity that would follow if I told just who you are? There are certain incidents which you do not care to have recalled. I made sure of that at the hotel, you remember."

"I don't want to know anybody. I came here to eat. If I can't do that without being introduced to a lot of folks, I'll beat it and find some lunch counter that will feed me without trying to make a boob outa me. I ain't dressed to meet company, anyway. And I don't want anything from this bunch except to be left alone."

"Fair enough," Cliff sighed contentedly and leaned back at his ease. "You're wiser than you realize. Knowing this bunch wouldn't get you anywhere, except at the bottom of your pile, maybe. What you want is to steer clear of everything that will interfere with what you're after. Here come the eats-you'll know presently why I brought you here."

Waiters came, brought strange preparations of food which were a revelation to Johnny, to whom meat had meant just meat, boiled, roasted or fried, to whom salad meant two or three kinds of vegetables hashed together and served sour. Girls' glances were wasted upon him while he tasted dubiously, succumbed to each new and delicious viand, and explored farther, secretly eager for more wonders.

"I know now why you brought me here," he sighed contentedly after the coffee was served. "It wasn't to see the girls, either. Grub's got possibilities I never dreamed about."

Lowell smiled, sent a negligent nod toward a group that had just come in and recognized him, and tendered Johnny his tooled leather cigarette case.

"I never talk business until after I am fed," he observed. "But now-since you have nothing definite in view except the making of money, suppose you listen to a little proposition I am going to make you. It's rather confidential, however —"

"My ears are open," said Johnny, "and my mouth is shut. I don't have to like your proposition, but in case I don't I can forget things mighty easy."

"Good. I'll make it short, and you can take it or leave it. I am not a reporter; not the kind of reporter you mean. I gather special stuff for a big news syndicate. Big stuff, stuff the little fellows never dream of going after. I get, of course, big returns.

"My real object in seeing you to-night was not exactly the getting of a news item for any paper. I saw your name on the register, found that you had flown over here, and wanted to see you and take your measure for the job I have in mind.

"Briefly, the proposition is this: I need a flyer who can fly, knows a little of the desert, has got some nerve on the ground as well as in the air, and who can keep his mouth shut. It's harder than you may think to find one who measures up, and who is willing to avoid the limelight. They all want publicity, and publicity is what this job must shun. What I am working on now is big stuff across the border. I can get the news, all right —I am in touch with some of the big men over there-but the deuce of it is the going back and forth. This embargo business that has been framed lately is interfering with my work. I could get a passport, yes. Perfectly simple. I could go across, and I could get the news I want. But the bother of it, and the delay here and there is-well, it's a big handicap. You can see that easily.

"My idea, therefore, and I think it's a good one, is to hire you to take me over and back. It might take all your time and it might not-but I should want to have you on call, ready to go anywhere, any time, at a moment's notice. It would make a tremendous difference in the time-saving alone. You would have to-what about your mechanic?"

"What about him? I don't just get you." Johnny looked at him startled.

Lowell sat leaning one elbow lightly on the table, his slim, manicured fingers tapping silently the rhythm of some tune which he was subconsciously following. It was the only sign of nervousness he displayed, save a frequent swift scanning of faces in the room. Any diner there who observed him would have said that Cliff was retailing some current scandal which concerned an acquaintance. Any diner would have said that the good-looking boy in flyer's togs was listening with mental reservations, ready to argue a point, but nevertheless eager to hear the whole story.

"I mean, what about the mechanic? Have you any contract with him, or are you tied up with him in any way? Can you get rid of him, in other words?"

Johnny studied his little cup of coffee, his subconscious mind registering the incongruity of such a skimpy amount of coffee after such an amazingly ample meal. Consciously he was having a hurried, whispered conversation with his native honesty.

"Well —I ain't married to Bland," he stated judicially, meeting candidly the other's intent stare. "I never made any contract with him. He agreed to do certain things for me if I'd bring him here-and I brought him. On top of that, he talked about our doing certain things when we got here-it was exhibition flying and taking up joyriders-and I kinda fell in with the idea.

I never said, right out in so many words, that I'd do it. I just kinda let it ride along the way he said. He sure expects me to go ahead, but —"

Lowell exhaled a mouthful of smoke and sipped his coffee as though he was relieved of some doubt. "That's all right, then. You are free to change your mind. And you're lucky that you have something to change to, if I may say what I think. There's nothing in that sort of thing any more. It would scarcely pay for the wear and tear on your machine, I imagine. You certainly could not pull down any real money doing that little stuff. Now let's see —"

He smoked and studied some mental question until Johnny grew restive and finished the demitasse at a gulp. "Let's see. Suppose we say a thousand dollars a week for you and your machine. It will be worth that to me if you make good and take me across where I want to go, whenever I want to go, and fetch me back without bringing all the border patrols buzzing around, asking why and how. That, frankly, is one point that must be taken care of. It is no crime to cross the border without a passport-if you can get across. Technically it is unlawful at the present time, but in reality it is all right, if you can get away with it. We could not walk up boldly and say, 'Listen, we want permission to fly across the line on business of our own.' They'd have to say no. That's their orders, issued to stop a lot of smuggling and that sort of thing. But we are not smugglers-at least," he qualified with a faint smile, "I am not. What I shall bring back will be legitimate news of international importance, gleaned in a legitimate way. In fact it will be of some use to the government, though the government could scarcely authorize me to gather it.

"Now as to credentials, you will do me a favor if you look me up. As to yourself, I know all about you, thanks to that adventurous spirit which brought you into the limelight and is really of tremendous value to me. Seriously now, as a sporting proposition and a chance to make money, how does it strike you?"

"Why-it looks all right, on the face of it." Johnny was trying to be extremely cautious. "I'll have to think it over, though. For one thing, I'll want to do some figuring before I can say whether the price is right. It costs money to keep an airplane in the air, Mr. Lowell. You'd be surprised to see just how much a fellow has to pay out to keep a motor in good mechanical shape. And, of course, I wouldn't look at it at any price unless I was dead sure it was straight. If you'll excuse my saying so, I ain't after dirty money. It's got to be clean."

"That's the stuff! I'm glad to hear you come right out and say so, because that's where I stand. I want you to look me up. Here's the card of the International News Syndicate-they handle nothing but big political stuff, you understand. A sort of secret service of newspaperdom. Ask them about me and about the proposition. They'll be paying you the money-not me. Ask any one else you like, only don't mention this particular matter we've been discussing. As the lawyers say, secrecy is the essence of this contract." He laughed and crooked a finger at the waiter who had served them so assiduously, got his dinner check and paid it with a banknote that, even deducting the high cost of eating in a regular place, returned him a handful of change. He tipped the waiter generously and rose.

"You'd have to keep under cover as much as possible," he continued planning, when they were again on the street. "How much attention did you attract, Mr. Jewel, when you landed?"

"Why, not any. It was about dark, and we lit in a beanfield over beyond Inglewood. We left the plane there and came in on a street car. I don't guess anybody saw us at all."

"Fine! This is playing our way from the start. If any one notices your name on the hotel register and asks you questions, you came after certain parts for your motor-any errand will do-and you expect to leave again at any time. This does not commit you to the proposition, Mr. Jewel. It is merely keeping our lines straight in case you do accept. I want you to sleep on it-but please don't talk in your sleep!" He laughed, and Johnny laughed with him and promised discretion.

The last he saw of Cliff Lowell that night, Cliff was talking with a group of important-looking men who treated him as though they had known him for a long, long while. Their manifest intimacy struck Johnny as a tacit endorsement of Cliff's character and reputation. It would seem almost an insult to go around quizzing people about a man so popular with the leading citizens, Johnny told himself. He would think the proposition over, certainly. He was not fool enough to jump headfirst into a thing like that at the first crook of a stranger's finger, but —

"Good golly! Talk about luck! Why, at a thousand dollars a week, I can pay old Sudden off in a month, doggone him. And have a thousand to the good. And if the job holds out for another month or two —"

That, if you please, is how Johnny "thought it over and did some figuring!"

The grinding clamor of passing street cars jarring over the Spring Street crossing woke Johnny to what he thought was moonlight, until it occurred to him that the pale glow must come from street lamps. The air was muggy, filled with the odor of damp soot. He sniffed, turned over with the bed covering rolled close around him, snuggled his cheek into a pillow, yawned, rooted deeper, opened his eyes again, and turned on the reading light by his bed. It was five-thirty — red dawn in Arizona where his dreaming had borne him swiftly to his old camp at Sinkhole. Five-thirty would be getting-up time on the range, but in Los Angeles the hour seemed an ungodly time to crawl out of bed. He reached for his "makings" and rolled a cigarette which he smoked with no more than one arm and his head exposed to the clamminess of the atmosphere.

He ought to return to the Thunder Bird by daylight, he mused, but he did not know how to get there. He needed Bland for pilot, but he did not know where to find Bland. Now that he came to consider finding people and places, it occurred to him that neither did he know where to find Cliff Lowell. Thinking of him made Johnny wonder what kind of news gathering it was that could make it worth a thousand dollars a week to a man to have a swift, secret means of locomotion at his command. It had sounded plausible enough last night, but now he was not so sure of it. It might be some graft-it might even be a scheme to rob him of his plane. It would be a good idea to look into matters a little before he went any farther, he decided. When Bland showed up, he'd go out and take a look at the Thunder Bird, and get her in shape to fly. Then they'd get to work. But a thousand dollars a week sure did sound good, and if the proposition was on the square —

He snuggled down and began to build an air castle. Suppose it was straight, and he went into the deal with Lowell; and suppose he worked for two months, say. That would be eight-well, say nine thousand, the way weeks lap over on the calendar. Suppose by Christmas he had eight thousand dollars clear money. (Five hundred a month ought to run the plane, with any kind of luck.) Well, what if he took the Thunder Bird and his eight thousand, and flew back to the Rolling R and lit in the yard just about when they were sitting down to their Christmas dinner. He'd walk in and lay three thousand dollars down on the table by old Sudden, and tell him kind of careless, "I happened to have a little extra cash on hand, so I thought I'd take up that note while I thought of it. No use letting it go on drawing interest."

Say, maybe Sudden's eyes wouldn't stick out! And Mary V would kind of catch her breath and open her eyes wide at him, and say, "Why, Johnny —?" And say-no, jump up and put her arms around his neck and-slide her lips along his cheek and whisper —

An hour and a half later he awoke, saw with dismay that it was seven o'clock, and piled out of bed as guiltily as though an irate round-up boss stood over him. The Thunder Bird to repair, a big business deal to be accepted or rejected, —whichever his judgment advised and the fates favored, —and he in bed at seven o'clock! He dressed hurriedly, expecting to hear an impatient rapping on the door before he was ready to face a critical business world. If he had time that day, he ought to get himself some clothes. He would not want to eat again in that place where Cliff Lowell took him, dressed as he was now.

He waited an impatient five minutes, went down to the lobby, —after some trouble finding the elevator, —and found himself alone with the onyx pillars and a few porters with brushes and things. A different clerk glanced at him uninterestedly and assured him that no one had called to see Mr. Jewel that morning. He left word that he would be back in half an hour and went out to find breakfast. Luck took him through the side entrance to Spring Street, where eating places were fairly numerous. He discovered what he wanted, ate as fast as he could swallow without choking on his ham and eggs or scalding his throat with the coffee, and returned to the hotel.

No, there had been no call for Mr. Jewel. Johnny bought a morning paper, but could find no mention of his arrival in Los Angeles. Cliff Lowell, he decided, must be playing the secrecy to the limit. It did not please him overmuch, in spite of his revilings of the press that had made a joke of his troubles. Couldn't they do anything but go to extremes, for gosh sake? Here he had made a record night,—he had distinctly told that clerk the time he had made it in,—and Cliff Lowell knew, too. Yet the paper was absolutely dumb. They ignored everything he did that was worth notice, and yawped his private affairs all over their front pages. That man Lowell was taking too much on himself. Johnny hadn't agreed to take the job yet; he very much doubted whether he would take it at all. He would rather be his own boss and fly when he pleased and where he pleased. This flying over into Mexico and back looked pretty fishy, come to think of it. If it was against the law, how did Lowell expect to get away with it? If it wasn't, why be so darned secret about it?

For three quarters of an hour, perhaps longer, Johnny dismissed the thousand-dollar-a-week job from his mind and waited with rising indignation for Bland. What had become of the darned little runt? Here it was nine o'clock, and no sign of him. The lobby was beginning to wear an atmosphere of sedate bustling to and fro. Johnny watched travelers arrive with their luggage, watched other travelers depart. Business men strayed in, seeking acquaintances. The droning chant of pages in tight jackets and little caps perched jauntily askew interested him. Would Bland, when he came, have sense enough to send one around calling out "Mr. Jew-wel—Mr. John-ny Jew-wel"? Johnny knew exactly how it would sound. Cliff Lowell might, but he did not want to see Cliff. The more he thought about him the more he distrusted that proposition. A thousand dollars a week did not sound convincing in the broad light of day. It was altogether too good to be true. Why, good golly! Nobody but a millionaire could afford to pay that much just for riding around; and if they could, they'd buy themselves an airplane. They wouldn't rent one, that was certain.

At ten o'clock Johnny mentally blew up. He had not come to Los Angeles to sit around in any doggone hotel like an old woman waiting for a train, and if Bland or anybody else thought he'd hang around there all day — He went to the desk, left word that he had gone out to Inglewood, watched the clerk scribble the information on a slip of paper and put it in his key box, and went out wondering how he was going to find his way to the Thunder Bird. But his natural initiative came to his aid. He saw an automobile with a FOR HIRE sign on it, held brief conversation with the driver, and was presently leaning back on the cushions watching luckless pedestrians dodge out of the way. The sight, I may add, restored his good humor to the point of forgetting his dignity and crawling over into the front seat where he proceeded to scrape acquaintance with the driver. Los Angeles was a great place, all right-when you can see it from the front seat of an automobile. Johnny began to talk automobiles to the man and managed to extract a good deal of information, that may or may not have been authentic, concerning the various "makes" and their prices and speed. Not that he intended to buy one; but still, with good luck, there was no reason why he should not, when he had that note paid. A car certainly did give class to a man-and according to this fellow it would be a real economy to own one. This man said he looked upon a car as a necessity; and Johnny very quickly adopted his point of view and began to think how extravagant he was not to own one. Why, take this trip, for instance. If he owned the car himself, all it would cost him to go to Inglewood would be the gas he would burn. As it was, it would probably mean ten or fifteen dollars before he was through. An automobile of your own sure did mean a big saving all around-time and money. Take a job like this man Lowell had offered, why, he could very soon own a car. A thousand dollars a week, for a few weeks-it was his to take, if he wanted to do it—

There he went again, playing with the thought until they slid through Inglewood and out on the boulevard that curved flirtatiously close to a railroad track, where he had tramped with Bland-good golly! Was that only last night? Tired and hungry and blue, with a broken plane to think of and Mary V and the Rolling R to forget-last night. And here he was, debating with himself the wisdom of accepting an offer of a thousand dollars a week, thinking seriously of buying himself an automobile! Was it two miles to where they had turned out of the bean field on to the highway? It certainly didn't seem that far today. Except for the curves which he remembered he would have thought the driver had made a mistake when he slowed and swung short into a rough trail that crossed the railroad. But there was the Thunder Bird sitting disconsolately with a broken nose and Lord knew what other disabilities, in the bean field where he had left her. He felt as though he had been away for a month.

With a pencil and paper he was carefully setting down what slight repairs he would need to make, when a big, dark red roadster swung off the boulevard and came chuckling toward them down the rough trail. Cliff Lowell was driving, and he greeted Johnny with a careless assurance of their unity of interest that would make it difficult for Johnny to hold off, if holding off proved to be his ultimate intention.

Cliff climbed out and came up to the Thunder Bird, standing with his feet slightly apart, pulling off his driving gloves that he might light a cigarette.

"They told me at the hotel you were out here, so I came on. Better send that car back to town," he suggested frugally. "I'll take you in. No use wasting money on car hire when you don't have to. I want to talk to you, anyway."

Johnny hesitated, then paid his driver and let him go.

"I've got to go around to a supply house and get me a new propeller," he said afterwards. "And a control wire snapped. We made a bum landing last night-or my mechanic did. He claimed he knew this field, so I let him go ahead."

"Where is he? Did you let him out?"

"I didn't, but I will if he don't show up; pronto." Johnny's tone was the tone of accustomed authority. "He failed to report, this morning."

Cliff reached into an inner pocket and drew out a flat package, which he proceeded to open, using a wing for a table. "I've been busy this morning," he announced, laying his cigarette down on the wing. Johnny promptly swept the cigarette to the ground and crushed it under his heel. Wing coverings are rather inflammable, and he was not taking any chances.

"Pardon the carelessness. I don't know much about airplanes, old man. Well, I went to the boss and had a talk with him, after I left you last night. I put the proposition up to him, and he is rather keen on it. He sees the value of getting news by airplane. The saving of time and the avoidance of publicity will double its value-to say nothing of the chance that we may be able to pick up something of immense importance to the government. Mexican situation, you know-all that sort of thing.

"So he put me in touch with parties that could furnish this. "*This*was a large photographic bird's-eye map of a country which looked very much like Arizona, or the wild places anywhere next the Mexican borderline. "Where I got it I am not at liberty to say. It's a practice map-done for the training in aerial photography that is essential nowadays in warfare. The government is going in rather strong on that sort of thing. This is authentic. Take a good look at it through this glass and tell me what you think of it. Can you see any place that would make a possible secret landing for an airplane, for instance?"

"Golly!" Johnny whispered, as Cliff's meaning flashed clean-cut through the last sentence. He studied the photograph with pursed lips, his left eye squinted that his right eye might peer through a small reading glass. "It would depend on the ground," he answered after a minute. "I'd want to fly over it before I could tell exactly. If it was soft sandy for instance —" (Bland would have snickered at that, knowing what reason Johnny had for realizing the disadvantages of soft sand as a landing place.) "But the topography looks very practicable for the purpose." (Nothing like talking up to your audience. Johnny was proud of that sentence.)

"All right. We'll lay that aside for further investigation. I'm glad you have the plane out here away from every one. We'll take a run over to that locality in my car-it's open season for ducks, and there's that lake you see on the map. A couple of shotguns and our hunting licenses will be all the alibi we'll need. You must know how to get about in the open country, living in Arizona as you have, and I'm counting a good deal on that. That's one reason why I made you the offer, instead of these flyers around here-and by the way, that's one point that made you look like a safe bet to the old man.

"I was talking to him about salary, and he's willing to go stronger than I said, if you make good. He said it would be worth about two hundred a day, which is considerably better than the thousand a week that I named."

Cliff knew when to stop and let the bait dangle. He fussed with a fresh cigarette, paying no apparent attention to Johnny, which gave that young man an idea that he was wholly unobserved while he dizzily made a mental calculation. Fourteen hundred a week-go-od golly! In a month-or would it last for a month?

"How long a job is this?" he demanded so suddenly that the words were out before he knew he was going to ask the question.

"How long? Well-that's hard to say. Until you fail to put me across the line safely, I suppose. There's always something doing or going to be done in Mexico, old man-and it's always worth reporting to the Syndicate. How long will people go on reading their morning paper at breakfast?" He smiled the tolerant, bored smile that Johnny associated with his first sight of Cliff. "I should say the job will last as long as you make good."

"Well, that puts it up to me, then. I'd want an agreement that I'd be paid a week in advance all the time. That's to cover the risk of costly breakage and things like that. At the end of every week I'd be free to quit or go on, and you'd be free to let me out if I didn't suit. With that understanding I'll try her out-for a week, starting to-morrow morning." He added, by way of clinching the matter, "And that goes."

Cliff Lowell blew a thin wreath of smoke and smiled again. "It goes, far as I am concerned. I think the old man will agree to it, providing you take oath you'll keep the whole thing secret. I haven't preached that to you, but the whole scheme blows up the minute it is made public. You understand that, of course, and I'm not afraid of you; but the old man may want some assurance. If he does, you can give it, and if he does not, it will be because he is taking my word that you are all right.

"Now let's get down to business. How long will it take you to get the machine in shape? And can't you make arrangements with the owner of this field to leave it here for the present-and perhaps get him to keep an eye on it? Wait. You leave him to me. I think he's a Jap, and I know Japs pretty well. I'll go hunt him up and talk to him. If we can run it under cover for a couple of days, all the better."

He climbed into his car and went off down the road to where the roofs of several buildings showed just above a ridge. His talk must have been well lubricated with something substantial in the way of legal tender, for presently he returned, and behind him a team came down the road hauling a flat hayrack on which four Japs sat and dangled their legs to the jolting of the wagon.

"He's a good scout, and he will keep the plane under cover for us," Cliff announced in a satisfied tone. "They're going to load it on the wagon and haul it home, where there's a shed I think will hold it. If it won't, we'll buy it and knock out an end or something."

The four Japs, chinning unintelligibly and smiling a good deal, loaded the Thunder Bird to Johnny's satisfaction, hauled it to the buildings over the ridge, and after they had knocked all the boards off one side to admit the wings, ran it under a shed. Afterwards they nailed all the boards on again while Johnny stood around and watched them uneasily, secretly depressed because his Thunder Bird was being penned in by gibbering brown men who might be unwilling to return it to him on demand.

For good or ill, he was committed now to Cliff Lowell's project. Even though he was committed for only a week, qualms of doubt assailed him at intervals during their roaring progress to the city. Cliff drove with an effortless skill which filled Johnny with envy. Some day-well, a car like this wouldn't be so bad. And if the job held out long enough — Why, good golly, think of it! And Mary V thought he couldn't make any money with his airplane. Wanted him to go to work for her dad-think of that!

Thinking of it; he tried to silence the qualms. Tried to reassure himself with Cliff's very evident sincerity, his easy assurance that all would be well. Johnny had been canny enough to make the agreement by the week-surely nothing much could go wrong in that little while, and if he didn't like the look of things after a week's try-out, he could quit, and that would be all there would be of it. It was too good a chance to let slip by without a trial, anyway. A man would be a fool to do that; and Johnny, whatever he thought of himself, did not consider himself a fool.

Under Cliff's direction, that afternoon Johnny did what a woman would call shopping. He bought among other things a suit of khaki such as city dwellers wear when they go into the wilds. Cliff had told him that he must not appear among people in the clothes of a flyer, but must be a duck hunter and none other when they left Los Angeles. When that would be, Johnny did not know; nor did he know where they were going. But a duck hunter he faithfully tried to resemble when he let Cliff into his room at five o'clock in the evening, which meant after the lights were on in the quiet hallways of the Alexandria, and the streets were all aglow. Cliff looked, if not like a hunter, at least picturesque in high, laced boots and olive-drab trousers and coat that had a military cut.

"Fine! We'll get under way and eat somewhere along the road, if you don't mind. What about that mechanic? Has he shown up yet?" Cliff's boredom was gone, along with his swagger stick.

"Naw. I guess the little runt went on a spree. I thought he'd be here when I got back, but he wasn't, and the clerk said nobody had called for me except you."

"All the better. You won't have to bother explaining to him without telling him anything. If you ever do run across him, give him a temperance talk-and the boot. That will be convincing, without your needing to furnish any other reason for letting him out. By the way," —reaching casually into a pocket, —"here is your first week's salary. The boss made it fifteen hundred a week, straight. And he said to tell you he would add a hundred every week that you deliver the goods. That is giving a tremendously square deal, in my opinion. But it's the boss's way, to make it worth a man's while to do his level best."

Round-eyed, Johnny took the roll of bank notes and flipped the ends with eager fingers. Golly! One with five hundred on it-he had never seen a five-hundred-dollar bill in his life, until this one. And fifties-six or seven of them, and four one-hundreds, and the rest in twenties and three or four tens for easy spending. He had a keen desire to show that roll to Mary V, and ask her whether he could make money flying, or whether she would still advise him to go to work for her dad! Why, right there in his hand was more money than Sudden thought he was worth in a year, and this was just one week's salary! Why, good gosh! In another week he could pay that note, and start right in getting rich. Why, in a month he could own a car like Cliff's. Why —

Cliff, watching him with sophisticated understanding of the dazzling effect of so much money upon a youth who had probably never before seen fifteen hundred dollars in one lump, smiled to himself. Whatever small voice of doubt Johnny had hearkened to, the voice would now be hushed under the soft whisper of the money fluttering in Johnny's fingers.

"Well, I'll call a porter to get these things down so you can settle for the room. You had better just check out without leaving any word of where you're going." Cliff turned to the 'phone.

"That'll be easy, seeing I don't know," Johnny retorted, crowding the money into his old wallet that bulged like the cheeks of a pocket gopher, busy enlarging his house.

"Fine," Cliff flung sardonically over his shoulder. He called for a porter to remove the luggage from room six-seventy-eight, and laid his fingers around the door knob. "I'll be down at the S.P. depot waiting for you, Jewel. There's a train in half an hour going north, so it will be plausible enough for you to take a taxi to the depot. Go inside, just as though you were leaving, see. And when the passengers come off the train, you join the crowd with your gun case and grip, and come on out to where I'll be waiting. Can you do that?"

"I guess I can, unless somebody runs over me on the way."

"Then I'll be going. The point is, we must not leave here together-even on a duck hunt!" He smiled and departed, at least three minutes before the porter tapped for admission.

There was no hitch, although there was a margin of safety narrow enough to set Johnny's blood tingling. He had "checked out" and had called his taxi and watched the porter load in gun case and grip, had tipped him lavishly and had slipped a dollar into the willing palm of the doorman, when he leaned in to get the address to give the driver. And then, just as the taxi was moving on, over the doorman's shoulder Johnny distinctly saw Bland turn in between the rubber plants that guarded the doorway. A pasty-faced, dull-eyed Bland, cheaply resplendent in new tan shoes, a new suit of that pronounced blue loved by Mexican dandies, a new red-and-blue striped tie, and a new soft hat of bottle-green velour.

For ten seconds Johnny was scared, which was a new sensation. For longer than that he had a guilty consciousness of having "double-crossed" a partner. He had a wild impulse to stop the taxi and sprint back to the hotel after Bland, and give him fifty dollars or so as a salve to his conscience, even though he could not take him into this new enterprise or even tell him what it was. Uncomfortably his memory visioned that other day (was it only yesterday morning? It seemed impossible!) when he had wandered forlornly out to the hangar in Tucson and had found Bland true to his trust when he might so easily have been false; when everything would seem to encourage him to be false. How much, after all, did Johnny owe to Bland Halliday? Just then he seemed to owe Bland everything.

It was all well enough for him to argue that his debt to Bland had been paid when he brought him to Los Angeles, and that Bland could have no just complaint if Johnny declined to continue the partnership longer. Bland, he told himself, would have quit him cold any time some other chance looked better. It was Johnny's plane, and Johnny had a right to do as he pleased with it.

For all that, Johnny rode to the S.P. depot feeling like a criminal trying to escape. He took his luggage and sneaked into the waiting room, sought an inconspicuous place and waited, his whole head and shoulders hidden behind a newspaper which he was not reading. Cliff Lowell could have found nothing to criticize in Johnny's manner of screening his presence there; though he would probably have been surprised at Johnny's reason for doing so. Johnny himself was surprised, bewildered even. That he, who had lorded over Bland with such patronizing contempt, should actually be afraid of meeting the little runt!

A stream of hurrying people, distinguished from others by their seeking glances and haste and luggage, warned him presently that he would be expected outside. He picked up his belongings and joined the procession, but he came very near missing Cliff altogether. He was looking for the dark-red roadster that had eaten up distance so greedily between Inglewood and the city, and he did not see it. He was standing dismayed, a slim, perturbed young fellow in khaki, with a grip in one hand and a canvas gun case in the other, when some one touched him on the arm. He needed the second glance to tell him it was Cliff, and even then it was the smooth, bored voice that convinced him. Cliff wore a motor coat that covered him from chin to heels, a leather cap pulled down over his ears, and driving goggles as concealing as a mask. He led the way to a touring car that looked like any other touring car-except to a man who could know the meaning of that high, long, ventilated hood and the heavy axles and wheels, and the general air of power and endurance, that marked it a thoroughbred among cars. The tonneau, Johnny saw as he climbed in, was packed tight with what looked like a camp outfit. His own baggage was crowded in somehow, and the side curtains, buttoned down tight, hid the load from passers-by. Cliff pulled his coat close around his legs, climbed in, set his heel on the starter.

A pulsing beat, smooth, hushed, and powerful, answered. Cliff pulled the gear lever, eased in the clutch, and they slid quietly away down the street for two blocks, swung to the left and began to pick up speed through the thinning business district that dwindled presently to suburban small dwellings.

"Put on that coat and the goggles, old man," Cliff directed, his eyes on the lookback mirror, searching the highway behind them. "We've got an all-night drive, and it will be cold later on, so the coat will serve two purposes. It's hard to identify a man in a passing automobile if he's wearing a motor coat and goggles. You couldn't swear to your twin brother going by."

"This is a bear of a car," Johnny glowed, all atingle now with the adventure and its flavor of mystery. "I didn't know you had two. I was looking for the red one."

"I forgot to tell you." Which Johnny felt was a lie, because Cliff Lowell did not strike him as the kind of man who forgot things. "Yes, I keep two. This is good for long trips when I want to take luggage-and so on." His tone did not invite further conversation. He seemed absorbed now in his driving; and his driving, Johnny decided, was enough to absorb any man. Yard by yard he was sending the big-nosed car faster ahead, until the pointer on the speedometer seemed to want to rest on 35. Still, they did not seem to be going so very fast, except that they overhauled and passed everything else on the road, and not once did a car overhaul and pass them. Cliff glanced often into the mirror, watching the road behind them for the single speeding light of a motor cop-because Los Angeles County, as you are probably aware, does not favor thirty-five miles an hour for automobiles, but has fixed upon twenty-five as a safe and sane speed at which the general public may travel.

But Cliff was wary, chance favored them with fairly clear roads, and the miles slid swiftly behind. They ate at San Juan Capistrano not much past the hour which Johnny had all his life thought of as supper time. Cliff filled the gas tank, gave the motor a pint of oil and the radiator about a quart of water, turned up a few grease cups and applied the nose of the oil can here and there to certain bearings. He did it all with the fastidious air of a prince democratically inclined to look after things himself, the air which permeated his whole personality and made Johnny continue calling him Mr. Lowell, in spite of a life-long habit of applying nicknames even to chance acquaintances.

Cliff climbed in and settled himself. "We want to make it in time to get some hunting at daylight," he observed in a tone which included the fellow at the service station who was just pocketing his money for the gas and oil. "I think we can, with luck."

Luck seemed to mean speed and more speed, The headlights bored a white pathway through the dark, and down that pathway the car hummed at a fifty-mile clip where the road was straight. Johnny got thrills of which his hardy nerves had never dreamed themselves capable. Riding the sky in the Thunder Bird was tame to the point of boredom, compared with riding up and over and down and around a squirmy black line with the pound of the Pacific in his ears and the steady beat of the motor blending somehow with it, and the tingle of uncertainty as to whether they would make the next sharp curve on two wheels as successfully as they had made the last. Mercifully, they met no one on the hills. There were straight level stretches just beyond reach of the tide, and sometimes two eyes would glare at them, growing bigger and bigger. There would be a *swoo-sh* as a dark object shot by with mere inches to spare, and the eyes would glare no longer. By golly, Johnny would have a car or know the reason why! He'd bet he could drive one as well as Cliff Lowell too, once he had the feel of the thing.

"Too fast for you?" Cliff asked once, and Johnny felt the little tolerant smile he could not see.

"Too fast? Say, I'm used to *flying*!" Johnny shouted back, ready to die rather than own the tingling of his scalp for fear. He expected Cliff to let her out still more, after that tacit dare, but Cliff did not for two reasons: he was already going as fast as he could and keep the road, and he was convinced that Johnny Jewel had hardened every nerve in his system with skyriding.

Oceanside was but a sprinkle of lights and a blur of houses when they slipped through at slackened speed, lest their passing be noted curiously and remembered too well. On again, over the upland and down once more to the very sand where the waves rocked and boomed under the stars. Up and around and over and down-Johnny wondered how much farther they would hurl themselves through the night. Straight out along a narrow streak of asphalt toward lights twinkling on a blur of hillside. Up and around with a skidding turn to the right, and Del Mar was behind them. Down and around and along another straight line next the sands, and up a steep grade whose windings slowed even this brute of a car to a saner pace.

"This is Torrey Pine grade," Cliff informed him. "It isn't much farther to the next stop. I've been making time, because from San Diego on we have rougher going. This is not the most direct route we could have taken, but it's the best, seeing I have to stop in San Diego and complete certain arrangements. And then, too, it is not always wise to take a direct route to one's destination. Not-always." He slowed for a rickety bridge and added negligently, "We've made pretty fair time."

"I'd say we have. You've been doing fifty part of the time."

"And part of the time I haven't. From here on it's rough."

From there on it was that, and more. There had been a rain storm which the asphalt had long forgotten but the dirt road recorded with ruts and chuck-holes half filled with mud. The big car weathered it without breaking a spring, and before the tiredest laborer of San Diego had yawned and declared it was bedtime, they chuckled sedately into San Diego and stopped on a side street where a dingy garage stood open to the greasy sidewalk.

Cliff turned in there and whistled. A lean figure in grease-blackened coveralls came out of the shadows, and Cliff climbed down.

"I want to use your 'phone a minute. Go over the car, will you, until I come back. Where can I spot her-out of the way?"

The man waved a hand toward a space at the far end, and Cliff returned to his seat and dexterously placed the car, nose to the wall.

"You may as well stay right here. I'll not be gone long. You might curl down and take a nap."

It was not an order, but Johnny felt that he was expected to keep himself out of sight, and the suggestion to nap appealed to him. He found a robe and covered himself, and went to sleep with the readiness of a cat curled behind a warm stove. He did not know how long it was before Cliff woke him by pulling upon the car door. He did not remember that the garage man had fussed much with the car, though he might have done it so quietly that Johnny would not hear him. The man was standing just outside the door, and presently he signalled to Cliff, and Cliff backed out into the empty street. He nodded to the man and drove on to the corner, turned and went a block, and turned again. The streets seemed very quiet, so Johnny supposed that it was late, though the clock set in the instrument board was not running.

They went on, out of the town and into a road that wound up long hills and down to the foot of others which it straightway climbed. Cliff did not drive so fast now, though their speed was steady. Twice he stopped to walk over to some house near the road and have speech with the owner. He was inquiring the way, he explained to Johnny, who did not believe him; Cliff drove with too much certainty, seemed too familiar with certain unexpected twists in the road, to be a stranger upon it, Johnny thought. But he did not say anything-it was none of his business. Cliff was running this part of the show, and Johnny was merely a passenger. His job was flying, when the time came to fly.

After a while he slid farther down into the seat and slept.

Chapter Seventeen. "My Job's Flying"

The stopping of the motor wakened him finally, and he sat up, stretching his arms and yawning prodigiously. His legs were cramped, his neck was stiff, he was conscious of great emptiness. By the stars he knew that it was well toward morning. Hills bulked in the distance, with dark blobs here and there which daylight later identified as live oaks. Cliff was climbing out, and at the sound of Johnny's yawn he turned.

"We'll camp here, I think. There's no road from here on, and I rather want daylight. Perhaps then we will decide not to go on. How would a cup of coffee suit you? I can get out enough plunder for a meal."

"I can sure do the rest," Johnny cheerfully declared. "Cook it and eat it too. Where's there any water?"

"There's a creek over here a few yards. I'll get a bucket." With his trouble-light suspended from the top of the car, Cliff moved a roll of blankets and a bag that had jolted out of place. In a moment he had all the necessary implements of an emergency camp, and was pulling out cans and boxes of supplies that opened Johnny's eyes. Evidently Cliff had come prepared to camp for some time.

Over coffee and bacon and bread Johnny learned some things he had wanted to know. They were in the heart of the country which Cliff had shown him on the relief map, miles from the beaten trail of tourists, but within fifteen miles of the border.

"There's a cabin somewhere near here that we can use for headquarters," Cliff further explained. "And to-day a Mexican will come and take charge of camp and look after our interests while we are over the line. I have ordered a quantity of gas that will be brought here and stored in a safe place, and there is a shelter for the plane. I merely want you to look over the ground, make sure of the landing possibilities, and fix certain landmarks in your mind so that you can drop down here without making any mistake as to the spot. When that is done we will return and bring your airplane over. It is only about a hundred and forty miles from Los Angeles, air line. You can make that easily enough, I suppose?"

"I don't see why not. A hundred and forty miles ain't far, when you're lined out and flying straight for where you're going."

"No. Well, one step at a time. We'll just repack this, so that we can move on to the cabin as soon as it's light enough. I don't think it can be far."

Daylight came and showed them that the cabin was no more than a long pistol shot away. Johnny looked at Cliff queerly. City man he might be-city man he certainly looked and acted and talked, but he did not appear to rely altogether upon signposts and street-corner labels to show him his way about. Just who and what was the fellow, anyway? Something more than a high-class newspaper man, Johnny suspected.

That cabin, for instance, might have been built and the surroundings ordered to suit their purpose. It was a commonplace cabin, set against a hill rock-hewn and rugged, with a queer, double-pointed top like twin steeples tumbled by an earthquake; or like two "sheep herders' monuments" built painstakingly by giants. The lower slope of the hill was grassy, with scattered live oaks and here and there a huge bowlder. It was one of these live oaks, the biggest of them all, with wide-spreading branches drooping almost to the ground, that Cliff pointed out as an excellent concealment for an airplane.

"Run it under there, and who would ever suspect? Mateo is there already with his woman and the kiddies. Has it ever occurred to you, old man, how thoroughly disarming a woman and kiddies are in any enterprise that requires secrecy?"

"Can't say it has. It has occurred to me that kids are the limit for blabbing things. And women —"

"Not these," Cliff smiled serenely. "These are trained kiddies. They do their blabbing at home, you'll find. They're better than dogs, to give warning of strangers prowling about."

He must have meant during the day they were better than dogs. They drove up to the cabin, swung around the end and turned under a live oak whose branches scraped the car's top, while four dogs circled the machine, barking and growling. Still no kiddies appeared, but their father came out of a back door and drove the dogs back. He was low-browed, swart and silent, with a heavy black mustache and a mop of hair to match. Cliff left the car and walked away with him, speaking in an undertone what Johnny knew to be Spanish. The low-browed one interpolated an occasional "Si, si, senor!" and gesticulated much.

"All right, Johnny, this is Mateo, who will look after us at this end-providing there's nothing to hinder our using this as headquarters. How about that flat, out in front? Is it big enough for a flying field, do you think? You might walk over it and take a look."

Stiffly, Johnny climbed down and walked obediently out across the open flat. It was fairly smooth, though Mateo's kids might well be set gathering rocks. The hills encircled it, green where the rocks were not piled too ruggedly. He inspected the great oak which Cliff had pointed out as a hiding place for the plane. Truly it was a wonder of an oak tree. Its trunk was gnarled and big as a hogshead, and it leaned away from the steep slope behind it so that its southern branches almost touched the ground. These stretched farther than Johnny had dreamed a tree could stretch its branches, and screened completely the wide space beneath. It was like a great tent, with the back wall lifted; since here the branches inclined upward, scraping the hillside with their tips. The Thunder Bird could be wheeled around behind and under easily enough, and never seen from the front and sides. It was so obviously perfect that Johnny wondered why Cliff should bother to consult him about it. He wondered, too, how Cliff had found the place, how he had completed so quickly his plans to use it for the purpose. It looked almost as though Cliff had expected him and had made ready for him though that could not be so, since not even Johnny himself had known that he was coming to the Coast so soon. But to have the place all ready, with a man to take charge and all in a few hours, was an amazing accomplishment that filled Johnny with awe. Cliff Lowell must be a wizard at news-gathering if his talents were to be measured by this particular achievement.

"Well, do you think it will serve?" Catlike, Cliff had come up behind him.

"Sure it will serve. If you can think up some way to hide the track of the plane when it lands, it wouldn't be found here in a thousand years. But of course the marks will show —"

"Just what kind of marks?"

"Well, the wheels themselves don't leave much of a track, and the wind fills them quick, anyway. But the drag digs in. If you've ever been around a flying field you've noticed what looks like wheel-barrow tracks all over, haven't you? That's something you can't get away from, wherever you land. Though of course some soil holds the mark worse than others."

"That will be attended to. Now I'll show you just where this spot is on the map." He produced the folded map and opened it, kneeling on the ground to spread it flat. "You see those twin peaks up there? They are just here. This is the valley, and right here is the cabin. You might take this map and study it well. You will have to fly high, to avoid observation, and land with as little manoeuvering as possible. For ten or fifteen miles around here there is nothing but wilderness, fortunately. The land is held in an immense tract-and I happen to know the owners so that it will be only chance observers we need to fear. You will need to choose your landing so that you can come down right here, close to the oak, and be able to get the machine under cover at once. I'll mark the spot-just here, you see.

"Now, I shall have Mateo bring the blankets here under the tree. I feel the need of a little sleep, myself. How about you? We start back at dark, by the way."

"How about that duck hunting?"

"Ducks? Oh, Mateo will hunt the ducks!" Cliff permitted himself a superior smile. "We shall have sufficient outlet for any surplus energy without going duck hunting. You had better turn in when I do."

"No, I slept enough to do me, at a pinch. If Mateo can get a horse, I want to ride up on this pinnacle and take a look-see over the country. I can get the lay of things a whole lot better than goggling a month at your doggone maps."

Cliff took a minute to think it over and gave a qualified consent. "Don't go far, and don't talk to any one you may meet-though there is no great chance of meeting any one. I suppose," he added grudgingly, "it will be a good idea for you to get the lay of the country in your mind. Though the map can give you all you need to know, I should think."

On a scrawny little sorrel that Mateo brought up from some hidden pasture where the feed was apparently short, Johnny departed, aware of Mateo's curious, half-suspicious stare. He had a full canteen from the car and a few ragged slices of bread wrapped in paper with a little boiled ham. In spite of the fact that he had lately forsworn so tame a thing as riding, he was glad to be on a horse once more, though be wished it was a better animal.

He climbed the hill, zigzagging back and forth to make easier work for the pony, until he was high above the live-oak belt and coming into shale rock and rubble that made hard going for the horse. He dismounted, led the pony to a shelving, rock-made shade, and tied him there. Then, with canteen and food slung over his shoulder, Johnny climbed to the peak and sat down puffing on the shady side of one of the twin columns.

Seen close, they were huge, steeple-like outcroppings of rock, with soil-filled crevices that gave foothold for bushes. In all the country around Johnny could see no other hilltop that in the least resembled this, so it did not seem to him likely that he would ever miss his way when he travelled the air lanes.

For awhile he sat gazing out over the country, which seemed a succession of green valleys, hidden from one another by high hills or wooded ridges. Mexico lay before him, across the valley and a hill or two-fifteen miles, Cliff Lowell had told him. It would be extremely simple to fly straight toward this particular hill, circle, and land down there in front of the oak. Cliff had spoken of risk, bat Johnny could not see much risk here. It must be across the line, he thought. Still, Cliff had said he had friends there, which did not sound like danger. They had considered it worth fifteen hundred a week, though, to fly across these fifteen miles into Mexico and back again. Johnny shook his head slowly, gave up the puzzle, and took out his wallet to count the money again.

Half an hour he spent, fingering those bank notes, gloating over them, wondering what Mary V would say if she knew he had them, wishing he had another fifteen hundred, so he could pay old Sudden and be done with it. An unpleasant thought came to him and nagged at him, though he tried to push it from him; the thought that it would be Sudden's security that he would be risking-that the Thunder Bird was not really his until he had paid that note.

The thought troubled him. He got up and moved restlessly along the base of the towering rock, when something whined past his ear and spatted against a bowlder beyond. Johnny did not think; he acted instinctively, dropping as though he had been shot and lying there until he had time to plan his next move. He had not been raised in gun smoke, but nevertheless he knew a bullet when he heard it, and he did not think himself conceited when he believed this particular bullet had been presented to him. Why?

On his stomach he inched down out of range unless the shooter moved his position, and then, impelled by a keen desire to know for sure, he adopted the old, old trick of sending his hat scouting for him. A dead bush near by furnished the necessary stick, and the steep slope gave him shelter while he tested the real purpose of the man who had shot. It might be just a hunter, of course-only this was a poor place for hunting anything but one inoffensive young flyer who meant harm to no one. He put his hat on the stick, pushed the stick slowly up past a rock, and tried to make the hat act as though its owner was crawling laboriously to some fancied shelter.

For a minute or two the hat crawled unmolested. Then, *pang-g* came another bullet and bored a neat, brown-rimmed hole through the uphill side of the hat, and tore a ragged hole on its way out through the downhill side. Johnny let the hat slide down to him, looked at the holes with widening eyes, said "Good gosh!" just under his breath, and hitched himself farther down the slope.

His curiosity was satisfied; he had seen all of the country he needed to see and there was nothing to stay for, anyway. When he reached. the patient sorrel pony a minute or two later (it had taken him half an hour or more to climb from the pony to the peak, but climbing, of course, is much slower than coming down-even without the acceleration of singing rifle bullets) he was perspiring rather freely and puffing a little.

For a time he waited there under the shelf of rock. But he heard no sound from above, and in a little while he led the pony down the other way, which brought him to the valley near a small pasture which was evidently the pony's home, judging from the way he kept pulling in that direction. Johnny turned the horse in and closed the gate, setting the old saddle astride it with the bridle hanging over the horn. He did not care for further exploration, thank you.

What Johnny would like to know was, what had he done that he should be shot at? He was down there by Cliff Lowell's invitation — Straightway he set off angrily, taking long steps to the cabin and the great oak tree beside it. The two dogs and five half-naked Mexican children spied him and scattered, the dogs coming at him full tilt, the children scuttling to the cabin. Johnny swore at the dogs and they did not bite. He followed the children and they did not stop. So he came presently to the oak and roused Cliff, who came promptly to an elbow with a wicked looking automatic pointed straight at Johnny's middle.

"Say, for gosh sake! I been shot at twice already this morning. What's the idea? I never was gunned so much in my life, and I live in Arizona, that's supposed to be bad. What's the matter with this darned place?"

Cliff tucked the gun out of sight under his blanket, yawned, and lay down again. "You caught me asleep, old man. I beg your pardon-but I have learned in Mexico that it's best to get the gun first and see who it is after that. Did you say something about being shot at?"

"I did, but I could say more. Here I am down here without any gun but that cussed shotgun, and I didn't have that, even, when I coulda used it handy. And look what I got, up here on the hill!" He removed his hat and poked two fingers through the two holes in the crown. "Some movie stuff! What's the idea?"

Cliff nearly looked startled. He called, "Oh, Mateo!" And Mateo came in haste, bent down, and the two murmured together in Mexican. Afterwards Cliff turned to Johnny with his little smile.

"It's all right, old man-glad you weren't hurt. It was a mistake, though. You were a stranger, and it was thought, I suppose, that you were spying on this place. While it was a close call for you, it proves that we are being well cared for. Better forget it and turn in."

He yawned again and turned over so that his back was toward Johnny, and that youth took the hint and departed to find blankets to spread for himself. He was tired enough to lie down and sleepy enough to sleep, but he could not blandly forget about those bullets as Cliff advised. There were several things he wanted to know before he would feel perfectly satisfied.

Since the Thunder Bird was not here, why should strangers be shot at? Their only trouble would be with the guards along the boundary, when they tried to cross back from Mexico. But they had not tried it yet. The guards were still happily unaware of how they were going to worry later on, so why the shooting?

"Oh, well, thunder! They didn't hit me-so I should care. If Cliff wants to set guards around this camp before there's anything to guard, that's his business. Like paying me before I fly, I guess. He's got the guards up there practising, maybe. I should worry; my job's flying."

Bright-eyed, eager for the adventure trail, Johnny swung the propeller of the Thunder Bird over three times and turned to Cliff. "Here's where you learn one of the joys of flying. Hold her there while I climb in. When I holler contact, you kick her over-if you're man enough."

Cliff smiled, dropped his cigarette and ground it under his heel, then reached up and grasped the propeller blade. "I never actually did this, but I've watched others do it. I suppose I must learn. Oh, before we go up, I ought to tell you that I'd like to go on over the line this morning if possible. If you can fly very high, and when you near the line just glide as quietly as possible, I think it can be managed without our being seen. And since it is only just daylight now, it should not be late when we arrive."

"It should not," Johnny agreed. "Arriving late ain't what worries a flyer-it's arriving too doggone unexpected. Where do we light, in Mexico? Just any old place?"

"Straight toward Mateo's camp, first-flying very high. From there on I'll direct you. Shall we start?"

"You're the doctor," grunted Johnny, not much pleased with Cliff's habit of giving information a bit at a time as it was needed. It seemed to betray a lack of confidence in him, a fear that he might tell too much; though how Johnny could manage to divulge secrets while he was flying a mile above the earth, Cliff had probably not attempted to explain.

Because he was offended, Johnny gave Cliff what thrills he could during that flight. He went as high as he dared, which was very high indeed, and hoped that Cliff's ears roared and that he was thinking pleasant thoughts such as the effect upon himself of dropping suddenly to that sliding relief map away down below. He hoped that Cliff was afraid of being lost, and of landing on some high mountain that stuck up like a little hill above the general assembly of dimpled valleys and spiny ridges and hills. But if Cliff were afraid he did not say so, and when the double-pointed hill that Johnny had reason to remember slid toward them, Cliff pointed ahead to another, turned his head and shouted.

"See that deep notch in the ridge away off there? Fly toward that notch."

Johnny flew. The double-pointed hill drifted behind them, other hills slid up until the two could gaze down upon their highest peaks. Beyond, as Cliff's maps had told him, lay Mexico. At eight thousand feet he shut off the motor and glided for the notched ridge. The patrol who sighted the Thunder Bird at that height, with no motor hum to call his attention upward, must have sharp eyes and a habit of sky-gazing. Cliff, peering down over the edge of the cockpit, must have thought so, for he laughed aloud triumphantly.

"Fine! I think we are putting one over on my friends, the guards," he cried, with more animation than Johnny had yet observed in him. Indeed, it occurred to Johnny quite suddenly that he had never heard Cliff Lowell laugh heartily out loud before. "How far can you keep this up-without the motor?"

"Till we hit the ground," drawled Johnny, who was enjoying his position of captain of this cruise. He had been taking orders from Cliff for about forty-eight hours now without respite save when he slept, and even his sleep had been ordered by Cliff.

"I could make that twelve miles or so from here, though. Why?"

"In the twelve miles you would not be using gas-could you glide to the ridge, circle and fly high again, and back to Mateo's camp without stopping for gas?"

Johnny gave a grunt of surprise. "I guess I could," he said. "Why?"

"Then do it. Just that. On this side of the notch you will see-when you are close enough —a few adobe buildings. I want to pass over those buildings at a height of, say, five hundred feet; or a little lower will be better, if you can make it. Then circle and come back again. And try and make the return trip as high as you did coming down, until you are well past those mountains we passed over, just inside the line. Then come down at camp as inconspicuously as possible. I may add that as we pass over the buildings I mentioned, please start your motor. I am not expected at just this time, and I wish to attract attention."

"Hunh!" grunted Johnny. "You'd sure attract attention if I didn't —because how the deuce would you expect me to climb back from five hundred feet to eight thousand or so, without starting the motor?"

Cliff did not answer. He was busy with something which he had brought with him; a square package to which Johnny had paid very little attention, thinking it some article which Cliff wanted to have in camp.

Evidently this was not to be a news-gathering trip, though Johnny could not see why not, now they were over here. Why just sail over a few houses and fly home? He could see the houses now, huddled against the ridge. A ranch, he guessed it, since half the huddle appeared to be sheds and corrals. A queer place to gather news of international importance, thought Johnny, as he volplaned down toward the spot. He threw in the motor and was buzzing over the buildings when Cliff unstrapped himself, half rose in his seat and lifted something in his arms.

"Steady," he cried. "I want to drop this over." Whereupon he heaved it backward so that it would fall clear of the wing, and peered after it through his goggles for a minute. "You can go home now," he shouted to Johnny, and settled down in his seat with the air of a man who has done his duty and has nothing more on his mind.

Mystified, Johnny spiraled upward until he had his altitude, and started back for the United States. Clouds favored him when he crossed the boundary, hiding him altogether from the earth. Indeed, they caused him to lose himself for a minute, so that when he dropped down below the strata of vapor he was already nearly over the double-pointed hill that was his landmark. But Cliff did not notice, and a little judicious manoeuvering brought him into the little valley and headed straight for the oak, easily identified because Mateo was standing directly in front of it waving a large white cloth.

They landed smoothly and stopped exactly where Johnny had planned to stop. He climbed out, Cliff following more awkwardly, and the three of them wheeled the Thunder Bird under the oak where it was completely hidden.

It was not until he had come out again into the warm sunshine of mid-morning that Johnny observed how the kiddies were playing their part. They had a curious little homemade wheelbarrow rigged, and were trundling it solemnly up and down and over and around the single mark made by the tail drag. A boy of ten or twelve rode the barrow solidly and with dignity, while a thin-legged girl pushed the vehicle. Behind them trotted two smaller ones, gravely bestriding stick horses. Casually it resembled play. It would have been play had not Mateo gone out where they were and inspected the result of stick-dragging and barrow-wheeling, and afterwards, with a wave of his hand and a few swift Mexican words, directed them to play farther out from the oak, where the Thunder Bird had first come to earth. Solemn-eyed, they extended the route of their procession, and Johnny, watching them with a queer grin on his face, knew that when those children stopped "playing" there would be no mark of the Thunder Bird's landing left upon that soil.

"I've sure got to hand it to the kids," he told Cliff, who merely smiled and pulled out his cigarette case for a smoke.

Chapter Nineteen. But Johnny was Neither Fool nor Knave

Cliff smiled faintly one morning and handed Johnny a long manila envelope over their breakfast table in Mateo's cabin. "Your third week's salary," he idly explained. "Do you want it?"

"Well, I ain't refusing it," Johnny grinned back. "I guess maybe I'll stick for another week, anyway." He emptied his coffee cup and held it up for Mateo's woman to refill, trying to match Cliff Lowell's careless air of indifference to the presence of seventeen hundred dollars on that table. "That is, if you think I'm making good," he added boyishly, looking for praise.

"Your third week's salary answers that, doesn't it? From now on it may not be quite so easy to make good. Perhaps, since I want to go across this evening as late as you can make a safe landing over there, I ought to tell you that a border patrol saw us yesterday, coming back, and wondered a little at a government plane getting over the line. He did not report it, so far as I know. But he will make a report the next time he sees the same thing happen."

"I wish I didn't have that name painted clear across her belly," Johnny fretted. "But if I went and painted it out it would all be black, and that would be just as bad. And if I took off the letters with something, I'm afraid I'd eat off the sizing too, or weaken the fabric or something. I ought to recover the wings, but that takes time —"

Cliff gave him that tolerant smile which Johnny found so intolerable. "It is not at all necessary. I thought of all possible contingencies when I first saw the Thunder Bird. Across the line the name absolutely identifies it, which is rather important. On this side it is known as a bird fond of doing the unusual. Your reputation, old man, may help you out of a tight place yet. Now we are duck hunters, remember. Hereafter we shall be hunting ducks with an airplane-something new, but not at all improbable, especially when it is the Thunder Bird doing the hunting. We must carry our shotguns along with us, and a few ducks as circumstantial evidence. If we stray across the line accidentally, that will be because you do not always look where you are flying, and watch the landmarks."

"This, of course, in case we are actually caught. Though I do not see why that should happen. They have no anti-aircraft guns to bring us down. It may be a good idea to carry an auxiliary tank of gasoline in case of an emergency."

"I don't see why-not if I fill up over there every time I land. I can stay up three hours-longer, if I can glide a lot. Of course that high altitude takes more, in climbing up, and flying while you're up there, but the distance is short. I'll chance running outa gas. I don't want the extra weight, flying high as we have to. The motor's doing all she wants to do, just carrying us."

Cliff did not argue the point, but went out to his car, fussed with it for a few minutes, and then drove off on one of the mysterious trips that took him away from Mateo's cabin and sometimes kept him away for two days at a time. Johnny did not know where Cliff went; to see the boss, perhaps, and turn in what news he had gleaned-if indeed he had succeeded in gleaning any. Sometimes the long waits were tiresome to a youth who loved action. But Johnny had been schooled to the monotony of a range line-camp, and if he could have ridden over the country while he waited, he would not have minded being left idle most of the time.

But he did not dare leave camp for more than half an hour or so at a time, because he never knew what minute Cliff might return and want him; and when one is being paid something like ten dollars an hour, waking or sleeping, for his time, one feels constrained to keep that precious time absolutely available to his employer. At least, Johnny felt constrained to do so. He could not even go duck hunting. Mateo hunted the ducks, using Johnny's gun or Cliff's, and seldom failing to bring back game. It would be ducks shot by Mateo which would furnish the circumstantial evidence which Cliff mentioned that morning.

Johnny went out to the Thunder Bird, shooed three kids from under the wings, and began to fuss with the motor. One advantage of being idle most of the time was the easy life the Thunder Bird was leading. The motor was not being worn out on this job, at any rate.

So far he had not spent a hundred dollars of his salary on the upkeep of his machine. He was glad of that, because he already had enough to pay old Sudden and have the price of a car left over. With the Thunder Bird clear, and a couple of thousand dollars to the good-why, he would not change places with the owner of the Rolling R himself! He could go back any time and vindicate himself to the whole outfit. He could pick Mary V up and carry her off now, without feeling that he was taking any risk with her future. Poor little girl, she would be wondering what had become of him; he'd write, or send a wire, if Cliff would ever open his heart enough to take a fellow with him to where there was a post-office or something.

He was beginning to feel a deep need of some word from Mary V, was Johnny. He was beginning to worry, to grow restive down here in the wilderness, seeing nothing, doing nothing save kill time between those short, surreptitious flights across to the notched ridge and back again. Two weeks of that was beginning to pall.

But the money he was receiving did not pall. It held him in leash, silenced the doubts that troubled him now and then, kept him temporizing with that uneasy thing we call conscience.

He climbed now into the cockpit, testing the controls absent-mindedly while he pondered certain small incidents that caused him a certain vague discomfort whenever he thought of them. For one thing, why must a gatherer of news carry mysterious packages into Mexico and leave them there, sometimes throwing them overboard with a tiny parachute arrangement, as Cliff had done on the first trip, and flying back without stopping? Why must a newspaper man bring back certain mysterious packages, and straightway disappear with them in the car? That he should confer long and secretly with men of florid complexions and an accent which hardens its g's and sharpens its s's, might very plausibly be a part of his gathering of legitimate news of international import. Though Johnny rather doubted its legitimacy, he had no doubt whatever of its world-wide importance. Certain nations were at war-and he was no fool, once he stopped dreaming long enough to think logically.

Those packages bothered him more than the florid gentlemen, however. At first he suspected smuggling, or something like that. But gun-running, that staple form of border lawbreaking, did not fit into any part of Cliff's activities, though opium might. But when he had made an excuse for handling one or two of the packages, they routed the opium theory. They were flat and loosely solid, as packages of paper would be. Not state documents such as melodramas use to keep the villains sweating-they did not come in reams, so far as Johnny knew. He could think of no other papers that would need smuggling into or out of a country as free as ours where freedom of the press has become a watchword; yet the idea persisted stubbornly that those were packages of paper which he had managed to take in his hands.

As a pleasing relief from useless cogitation on the subject, Johnny took his bank roll from a pocket he had sewed inside his shirt. Like a miser he fingered the magic paper, counting and recounting, spending it over and over in anticipatory daydreams. Thirty-two hundred dollars he counted in bills of large denomination-impressively clean, crisp bills, some of them-and mentally placed that amount to one side. That would pay old Sudden, interest and all. What was left he could do with as he pleased. He counted it again. There were three hundred dollars left from what Bland had earned-Bland — What had become of Bland, anyway? Little runt might be broke again; in fact, it was practically certain that he would be broke again, though he must have had close to a hundred dollars when they landed in Los Angeles. Oh, well-forget Bland!

So there were the three hundred-gee golly, but it had cost, that short stay in the burg of Bland's dreams. A hundred dollars gone like the puff of a cigarette! Well, there were the three hundred left-he'd have been broke, pronto, if he had stayed there much longer. Another hundred he had spent on the Thunder Bird-golly, but propellers do cost a lot! And that shotgun he never had had a chance to shoot-Cliff sure was a queer guy, making him buy all that scenery, and then caching him away so no one ever got a chance to size him up and see whether he looked like a duck hunter or not. Well, anyway, let's see. There were a thousand in big juicy hundreds; and five hundred more in fifties and twenties —

Out beyond the oak's leafy screen the dogs were barking and growling and the children were calling shrilly. Johnny hastily put away his wealth and eased himself up so that he could peer out through the branches. He had not consciously feared the coming of strangers, yet now he felt his heart thumping noisily because of the clamor out in the yard. While he looked, two horsemen rode past and stopped at the cabin.

Now Johnny had been telling himself what a godsend some new face would be to him, yet he did not rush out to welcome the callers and ask the news of the outside world which Cliff was so chary of giving. He did not by any sound or movement declare his presence. He simply craned and listened.

One of the men he could not see because of a great, overhanging limb that barred his vision. The other happened to stop just opposite a very good peephole through the leaves. The kiddies were standing back shyly, patently interrupted in their pretended play of trundling the wheelbarrow and dragging the stick horses over the yard. Rosa, the thin-legged girl, stood shyly back with her finger in her mouth, in plain sight of Johnny, though she could not see him in the deep shadow of the leaves.

It was the man that interested Johnny, however. He was a soldier, probably one of the border patrol. He sat his horse easily, erect in the saddle, straight-limbed and alert, with lean hard jaw and a gray eye that kept glancing here, there, everywhere while the other talked. It was only a profile view that Johnny saw, but he did not need a look at the rest of his face with the other gray eye to be uncomfortably convinced that not much would escape him.

"It circled and seemed to come down somewhere on this side the Potreros and it has not been seen since. Ask the kids if they saw something that looked like a big bird flying." This from the unseen one, who had raised his voice as impatience seized him. These Mexicans were so slow-witted!

Johnny heard Mateo's voice, speaking at length. He saw Rosa take her finger from her mouth, catch up a corner of her ragged, apron and twist it in an agony of confusion, and then as if suddenly comprehending what it was these senores wished to know, she pointed jerkily toward the north. Perhaps the others also pointed to the north, for the lean-jawed soldier tilted his head backward and stared up that way, and Mateo spoke in very fair English.

"The kids, she's see. No, I dunno. I'm busy I don' make attenshions. I'm fine out when —"

"We know when," the efficient looking soldier interrupted. "You keep watch. If you see it fly back, see just where it comes from and where it goes, and ride like hell down to camp and tell us. You will get more money than you can make here in a year. You sabe that?"

"Yo se, senor-me, I'm onderstan'."

"You know where our camp is?"

"Si, senor capitan. Me, I'm go lak hel_."

"Well, there's nothing more to be got here. Let's get along." And as they moved off Johnny caught a fragmentary phrase "from Riverside."

The children had taken up their industrious play again, and their mother had turned from the open doorway to hush the crying of Mateo's youngest in the cabin. Mateo called the children to him and patted them on the head, and the senora, their mother, brought candy and gave it to them. They ran off, sucking the sweets, gabbling gleefully to one another. Cliff Lowell had been right, nothing is so disarming as a woman and children about a place where secrets are kept.

There had been no suspicion of Mateo's cabin and the family that lived there in squalid content. The incident was closed.

But Johnny slumped down in the seat again and glowered through the little, curved windshield at the crisply wavering leaves beyond the Thunder Bird's nose. He was not a fool, any more than he was a crook. He was young and too confiding, too apt to take things for granted and let the other fellow do the worrying, so long as things were fairly pleasant for Johnny Jewel. But right now his eyes were open in more senses than one, and they were very wide open at that.

There was something very radically wrong with this job. The fiction of legitimate news gathering in Mexico could no longer give him any feeling save disgust for his own culpability. News gathering did not require armed guards-not in this country, at least-and such mysteries as Cliff Lowell dealt in. The money in his possession ceased to give him any little glow of pleasure. Instead, his face grew all at once hot with shame and humiliation. It was not honest money, although he had earned it honestly enough. If it had been honest money, why should those soldiers go riding through the valleys, looking for him and his plane? It was not for the pleasure of saying howdy, if Johnny might judge from the hard-eyed glances of that one who had stopped in plain view.

It was not honest money that he had been taking. Why, even the kids out there knew it was not honest! Look at Rosa, playing shrewdly her part of dumb shyness in the presence of strangers-and she thinking all the while how best she could lie to them, the little imp! It was not the first time she had shown her shrewdness. Why, nearly every time Cliff wanted to make a trip across the line, those kids climbed the hill to where they could look all over the flat and the near-by hills, and if they saw any one they would yell down to Mateo. If the interloper happened to be close, they had orders to roll small rocks down for a warning, so Cliff one day told Johnny with that insufferably tolerant smile. Cliff brought them candy and petted them, just for what use he could make of them as watchdogs. Would all that be necessary for a legitimate enterprise? Wouldn't the guards have orders to shut their eyes when an airplane flew high, bearing a man who gathered news vital to the government?

Once before Johnny had been made a fool of by horse thieves who plied their trade across the line. They had given him this very same airplane to keep him occupied and tempt him away from his duty while they stole Rolling R horses at their leisure. Wasn't this very money-thirty-two hundred dollars of it-going to pay for that bit of gullibility? Gulled into earning money to pay for an earlier piece of gross stupidity!

"The prize-mark!" he branded himself. "By golly, they've got me helping 'em do worse than steal horses from the Rolling R, this time; putting something over on the government is their little stunt-and by golly, I fell for the bait just like I done the other time! *Huhn!*" Then he added a hopeful threat. "But they had me on the hip, that time-this time it's going to be different!"

For the rest of that day he brooded, waiting for Cliff. What he would do he himself did not know, but he was absolutely determined that he would do something.

Chapter Twenty. Mary V Takes the Trail

On a Saturday afternoon Spring Street at Sixth is a busy street, as timid pedestrians and the traffic cop stationed there will testify. In times not so far distant the general public howled insistently for a subway, or an elevated railway-anything that would relieve the congestion and make the downtown district of Los Angeles a decently safe place to walk in. But subways and elevated railways cost money, and the money must come from the public which howls for these things. Gradually the public ceased to howl and turned its attention to dodging instead. For that reason Sixth and Spring remains a busy corner, especially at certain hours of the day.

On a certain Saturday, months before the traffic cops grew tired of blowing whistles and took to revolving silently at stated intervals with outspread wings after the manner of certain mechanical toys, Mary V Selmer came from the Western Union's main office, and thanked heaven silently that her new roadster of the type called the Bear Cat was still standing at the curb where she had left it. Just beyond it on the left a stream of automobiles grazed by-but none so new and shiny, so altogether elegantly "sassy" as the Bear Cat. Mary V, when she stepped in and settled herself behind the steering wheel, matched the car, completed its elegant "sassiness," its general air of getting where it wanted to go, let the traffic be what it might and devil-take-the-fenders.

Mary V was unhappy, but her unhappiness was somewhat mitigated by the Bear Cat and her new mole collar that made a soft, fur wall about her slim throat to her very ears and the tip of her saucy chin, and the perky hat-also elegantly "sassy" —turned up in front and down behind, and the new driving gauntlets, and the new coat that had made dad groan until he had seen Mary V inside it and changed the groan to a proud little chuckle of admiration.

Mary V was terribly worried about Johnny Jewel. She had been sure that he had come to Los Angeles, and she had pestered her dad into bringing her here in the firm belief that she would find him at once and "have it out with him" once and for all. (Just as though Mary V could ever settle a quarrel once and for all!) But though she had haunted all the known and some of the unknown flying fields, she had found no trace of Johnny. That messenger boy in Tucson had insisted that the plane climbed high and then flew toward the Coast. And at Yuma she had learned that the Thunder Bird had alighted there for gas and oil and had flown toward Los Angeles. But so far as Mary V could discover, it was still flying.

Hoping to wean her from worrying about Johnny, dad had bought the Bear Cat. Mary V had owned it for ten days now, and its mileage stood at 1400 and was just about ready to slide another "1" into sight. The Bear Cat had proven itself a useful little Cat.

Now she shifted from neutral to second, disdaining low speed altogether, and swung boldly out into the stream of traffic. A Ford shied off with a startled squawk to let the Bear Cat by. A hurrying truck that was thinking of cutting in to get first chance within the safety zone passage thought better of it when Mary V honked her big Klaxon at him, and stopped with a jolt that nearly brought the Ford to grief behind it.

But Mary V ignored these trifles. She was busy wondering where she should go next, and she was scanning swiftly the faces of the passers-by in the hope of glimpsing the one face she wished most of all to see.

She reached the corner just as the frame closed against her, and with one small foot on the clutch pedal and the other on the brake, she leaned back and scanned the crowd. Abruptly she leaned and beckoned, saw that her signal went unregarded, and gave three short but terrific blasts of her Klaxon. Five hundred and forty-nine persons reacted sharply to the sound and sent startled glances her way. The traffic cop whirled and looked, the motorman on the car waiting beside her leaned far out and craned, and the conductor grasped both handrails and took a step down that he might see the better.

Mary V ignored these trifles. Bland, for whom she had meant it, jumped and turned a pale, startled pair of eyes her way, and to him she beckoned imperiously. He hesitated, glanced this way and that, making a quick mental decision. Mary V had once been candidly tempted to shoot him and had dallied with the temptation to the point of cocking her sixshooter and aiming it directly at him. She looked now quite capable of repeating the performance and of completing what she had merely started last summer. He went to the edge of the curb, obeying her expectant stare. The expectant stare continued to transfix him, and he stepped off the curb and close to the Bear Cat that was growling in its throat.

"Bland Halliday, where have you *been*, for gracious sake? And where's Johnny?"

"I ain't been anywhere but here-and I wisht I knowed where Johnny was. I—"

"Bland Halliday, you tell me instantly! Where's Johnny?"

"Honest, I don't know. I been looking for him myself, and —"

"Bland Halliday, do you want to be torn limb from limb, right here on the public street before everybody? I want to know where Johnny is, and I want to know *now*."

"Aw, f'r cat's sake! I ain't saw Johnny f'r three weeks-not since the night we got here. I been looking —"

Behind them sounded a succession of impatient honks that extended almost to Seventh Street. The traffic cop had blown his whistle, the street car had clanged warning and gone on. The truck had shaved past Mary V and the Ford had followed. Other cars coming up behind had mistaken the Bear Cat's inaction for closed traffic and had stopped. Others had stopped behind them; then two other street cars slid up and blocked the way around.

Mary V was quite oblivious to all this. She was glaring at the one link between herself and Johnny Jewel. She was bitterly regretting the fact that she had no gun with which to scare Bland into telling the truth, and she was wondering what other means of coercion would prove effective. Bland knew where Johnny was, of course. He was lying, for some reason-probably because he had the habit and couldn't stop.

Bland kept an eye on Mary V's right hand. He suspected a gun, and when, in involuntary obedience to the frantic honkings behind her, she let her hand drop to the gear lever, Bland turned to flee.

"Bland, you come back here!" Bland came. "What do you mean, trying to avoid answering a perfectly civil question?"

"I did answer it," Bland protested in his whining tone. "I said I didn't know —"

"That's no answer; that's nothing but a plain old lie. You do know perfectly well where he is. You left Tucson with Johnny, and you left Yuma with him. Bland Halliday, what have you done with him?"

Bland's eyes turned slightly glassy. Like a trapped animal, he sent roving glances here and there-and took in the purposeful approach of the traffic cop. He turned again toward the curb.

"Don't you dare attempt to leave before —"

"What's the matter here? What you blocking traffic for? Don't you know I can —"

"Oh! Am I in the way here? I shall move immediately, of course. Thank you so much! It's really no trouble at all, and I'm tremendously sorry if I have inconvenienced you or the general public any. I believe you are really *glad*, down deep in your heart, when somebody gives you an excuse to leave that horrid little square spot for a minute. Don't you nearly go wild, having to-Bland! What are you standing there holding up traffic for? Get in!"

Looking completely dazed and helpless, Bland got in.

"Now we're all ready, Mr. Policeman. Run along back and point the herd again before all the nice little tame Fords get walked on. I hear one squalling now. And thank you so much."

Mary V let in the clutch. The Bear Cat slid out across the street, scattering pedestrians and jeopardizing wheels and fenders as it ducked past them. The traffic cop stood still for a minute, rubbing his chin vaguely and staring after Mary V. Then he went back to his post, grinning and frowning-which gave him a strange, complex expression.

"Aw, say, Miss Selmer —"

"Will you be quiet? Haven't you done harm enough, for gracious sake? Aren't you satisfied with getting me almost put in jail innocently? If you had told me at once where Johnny is, I'd be miles away by now. But no-you hold up traffic trying to deceive me, and I almost get pinched. I should think you'd be ashamed. Where is Johnny? If you have done anything to him, Bland Halliday, I'll-hang you!"

"I been telling yuh all I know about it. I don't know where he is, and I don't know where the plane is. They're both of 'em gone, and that's Gawd's truth, Miss Selmer. Last I seen of Johnny he was goin' in the Alexandria. He said he was going to stop there. He registered all right—I seen his name. He stayed all night, and he was gone the next day when I went after him. And the plane's gone, I been out there, and I can't find so much as a sign of it. And that was three weeks ago. And you kin hang me till I'm dead, but I can't tell nothin' more. Don't yuh spose I want to know where's he at?"

"Well—" Mary V crossed the path of a street car, leaving the motorman shivering while he stood on the bell that clamored wildly. "Maybe you are telling the truth-but I doubt it." They were across Figueroa Street and speeding out toward Westlake. The Bear Cat was breaking the speed law, and Mary V had no time to say more.

"Where you takin' me, f'r cat's sake?"

"Oh-for a ride. Don't you like to ride?" Mary V's voice was filled with amiability; too much so to satisfy Bland, who eyed her with suspicion.

"Aw, a fellow can't never git a square deal no more. Here I been hunting the town over trying to git some line on Skyrider. Went and left me in the lurch after me helping him to a roll of kale that would choke a nelephant! And I never charged him nothin' for flying, except just what we agreed on before he got throwed in jail. Handed him over close to five hundred dollars when he come out-piloted him here, took him into town, and was planning on helping him to make more money, and what does he do? Ducks into the Alexandria, leavin' me waitin' outside, hungry and thirsty and tired as a dog. Him with five hundred, me with seventy-five! And *he* wouldn't a knowed any different if I'd trimmed him! Who was to keep tabs on how many passengers I took up? And what does he do? Gives me the slip right there in the Alexandria, that's what he done. I ain't been able to locate him yet, but if ever I do —"

Mary V swung the Bear Cat out and passed a limousine as though it were standing still-which it emphatically was not. What if Bland were telling the truth? What if Johnny had actually dropped out of sight with five hundred dollars in his possession? That would mean-she refused to consider just what it would mean. She would wait until her dad had gotten the truth out of Bland Halliday. She was taking Bland home, hoping that her dad was there so that she would not be compelled to keep Bland any longer than was necessary. Bland was seedier than he had been in Tucson, if that were possible. Too evidently he had no part of the seventy-five dollars left, if he had ever possessed that much. Mary V would like to disbelieve everything he said, but a troubled doubt of his falsity assailed her.

She drove a little faster and presently brought Bland to the door of a cheerful, wide-porched bungalow patterned somewhat after the Rolling R home. Old Sudden was just pulling on his driving gloves ready to step into his own car when the Bear Cat slid up and stopped. He looked at Bland casually, looked again quickly, pursing his lips. Whereupon his poker face hid what he thought.

"Dad, come back into the house and talk to Bland Halliday. He told me the strangest story about Johnny, and-and I wish you'd just talk to him and see if it's true." Mary V was not altogether without consideration for the feelings of another, but candor was the keynote of her nature, and she was very much perturbed, and she did not really feel that a fellow like Bland Halliday had any feelings to consider.

Sudden smoothed a smile off his mouth. "Well, now, this is very thoughtful of you; very thoughtful. I appreciate your coming to consult me before you have settled the whole thing yourself. Come into the house, young man."

An hour later, Sudden leaned back in his chair and looked at Mary V. Tight-lipped, paler than she had any right to be, Mary V met the look wide-eyed. Bland moved his feet anxiously, watching them both.

"I played square with him," he whined. "Either he didn't, or else —"

Sudden's eyes turned to Bland and settled there meditatively. "Yes, I guess you did," he admitted. "Looks like you had played fair. Where are you stopping? I'll take you back down town. Need money?"

"Dad! Aren't you going to *do* anything? If Bland is telling the truth, don't you see what it means? Something must have happened —"

"Well, now, that will all be attended to, kitten. According to Bland, Johnny checked out before he disappeared. Also his airplane disappeared with him. That doesn't look like he'd been made away with, exactly. He's all right, probably-but we'll find out. I've a right to know what he did with that flying machine; it's security for that note of his!"

Mary V sprang to her feet and faced him. "Dad Selmer, I would never have believed a person on oath if they had said you could be so perfectly mean and mercenary! If that's all you care about, why take the Bear Cat and give me that note! Go on-take it! I guess Johnny has a right to do as he pleases until the note is due, at any rate. You might at least treat Johnny with ordinary business courtesy, I should think. You know perfectly well that you wouldn't dare hound your other creditors like that. But if you are really worried about that note, I shall deem it a pleasure and a privilege to pay it myself, and I'm sure the Bear Cat is good for the amount, or if you prefer you may hold back my allowance, and I shall go without clothes and everything until it is paid. It's a perfect outrage to keep nagging Johnny when he's doing his level best and not asking any help from you or any one else. I'm sure I honor and respect him all the more, and you would too if you had a drop of human blood-now what are you grinning for-and trying to hide it? Dad Selmer, you do make me perfectly furious at times!"

Mary V laid hands upon her father and for his shortcomings she "woolled" him until his grizzled hair stood straight on end. Sudden protested, tried to hold her off at arm's length and found her all claws, like an excited wildcat.

"Now, now —"

"Tell me then what you are going to do. And don't try to make me believe you only care for that horrid note. Every time I think of you making that poor boy sign over everything he had on earth, except me, of course, and you wouldn't let him have me when he wanted-why, dad, I could shake you till —"

Bland was edging to the door. He had no experience with families and domestic upheavals, and he did not know just how serious this quarrel might prove. He expected Sudden to order Mary V from the house-to disown her, at the very least. He did not want to be a witness when Sudden broke loose. But Sudden called him back and turned to Mary V.

"Here, let me go. You're scaring off the only evidence we've got that Johnny landed here. You stay right here and behave yourself, young lady. I might want to 'phone you, if I get a clue —"

"Oh, dad! Cross your heart you'll 'phone the very instant you find out anything? Here's your hat-do, for gracious sake, hurry!"

Chapter Twenty-One. Johnny is not Paid to Think

On that same Saturday afternoon, at about the time when Mary V sighted Bland at the southeast corner of Sixth and Spring, Johnny stood just under the peak behind Mateo's cabin and saw a lone horseman ride across the upper neck of the little valley and disappear into the brush on the side opposite him. He waited impatiently. The rider did not reappear, but presently he saw what looked like a human figure crouched behind a rock well up the slope. Johnny stared until his eyes watered with the strain, but he could not be sure that the object was a man. If it were, the man was without a doubt placed there for purposes of observation. The thought was not a pleasant one.

He waited, himself crouched now behind a jutting fragment of rock, and thought he saw the object move. A little later the sun, sliding farther down the sky, reflected a glittering something just above that rock. A bit of glass would do that-the lenses of a field glass, for instance. Two lenses would shine as one, Johnny believed, and was thankful that his slope was in shadow.

Taking it for granted that some one was watching the valley, he studied the spot where the glitter had already winked out-possibly because the man had moved the field glasses, sweeping the valley. It was a good place for a spy, Johnny admitted. There was a slight ridge just there, so that the view was clear for some distance in either direction; Mateo's cabin was in plain sight, and the surrounding hills. He hoped the fellow would see nothing suspicious and would presently give up that post; in the meantime he was effectually treed. There was no shelter that he dared trust on the first rocky half of the descent, and to climb up and over the peak he would surely reveal himself, unless the fellow's attention happened to be centered on something else.

Johnny studied his predicament. The man could see everything-but could he hear? He was half a mile off, Johnny judged, estimating the distance with an accuracy born of long living in the country of far skylines. The spy would need sharp ears indeed to hear anything less than a shout.

Johnny picked up a pebble, aimed, and threw it at the roof of Mateo's cabin. The pebble landed true and rattled off, hitting the ground with a bounce and rolling away in the grass. The children, playing in the open as they always did, stopped and looked up inquiringly, then went on with their play. Mateo came cautiously from the back door and to him Johnny called, thankful that the observer on the hillside could not see through the cabin to where Mateo stood.

"Stay where you are," he called. "Can you hear me?"

Mateo nodded emphatically.

"All right. Take your gun and start off across the flat, down the way Cliff will come. Act like you didn't want to be seen. There's somebody across on the hill, up here, and I want to see if he'll follow you. You get me?"

"Si, yes. I'm go."

"After awhile you can come back. If you see Cliff, tell him he's after ducks. Sabe?"

"Yo se. I'm onderstan'."

"All right. Go back in the house and come out the front door and start off."

Mateo waved his hand and disappeared. In five minutes or less Johnny saw him walking away from the cabin and glancing frequently at the hills upon either hand. His manner might have been called stealthy, if one were looking for stealth. Johnny was looking for something else, and presently he gave a grunt of satisfaction. The object behind the rock stood up and levelled his glasses at Mateo. Johnny waited until he was sure and then scrambled down to the protection of another bowlder. He peered from there up the valley and after some searching discovered his man working carefully along a side hill, evidently anxious to keep Mateo in sight. Johnny worked down another rod or two, reconnoitered again, made another sliding run for it, and stopped behind a clump of brush. In that way he reached the shelter of the oak, feeling certain that he had not been seen.

Through the screen of branches he looked out across the little valley, but he could not see any one at all, not even Mateo. So he turned to his one solace, The Thunder Bird, and dusted it as carefully as a young girl dusts her new piano. With a handful of waste he went over the motor, wiping it until it shone wherever shining was possible, and tried not to think of the man on the hillside. That was Cliff's affair-until Johnny was ready to make the affair his.

"I wish I knew just what he's up to," Johnny fretted. "If I just *knew* something! I'd look like a boob now, wouldn't I, if the guards nabbed us? They might try to pin most anything on me, and I wouldn't have any comeback. It don't look good, if anybody asks me! And if they —"

"Man's come here," Rosa announced close behind him in a tense whisper. "Walking."

Johnny jumped and went on his toes to a spot where he could look through the foliage.

"Walking down," explained Rosa, and waved a skinny hand toward the hill behind them.

"Did you see him?"

"No, senor. I'm seeing rocks falling where somebody walks down."

There was nothing to do but wait. Johnny pushed the girl toward the cabin and saw her scramble under the lowest branches and join the others unconcernedly, tagging the boy Josef, and, then running off into the open-where she could see the hillside-with Josef running after. She did not seem to be watching the hill, while she was apparently absorbed in dodging Josef, but Johnny gathered from her gestures that the man was still coming and that he was making for the cabin. He was wondering what she meant by suddenly sinking to the ground in shrill laughter, when he heard a step behind him. He whirled, startled, his hand jerking back toward the gun he wore.

"I approve your watchfulness, but you happened to be watching in the wrong direction," said Cliff, brushing dirt from his hunting clothes. "Well, they are getting warm, old man. They have eliminated Riverside as a probable hang-out for the mystery plane, and —" He waved a hand significantly while he stood his shotgun against the bole of the tree.

"Some one saw us land in this valley," he added. "Luckily they do not suspect Mateo yet. I saw him going down the flat and sent him on to tell the patrol a lot they already knew. He saw the plane come down, but has not been able to find the exact spot. He thinks it took the air again. His ninos told him of a big bird flying east. Great boy, Mateo. Great kids. Did they see me coming?"

"Sure they did. Rosa's eagle eye spotted a rock or two rolling down and came and told me."

"Good girl, Rosa. The car's over in another valley, parked under a tree very neatly and permanently and in plain sight. Its owner is off hunting somewhere. By its number plates they will never know it. Good old car."

"You seem tickled to think they're after you," Johnny observed, rolling a cigarette by way of manifesting complete unconcern. "What's the next move?"

"Get me across without letting them see where we come from. Can you fly at night?"

"Sure, I can fly at night. Don't the Germans fly at night all over London? I won't swear I'll light easy, though."

"There'll be a moon," said Cliff. "I've got to get over, and I've got to light, and I've got to get back again. There are no if's this time; it's *got* to be done."

"A plane chased us, day before yesterday," Johnny informed him, fanning the smoke from before his face and squinting one eye while he studied Cliff. "It was a long way off, and I got down before it was close enough to see just where I lit. It came back yesterday and scouted around, flying above five thousand feet up. To-day I saw two of them sailing around, but they didn't fly over this way. They were over behind this hill, and high. We'd better do our flying at night, old-timer."

"You can dodge them. You've got to dodge them," said Cliff.

"If I fly," Johnny qualified dryly.

"You've got to fly. You're in to your neck, old man-and there's a loop ready for that." Then, as though he had caught himself saying more than was prudent, he laughed and amended the statement. "Of course, I'm just kidding, but at that, it's important that you make this flight

and as many more as you can get away with. There's something to be brought back to-night —
legitimate news, understand, but of tremendous value to the Syndicate." He reached into his
pocket and drew out an envelope such as Johnny had learned to associate with money.

"Here's two thousand dollars, old man. The boss knows the risk and added a couple of
hundred for good measure, this week. When you land me over there to-night I'll give you
this." He smiled disagreeably. "I think you'll fly, all right-for this."

"Sure, I'll fly-for that. I was kidding. For two thousand I'd fly to Berlin and bring back a
lock of old Kaiser Bill's hair."

"That's the way to talk, old man! I knew you were game. I told the boss so, when he asked
if we could count on you. I said you had nerve, no political prejudices, and-that you need
the money."

"That's my number, I guess," Johnny admitted, grinning.

Cliff laughed again, which made three distinct impulses to laughter in one conversation. This
was not like Cliff's usual conservatism. As Johnny had known him he laughed seldom, and then
only at something disagreeable. He was keyed up for something; a great coup of some sort was
in sight, Johnny guessed shrewdly, studying Cliff's face and the sparkle in his eyes. He was
like a man who sees success quite suddenly where he has feared to look upon failure. Johnny
wondered just what that success might mean-to others.

"I bet you're putting over something big that will tickle Uncle Sam purple," he hazarded,
giving Cliff a round-eyed, admiring glance.

"It will tickle him-purple, all right!" Cliff's tone had a slight edge on it. "You're sitting in
a big game, my boy, but you aren't paid to ask questions. You go ahead and earn your two
thousand. You do the flying, and let some one else do the thinking."

"I get you," said Johnny laconically and took himself and his thinkless brain elsewhere.

Chapter Twenty-Two. Johnny Makes up his Mind

"No political prejudices-hunh!" Johnny was filling the gas tank, and while he did it he was doing a great deal of thinking which he was not paid to do. "This newspaper business-say, she's one great business, all right. It's nice to have a boss that jumps your wages up a couple of hundred at a lick, and tells you you needn't think, and you mustn't have any political prejudices. Fine job, all right. Will I fly by moon-light? Will I? And them government planes riding on my tail like they've been doing the last two trips? Hunh!"

Cliff came then with a bundle under his arm. Johnny cast a suspicious eye down at him, and Cliff held up the package.

"I want to take this along-rockets; to let them know we're coming. Then they'll have flares for us to land by."

"Been planning on some night-riding, hunh?"

"Naturally; I would plan for every contingency that could possibly arise."

"Hunh. That covers them planes that have been line-riding over this way, too, I reckon." Johnny climbed down and prepared to pump a little more air into one tire.

"Possibly. Don't let those airplanes worry you, old man. They have to catch us, you know."

"No? I ain't worrying about 'em. The one that does the thinking on this job can do the worrying. I'm paid to fly." Johnny laughed sourly as he glanced up from where he squatted beside the wheel.

"Let it go at that. Are you about ready? It will be dark in another half hour-dark enough to fly, at least." Cliff was moving about restlessly in the gloom under the tree. For all his earlier exhilaration he seemed nervous, in haste to be done.

"You said moonlight," Johnny reminded him, putting away the pump.

"I know, but it's best to get out of here and over the line in the dark, I think. The moon will be up in less than an hour. Be ready to leave in half an hour-and don't start the motor until the very last minute. Mateo has not come back yet. If they are holding him —"

"I'm ready to go when you are. Let's run her out before it's plumb dark under here. She can't be seen in this light very far-and if a man comes close enough to see her, he'd get wise anyway. Uh course," he apologized quickly, "that's more thinking than I'm paid to do, but you got to let me think a little bit now and then, or I can't fly no two thousand dollars worth to-night."

"I meant thinking about my part in the game. All right, I've got her right, on this side. Take up the tail and let's run her out."

In the open the children were running back and forth, playing tag and squealing over the hazards of the game. When the Thunder Bird rolled out with its outspread wings and its head high and haughty, they gave a final dash at one another and rushed off to get wheelbarrow and stick horses. They were well trained-shamefully well trained in the game of cheating.

Johnny looked at them glumly, with an aversion born of their uncanny obedience, their unchildlike shrewdness. Fine conspirators they would make later on, when they grew a few years older and more cunning!

"Head her into the wind so I can take the air right away quick," he ordered Cliff, and helped swing the Thunder Bird round.

Dusk was settling upon the very heels of a sunset that had no clouds to glorify and therefore dulled and darkened quickly into night, as is the way of sunsets in the southern rim of States.

Already the shadows were deep against the hill, and in the deepest stood the Thunder Bird, slim, delicately sturdy, every wire taut, every bit of aluminum in her motor clean and shining, a gracefully potent creature of the air. Across her back her name was lettered crudely, blatantly, with the blobbed period where Johnny had his first mental shock of Sudden's changed attitude toward him.

While he pulled on his leather helmet and tied the flaps under his chin, and buttoned his leather coat and pulled on his gloves, Johnny stood off and eyed the Thunder Bird with wistful affection. She was going into the night for the first time, going into danger, perhaps into annihilation. She might never fly again! He went up and laid a hand caressingly on her slanted propeller, just as he used to stroke the nose of his horse Sandy before a hard ride.

"Good old Thunder Bird! Good old Mile High! You've got your work cut out for yuh to-night, old girl. Go to it-eat it up."

He slid his hand down along the blade's edge and whispered, "It's you and me for it, old girl. You back my play like a good girl, and we'll give 'em hell!"

He stepped back, catching Cliff's eye as Cliff took a last puff at his cigarette before grinding it under his heel.

"Thought I saw a crack in the blade," Johnny gruffly explained his action. "It was the way the light struck. All right; turn her over, and we'll go."

He climbed in while Cliff went to the propeller. Never before had Johnny felt so keenly the profanation of Cliff's immaculate, gloved hands on his beloved Thunder Bird.

"Never mind, old girl. His time's short-or ours is," he muttered while he tested his controls. "All right-contact!" he called afterwards, and Cliff, with a mighty pull, set the propeller whirling and climbed hastily into his place.

The kiddies, grouped close to watch the Thunder Bird's flight, blinked and turned their faces from the dust storm kicked up by the exhaust. The plane shook, ran forward faster and faster, lifted its little wheels off the ground and went whirring away toward the dark blur of the mountains that rimmed the southern edge of the valley.

Johnny circled twice, getting sufficient altitude to clear the hills, then flew straight for the border. In the dark Cliff would not know the difference between one thousand feet and five thousand, and Johnny wanted to save his gas. He even shut off his motor and glided down to one thousand before he had passed the line, and picked up again and held the Thunder Bird steady, regardless of the droning hum, that would shout its passing to those below.

"Isn't this rather low?" Cliff turned his head to shout.

Johnny did not read suspicion in his voice, but vague uneasiness lest the trip be brought to a sudden halt.

"It's all right. They can't do anything but listen to us go past. I've got to keep my landmarks."

Cliff leaned and peered below, evidently satisfied with the explanation. A minute later he was fussing with the flare he meant to set off for a signal, and Johnny was left free to handle the plane and do a little more of that thinking for which he was not paid.

The night sky was wonderful, a deep translucent purple studded with stars that seemed closer, more humanly intimate than when seen from earth even in the higher altitudes. The earth was shadowy, remote, with now a growing brightness as the moon slid up into sight. Before its light touched the earth the Thunder Bird was bathed in its glow. Cliff's profile emerged clear-cut from the dusk as he gazed toward the east. Johnny, too, glanced that way, but he was not thinking then of the wonderful effect of the rising moon upon the drifting world below. He was wondering just why this trip to-night should be so important to Cliff.

It would not be the first time that Johnny had gone ahead with his eyes shut, but that is not saying he would not have preferred travelling with them open. His lips were set so stubbornly that the three tiny dimples appeared in his chin, —his stubborn-mule chin, Mary V had once called it, —and his eyes were big and round and solemn. Mary V seeing him then would surely have asked herself, "What, for gracious sake, is Johnny up to now?"

But Mary V was not present, and Cliff Lowell was fully absorbed in his own thoughts and purposes; wherefore Johnny's ominous expression went unnoticed.

In the moonlight the notched ridge showed clear, and toward it the Thunder Bird went booming steadily, as ducks fly south with the first storm wind of November. A twinkling light just under the notch showed that Cliff's allies were at home, whether they expected him or not. Johnny veered slightly, pointing the Thunder Bird's nose straight toward the light.

Cliff half turned, handing something back over his shoulder.

"Can you drop this for me, old man, when we are almost over the hacienda? The fuse is lighted, and I'm afraid I might heave it on to the wing and set us afire."

Johnny heard only about half of what Cliff was saying, but he understood what was wanted and took the bomb-like contraption and balanced it in his hand. Cliff had said rockets, but this thing was not like any rocket Johnny had ever seen. Some new aerial signal bomb, he guessed it, and thought how thoroughly up-to-date Cliff was in all his tools of trade.

He poised the thing on the edge of the cockpit, waited until they were rather close, and then gave it a toss overboard. For a few seconds nothing happened. Than, halfway to the ground a great blob of red light burst dazzlingly, lighting the adobe building with a crimson glow that floated gently earthward, suspended from its little parachute.

Cliff handed back another, and Johnny heaved it away from the plane. It flared white; the third one, dropped almost before the door of the main building, revealed three men standing there gazing upward, their faces weird in its bluish glare. Red, white and blue —a signal used sacrilegiously here, he thought.

Johnny circled widely and came back to find the landing place lighted by torches of some kind. He was not interested in details, and what they were he did not know or care. The landing was marked for him plainly, though he scarcely needed it with the moon riding now above the low rim of hills.

He came down gently, and Cliff, remembering to give Johnny his money, climbed out hurriedly to meet the florid gentleman who had never yet failed to appear when the Thunder Bird landed. Johnny did not know his name, for Cliff had never mentioned it. The two never talked together in his presence, but strolled away where even their voices would not reach him, or went inside the adobe house and stayed there until Cliff was ready to return. News gathering, as Johnny saw the news gathered, seemed to be mighty secret business, never to be mentioned save in a whisper.

The florid gentleman came strolling toward them through the moonlight, smoking a big, fat cigar whose aroma reminded Johnny of something disagreeable, like burning rubbish. Tonight the florid gentleman's stroll did not seem to match his face, which betrayed a suppressed excitement in spite of the fat cigar. He reached out, caught Cliff's arm, and turned back toward the house, forgetting all about his stroll as soon as he began to speak. He forgot something else, for Johnny distinctly heard a sentence or two not meant for his ears.

"I've put it through all right. I got them to sign with the understanding that they don't turn a hand till you bring the money. You can take —"

That was all, for even on that still night the florid gentleman's voice receded quickly to an unintelligible mumbling. They went inside, and the door closed. Johnny and the Thunder Bird were once more shut out from their conference.

Johnny spied a Mexican who was leaning against the wall of a smaller building, smoking and staring pensively across the moonlighted plain toward that portion of the United States where the Potreros hunched themselves up against the stars.

"Bring me some gas, you!" he called peremptorily.

The Mexican pulled his gaze away from the vista that had held him hypnotized and straightened his lank form reluctantly. From a bench near by he picked up a square kerosene can of the type made internationally popular by a certain oil trust, inspected it to see if the baling-wire handle would hold the weight of four gallons of gasoline, and sauntered to a shed under which a red-leaded iron drum lay on a low scaffold of poles. A brass faucet was screwed into the hole for a faucet. He turned it listlessly, watched the gasoline run in a sparkling stream the size of his finger, went off into a moon-dream until the oil can was threatening to run over, and then shut off the stream at its source. He picked up the can with the air of one whose mind is far distant, came like a sleepwalker to where Johnny waited, set the can down, and turned apathetically to retrace his steps to where he could lean again.

"That ain't all. Bring me a can of water as fast as you brought the gas. We may want to go back to-night."

"Si," sighed the Mexican and continued to drift away.

"Don't be in a hurry. Come and lift the can up to me."

The Mexican returned as slowly as he had departed, and picked up the can. Johnny dropped a half dollar into it, whereat the Mexican's eyes opened a trifle wider.

"What's the name of that red-faced friend of Cliff's?" Johnny asked, taking the can and beginning to pour gas into the Thunder Bird's tank.

"Quien sabe?" murmured the listless one.

Johnny paused, and another coin slipped tinkling into the can.

"What did you say?"

The Mexican hesitated. He would like very much to see that other coin. It had sounded heavy-almost as heavy as a dollar. He turned his head and looked attentively at the house.

"Quien sabe, senor." The senor he added for sake of the coin he had not seen. "Mucho name, Ah'm theenk."

"Think some more." Johnny poured the last of the gas and caused another clinking sound in the can. The Mexican's eyes were as wide open now as they would ever be, and he even called a faint smile to his countenance.

"Some-*times* —Sawb," he recollected, and reached for the can.

"Sawb-What y'mean, Sawb? That's no name for a man. You mean Schwab?"

"Si, senor-Sawb." He glanced again at the house distrustfully, as if he feared even his murmur might be overheard.

"All right. Get the water now."

"Si, senor." And he went for it at a trot, that he might the sooner investigate the source of those clinking sounds.

"Schwab! Uhm-hm —he looks it, all right." He stepped down to the ground, pulled a handful of silver from his pocket and eyed it speculatively, glancing now and then after the receding Mexican. "He'd tell a lot to get it all," he decided. "He'd tell so much he'd make up about four thirds of it. I guess those birds ain't taking greasers like him into their secrets, and he's spilled all he knows when he spilled the fellow's name. Four bits more will do him fine." Wealth, you will observe, was inclining Johnny toward parsimoniousness.

He got the water from the hopeful Mexican, gave him the half dollar and brief thanks, filled the radiator, and waited for Cliff. And in a very few minutes Cliff came out, walking as though he were in a hurry. The florid gentleman stood framed in the doorway, watching him as friendly hosts are wont to gaze after departing guests, out west where guests are few. Like a departing guest Cliff turned for a last word.

"I'll be back soon as possible," he called to the man Schwab. "A little after sunrise, probably. Better wait here for me."

Schwab nodded and waved his cigar, and Johnny grinned to himself while he straddled into his seat.

Cliff went straight to the propeller. "Take me to Los Angeles, old man. You can light where you did before; there won't be any bean vines in the way this time. I had the Japs clear off and level a strip for a landing. It's marked off with white flags, so you can easily see it in this moonlight. Luck's with us; I was afraid we might have to wait until morning, but this is fine. Several hours will be saved."

"I've got you," Johnny said-and he did not mean what Cliff thought he meant. "All ready? Contact!"

Off to the right and flying high, two government planes circled slowly over the boundary line. Long before the Thunder Bird had put the map of Mexico behind her the two planes veered that way, their fishlike fuselages and the finned rudders gleaming like silver in the moonlight. Cliff, happening to glance that way, moved uneasily in his seat and cursed the moon he had so lately blessed.

"Better duck down somewhere; can't you dodge 'em?" he yelled back at Johnny, who was himself eyeing perturbedly the two swift scouts.

"You let me handle this. It's what I'm paid for," he yelled back, and banked the Thunder Bird sharply to the left. He had not yet crossed the border; until he did so those scouting machines dare not do more than keep him in view. But keeping him in view was absurdly simple in that cloudless sky, white-lighted by the moon.

To a person looking up from the earth, the situation would have appeared to be simple —a matter of three planes zooming homeward after a long practice flight. The five-pointed star in the black circle, painted on each wing Of the government planes, would probably have been invisible at that height, and the bold lettering of THE THUNDER BIRD indistinguishable also on the shadowed underside of the outlaw plane. To the government planes she was branded irrevocably as they looked down upon her from their superior height. There was no mistaking her, no hope whatever that the scouts might think her anything but the outlaw plane she was, flying in the face of international law, trafficking in treason, fair game if she once crossed the line.

On she went, boring through the night, heading straight for Tia Juana, which lies just south of the line. Just north of that invisible line her pursuers held doggedly to the course.

"Turn back," Cliff turned to shout to Johnny who was driving big-eyed, his lips pursed with the tense purpose that held him to his work. "Turn back and land at the rancho. We'll never make Los Angeles with those damned buzzards after us. I'll have to notify Sch-somebody."

"Send him a thought message, then."

"Turn back when I tell you!" Cliff twisted around as far as his safety belt would permit, that he might glare at Johnny. His tone was the long of stern authority.

"Can't be done! The Thunder Bird's took the bit in her teeth. I'm just riding' and whippin' down both sides!" Johnny laughed aloud, Cliff's tone releasing within him a sudden, reckless mood that gloried in the sport of the chase and forgot for a moment its grim meaning. "Whooee! Go to it, old girl! They gotta go some to put salt on *your* tail-whoo-ee!"

"Are you crazy, man? Those are government planes! They're probably armed. They'll get us wherever we cross the line-turn back, I tell you! You're under orders from me, and you'll fly where I tell you! This is no child's play, you fool. If they get me with what papers-it'll be a firing squad for you if they catch you-don't forget that! Damn you, don't you realize —"

"Sit down!" roared Johnny. "And shut up!"

"I won't shut up!" Cliff's eyes, as Johnny saw them facing the moon, looked rather wild. "You're working for me, and I order you to take me back to Schwab's. You better obey-it will go as hard with you as it will with me if those planes get in their work. Why, you fool, they —"

"What the heck do I care about them? I'm working for a bigger man than you are right now. Sit down!"

"Stop at Tia Juana then and let me out. But I warn you —"

"Shut up!"

"I will not! You'll do as I tell you, or I'll —"

"Now will you shut up?" Johnny swung his gun, a heavy, forty-four caliber Colt, of the type beloved of the West. Its barrel came down fairly on the top of Cliff's leathern helmet and all but cracked his skull. Cliff shut up suddenly and completely, sliding limply down into his seat.

"By gosh, you had it coming!" Johnny muttered as he settled back into his seat. He had never knocked a man cold before, and his natural soft-heartedness needed bracing. He had let Cliff rave as long as he dared, dreading the alternative. But now that it was done he felt a certain relief to have it over. He could turn his mind wholly to the accomplishment of another feat which would take all his nerve.

That other thing had looked simple enough in contemplation, but the actual doing of it presented complications. The simplicity of the plan vanished with the sighting of those two scouting planes that persisted in paralleling his course and herding him away from the line he fain would cross.

Tia Juana with its flat-roofed adobes lay ahead of him now, its lights twinkling like fallen stars. Away off to the right he could see the blurred lights of San Diego and the phosphorescent gleam of the bay and ocean beyond. Beautiful beyond words was the broad view he got, but its beauty could only vaguely impress him then, though he might later recall it wistfully.

He looked toward San Diego with longing; looked at the two planes that hounded him, then gazed straight ahead at the ocean. Perhaps they would not follow him beyond their station at North Island. They would maybe circle and come back, watching for his return, or they might keep to the shore line, flying north, and thinking to head him off when he turned inland. At least, he reasoned, that is what he would do if he were following an outlaw plane and saw it head out over the ocean, straight for Honolulu.

So over Tia Juana he flew and made for the sea like a gull that has flown too far from its nesting place. He watched and saw the two planes spiraling upward, climbing to a higher altitude where it would be easy to dart down at him if he swung north. They suspected that trick, evidently, and were preparing to swoop and follow.

The beach, pale yellow in the moonlight, with a riffle of white at its edge, slid beneath him. The ocean, heaving gently, rolled under, the moon reflected from its depths.

Cliff sat slumped down in his seat, his head tilted upon one shoulder. He had not moved nor made a sound, and his limp silence began to worry Johnny. What if he had struck too hard, had killed the man? A little tremor went over him, a prickling of the scalp. Killing Cliff had no part in his plans, would be too horrid a mischance. He wished now that he had left him alone, had let him bluster and threaten. Perhaps Cliff would not have had presence of mind enough to do what Johnny had feared he would do when he saw capture was inevitable: drop overboard what papers he carried that would incriminate him with the United States Federal officers. With empty pockets Cliff would be as free of suspicion as Johnny himself—a mere passenger in a plane that had flown too far south. He would then be fairly safe in assuming that Johnny would never dare to cross the line with him under the eye of those who watched from the sky. It had been the fear of that ruse that had brought Johnny to the point of violence to Cliff's person, but he was sorry now that he had not risked taking that chance.

Flying has its inconveniences, after all, for Johnny could not stop to investigate the injury he had done to Cliff. He would have to go on, now that he was started, but the thought that he might be flying with a dead man chilled what enthusiasm he had felt for the adventure.

On over the ocean he flew until he had passed the three-mile limit which he hazily believed would bar the planes of the government unless they had express orders to follow him out. Looking back, he saw that his hunters seemed content to wheel watchfully along the shore line, and presently he banked around and flew north.

From the Mexican line to San Diego is not far —a matter of twenty miles or so. Across the mouth of San Diego bay, on the inner shore of which sits the town, North Island stretches itself like a huge alligator lying with its back above water; a long, low, sandy expanse of barrenness that leaves only a narrow inlet between its westernmost tip and the long rocky finger of Point Loma.

Time was when North Island was given over to the gulls and long-billed pelicans, and San Diego valued it chiefly as a natural bulkhead that made the bay a placid harbor where the great combing rollers could not ride. But other birds came; great, roaring, man-made birds, that rose whirring from its barrenness and startled the gulls until they grew accustomed to the sight and sound of them. Low houses grew in orderly rows. More of the giant birds came. Nowadays the people of San Diego, looking out across the bay, will sometimes look again to make sure whether the sailing object they see is an airplane or only a gull. In time the gull will flap its wings; the airplane never does. All through the day the air is filled with them-gulls and airplanes sharing amicably the island and the air above it.

Up from the south, with her nose pointed determinedly northward and her rudder set steady as the tail of a frozen fish, the Thunder Bird came humming defiantly, flying swift under the moon. Over San Diego bay, watching through night-glasses the outlaw bird, the two scouting planes dipped steeply toward their nesting place on North Island. Three planes were up with students making practice flights and doing acrobatics by moonlight. These saw one scout go down and land, saw the other circle over the field and climb higher, bearing off toward the mainland to see what the outlaw plane would do.

The Thunder Bird swung on over the island, banked and came back over Point Loma, heading straight for the heart of the flying station. She was past the finlike reef where the pelicans foregather, when the searchlight brushed its white light over that way, seeking her like a groping finger; found her and transfixed her sternly with its pitiless glare.

There was no hiding from that piercing gaze, no possibility of pretending that she was a government plane and flying lawfully there. For straight across her middle, from wing-tip to wing-tip, still blazoned THE THUNDER BIRD in letters as bold and black as Bland's brush and a quart of carriage paint could make them.

She volplaned, flattened out a thousand feet or so above the island, circled as the searchlight, losing her when she dipped, sought her again with wide sweeping gestures of its accusing white finger.

Blinded by the glare, poor Johnny was banking to find a landing place among that assemblage of tents, low-eaved barracks, hangars, shops-the city built for the purpose of teaching men how to conquer the air. Something spatted close beside him on the edge of the cockpit as he wheeled and left a ragged hole in the leather. Johnny's brain registered automatically the fact that he was being shot at. They probably meant that as a hint that he was to clear out or come down, one or the other. Well, if they'd take that darned searchlight out of his eyes so he could see, he would come down fast enough.

In desperation he slanted down steeply toward an open space, and the open space immediately showed a full border of lights, revealing itself a landing field such as he had read of and dreamed of but had never before seen. It shot up at him swiftly; too swiftly. He came down hard. There was a jolt, a bounce and another jolt that jarred the Thunder Bird from nose to tail.

After a dazed interval much briefer than it seemed, Johnny unstrapped himself and climbed out unsteadily. He looked fearfully at Cliff, but there was no sign of life there. Cliff's head had merely tilted from the right shoulder to the left shoulder, and rested there.

Uniformed young men came trotting up from all sides. Two carried rifles, and their browned faces wore a look of grim eagerness, like men looking forward to a fight. Johnny pushed up his goggles and stared around at them.

"Where's your captain or somebody that's in charge here? I want to see the foreman of this outfit, and I want to see him quick," he demanded, as the two armed young athletes hustled him between them. "Here, layoff that grabbing stuff! Where do you get that? I ain't figuring on any getaway. I'm merely bringing a man into camp that stacks up like a spy or something like that. Better have a doctor come and take a look at him; I had to land him on the bean with my six-gun, and he acts kinda like he's hurt. He ain't moved since."

"Well, will you listen to that!" One of the foremost of the unarmed group grinned. "This here must be Skyrider Jewel, boys, no mistake about that-he's running true to form. 'Nother elopement-only this time he's went and eloped with a spy, he claims."

"Here comes the leatherneck. You'll wish you hadn't of lit, Skyrider. You'll be shot at sunrise for this, sure!"

"You know it! It's a firing squad for yours, allrighty!"

Johnny gave them a round-eyed, disgusted glare. "They can shoot and be darned; but the boss has got to see Cliff Lowell and the papers he's got on him, if I have to wade through the whole hunch of you! Do you fellows think, for gosh sake, I just flew over here to give you guys a treat? Why, good golly! You—"

"Here, you come along with me and do your talking to the commandant," a gruff voice spoke at his shoulder.

"And let these gobblers fool around here and maybe lose the stuff this man's got in his clothes! Oh-h, no! Bring him along, and I'll go. I'd sure like a chance to talk to somebody that can show a few brains on this job. That's what I came over here for. I didn't have to land, recollect."

The petty officer gave an order or two. The guards fell in beside Johnny with a military preciseness that impressed him to silence. From somewhere near two men trotted up with a field stretcher, and upon it Cliff was laid, still unconscious.

"You sure beaned him right," one of them observed, looking up at Johnny with some admiration.

"Yes, and I'd like to bean the whole bunch of you the same way. You fellows ain't making any hit with me at all," Johnny retorted uncivilly as he left under guard for headquarters.

A few minutes later he was standing alone before a man whose clean-cut, military bearing, to say nothing of the insignia of rank on his uniform, awed Johnny to the point of calling him "sir" and of couching his replies in his best, most grammatical English. The guards had been curtly dismissed, for which he was grateful, and he had the satisfaction of stating his case in private. Johnny did not want those fellows out there to hear just how easily he had been fooled. They seemed to know altogether too much about him as it was.

The commandant listened attentively to what John Ivan Jewel had to say. John Ivan Jewel had nearly finished his story when he thought of another phase of the affair, and one that had begun to worry him considerably.

"I forgot to tell you about the money. I've got a good deal from them since I started. They paid me on a sliding scale, beginning with fifteen hundred dollars a week and ending with two thousand that Cliff paid me this evening. I've got it all with me."

Prom his secret pocket Johnny drew all his wealth, counted off four hundred dollars and handed the rest to his inquisitor.

"This four hundred dollars is my own, that I brought from Arizona," he explained, flushing a little under the keen eyes of Captain Riley. "This is honest money; the rest is what they paid me for flying back and forth across the line."

The commandant turned the big roll of bank notes over, looking at it quizzically.

"Who is really entitled to this money?" he asked Johnny crisply.

"Well, I—I don't know, sir. It's what they paid me for flying."

"And did you fly as agreed upon?"

"Yes, sir; I made trips back and forth whenever Cliff wanted me to. That is, up to the time I lit out for here, so you could see for yourself what he's up to. He ordered me to go back to Schwab's place, but I wouldn't. I—I knocked him on the head and came on. But until then I flew as agreed upon."

"Do you feel that you earned this money?"

"Well-taking everything into consideration-yes, sir, I do. I think now I worked for them much cheaper than any other aviator would have done.

"Yes. Well, you spoke of that four hundred being honest money, thus differentiating it from this money. Don't you consider this is honest money? What do you mean by honest?"

Johnny flushed unhappily. "Well, it's kinda hard to explain, but I guess I meant that I wasn't doing the right thing when I was earning that money you've got. I meant it wasn't clean money, the way I look at it now. Because it was crooks I was working for, and I don't know how they got it. I worked honestly for it, for them, but the work wasn't honest with the government. It's kinda hard—"

"I think I'll just give you a receipt for this. How much is it?"

"There ought to be about seventy-two hundred there, all told, sir."

Captain Riley looked at him queerly and proceeded to count the astounding wealth of John Ivan Jewel. Then he very matter-of-factly wrote a receipt, which Johnny accepted with humility, not at all sure of what the captain thought or intended.

"Now, tell me this. Is this young man —-the one you brought in-is he the only one you know who has been concerned in this-er-business?

"Yes, sir, on this side he is. Cliff spoke about his boss several times, but he never told me who his boss was. An International News Syndicate, he claimed. But I know now that was just a stall. I don't think there was any such thing. There's a Mexican, Mateo, down where we kept the plane —"

"Mateo-yes, we have Mateo." Captain Riley sat drumming his fingers gently on the table, studying Johnny with his chin dropped a little so that he looked up under his eyebrows, which grew long, unruly hairs here and there.

Johnny's eyes rounded with surprise. He wanted to ask how they had come to suspect Mateo when they had seemed so unsuspicious, but he let it go.

"There's another one, named Schwab, over in Mexico where we always went," he divulged. "He's the one Cliff got those papers from-whatever they were. And he's the one that expects to get some money in the morning. I heard that much. I —I could get him, too," he added tentatively.

"Out of Mexico?" Captain Riley stirred slightly in the chair.

"Yes, sir. I'm pretty sure I could. I was planning to nab him, if you'd let me."

"You mean you could bring him-as you brought this man Lowell?"

Johnny's lips tightened. "If I had to-yes, sir. I'd knock him on the head same as I did Cliff. Only I wouldn't hit quite so hard next time."

Captain Riley bit his lip. "Better hit hard if you hit at all," he advised. "That's a very good rule to remember. It applies to a great many things."

Then he straightened his shoulders a bit and called his orderly, who again impressed Johnny with his military preciseness when he stood at attention and saluted. Captain Riley's whole manner seemed to stiffen to that military preciseness, though Johnny had thought him stiff enough before.

"Detain this man," he commanded crisply, "until further orders. If he is hungry, feed him; and see that he has a decent place to sleep. The petty officers' quarters will do."

He watched the perturbed John Ivan Jewel depart under guard, and his eyes were not half so stern as his tone had been. Then he reached for his desk 'phone and called up the repair shop.

"Run that Thunder Bird plane into the shop and repair it to-night," he commanded. "You will probably need to shift motors, but preserve the present appearance of the plane absolutely. It must be ready to fly at sunrise."

Then, being all alone where he could afford to be just a human being, he grinned to himself, "So-ome boy," he chuckled. "Hope he doesn't lose any sleep to-night. So-ome boy."

Chapter Twenty-Four. The Thunder Bird's Last Flight for Johnny

Over North Island the high, clear notes of the bugle sounding reveille woke Johnny. Immediately afterward a guard appeared to take him in charge, from which Johnny gathered that he was still being "detained." He did not want to be detained, and he did not feel that they had any right to detain him. He flopped over and pulled the blankets over his ears.

"Here, you get up. Captain wants you brought before him right after chow, and that's coming along soon as you can get into your pants. You better be steppin'."

"Aw, what's he want to see me for?" Johnny growled. It would be much pleasanter to go back to his dream of Mary V.

"Why, to shoot you, stupid. Whadda yuh think?"

"I'd hate to tell yuh right to your face, but at that I may force myself to it if you hang around long enough," Johnny retorted, getting into his clothes hurriedly, for the morning was chill and bleak. "Where's that chuck you was talking about? Say, good golly, but you're a sorry looking bird. I'm sure glad I ain't a soldier."

"Whadda yuh mean, glad? It takes a man to do man-size work. That's what I mean. Wait till about twelve of us stand before yuh waiting for the word! Lucky for you this sand makes soft digging, or you wouldn't have pep enough left to dig your own grave, see."

"You seem to know. Is yours dug already? They musta had you at it last night."

The guard grinned and suspended hostilities until after Johnny had eaten, when he led him out and across to where Johnny's inquisitor of the night before awaited his coming. Captain Riley was not so terrifying by daylight. For one thing, he betrayed the fact that he wore large, light-tan freckles, and Johnny never did feel much awe of freckles. Captain Riley also wore a smile, and he was smoking a cigar when Johnny went in.

"Good morning, Mr. Jewel. I hope you slept well."

"I guess I did ——I never stayed awake to see," Johnny told him quite boldly for a youth who had blushed and said "sir" to this man last night.

"You landed pretty hard last night, I hear."

"Why-yes, I guess I did. It looked to me around here last night as though I had fallen down bad."

"And what has made you so cheerful this morning?" Captain Riley actually grinned at Johnny. He could afford to, since Johnny was not in service and therefore need not be reminded constantly of the difference between officer and man.

"I dunno-unless maybe it's because the worst is done and can't be helped, so there's no use worrying about it."

"Well, I can't agree with you, young man. You may possibly do worse to-day. Last night, for instance, you brought in a man who has been very much wanted by the government. We did not know that he was the man until you landed with him, but certain papers he carried furnished what proof we needed. You spoke of another —a man named Schwab. Now I am not going to ask you to bring him in. He is in Mexico, and the laws of neutrality must be preserved. I shall have nothing whatever to do with the matter. I wish he were on this side, though. There's quite a good-sized reward offered for his arrest-in case he ever does get back on our side of the line."

"Mhm-hmh —I —see," said Johnny, in his best, round-eyed judicial manner.

"Yes. He's a criminal of several sorts, among them the crime of meddling with the government. He's over there now-where he can do the most harm.

"Y-ess-he's over there —*now*," Johnny agreed guardedly.

"However, I can't send you over after him, I am sorry to say. It is impossible. If ever he comes back, though —"

"He'd be welcome," Johnny finished with a grin.

"We'd never part with him again," the captain agreed cheerfully. "Well, that Thunder Bird plane of yours had quite a jolt, from the report. You cracked the crank-case for one thing, and broke the tail. I had the plane run in and repaired last night, so it's all ready now for you to go up. We really are much in your debt for bringing in this man Lowell; though your manner of doing it was rather unusual, I must admit. Are you-er-ready to fly?"

"Fly where?" Johnny nerved himself to ask, though he knew well enough where he intended to fly.

"Fly away from North Island," smiled Captain Riley, who was not to be caught. "Civilian planes are not permitted here."

"If I come back would I be shot at?"

"Oh, no —I think not, so long as you come peacefully."

"I'll come peacefully all right; what I'm wondering now is, will the other fellow?" Johnny looked toward the door suggestively.

Captain Riley laughed and rose to his feet. "Young man, you seem to know a sure way of making men peaceful! They tell me that Cliff Lowell came to himself about two o'clock this morning. For awhile they thought you had finished him."

"Well, it's time all good flyers were in the air; I'll go with you and see you start. I'm rather curious over that Thunder Bird of yours. I want a look at her."

In his youth and innocence-John Ivan Jewel wondered why it was that the soldiers looked astonished even while they saluted their commanding officer. He did not know that he was being especially honored by Captain Riley, which is perhaps a good thing. It saved him a good deal of embarrassment and left him so much at ease that he could talk to the captain almost as freely as if he had not worn a uniform.

"Good-by —and good luck," said Captain Riley, and shook hands with Johnny. "I'll be glad to see you again-and, by the way, I'm just keeping that money until you call for it."

Johnny climbed in and settled himself, then leaned over the edge where the bullet had nicked so that his words would not carry to the man waiting to crank the motor.

"I'll call for that money in about two hours," he said. "I ain't saying good-by, Captain. I'll see yuh later."

Captain Riley stood smiling to himself while he watched the Thunder Bird take the air. That it took the air smoothly, spiraling upward as gracefully as any of his young flyers could do, did not escape him. Nor did the steadiness with which it finally swung away to the southeast.

"That boy's a born flyer," he observed to his favorite first lieutenant, who just happened to be standing near. "They say he never has had any training under an instructor. He just *flew*. He'll make good —a kid like that is bound to."

Up in the Thunder Bird Johnny was thinking quite different thoughts. "He thinks I won't be able to deliver the goods. He was nice and friendly, all right-good golly, he'd oughta be! He admitted right out plain that they wanted Cliff bad. But he's hanging on to my money so he'll have some hold over me if I don't bring in Schwab for him. And if I don't, and go back for my money, he'll-well, firing squad won't be any kidding, is what I mean.

"O-h-h, no! Captain Riley can't fool me! Wouldn't tell me to get Schwab over here-didn't dare tell me. But he makes it worth a whole lot to me to get him, just the same. He knows darn well if I don't I'll never dare to go back, and he'll be over seven thousand dollars better off." Johnny, you will observe, had quite forgotten that receipt in his pocket, which Captain Riley might find it hard to explain if he attempted to withhold the money.

His doubt of the Captain increased when, looking back, he spied two swift scouting planes scudding along a mile or two behind him. That they might be considered a guard of honor rather than spies sent out to see that he did not play false never occurred to him.

"Aw, you think maybe I won't do it!" he snorted angrily, his young vanity hurt. "All right, tag along and be darned. I'll have Schwab and be flying back again before you can bank around to fly hack and tattle where I went. That's what I mean. I ain't going to be done outa no seven thousand dollars; I'll tell the world I ain't."

Getting Schwab was absurdly simple, just as Johnny had felt sure it would be. He flew to where he would be expected to cross the line had he come from Los Angeles. Schwab would be impatient, anxious to get in his fingers the money Cliff was supposed to bring. He did not wait at the house, but came out to meet the Thunder Bird. Johnny had been sure that he would do that very thing.

To keep the nose of the Thunder Bird toward Schwab so that he could not see that only one man returned with her was simple. Until he was close Schwab did not suspect that Cliff was not along. Even then he was not suspicious, but came hurrying up to know why Johnny came alone. Schwab wanted that money-they always do.

"Where's my man?" he demanded of Johnny, who had brought the landing gear against an old fence post used to block the wheels, and shut the motor off as much as he could and keep it running.

"Your man is sick." Which was true enough; Cliff was a very sick man that morning. "You'll have to come to him. Get in-it won't take long."

Schwab hung back a little, not from fear of Johnny but because he had no stomach for flying. "Well, but didn't he send —"

"He didn't send a darned thing but me. He wouldn't trust me to bring anything else. Get in. I'm in a hurry."

"What's the matter with him? He was all right last night." Still Schwab hung back. "I'll wait until he can come. I —I can't leave."

Then he found himself looking up into the barrel of Johnny's six-shooter. "I was told to bring you back with me. Get in, I said."

"This is some trick! I —"

"You get —in!"

So Schwab climbed in awkwardly, his face mottled and flabby with fear of the Thunder Bird.

"Fasten that strap around you-be sure it's fast. And put on this cap and goggles if you like. And sit still." Then he called to the languid Mexican who was idly watching him from afar. "Hey! Come and pull the block away from the wheels."

The Mexican came trotting, the silver of the night before clinking in his overalls pocket. Grinning hopefully, he picked up the post and carried it to one side. But Johnny was not thinking then of tips. He let in the motor until the Thunder Bird went teetering around in a wide half circle and scudded down the level stretch, taking the air easily.

"This is an outrage!" Schwab shouted.

"Where are you taking me?"

"Oh, up in the air a ways," Johnny told him, but the roar of the motor so filled Schwab's unaccustomed ears that he could hear nothing else. And presently his mind became engrossed with something more immediately vital than was his destination.

They were getting too high up, he shouted. Johnny must come down at once-or if he would not do that, at least he must fly lower. Did Johnny mean to commit suicide?

For answer Johnny grinned and went higher, and the face of Schwab became not mottled but a sickly white. He sat gripping the edges of the cockpit and gazing fearfully downward, save when he turned to implore, threaten, and command. He would report Johnny to his employers. He could make him sorry for this. He would make it worth his while to land. He would do great things for Johnny-he would make him rich.

From five thousand feet Johnny volplaned steeply to four thousand, and Schwab's sentences became disconnected phrases that ended mostly in exclamation points. So pleased was Johnny with the effect that he flew in scallops from there on-not unmindful of the two scouting planes that picked him up when he recrossed the line and dogged him from there on.

"I suppose," snorted Johnny to the Thunder Bird, "they think they're about the only real flyers in the air this morning. What? Can't you show 'em an Arizona sample of flying? What you loafing for? Think you're heading a funeral? Well, now, this is just about the proudest moment you've spent for quite some time. This man Schwab —he craves excitement. Can't you hear him holler for thrills? And don't you reckon that Captain Riley will be cocking an eye up at the sky about now, looking to see you come back. Come, come-shake a wing, here, and show 'em what you're good for!"

Whether the Thunder Bird heard and actually did shake a wing does not matter. Johnny remembered that he had yet some miles to fly, and proceeded to put those miles behind him in as straight a line as possible. Schwab's voice came back to him in snatches, though the words were mostly foreign to Johnny's ears. Schwab seemed to be indulging in expletives of some sort.

"Don't worry, sauerkraut, we'll show you a good time soon as we get along a few miles. There's some birds behind us I'm leading home first."

"My God, don't go straight down again! It makes me sick," wailed Schwab.

"Does? Oh, glory! That ain't nothing when you get used to it, man. Be a regular guy and like it. I'll *make* you like it, by golly. Come on, now-here's San Diego-let's give 'em a treat, sauerkraut. You never knew you'd turn out to be a stunt flyer, hey? Well, now, how's this?"

"Whee-ee! See the town right down there? Head for it and keep a-goin', old girl! *Whee-ee!* Now, here it goes, sliding right up over our heads! Loop 'er, Thunder Bird, loop 'er! You're the little old plane from Arizona that's rode the thunder and made it growl it had enough! In Mexico I got yuh, and to Mexico you went and got me a regular jailbird that Uncle Sammy wants. You're takin' him to camp-whoo-ee! Give your tail a flop and over yuh go like a doggone tumbleweed in the wind!

"Come on, you little ole cop planes that thinks you're campin' on my trail! You'll have to ride and whip 'em, now I'm tellin' yuh, if you want to keep in sight of our dust! Sunfish for 'em, you doggone Thunder Bird! You're the flyin' bronk from Arizona, and it's your day to fly!"

With the first loop Schwab went sick, and after that he had no wish except to die. Whether the Thunder Bird rode head down or tail down he neither knew nor cared. Nor did Johnny. As he yelled he looped and he dived, he did tail spins and every other spin that occurred to him. For the time being he was "riding straight up and fanning her ears," and his aerial bronk was pulling off stunts he would never have attempted in cold blood.

He thought it a shame to have to stop, but North Island was there beneath him, a flock of planes were keeping out of his way and forgetting their own acrobatics while they watched him, and Johnny, with an eye on his gas gauge and his mind recurring to his parting words with Captain Riley, straightened out reluctantly and got his bearings. There was room enough for one more nose dive, and he took it exuberantly, trying to see how many turns he could make before he must quit or smash into a building or something.

There was the field, just ahead of him. He flattened, banked, and came down circumspectly enough, considering how his head was whirling when he finally came to a stand. He crawled out, looking first at Schwab to see what he was doing.

What Schwab was doing has no bearing whatever on this story. Schwab was not feeling well, wherefore he was not showing any interest whatever in his surroundings and probable future. John Ivan Jewel laughed unfeelingly while he beckoned a guard who was coming up at a trot and needed no beckoning.

"Here's another man for your boss to take charge of," Johnny announced. "And lead me to him right now. I've got a date with him."

This guard was a new guard and looked dubious. But presently the captain's orderly appeared and took charge of the situation, so Johnny straight-way found himself standing before Captain Riley "Well, I'm back," he announced cheerfully. "And I've got Schwab out there."

Captain Riley dismissed the orderly before he unbent enough to reply. But then he shook hands with John Ivan Jewel just as though he had not seen him a couple of hours before. He was a very pleased Captain Riley, as he showed by the broad grin he wore on his freckled Irish face.

"Schwab," he said, "will be taken care of. He's a deserter from the army, you know. Held a captaincy and disgraced the uniform in various ways, the crowning infamy being the sale of some important information, a year or so ago when things were at the touchiest point with Mexico. We nearly had him, but he deserted and got across the line, and since then he has been raising all kinds of cain in government affairs. Of course, his capture is a little out of my line, but I don't mind telling you that it's a big thing for me to have both these men turned over to me. I can't go into details, of course-you would not be especially interested in them if I could. But it's a big thing, and I want you to know—"

The telephone interrupted him, and he turned to answer it.

"Yes, yes, this is Captain Riley speaking. Yes, who is this, please? Who? Oh, yes! Yes, indeed, no trouble at all, I assure you. Yes, I will give the message-yes, certainly. I shall send him right over. At your command, believe me. Not at all—I am delighted, yes; just one moment. Would you like to talk with him yourself? Just hold the line, please."

One should not accuse a man like Captain Riley of smirking, but his smile might have been mistaken for a smirk when he turned from the telephone. He straightened it out at once, however, so that he spoke with a mere twinkle to Johnny.

"Some one in San Diego," he said, "would like to speak with you. I judge it's important."

Chapter Twenty-Five. Over the Telephone

"Hello?" cried Johnny, wondering vaguely who could be calling him from San Diego. "Oh-who? Mary V! Why, good golly, where did you come from? . . . Oh, you did? . . . Say, that was some bronk-riding I did up there among the clouds-what? . . . Oh, yes, I just happened to feel that way."

In the U.S. Grant hotel Mary V was talking excitedly into the 'phone. "I don't know why I happened to drive down here, but I did, and I just got here in time to see you come flying over and then you did all those flip-flops —Johnny Jewel, do you mean to tell me *that's* the way you have been acting all the time?"

"Oh, no —I happened to have a fellow along that I wanted to give him a treat!"

"A *treat*! Do you call that a treat, for gracious sake? What are you doing over there? I want you to come over here just as quick as ever you can, Johnny. Bland is here; I brought him down with me because he's a very good mechanic and besides, he was very much worried and trying to find you, so I thought he could help, and he did. He saw the Thunder Bird come sailing overhead before I noticed it, for I was driving, and a street car was hogging the crossing and trying to head me off, so I didn't happen to look up just then. And when I did-why, Johnny, I thought sure you were coming right down on top of us! Did you do that deliberately just to scare me, you bad boy? Now you come right over here just as quick as ever you can! I am sure I have been kept waiting long enough —"

"You have," Johnny agreed promptly. "I'm coming, Mary V, and when I get there you're going to marry me or I'll turn the town bottom side up. You get that, do you? Your dad ain't going to head us off this time, I've made good, and doggone him, I can pay that note and have enough left over to buy me an airplane, or you an automobile or both, by golly! And tell Bland I'll make it all right with him, too. I kinda left him in the lurch for awhile, but I couldn't help that. I've been thinking, Mary V, what I'll do. I'm going to give Bland the Thunder Bird. Doggone it, he's done a whole lot for me, and I guess he's got it coming. There's planes here that can fly circles around the old Thunder Bird, and I'm going to have one or break a leg. I'll . . . What's that? . . . Oh, all right, I'll come on and do my talking later. Being a government line, I guess maybe I'd better not hold this telephone all day. Sure, I'm crazy to see you! All right, all right, I'm coming right now!"

"With apologies for overhearing a private conversation," said Captain Riley, "speaking of getting a new plane, why don't you enlist as an aviator? I can use you very nicely and would like to have you here. How would a second lieutenancy strike you, Jewel? I can arrange it for you very easily-and let me tell you something: Before many months roll by it will be a matter of patriotism to serve your country. We shall be at war before long, unless I miss my guess. Better come in now. You-your being married will not interfere, I should think-seeing you intend to continue flying, anyway. I wonder, by the way, why I am not invited to be present at that wedding?"

"Well, good golly! You're invited right now, if you mean you'll go. Mary V will be one proud little girl, all right. And say, Captain, of course I'll have to talk it over with Mary V first, but that offer you just made me sure listens good. I tried to enlist-that's what I wanted all along-but I was turned down. But if you'll say a word for me —"

"Your Mary V is wanting," Captain Riley grinned. "And if I may judge from the brief conversation I had with her over the 'phone just now, we had better be on our way!"